TRUE NAMES

In 1981 Vernor Vinge, SF author and mathematics and computer science professor at San Diego State University, wrote the novella *True Names*. It was set in the real world more than thirty years in the future, and also in something called "The Other Plane." The Internet was still aborning in 1981, the ARPAnet; in his story it had become a worldwide network with a consensual reality more like a fantasy world than the real world.

True Names became an immediate sensation, firing the imaginations of science fiction writers . . . and of scientists as well. Many researchers in computer science and artificial intelligence saw *True Names* as a vastly intriguing story of what their work was just bringing into the light of day.

Twenty years later the Internet and its World Wide Web are part of the fabric of life in the new millennium. And *True Names* looms as an eerily prophetic story, almost precognitive in its projection of trends which have become reality. Here is that story, along with cautionary tales, reports from the frontier, visionary ideas, a cornucopia of fascinating notes from the cyberspace underground of the past twenty years.

Also by Vernor Vinge

TRUE NAMES

BY VERNOR VINGE

and

The Opening of the Cyberspace Frontier

EDITED BY JAMES FRENKEL

TOR®

A Tom Doherty Associates Book
New York

TRUE NAMES AND THE OPENING OF THE CYBERSPACE FRONTIER

Copyright © 2001 by Vernor Vinge
Preface Copyright © 2001 by James Frenkel

Edited and with Introductions by James Frenkel

This book is printed on acid-free paper.

Book design by Jane Adele Regina

A Tor Book
Published by Tom Doherty Associates, LLC
175 Fifth Avenue
New York, NY 10010

www.tor.com

ISBN 0-312-86207-5

First Edition: December 2001

Printed in the United States of America

0 9 8 7 6 5 4 3 2 1

Copyright Acknowledgments

To Marvin Minsky,
godfather to a new age

Contents

Preface

Work on the volume you hold in your hands was begun in 1995. As Vernor Vinge's editor at Tor Books (and elsewhere, beginning, appropriately, with the Dell Books publication of "True Names" in *Binary Star 5* in 1981), I had long been aware of the great interest in that novella.

However, since its first publication, "True Names" had been difficult to keep in print, for reasons Vernor explains in his Introduction, which follows this Preface. By 1995 it had become quite apparent that the Internet, which was the core of or at least the environment in which the majority of the story took place, had become an integral part of modern life.

Both within and outside the field of science fiction, people discuss the notion that there are times when reality "catches up" with science fiction. Often this is said by those who don't understand science fiction. Some think that somehow SF writers are going to run out of new ideas, simply because developments in the real world either have brought into being something that was once written about in some science fiction tale, or because something that had been speculated about in some science fiction tale has been shown to be quite unlikely in the face of some entirely unpredictable development that makes the science fictional notion seem suddenly quaint, or worse.

My favorite instance of the latter is the development of smaller, more powerful computers. In the 1940s and '50s Isaac Asimov wrote a few stories in which he posited that computers would get more powerful—and bigger—until they were as big as whole planets. I personally found this vision pretty cool, though also a little daunting, since the ultimate result of this trend was a computer that essentially became God.

Then the microchip was developed, and since then computers have gotten increasingly powerful . . . but *smaller*. Which brings us back to this book.

When my then-assistant, Jim Minz, and I set out to get articles or essays that related to or were inspired by "True Names," we received many excellent pieces, a number of which are included here. Then the project was delayed by a number of factors that had nothing to do with the material itself. Therefore this book is being published nearly six years after its inception.

The articles and essays here were written at various times, the oldest being "True Names" itself and then Marvin Minsky's Afterword, and the most recent being Richard M. Stallman's addendum to his "The Right to Read." During the editing it became clear that some of the articles contain material that seems somewhat dated in the face of more recent developments. In a way, it's like science fiction from a previous time which has been superseded by (contradictory) reality.

The other thing that became clear during the editorial process, however, was that the one constant in cyberspace is rapid change. Things that were new and unique just a few years ago are old hat today, and the rate of change doesn't seem likely to slow down any time soon. So it's quite likely that all the nonfiction in this book will seem like outdated science fiction within just another few years.

But this book isn't intended to provide a report on what's about to happen in cyberspace, or necessarily on what's happening at the moment we go to press. Our intention from the start has been to provide something of a historical perspective, and to give readers a window on developments and theories that have contributed to some of the more intriguing aspects of the Internet and the World Wide Web, set against a story that provided the first seriously imaginative depiction of what the Internet could become. When *True Names* was written, it was considered visionary. And it was read by some of those who have had a great deal to do with shaping the Internet to date. Therefore, we've chosen to do the only really sensible thing—let the authors' ideas speak for themselves, without attempting to second-guess them.

—JAMES FRENKEL
August 2001

Introduction

Vernor Vinge

I'm writing this in August 1999. It's almost exactly twenty years since I wrote the first draft of *True Names*. This new appearance of the story as part of *True Names and the Opening of the Cyberspace Frontier* is the first that has included multiple essays by other people. And these are very interesting people. All but one I've met, in one way or another, because of *True Names*. If there were no other reason for writing the story, these friendships would suffice. I'm very grateful to Jim Frenkel for bringing all these essays together.

Word for word, *True Names* was one of the easiest projects I've ever worked on. I think there were several reasons for this. I went to college back before there were computers. Well, not really—but my college days are so far back along the exponential run of technology, it almost seems that way. In the early 1960s there were computers but as far as I know there were no computer-science departments. It's so far back that many of the computer services we use every day were not even imagined—and that is a terrible thing for a science-fiction writer to confess.

From well before the 1960s, however, there was one computer application that was imagined, and that still waits in our future: machine intelligence, in particular, superhuman machine intelligence. That did catch my attention. From the early 1960s onward, computer technology joined space travel as my central speculative interest.

And yet, in college I never took any computer courses. Sometimes, I wonder if this ignorance was an advantage,

saving me from getting lost in the irrelevancies of the moment. After all, I figured I knew where things were *ultimately*
going! (John Ford's essay here is an interesting look back on
this. What of the machine archaeologists in our future, digging around in their prehistory trying to make sense of
things as bizarre as human cinema?)

By 1979, I did know a little about contemporary computing. I had been teaching computer-science courses at San
Diego State University for several years; I did a lot of what
is now called telecommuting. One night I was working at
home, logged on to SDSU's principal computer (a PDP-11/
45 running RSTS; it had about the computing power of the
digital camera I have sitting on my desk today). As usual, I
sneaked around in anonymous accounts—no need for the
whole world to see I was on the machine. Every so often,
I'd take a look at the other users, or surface in my official
account. Suddenly I was accosted by another user via the
TALK program (which for some reason I had left enabled).
The TALKer claimed some implausible name, and I re-
sponded in kind. We chatted for a bit, each trying to figure
out the other's true name. Finally I gave up, and told the
other person I had to go—that I was actually a personality
simulator, and if I kept talking my artificial nature would
become obvious.

Afterward, I realized that I had just *lived* a science-fiction
story, at least by the standards of my childhood. For several
years (ever since reading Ursula K. Le Guin's *A Wizard of
Earthsea*) I'd had the idea that the "true names" of fantasy
were like object ID numbers in a large database. Now I saw
how that could be turned into a story.

IT WAS THE SUMMER OF 1979. *TRUE NAMES* WAS THE FIRST STORY I
ever wrote with a word processor: a TECO editor running on a
Heathkit LSI 11/03. For me, the writing environment was

heaven on earth! (And somewhere in the following years, in upgrading from RT-11 8-inch floppies to IBM 5.25-inch floppies to my first hard disk . . . the machine-readable form of the original manuscript was lost. Sigh.) I sent the manuscript around— in hardcopy, of course. Jim Frenkel suggested that I make it longer, mainly to have additional action after the battle with the Mailman and provide a satisfying denouement. I think that rewrite was done in early 1980, producing the form of the story that you see here. Dell published *True Names* early in 1981 as half of a Binary Star "double novel" book (the other half being George R. R. Martin's "Nightflyers"), all illustrated by Jack Gaughan.

In the years after the Dell Books edition, *True Names* was in and out of print: Jim Frenkel's Bluejay Books had an edition illustrated by Bob Walters with an afterword by Marvin Minsky (which has been recaptured here). Jim Baen published the story in a collection of my other short fiction, *True Names and Other Dangers*. The only other U.S. publication is in Hartwell and Wolf's *Visions of Wonder* from Tor Books. This on-again, off-again publishing history has been frustrating to some readers—and it has certainly been frustrating to me! Part of the problem is that *True Names* is thirty thousand words long, too small to be a stand-alone novel but too large for most story collections.

As the years pass, I've been very interested in the reaction of readers to *True Names*. I have a knowledgeable friend who first read it in 1980. At that time she liked it, but thought the story was a bit "off the wall." She reread it several years later and still liked it, but by then it seemed much less radical. By the middle 1980s, the ideas in the story had appeared (independently) in a number of other places. By the late 1980s, there were television shows with these ideas. In the early 1990s I noticed another kind of interest—not inspired by the Internet aspects of the story so much as by the autonomous sprites and guardians that inhabited the Other Plane. This was largely because such things were actually being made (and that is so much more impressive than any fiction!). Both Pattie Maes and Lenny Foner (Pattie's PhD student, now graduated) are in the middle of this research, and they both have essays here.

I'VE ALSO LOOKED FOR ANTECEDENTS TO TRUE NAMES. THERE'S POUL Anderson's "Kings Who Die" (1962) and John Brunner's Shockwave Rider (1975). In the late 1970s, I believe there was an interactive role-playing program being marketed for use on a computer network (and I'd be grateful for a solid reference on this). And, of course, there's Vannevar Bush's incredible essay "As We May Think" (1945) and Theodor Nelson's Xanadu system (1965–).

Many of the best things about True Names grew almost subconsciously as I worked on the story; others came out of the constraints that the plot put on me. (So some of the following is undocumented archeology on my recollections of the time!) The network aspect was inspired by my interactions on SDSU's dial-in computer. Scaling up from that and imagining consequences was easy, and pointed to many important things. I was aware of Moore's Law in some form when I wrote True Names. I think I had the raw hardware power fairly well targeted. The story took place just on the near side of a network-mediated Technological Singularity, but superhuman automation was still mostly offstage. (There were numerous things about the future that the story misses—or that have not yet happened. The version of True Names appearing in this book contains some small corrections, but as far as I know they are all spelling, punctuation, and typography. For this story, I felt that larger "fixes" would not be as interesting as seeing what went right and what went wrong.)

Some things in True Names were simply very happy accidents. For instance, the Vandals used "fifty thousand baud" connections from their home machines. The "baud" was just a misuse of jargon; I should have said "bits per second." But "fifty thousand bits per second" *is* correct, even though many home users in 1999 already have better connections to the Net. Home connections in *True Names* were much much larger, but it seemed to me that covert, untraceable channels would be very small by comparison, because of all the overhead involved in hiding one's tracks. (Actually, latencies would probably be a lot worse on the covert connections, but I didn't get that.) It was this low bit rate that made me put the responsibility for picture generation at the user end (the "EEG Portal," mediated by the user's imagination). It was fascinating, at Hackers several years later, to talk to Chip Morningstar and Randy Farmer about what they had done with Habitat. Chip and Randy did the real thing, using a 300-bit-per-second link and a protocol that evoked image fragments stored on the user's local disk.

The user environment of the 1999-era Internet is not nearly as magical as the one in *True Names* (which was targeted to take place around 2014). But in writing the story, magic was everywhere I looked. The concept of "true names" is entrenched in fantasy and seemed an excellent fit to the real importance of true names in a network environment. And even in serious commerical programming, the magic metaphors are very common, partly as humor, partly because they provide useful terminology to hang reasoning on. (Interestingly, there is even a rational reemergence of superstition. Very few people nowadays believe that if you spill salt, then—to avoid bad luck—you should throw a pinch of it over your shoulder. But I'll bet almost every computer user notices and acts on correlations that are almost as unsubstantiated. For example, a user notes, "My VeryComplexApplication often crashes when I pop up a calendar window in this other application"—and therefore avoids looking at the calendar when running the VeryComplexApplication. Before computers, things moved slowly enough that such correlations could be tested and verified, and lead to logical insights. With computer programs, things are very complex and interrelated, and in many situations we don't have time to go beyond the superstition stage in analyzing coincidences.)

So the magical terminology fit with some things that go on in real programming. And of course, magical imagery was a ready tool for me as author in describing the Other Plane. There are many ironies that grew from the magic—and what it represented in the real world. In fact, these ironies may be the most important reason that it was easy to write the story. The magic metaphor was a powerful guide in the choosing of terms (for instance, "true names"). But even a good metaphor cuts you off from other insights, and I ended up providing an excellent example of Mark Twain's notion that "the difference between the right word and the almost right word is the difference between lightning and a lightning bug." One of the central features of *True Names* is the notion that a worldwide computer network would be a kind of *place* for its users. I needed a word for that place, and the best I came up with was "the Other Plane." Alas, that is a lightning bug compared with the lightning bolt that is "cyberspace." (Heh, heh: And yet there is still hope for the term "the Other Plane" . . . the folks working with the movie option on *True Names* talk in terms of being "on TOP"— that is, being on The Other Plane.) In the long run, I think the inhabitants (users) of cyberspace will adapt different metaphors for dealing with what they find there and how they access it: almost offstage in *True Names*, we saw the werebots and other groups with other visions. In their essays, Marvin Minsky and Mark Pesce do a much better job with these ideas than I can. And the essay of Chip Morningstar and Randy Farmer illustrates some of these issues with an actual implementation.

The appearance of *True Names* revealed to me a new virtue of writing hard science fiction. *Omni* magazine wanted to send some science fiction writers to the 1982 conference of the American Association for Artificial Intelligence (Jim Hogan, Fred Pohl, Bob Sheckley, and me, as it worked out). There I met Marvin Minsky and Hans Moravec. In later years, Marvin invited me to MIT for talks and meetings. Between the MIT Media Lab and Thinking Machines and Hackers and Aether Wire, I've had marvelous opportunities to talk to people who are at the edge of wonderful things. Asking them questions, listening to them, has been an inspiration. Sometimes the witness-to-history feeling gets to be very very strong!

I notice that four of the essays in this book are strongly focused on political and crypto issues. There is certainly a lot of political *attitude* in *True Names*. The political situation of the era is a pervasive background noise: people live with it. Lots of problems are envisaged—and many of them have turned out to be very real—but I provide very little in the way of solutions. One amusing misprediction (at least I hope it is a misprediction) is that network access would be licensed: having your "license to operate" revoked was as effective a career-ender as losing your automobile driver's license is in the twentieth century. The idea is typical of a writer who doesn't quite have his head around all the consequences. Network access is *so* ubiquitous nowadays that it would take some weird and retro surprise to make licensing practical. It looks like such a law would be much more difficult to enforce than the drug laws ever were.

The essays that Tim May and Alan Wexelblat and Lenny Foner and Richard Stallman have in this book are much more substantive than *True Names* in outlining problems and advocating policies. Tim May's piece is certainly the most outspoken in its predictions about power for the individual. I got a laugh at CFP '96 when I drew a spectrum of opinion on the wall: it was labeled something like "What Different People See as the Impact of Computers on Freedom." At one end of the spectrum was George Orwell and at the other end was . . . Tim May. I think my CFP '96 audience recognized that Tim's ideas deserve first place as the antithesis of Orwell's vision. Up until the personal computer came along, Orwell's vision of technology as the enabler of tyranny was the mainstream view. But in the 1980s (ironically beginning about calendar year 1984) people with PCs began to realize that computers might bring the end of tyranny, perhaps the end of national governments. . . . Then came the 1990s and the various schemes to control crypto and maybe even use distributed automation to give Enforcement a better grip than ever before. It seems to me that it's still an open question whether computers and networks will help or hurt human freedom—but this is one place where the extreme scenarios are also the most plausible. I think we could easily go in the direction Tim May indicates, perhaps ending up with a world very like the one in Neal Stephenson's *Diamond Age*. On the other hand, there are the "Four Horsemen" that Tim, Alan, and Lenny remark upon. All four Horsemen are good excuses for the incremental tightening of regulation and enforcement (some being more effective with one constituency than another), but I think the "Terrorist Horseman" is the one that could shift our whole society toward strict controls. Just a few really ghastly terrorist incidents would be enough to cause a sea change in public opinion. It's not hard to imagine the entire country run the way airports were run in the late twentieth century. But there are worse nightmares: Imagine a government that mandated control of some part of each communicating microchip. In that case, the computing power of the Internet could be used for much tighter control than George Orwell described.

Richard Stallman's "The Right to Read" is the only other fiction in this book. It has one of the best features of science fiction: at first it seems to be an over-the-top parody . . . but then you see the seeds of the story in our present, and feel a chill. Intellectual Property rights are at a crossroads. Maybe the Information Age will force an end to such rights. Maybe technology will be exploited to enforce them in the terrifying way that Richard Stallman describes in "The Right to Read." In any case, the next decade should be witness to incredible turbulence in this area, as new models of Intellectual Property management are devised and experimented with. However it turns out, Richard Stallman's work with the free software movement and the GNU "copyleft" agreement are among the happiest developments of the late twentieth century.

Danny Hillis's essay begins this book. He's not talking about policy issues or nightmares. He looks at the trend curves and the real world around him. The cautious hopefulness of this essay could be both the prologue and the epilogue for this book. We are all so much in the middle of things. We can't really know how high we can fly (or if we might crash). But we can see that our children may soar beyond our imagination. . . .

TRUE NAMES

and

The Opening of the

Cyberspace Frontier

A Time of Transition/The Human Connection

Danny Hillis

Founder of Thinking Machines and the first Disney Fellow, Danny Hillis has feet both in the world of the past and in the future world that is being built every day by new technological developments. In the following essay he neatly encapsulates some of the issues faced by people today.

Faced by hitherto unheard-of rapidity of change, we have problems today vastly different from those faced by any previous generation of humans. And while many people think humans will change before long into a different kind of intelligent being, Hillis deals with the questions and problems posed by the pace and tenor of change as a human being already born and not likely to change radically. His perceptive, poignant essay is a fitting prelude to the others that follow. This piece was first published in 1997.

You can tell that something unusual is going on these days by the way we draw our graphs. In normal times, we would use a linear scale to plot progress. The height of our graph would be proportional to the measure of progress. But we live at a remarkable moment in history, when progress is so rapid that we plot it on a logarithmic scale.

In the field of computing we have become accustomed to measures that double every few years—processor speeds, communication bandwidths, the number of sites on the Internet—so we plot them on a scale that shows each order of magnitude as an equal step. By plotting on a log-labeled scale (1,10,100,1000) we can imagine progress as a straight line, moving steadily upward with the advance of time. This gives us a comfortable illusion of predictability.

Of course, if we used a linear scale to plot these same curves, they would not look so tame. They would be exponentials, shooting uncontrollably off the page. They would make it look as if everything that has happened so far is an insignificant prelude to what will happen next. On a linear scale, the exponents look unpredictable. The curves approach vertical, converging on a singularity, where the rules break down and something different begins.

The two ways of plotting progress correspond to different attitudes about technological change. I see the merits in both. As an engineer, I am an extrapolator. I am a believer in, and a participant in, the march of progress. As an engineer, I like semi-log scales. But I am also a parent, a citizen, a teacher, and a student. I am an object, not just an agent of change. As an object and as an observer, I can see clearly that there is something extraordinary going on. The explosion of the exponentials reveals a truth: We are alive at a special and important moment. We are becoming something else.

This century, fifty years back and fifty forward, is one of those rare times in history when humanity transforms from one type of human society to another. To use a physical analogy, we are in the midst of a phase transition, when the configuration of the system is switching between two locally stable states. In this transition, technology is the catalyst. It is a self-amplifying agent of change, in the sense that each improvement tends to increase its capacity to improve. Better machines enable us to build even better machines. Faster computers let us design faster computers, faster.

Change was not always like this. For most of human history, parents could expect their grandchildren to grow up in a world much like their own. For most of human history, parents knew what they needed to know to teach their children. Planning for the future was easier then. Architects designed cathedrals that would take centuries to complete. Farmers planted acorns to shade their descendants with oaks. Today, starting a project that would not be completed for century or two would seem odd. Today, any plan more than a year is "long-term."

Why have we become so shortsighted? We have no less goodwill than our ancestors. Our problem is that, literally, we cannot imagine the future. The pace of technological change is so great that we cannot know what type of world we are leaving for our children. If we plant acorns, we cannot reasonably expect that our children will sit under the oak trees. Or that they will even want to. The world is changing too fast for that. People move. Needs change. Much of our generation is employed at jobs our parents never imagined. Entire industries, indeed entire nations, can wither in the blink of an eye.

All of this confusion becomes understandable, even expected, if we accept the premise that we are in a time of transition from one type of society to another. We should expect to understand the occupations of our grandchildren no more than a hunter-gatherer would understand the life of a farmer, or than a preindustrial farmer would understand the life of a factory worker. All we can really expect to understand is the good in what we leave behind.

So what are we humans becoming? Whatever it is is more connected, more interdependent. Few individuals today could survive outside the fabric of society. No city could stand alone without being continuously fed from the outside by networks of power, water, food, and information. Few nations could maintain their lifestyles without trade. The web of our technology weaves us together, simultaneously enabling us and forcing us to depend more on one another.

As we are becoming more deeply connected to each other, we are simultaneously becoming more connected with our creations. Each time I watch a worker on an assembly line, a violinist with a violin, or a child with a computer, I am struck by how intimate we have become with our technology. Already, our contact lenses and our pacemakers are as much a part of us as our hair and teeth. With recombinant biotechnology we will blur the final boundary between artifacts and ourselves.

In 1851, Nathaniel Hawthorne wrote, "Is it a fact—or have I dreamed it—that, by means of electricity, the world of matter has become a great nerve, vibrating thousands of miles in a breathless point of time? Rather, the round globe is a vast head, a brain, instinct with intelligence!" Now, more than a century later, we can see the signs of his vision. The collective intelligence of the world's minds, biological and electronic, already make many of our economic decisions. The prices of commodities and the rates of global growth are determined by this network of people and machines in ways that surpass the understanding of any single human mind. The phone system and the Internet have short-circuited distance, literally "vibrating thousands of miles in a breathless point of time."

There are other, subtler signs that we are becoming a part of a symbiotic whole. It is obvious that we have become more narrowly specialized in our professions, but we are also becoming more specialized in the activities of our daily lives.

Increasingly we fragment our activities into pure components. We either work or play, exercise or relax, teach or learn. We divide our art, our science, our politics, and our religion into carefully separated spheres. There was an older kind of human that kept these things together, a kind a person who worked and played and taught and learned all at the same time. That kind of person is becoming obsolete. Integration demands standardization. Just as a single cell in our body is adapted to a specific function and a specific time, we too must focus our roles. An earlier kind of cell could sense, move, digest, and reproduce continuously, but such a self-sufficient unit cannot function as a part of a complex whole.

I cannot help but feel ambivalent at the prospect of this brave new world, in which I will be a small part of a symbiotic organism that I can barely comprehend. But then, I am a product of another kind of society, one that celebrates the individual. My sense of identity, my very sense of survival, is based on a resistance to becoming something else. Just as one of my hunting-gathering ancestors would surely reject my modern city life, so do I feel myself rebelling at this metamorphosis. This is natural. I imagine that caterpillars are skeptical of butterflies.

As frightened as I am by the prospect of this change, I am also thrilled by it. I love what we are, yet I cannot help but hope that we are capable of turning into something better. We humans can be selfish, foolish, shortsighted, even cruel. Just as I can imagine these weaknesses as vestiges of our (almost) discarded animal past, I can imagine our best traits—our kindness, our creativity, our capacity to love—as hints of our future. This is the basis for my hope.

I know I am a relic. I am a presymbiotic kind of person, born during the time of our transition. Yet, I feel lucky to have been given a glimpse of our promise. I am overwhelmed when I think of it . . . by the sweet sad love of what we were, and by the frightening beauty of what we might become.

True Nyms and Crypto Anarchy

Timothy C. May

One of the biggest issues in cyberspace these days, one that will continue to be an issue as long as there is such a venue as the Internet, is the safety of communication from prying eyes. In the detailed and persuasive essay that follows, Tim May, formerly a physicist at Intel and one of the founding members of the Cypherpunks, discusses the big issues involved—invasion of privacy, the specter of government interference in personal affairs, the use of electronically forwarded information by a variety of people, entities, and organizations for purposes other than those intended by the forwarder . . . these are all issues of tremendous importance to anyone who uses the Internet—and that means just about everyone, in one way or another.

In a previous age, these issues were not of such great importance, for there was never the possibility that anyone could find and gather enough information to do harm to others in the ways that are now possible with the Internet. Today, however . . . Read Tim May's essay and you'll never feel quite as safe as you did a moment before you read these pages. This article was written in 1996.

"True Names" came to my attention in 1986, when a friend of mine gave me a dog-eared Xerox copy and said "You need to read this." But before I even started reading this samizdat edition, the Bluejay Books trade paperback edition appeared and that's what I read, saving my eyesight and giving Vernor Vinge his proper cut of the action. *True Names* certainly riveted me, and it fit with other developments swirling around in computer circles at the time. Namely, digital money, anonymous e-mail, and all of the other issues connected with "strong cryptography" and "public key cryptography."

Some friends were setting up a company to develop "information markets" for the Net, though this was half a dozen years before the World Wide Web and wide public access to the Internet. It was clear to me that the ideas of anonymous interaction, reputation-based systems, digital pseudonyms, digital signatures, data havens, and public-key encryption in general would all be important for these markets in cyberspace. The work of Holland-based David Chaum, an American cryptographer who developed most of the early ideas about digital money and untraceable e-mail, looked to be of special relevance. Chaum's work on untraceable electronic cash, reported in a 1985 "Communications of the ACM" cover story (November 1985), sparked the realization that a digital economy could be constructed, with anonymity, untraceability, and ancillary anarcho-capitalist features, such as escrow agents to hold money for completion of services, reputation rating services and tools, and "persistence" for various kinds of constructs. In other words, a cryptographically based version of Vinge's *True Names*, and even of Ayn Rand's "Galt's Gulch" in *Atlas Shrugged*.

The full-blown, immersive virtual reality of *True Names* may still be far off, but the technologies of cryptography, digital signatures, remailers, message pools, and data havens make many of the most important aspects of *True Names* realizable today, now, on the Net. Arguably, Mr. Slippery is already here and, as Vernor predicted, the Feds are already trying to track him down. In 1988 these ideas motivated me to write and distribute on the Net "The Crypto Anarchist Manifesto," a section of which is quoted here:

"A specter is haunting the modern world, the specter of crypto anarchy.

"Computer technology is on the verge of providing the ability for individuals and groups to communicate and interact with each other in a totally anonymous manner. Two persons may exchange messages, conduct business, and negotiate electronic contracts without ever knowing the True Name, or legal identity, of the other. Interactions over networks will be untraceable, via extensive re-routing of encrypted packets and tamper-proof boxes which implement cryptographic protocols with nearly perfect assurance against any tampering. Reputations will be of central importance, far more important in dealings than even the credit ratings of today. These developments will alter completely the nature of government regulation, the ability to tax and control economic interactions, the ability to keep information secret, and will even alter the nature of trust and reputation."

These ideas have evolved over the years since this was written, but the basic ideas remain unchanged. The Cypherpunks group has been instrumental in implementing many of the concepts.

In this article I'll be exploring some of the implications of strong cryptography and crypto anarchy and the connections with *True Names*. Because this article will be in a book, with presumably a shelf life of many years, I'm avoiding giving specific article citations and URLs to Web sites, as they tend to change quickly. Searching on the names of authors should be a more reliable way of finding current locations and information.

Cypherpunks

The time was right in 1992 to deploy some of these new ideas swirling around in the cryptography and computer communities and reify some of these abstractions. Eric Hughes and I gathered together some of the brightest folks we knew from the annual Hackers Conference and from the Bay Area computer community to discuss the implications of these ideas, and to look into translating some of the academic work on cryptography into real-world programs. The initial meeting led to larger, monthly meetings, and to an active mailing list. Jude Milhon suggested the pun "Cypherpunks," a play on "cyberpunk" and on the British spelling "cypher." The name stuck, and the Cypherpunks mailing list has been active ever since. It was on this list that several of the most important security breaches in Netscape and other Internet programs were revealed, and the Cypherpunks list has played an important role in the ongoing cryptography debate, including fruitful discussions of the Clipper chip, key escrow, export laws, private access to strong cryptography, the implications of digital money, and other issues. We were also fortunate that Phil Zimmermann's Pretty Good Privacy, or PGP, appeared in a usable form just as we were getting started. PGP is the leading user-friendly encryption program, available on nearly all platforms, and it was used as a building block for many of the cryptographic tools we and others developed.

The Cypherpunks group is also a good example of a "virtual community." Scattered around the world, communicating electronically in matters of minutes, and seemingly oblivious of local laws, the Cypherpunks group is indeed a community; a virtual one, with its own rules and its own norms for behavior. Some members use pseudonyms, and use anonymous remailers to communicate with the list, using PGP to digitally sign posts. These digital pseudonyms are in some sense their true names, their "true nyms." On the Cypherpunks list, a number of well-respected nyms have appeared and are thought of no less highly than are their "real" colleagues. The whole subject of digitally authenticated reputations, and the reputation capital that accumulates or is affected by the opinions of others, is one that combines economics, game theory, psychology, and expectations. Reputations play a critical role in how anonymity and pseudonyms work in cyberspace; many of the predicted problems with nyms vanish when reputations are taken into account.

There were several books we frequently recommended to new members: *True Names* led the list, along with John Brunner's *Shockwave Rider*, Orson Scott Card's *Ender's Game*, Neal Stephenson's *Snow Crash*, Hakim Bey's *TAZ*, and, of course, various cryptography and computer references, notably Bruce Schneier's *Applied Cryptography*. At our first meeting, in fact, we simulated some of the notions out of "True Names," using cryptographic protocols. Most of the issues about pseudonyms, digital personas, and anonymity have since been explored directly using "Cypherpunks remailers" and related technologies.

Anonymous Remailers

Anonymous remailers, also called digital mixes, provide an excellent example of the possibilities inherent in cryptographic technology. David Chaum originally developed most of the important ideas in a 1981 paper on "Untraceable E-Mail," years before e-mail achieved the wide prominence it now has. And he later refined the ideas in a paper on so-called "DC-Nets," an interesting topic a bit beyond the scope of this article.

There are many reasons people may wish to occasionally communicate without being traced or identified. A digital pseudonym is obviously useless if e-mail programs identify the origin of e-mail. People may wish to be anonymous for many reasons: privacy, fear of reprisal by employers or other groups, avoidance of profiles of their activities and interests, posting to controversial newsgroups or support groups (such as "alt.recovery" or rape and incest recovery groups), whistleblowing, and floating of controversial ideas. Writers have long used pseudonyms for some of the same reasons. (And the U.S. Supreme Court ruled in 1956 that writers may not be compelled to put their true names on their writing.)

To see how anonymous remailers work, imagine a person—call her Alice—trying to avoid being followed by someone—call him Bob. Wherever she goes, Bob follows. As she enters a store, Bob waits outside and watches for her to leave, and picks up the tail. However, suppose she enters a large department store, along with many others, and emerges some time later with many others, wearing different clothes and generally not being recognizable. Bob has no idea of which person leaving the store is Alice, and so he must either give up the tail, or follow all of the people leaving the store. She repeats this process many times, each time becoming more and more "mixed" with others. With even a small number of such mixings, the number of paths Bob must follow can become astronomically high. Alice has thus used department store mixes to shake her tail.

This is the way anonymous remailers or digital mixes work. An e-mail message is sent to a remailer, encrypted to the public key of the remailer operator or his machine. The contents of the message look essentially random to any observer (who might be tapping the lines, for example). The remailer operator decrypts the message, holds it for some period of time or until sufficient other messages have accumulated, adds any needed padding to make the message size not a correlatable factor, and sends the accumulated messages out to their next destinations. Very importantly, the messages he remails are usually encrypted by the originator to the *next* remailer's public key, so any given remailer cannot read the contents of any message. Nor can any remailer in the chain modify the messages, or tag them in any way (as any modifications would make the message unreadable, undecipherable, by the next remailer in the chain). Using encryption at each stage completely obscures the mapping between origin and destination, to both the final recipient and to all of the remailers. The recipient receives only the "innermost" message, with all of the earlier stages progressively stripping off headers. Any given remailer can only open the envelope "addressed" (encrypted) to him, and cannot read the messages that remain in the text block he does see . . . all he can do is read the next destination, which is included in the clear. Think of envelopes within envelopes, each addressed to a particular remailer.

The originator of a message decides on a chain of remailers he plans to use, encrypts and addresses his messages in reverse order, and then sends the resulting message to the first remailer, who decrypts it and sends the result to the next remailer in the chain, and so forth. If, for example, the originator picks five remailers, and each remailer waits until ten messages have been accumulated before forwarding the accumulated batch, then in theory there are upward of one hundred thousand possible routings to be followed. There are not usually this many messages, so the correlation problem is not quite this hard. But any attempt at tracing the message is still effectively thwarted, unless the various remailers collude or are instructed by authorities to report all of the mappings between arriving and departing messages. Using some offshore remailers is an effective bar to this latter attack. And some people publish regular lists of remailers, with the results of ping tests, latency time measurements, reliability, etc.

The first Cypherpunks remailers were initially written in Perl and C by Eric Hughes and Hal Finney. They allowed e-mail to be sent to a remailer, have its origin stripped off, and then be remailed to a selected destination, including other remailers. They were first deployed in 1992, and by 1996 several dozen existed. These were used to anonymously publish ("liberate") ciphers that had not previously been published, to publish secrets of the Church of Scientology, to disclose a few military and security secrets, and, not surprisingly, for flames, insults, and anonymous attacks. Ideally, no mapping is kept of who sent what mail, so court orders and lawsuits are ineffective in revealing the identities of those sending mail. Further, hardware-based digital mixes, i.e. sealed modules with a public key present only inside the module and unreadable by outsiders, will mean no human is even involved in the process, even as a system administrator. Long chains of such mixes, operating quickly on high-speed networks, should make the task of tracing messages even more intractable. A commercial implementation of a digital mix, called MixMaster, is available; users can install such "instant mixes" on their Internet boxes and become remailers. This turns out to be a good example of what a simple application of strong cryptography, using PGP, can do. The Perl and C code is short and simple, and the security of the entire chain depends solely on the unbreakability of encrypted messages, on the number of hops, and on the unlikelihood of collusion between the various remailers. (If all of the remailers were to get together and compare notes, the system would of course be broken. But as the number of remailers increases, this strategy becomes less and less effective. Also, one can always remail messages through oneself, thus defeating most collusion or tapping efforts.)

Another approach to remailers is the one followed by Julf Helsingius, of Finland, who operated an anonymizing service that kept a database of mappings between pseudonyms and actual e-mail addresses. This system was easy to use, and allowed easy replies to senders. However, the database was a ripe target for civil lawsuit investigators (and criminal investigators), and Julf pulled the plug on his system in 1996. Cypherpunks remailers, by being distributed, in many jurisdictions, and robust against such requests, offer a more solid and scalable basis for anonymous remailer networks.

"Digital postage" is needed both to incentivize remailers to operate for-profit sites (and thus expand the number and robustness of these sites) and to provide a more solid economic basis for e-mail in general. E-mail currently costs most users nothing to send; this has led to widespread "spamming" of the Net. (Consistent with the themes of this article, what is needed is not global regulation but a market-based pricing mechanism for e-mail.) Some work on digital postage has been done, but true progress awaits wider deployment of digital cash systems.

This use of remailers is just one concrete example of the use of cryptography to alter institutions and interactions.

True Nyms

The controversy over naming and under what circumstances true names can be demanded is likely to rage for decades.

Why do we so often accept the notion that governments issue us our names and our identities, and that governments must ensure that names are true names? Governments like to be involved in identity issues because it gives them additional control. And it helps them to track the flow of money. For example, centuries ago, the rulers of various European countries forced the Jews to drop their traditional patronymic practices ("Jacob son of Israel") so as to allow taxes to be more efficiently collected, to monitor movements, and so forth. These rulers even sold the "best" family names to those who paid the most, leaving others with less desirable, or even insulting, names. The same practice was repeated in the U.S. with the naming of ex-slaves and the renaming of immigrants. As Nietzsche pointed out, "The master's right of naming goes so far that it is accurate to say that language itself is the expression of the power of the masters." Governments today even give themselves the rights to create/forge completely false identities, with false credit histories, false educational backgrounds, etc. Under the guise of "protecting witnesses," the Federal Witness Security Program, popularly called Witness Protection, has created upward of fifty thousand fabricated identities. The major credit reporting agencies are, of course, not fooled, as these "ghosts" pop into existence in their databases, and these agencies are most likely colluding in the support of these false identities. Imagine lending money to someone on the strength of an excellent credit report, only to find that you lent money to a convicted scam artist who sold out his partners so he could receive a fake ID. Who would you sue? (One of the things anonymous information services, to be covered later, will be good for is soliciting the truth behind such government lies, e.g., by offering money for a CD-ROM containing the true names and locations of those in the WitSec program. Anyone with access to this database is a potential seller, and can accept payment untraceably. It's going to be an interesting world.) There are strong pressures building for issuance of national identity cards, perhaps using smart cards, especially for control of immigration, travel, "deadbeat dads," and terrorism. In a free society, those who wish to deal only with actual, provable true names would, of course, be free to refuse interactions with nyms, true names being just another credential, sometimes offered, sometimes not.

Digital pseudonyms, the creation of persistent network personas that cannot be forged by others and yet are unlinkable to the "true names" of their owners, are finding major uses in ensuring free speech, in allowing controversial opinions to be aired, and in providing for economic transactions that cannot be blocked by local governments. The technology being deployed by the Cypherpunks and others means their identities, nationalities, and even which continents they are on are untraceable—unless their owners choose to reveal this information. This alters the conventional "relationship topology" of the world, allowing diverse interactions without external governmental regulation, taxation, or interference.

Public-Key Cryptography

Cryptography is about more than the stereotypical sending of secret messages. The combination of strong, unbreakable public-key cryptography and virtual network communities in cyberspace will produce profound changes in the nature of economic and social systems. Crypto anarchy is the cyberspatial realization of anarcho-capitalism, transcending national boundaries and freeing individuals to consensually make the economic arrangements they wish to make. The fundamental notion of modern public-key cryptography is that the key for locking, for example, a box, is different from the key for unlocking the box. The owner of a box can then publicize the form of the key needed to lock "his" box, and keep the unlocking key a secret. Anyone can then lock a message in Bob's box with his "public-key," but no one except Bob can ever unlock that box, not even with all the computer power in the world. From this basic point flow all sorts of variations and extensions. An alternative metaphor is that of the *envelope*: anyone can place something inside one of Bob's envelopes and seal it, but only Bob can open his envelopes. (In the chains of remailers we just discussed, envelopes-within-envelopes are used, for as many stages as are desired.)

Cryptography revolves around *local control* of some secret. For example, a user has a private key which only he knows. Others can send him messages, using his *public* key, but only he can decode or decrypt them. So long as this key is kept secret, the encrypted communication cannot be read by others. The security depends on the length of the keys, the number of bits in the keys. A "weak" key of forty or fifty bits, for example, can be cracked with a personal computer. Stronger keys of sixty-four or eighty bits are preferable, though they're still not truly secure. And it is no more difficult to use ciphers with an effective strength of several hundred bits; such ciphers should withstand brute-force attacks for centuries, perhaps millennia or longer. Public-key cryptography has the important property that it is much easier to encrypt with very large keys than it is to break a message (decrypt by brute force, without the secret key). The difference in effort widens exponentially with increasing key size. Advances in computer power are more than offset by the ability to use longer keys. Likewise, "massively parallel computers," often cited by the ignorant as a possible way to break these ciphers, offer only marginal, linear speedups on brute-force cracking . . . utterly inconsequential compared with the efforts needed to factor large numbers. Faster computers are a big win for strong cryptography.

The important distinction between modern cryptography and conventional, or classical, cryptography is that the keys are asymmetric in modern cryptography, whereas in classical cryptography the parties to a cipher had somehow to exchange the same key. Exchanging keys with hundreds or even thousands of correspondents is much harder than simply looking up a key in a public-key directory, or asking for it to be sent in e-mail. More important for our purposes here, only the public-key approach allows the uses described here. For example, digital signatures rely on keeping the secret key a secret. If conventional ciphers were used, then anyone sharing one's private key could forge signatures, withdraw money, and generally wreak havoc. (Digital signatures exploit this asymmetry property of keys by allowing anyone to easily authenticate a signature without having access to the key that would allow forgery of a signature.)

Appropriately for this book, encryption is like an unbreakable "force field" around an encrypted item, much like the "bobbles" described in Vinge's *The Peace War*. The amount of energy required to run the computers—not to mention the number of such computers and the time involved!—can be shown to be greater than all of the energy all of the stars in the universe will ever produce. This for a sufficiently large key, one with an RSA modulus of a few thousand digits. (This has not yet been mathematically proved, in that factoring large numbers has not been proved to be "hard." It is remotely possible that some fast factoring breakthrough will be discovered, but this is considered by nearly all mathematicians to be extremely unlikely. The speculation that the NSA knows how to quickly factor large numbers, and thus break RSA, seems equally unlikely.)

The Encryption Controversy

Governments are clearly afraid of strong cryptography in the hands of the citizenry. Governments around the world have attempted to deal with the implications of this threat by limiting the size of keys that citizens may use, by limiting the types of algorithms that may be used, by demanding that citizen-units "escrow" (deposit) their keys with the government or with registered government agents, and by banning strong cryptography altogether. This is a battle over whether one's thoughts and messages may be placed inside sealed envelopes or must be written on "postcards," for the government to read, as Phil Zimmermann points out. One U.S. government proposal, repeated in several variants, is that messages may be sealed in envelopes, but only if the government has a special key to open them. This is like allowing citizens to have curtains on windows, but only if the local police can trigger a special transparency mode. And the issues are quite comparable. Encryption, as we will see, makes certain kinds of crimes and revolutionary activities much more feasible, but so do locked doors, curtains, and whispered conversations. And yet we would not consider outlawing locked doors, curtains, and whispered conversations. As Zimmermann notes, "I should be able to whisper in your ear, even if you're a thousand miles away," referring of course to e-mail or to voice-scrambling technology (public-key cryptography is fast enough, when combined cleverly with conventional ciphers, to allow real-time audio and video streams to be encrypted). There are profound constitutional issues involved, in the U.S. at least. The various rights enumerated in the Bill of Rights would seem to make it impossible for the U.S. government to specify the forms of speech, to insist that locks have keys escrowed with the police, and so forth. Many observers expect cryptography restrictions to face strong challenge on constitutional grounds, and, in fact, a few cases are in the court system, challenging various provisions of U.S. cryptography policy (especially the export provisions of the Munitions Act and related restrictions).

This debate is still going on, and it's too soon to tell if the "Great Crypto Crackdown" will succeed. Certainly there are many reasons to expect that it's far too late to suppress such technologies, that millions of users will not lightly go to "postcards" for their communications, and that concerns about government corruption, secret FBI dossiers, and economic espionage will undermine Big Brother's efforts to control the communications of "citizen-units."

Digital Money and Electronic Commerce

This is one of the most exciting frontiers, and one of the most publicized. But it is also one of the hardest to implement correctly. Money intrinsically involves stores of value, transfers of value, institutions, and various interlocking webs of regulations, so implementing digital money correctly has not come easily. In fact, the history of digital money lies mostly in the future. The early years of the new century should see many of the current problems resolved.

Digital cash, untraceable and anonymous (like real cash), is coming, though various technical and practical hurdles remain. What have been dubbed "Swiss banks in cyberspace" will make economic transactions much more liquid and much less subject to local rules and regulations. Tax avoidance is likely to be a major attraction for many. One example to consider is the work under way to develop anonymous, untraceable systems for "cyberspace casinos." While not as attractive to many as elegant casinos, the popularity of "numbers games" and bookies in general suggests an opportunity to pursue; this is but one of many new opportunities digital money will offer.

By digital money I do not mean the various kinds of electronic funds transfers, automated teller machine transactions, wire transfers, etc. that already exist in so many forms. Nor do I mean the various "smart card" systems that some claim to be "digital money," even "untraceable digital cash" (in some notorious examples involving flawed protocols). Rather, our focus is on instruments that are actually *untraceable* in a strong sense. Again, Chaum was the pioneer in this area, and his company DigiCash is the exemplar of digital money at this time, with several large banks cooperating in joint ventures to issue DigiCash. Digital money probably will not be "digital currency," in the sense that dollars, yen, and marks are currency. Rather, it will be more like the various financial instruments, denominated in various currencies, such as checks, bearer bonds, letters of credit, promissory notes, chop marks, and even IOUs.

Alice and Bob can exchange digital cash in this way: Alice goes to a bank, submits to the bank a kind of number, and receives a modified form of this number from the bank. It's as if the bank has stamped her number with a "Good for 100 Digimarks" stamp. Ordinarily this number would of course be traceable, but Alice can perform a special operation on this number ("unblinding" it) which makes it unlinkable to her original purchase of the number. She can then send this number to Bob, perhaps even through an anonymous remailer, and Bob can then present this number to the bank for redemption. The bank can recognize the number as one that it issued, through some manipulations, but cannot link it with Alice. Full-blown digital cash is both payer- and payee-unlinkable. Some of the current proposals being floated limit the untraceability to only partial untraceability, presumably to satisfy the concerns of government and law-enforcement critics of full untraceability. Cypherpunks Ian Goldberg, Doug Barnes, and others have developed methods to make even this partially traceable form fully untraceable.

The actual details involve some complicated math and need careful thought to get straight, which this article cannot cover. Bruce Schneier's *Applied Cryptography* has a good explanation of how Chaumian digital cash works, and *Scientific American* has also carried some good articles.

It is often claimed that "digital currencies" will not gain widespread acceptance, let alone the support of governments. If digital money is viewed as a transfer mechanism, and not as a competitor to currency or specie (gold, silver, etc.), then the support of governments is less of an issue, perhaps even a non-issue, because banks have done quite well without explicit governmental sanction of their instruments. And in the international realm, there already is not much of a governmental role: banks have worked out mechanisms for dealing with each other, and for dealing with entities with a reputation for misbehavior. As we will see, international trade represents a kind of anarchy.

There are many reasons for using untraceable digital cash. Some people simply prefer to pay cash for various reasons, and see no reason why electronic transactions should have more traceability than ordinary folding-money transactions have. Others fear the compilation of dossiers on spending habits, travel agendas, and so forth. Untraceable digital money protects the privacy of economic transactions, just as cash does today. With increasingly powerful networks of ATM and check-processing systems, the development of "shopping profiles" is a concern for anyone interested in privacy. Having insurance companies and employers gaining access to purchasing habits is undesirable; such access could, at its extreme, lead to law enforcement midnight raids on persons suspected of various crimes because of legal purchases they might have made. Untraceable digital money provides protection against this.

Making automated toll-road payments with untraceable digital cash is one obvious use. Digicash is working with European governments to deploy digital money for this sort of application.

There are, of course, various transactions involving anonymity, digital pseudonyms, and illegal items that only an untraceable digital cash system makes possible. And some novel applications are new. For example, "perpetual trusts" could be constructed by purchasing a large number of digital money instruments, perhaps being converted regularly to other such instruments. Because they are untraceable, there is no means of, say, canceling the numbers to stop the perpetual trust. Thus, as a hypothetical, no one—certainly not the bankers—will know that which of the instruments are part of the perpetual trust Bill Gates creates in 2010 with ten billion dollars . . . and this trust could still exist a century later, untouched by taxation and not even really domiciled in any particular nation. Contracts using such digital money instruments could similarly be of this "fire and forget" sort. Thus can fortunes be directed toward specific purposes, beyond the reach of governments. (For the curious, digital time-stamping and cryptographic timed-release techniques are needed to insure that the humans involved don't violate the contract originally set up.)

There are, of course, many reasons *not* to use untraceable digital cash. Businesses typically need to show records of expenses to deduct against gross sales. The simplest example of this involves anonymous payments to employees: few corporations would be interested in doing this, even if they satisfied themselves that they wouldn't get caught, because they then could not use the employee expenses as a deduction against raw income. (One can imagine many situations where an employer *would* be interested in such arrangements, and under-the-table payments are common practice in certain types of businesses.)

There is still the possibility of fraud, of dissatisfaction with transactions, and of improperly completed transactions. Cryptography obviously cannot completely eliminate such disputes. But various measures, such as reputation-rating services, digital signatures, etc., should work fairly well in controlling these kinds of problems. Trade has been conducted for millennia without governments playing a central role; in fact, international trade is often cited as an example of anarchy in action, as clearly the laws of any one country are not easily applicable. That trade works so well is evidence that actions have consequences, that repeat business matters, and that even in a relative anarchy, behavior matters. An excellent survey of this kind of trade anarchy is contained in Bruce Benson's *The Enterprise of Law*.

The argument often made by critics of untraceable e-cash, that issuers will renege or abscond, refusing to honor their instruments, ignores the nature of e-cash. Because e-cash is untraceable, an issuer never really knows when he's merely being "tested" by a rating service (or, more direly, when the client might be a member of the Mafia!). Reliability testing and reputation ratings are important.

True digital cash—the fully untraceable form—admittedly will allow some new channels for criminal activity. Privacy has its price. The ability of people to plot crimes and commit them behind closed doors is obvious, and yet we don't demand secret cameras in homes, apartments, and hotel rooms. Some of the disadvantages of anonymous systems will be discussed later, along with some of the proposals by various governments to limit or even completely ban strong cryptography.

The Surveillance Society

Imagine you are entering a bar or nightclub, or a movie. You are asked to produce identification as proof that you are of legal age. Currently, these "credentials" are presumably only glanced at briefly. With the advent of computer scanners, bar codes, and networks, the very real possibility exists that such credentials will be scanned, read, and fed into various databases. Maybe for customer profiling, maybe for compliance auditing, maybe for other reasons. But the effect is that one's movements, habits, and preferences are now in a database, perhaps even fed to the local police (as is the custom in many countries). Even if the collected data is not explicitly planned for a dossier, or for the government, a trail is still created, and this presents serious problems, especially as networks and computers get much faster.

David Chaum, along with his other work, has also developed schemes for presenting a credential of some sort without revealing identity. Though this sounds impossible, modern cryptography provides an approach. Think of it as a sealed envelope with a movable transparent window that can be moved over, say, an "age" field. The owner of such a credential could present proof that he is of some age, or past some age, without providing his identity or any other information. How this works, and how forgeries are prevented, is beyond the scope of this chapter. Cryptographic protocols are used, and biometric authentication is generally needed, to prevent such a credential from being easily lent or sold to others.

One obvious use is for automated toll-road tokens that can be read remotely, either authorizing the holder to travel on the road, or, using digital cash, make a payment remotely. The dangers of having one's movements on toll roads compiled into records is obvious to nearly everyone, though Singapore has adopted just such a citizen-unit-tracking system!

This is a good example of how technology can provide the kind of protection that well-meaning "privacy laws" cannot actually provide. While special interest groups lobby the government for new laws and new wrinkles on old laws, technology can directly provide the protection many want. For example, which approach better solves the problem of people using scanners to monitor cellular telephone conversations: passing more laws saying such monitoring is illegal (except for the police), or adding encryption to cell phones? A basic credo of the Cypherpunks movement has been that technological solutions are preferable to administrative or legislative solutions.

The growing use of government-approved picture IDs for travel is becoming the modern equivalent of travel documents in the U.S. While I cannot see a situation in which citizen-units are ever told they may not travel without authorization, I can quite easily see the situation emerging in which airlines, bus companies, car rental agencies, hotels, and gas stations are expected to "run your card through." This is already the case with many hotels and nearly all car and truck rental agencies demanding credit cards (partly to insure payment, but also for law-enforcement purposes). This produces a de facto movement-tracking system. Expect more scrutiny, perhaps even time-consuming and hassling scrutiny, for those who try to pay in cash and for those who are reluctant to have their ID cards run through the system. Since 1995, airlines have insisted on picture IDs, on orders of the government.

As with the government interest in true names and the naming process for tracking, such ID cards are an essential tool for tracking movements, collecting taxes, and establishing dossiers on citizen-units. Credentials without identity are an important technology to have and to deploy widely. A recurring theme here is that technology, not so-called privacy laws (from which governments nearly always exempt themselves anyway), is the best protection against such a surveillance state.

Data Havens and Information Markets

Another science fiction writer, Bruce Sterling, popularized "data havens" in his 1988 novel *Islands in the Net*. He focused on *physical* data havens, but cyberspace data havens are more interesting, and are likely to be more important. That they are distributed in many legal jurisdictions, and may not even be traceable to any particular jurisdiction, is crucial. A data haven is a place, physical or virtual, where information may be stored or accessed. The usual connotation is that the data are illegal in some jurisdictions, but not in the haven.

Data havens and information markets are already springing up, using the methods described to make information retrievable anonymously and untraceably. Using networks of remailers and, of course, encryption, messages may be posted in public forums like the Usenet, and read by anyone in the world with access, sort of like a cyberspatial "Democracy Wall" where controversial messages may be posted. These "message pools" are the main way cyberspatial data havens are implemented. Offers may be in plaintext, so as to be readable by humans, with instructions on how to reply (and with a public key to be used). This allows fully untraceable markets to develop.

It is likely that services will soon arise which archive articles for fees, to ensure that a URL (Uniform Resource Locator) is "persistent" over a period of many years. Ross Anderson's "Eternity Service" provides a means of distributing the publication of something so that even later attempts to withdraw all copies are thwarted. This has obvious value in fighting censorship, but will also have implications when other types of publication occur (for example, a pirated work would not be withdrawable from the system, leaving it permanently liberated).

Examples of likely data haven markets are credit databases, doctor and lawyer databases, and other heavily regulated (or even unallowed) databases: information on explosives, drug cultivation and processing, methods for suicide, and other such contraband information. Data havens may also carry copyrighted material, sans payment to holders, and various national and trade secrets.

As one example, the "Fair Credit Reporting Act" in the U.S. limits the length of time credit records may be kept (to seven or eight years) and places various restrictions on what data may be collected or reported. What if Alice "remembers" that Bob, applying for credit from her, declared bankruptcy ten years earlier, and ran out on various debts? Should she be banned from taking this into account? What if she accesses a database that is *not* bound by the FCRA, perhaps one in a data haven accessible over the Net? Can Alice "sell" her remembrances to others? (Apparently not, unless she agrees to the various terms of the FCRA. So much for her First Amendment rights.) This is the kind of data haven application I expect will develop over the next several years. It could be in a jurisdiction that ignores such things as the FCRA, such as a Caribbean island nation, or it could be in cyberspace, using various cryptographic protocols, Web proxies, and remailers for access.

Imagine the market for access to databases on "bad doctors" and "rip-off lawyers." There are many interesting issues involved in such databases: inaccurate information, responses by those charged, the basis for making judgments,

etc. Some will make malicious or false charges. This is ostensibly why such databases are banned, or heavily regulated. Governments reserve the right to make such data
available. Of course, these are the same governments that
falsify credit records for government agents and that give the
professional guilds like the American Medical Association
and the American Bar Association the power to stop com-
petitors from entering their markets.

Information markets match potential buyers and sellers of
information. One experimental "information market" is
BlackNet, a system I devised in 1993 as an example of what
could be done, as an exercise in guerrilla ontology. It allowed
fully anonymous, two-way exchanges of information of all
sorts. The basic idea was to use a "message pool," a publicly
readable place for messages. By using chains of remailers,
messages could be untraceably and anonymously deposited
in such pools, and then read anonymously by others (because the message pool was broadcast widely, à la Usenet).
By including public keys for later communications, two-way
unreadable (to others) communication could be established,
all within the message pool. Such an information market
also acts as a distributed data haven.

As Paul Leyland succinctly described the experiment:

Tim May showed how mutually anonymous secure information trading could be implemented with a public forum
such as Usenet and with public key cryptography. Each
information purchaser wishing to take part posts a sales
pitch and a public key to Usenet. Information to be traded
would then have a public key appended so that a reply
can be posted and the whole encrypted in the public key
of the other party. For anonymity, the keys should contain
no information that links it to an identifiable person. May
posted a 1024-bit PGP key supposedly belonging to "Black-

net". As May's purpose was only educational, he soon admitted authorship.

An example of an item offered for sale early on, in plaintext, was proof that African diplomats were being blackmailed by the CIA in Washington and New York. A public key for later communications was included.

There are reports that U.S. authorities have investigated this market because of its presence on networks at Defense Department research labs. There's not much they can do about it, of course, and more such entities are expected. The implications such tools hold for espionage are profound, and their impact largely unstoppable. Anyone with a home computer and access to the Net or the Web, in various forms, can use these methods to communicate securely, anonymously or pseudonymously, and with little fear of detection. "Digital dead drops" can be used to post information obtained, far more securely than the old physical dead drops . . . no more messages left in Coke cans at the bases of trees on remote roads. Payments can also be made untraceably; this of course opens up the possibility that anyone in any government agency may act as a part-time spy.

Matching buyers and sellers of organs is another example of such a market, although one that clearly involves some real-world transfers (and so it cannot be as untraceable as purely cyberspatial transactions can be). There is huge demand for such transfers, but various laws tightly control such markets, thus forcing them into Third World nations. Fortunately, strong cryptography allows market needs to be met without interference by governments. (Those who are repelled by such markets are of course free not to patronize them.)

Whistleblowing is another growing use of anonymous remailers, with those fearing retaliation using remailers to publicly post their incriminating information. The Usenet news-groups "alt.whistleblowing" and "alt.anonymous.messages" are places where anonymously remailed messages blowing the whistle have appeared. Of course, there's a fine line between whistleblowing, revenge, and espionage. The same is true for "leaks" from highly placed sources. "Digital Deep Throats" will multiply, and anyone in Washington, or Paris, or wherever, can make his case safely and anonymously by digitally leaking material to the press. William Gibson foresaw a similar situation in his novel *Count Zero* (1987), in which employees of high-tech corporations agree to be ensconced in remote labs, disconnected from the Nets and other leakage paths. We may see a time when those with security clearances are explicitly forbidden from using the Net except through firewalled machines, with monitoring programs running.

Information selling by employees may even take whimsical forms, such as the selling of topless images of women who flashed for the video cameras on "Splash Mountain" at Disneyland (now called "Flash Mountain" by some). Employees of the ride swiped copies of the digital images and uploaded them anonymously to various Web sites. Such thievery and exposure has also been committed with the medical records of famous persons. DMV records have also been stolen by state employees with access, and sold to information brokers, private investigators, and even curious fans. The DMV records of notoriously reclusive author Thomas Pynchon showed up on the Net. It's been rumored that information brokers are prepared to pay handsomely for a CD-ROM containing the U.S. government's "key escrow" database.

The larger issue is that mere laws are not adequate to deal with such sales of personal, corporate, or other private information. The bottom line is this: if one wants something kept secret, it must be kept secret. In a free society, few personal secrets are compelled. Unfortunately, we have for too long been in a situation where governments insist that people give out their true names, their various government identification numbers, their medical situations, and so on. "And who shall guard the guardians?" The technology of privacy protection can change this balance of power. Cryptography provides for "personal empowerment," to use the current phrasing.

Holding Up the Walls of Cyberspace

In the virtual worlds described in the science fiction of Vinge, Gibson, Stephenson, and others, what holds up the "walls"? What keeps these worlds from collapsing, from crumbling to cyberdust as users poke around, as hackers try to penetrate systems? The virtual gates and doors and stone walls described in *True Names* are persistent, robust data structures, not flimsy constructs ready to collapse.

Certainly the robustness does not come from the hand-waving "consensual hallucination" referred to by some cyberspace pioneers such as Gibson (though he got it mostly right with his "ice"). Psychology and mental states will of course be important in virtual worlds, as is already so obviously the case on the Net and the Web, but true solidity and structure will come from more basic protocols.

Security and cryptography provide the ontological support for these cyberspatial worlds, for enduring structures that permit "colonization" of these spaces and structures. More precisely, the "owners" of a chunk of cyberspace—e.g., someone maintaining a virtual world on their owned machines and networks—establish the structure, persistence, access policies, and other rules. "My house, my rules." Those who disagree with the rules will be welcome to stay away. And those who disagree with the rules but want governments to change the rules will face an uphill battle. Owners can always re-site their machines in more favorable jurisdictions or choose to operate behind a veil of anonymity. The owners of cyberspaces will use cryptography and security measures to ensure against tampering by others.

Cryptography is not just about building the kinds of virtual realities described in *True Names*. The security of ordinary networks depends on cryptography. And yet the deployment of strong cryptography is being hobbled by the various laws and regulations limiting the use of cryptography, including export laws that affect domestic encryption products in several ways, especially because they decree that liability exists if a "foreign person" is "exposed" to an export-controlled product, even if he buys it in a U.S. store or sees it in a U.S. university lab! The U.S. is even limiting export and placement on public sites of virus protection and general security software, strongly suggesting they want the ability to knock out foreign sites and don't want Americans to protect foreign sites. Is the U.S. planning for information warfare?

Proposals for mandatory "key escrow," where the government gets access to a kind of spare key left with it, will weaken confidence in digital commerce, and could provide the "keys to the kingdom" to a spy or hostile power able to gain access to the master database. Unfortunately, the government's plans to put "Big Brother Inside" the networks and to restrict access to proper security measures means these hostile agents will face an easier job. When considering the "bad" implications of strong cryptography, keep this in mind.

Some years back, the National Security Agency was explicitly divided into two functions, one function doing signals and communications intelligence (SIGINT and COMINT), and the other doing communications security and information security (COMSEC and INFOSEC), i.e., working on mechanisms to better secure the nation's communications. At about this time, circa 1988, the NSA's COMSEC folks were *explicitly* warning that DES, the Data Encryption Standard, was long overdue for replacement and that new measures were urgently needed to secure the nation's communications and financial infrastructure. Yet, a decade later, with warnings of an impending "digital Pearl Harbor," the NSA and FBI are doing everything they can to limit access to strong cryptography and are throwing up roadblocks to hinder the deployment of strong and secure systems.

It looks like the user community will have to ignore their demands and secure things themselves. John Gilmore's SWAN program seeks to make links between machines on the Net routinely encrypted.

Virtual Communities

Virtual communities, mentioned earlier, are networks of individuals or groups which are not necessarily closely connected geographically. The word "virtual" is meant to imply a nonphysical linking, but should not be taken to mean that these are any less community-like than are conventional physical communities.

The "Coven" in *True Names* is such a virtual community. Other examples include churches, service organizations, clubs, criminal gangs, cartels, fan groups, etc. The Catholic Church and the Boy Scouts are both examples of well-established virtual communities that span the globe, transcend national borders, and create a sense of allegiance, of belonging—a sense of "community." Likewise, the Mafia, with its enforcement mechanisms, its own extralegal rules, etc., is a virtual community. There are many other examples: Masons, Triads, Red Cross, Interpol, religions, drug cartels, terrorist groups, political movements, to name a few. In an academic setting, "invisible colleges" are the communities of researchers. Linked by computer networks, these virtual communities are often of greater importance to members than are their physical communities, or even their universities.

There are undoubtedly many more such virtual communities than there are nation-states, and the ties that bind them are for the most part much stronger than are chauvinistic nationalist impulses. Each community will have its own rules, its own access policies, initiation rituals, censure policies, and so forth. Governments have had little power to penetrate such private groups, and even less penetration is likely when strong cryptography provides a new topology for connectivity. Essential to these communities is their essentially *voluntary* nature: it is difficult to coerce membership or interaction, though there are some obvious examples of such coercion. Self-selection and self-enforcement of rules are important aspects. Virtual communities may be attacked by those who disagree with their policies, or have some bone to pick; the Cypherpunks list has been attacked by spam attacks, subscribing the list to other high-volume lists, creating mail loops, posting of incredibly long rants on unrelated topics, and so forth. It is to be expected that hardening techniques will evolve to better protect such virtual communities. For the time being, kill files and twit filters are the best protection. Some on the Cypherpunks list choose to contract with others to filter for them, e.g., by creating "best of" compilations. This is the free market in action.

The corporation is a prime example of a virtual community, having scattered sites, private communication channels (generally inaccessible to the outside world, including governmental authorities), its own security forces and punishment systems (within limits), and its own goals and methods. In fact, many "cyberpunk" (not cypherpunk) fiction authors make a mistake in assuming the future world will be dominated by transnational megacorporate "states." Corporations are just one of many examples of such virtual communities that will be effectively on a par with nation-states.

These virtual communities are typically "opaque" to outsiders. Attempts to gain access to the internals of these communities are rarely successful. Law-enforcement and intelligence agencies may infiltrate such groups and use electronic surveillance (ELINT) to monitor these virtual communities. Not surprisingly, these communities are early adopters of encryption technology, ranging from scrambled cell phones to full-blown PGP encryption. Strong cryptography is already being used by various revolutionary and antigovernment movements, including rebels in Burma and Mexico. Usage is mounting daily; strong crypto makes for an ideal "revolutionary cell" system.

In addition to their own rules and access procedures, virtual communities typically have their own moral codes and ethical standards. Revolutionary or so-called terrorist groups are just one example; unbreakable cryptographic communications mean that the potential for coordinated activity by groups having their own moral standards is greatly increased.

A "politically incorrect" usage of these virtual communities is to use "race bits" to bar membership by certain races in such communities. This can even be done without violating the protection of a nym, using the idea of a "credential without identity." For example, the Aryan Cybernation could demand that a credential be displayed showing one to be a Caucasian. Ironically, an equivalent example, but one which is deemed politically correct by many, is the example of "women-only" forums on the Net. In this case, a woman could gain access to a women-only forum by demonstrating possession of a credential with the appropriate gender bit set. (At the simplest level, this can be done by having other women "vouch" for a candidate, digitally signing a statement the candidate presents.) A more robust system, with less opportunity for false use or false transfer, would be to implement Chaum's credentials-without-identity scheme. But the point is to show how virtual communities can establish their own access rules and their own enforcement mechanisms.

In this example, if the nexus of the virtual community is not known to be in a specific jurisdiction, but is "virtual," enforcement of national laws is problematic. Nations can ban membership in such unapproved groups, of course, but then members will access them through remailers, etc. (Which would inevitably lead to the next step: banning remailed messages, banning encrypted messages, registering personal computers and software, etc.)

The use of encryption by "evil" groups, such as child pornographers, terrorists, money launderers, and racists, is cited by those who wish to limit civilian access to crypto tools. I call these the "Four Horseman of the Infocalypse," as they are so often cited as the reason why ordinary citizen-units of a nation-state are not to have access to crypto. Newspaper headlines scream "Child Pornography Ring Using Secret Codes to Communicate," and the U.S. Department of Justice and the FBI send spokesmen out to speak at public conferences on the dangers of encryption.

This is clearly a dangerous argument to make, for various good reasons. The basic right of free speech is the right to speak in a language one's neighbors or governing leaders may not find comprehensible: encrypted speech.

Many of us believe we are already seeing the imminent

end of nation-states, with virtual communities attaining greater importance for many people. Certainly many of us are "closer" to our neighbors in cyberspace—those with whom we share certain interests—than we are to our physical neighbors. And the passions of these special interest groups (think of Aryan Nation, Greenpeace, Sendero Luminoso, Scientologists, etc.) are often vastly more intense than normal nationalistic sentiments. (This was the rap against the Catholic Church: that Catholics were often more loyal to the Pope and the Vatican than to their various provinces and kingdoms. Whether true or not, it has clearly been a concern for many centuries.)

In such "discretionary" communities, the time-honored enforcement mechanism of "shunning" is gaining new popularity. Using kill files or twit filters, nobody in these communities has to read the messages of those they dislike. They can just filter them out.

Reputations Matter

What will keep people from reneging on digital deals? What will keep them honest? If the government and the courts cannot track a person down, because they used untraceable or anonymous systems, how will digital societies and economies work?

Well, for starters, the systems are not really purely "anonymous." The ability to use digital signatures and persistent digital pseudonyms, or "true nyms," means that behaviors can and will be attributed to nyms. Some nyms will establish the reputation of being straight in dealings, others will establish a less savory reputation.

How does an escrow service (the classical definition of escrow, not the newspeak definition used by the U.S. government for key escrow) survive and prosper? By being in the business of releasing funds when conditions are met, and not otherwise. By not absconding with the funds. In the real world escrow services do quite well because the continuing future revenue stream from their good reputation exceeds what they could get by "burning" any particular customer. Sometimes this involves putting up a bond, which is a kind of secondary escrow.

Digital escrow services will operate along similar lines, with reputation playing the major role. Also, escrow services can be "pinged" (tested) by lots of small transactions. Inasmuch as digital money is untraceable, lots of small interactions can be used to test the trustworthiness of any bank or escrow service. Brand names, image, and product ratings will be as important in cyberspace as they are today, perhaps more so.

Private Law

As noted, virtual communities have their own rules, with usually little involvement of the outside world in the internal operations of the community. In some important examples, the virtual community is explicitly outside the law, as with the Mafia, Triads, and other such "outlaw" or "underworld" organizations—the very names suggest the status vis-à-vis the conventional legal system. For those who think of these groups as essentially criminal and coercive, à la truck hijackings and protection rackets, think also of the market services provided by the Mafia because government has decided to outlaw certain services: gambling, prostitution, high-risk loans, and "recreational" drugs. Since a bookie cannot use the court system to collect on bad debts, he has to use "private justice" systems, e.g., breaking legs. Other virtual communities have equally well developed private legal systems. The killing of informants is one obvious example. (Note that I am not condoning the killing of informants, cheats, whatever. I'm merely noting such examples in the context of this discussion.)

But more than just "voluntary" interactions are involved: the role of contracts becomes central. And contracts can be enforced in cyberspace. Bonding entities or escrow agents can hold digital money until some service is satisfactorily completed.

Most interactions in the real world depend more on these reputational effects than on actual enforcement of laws by governments. A "reputable" mail order company, for example, ships products because that's a more important long-term business for it to be in than ripping off a few customers would be. Just about any bank could, quite easily, forge simplistic withdrawal signatures and claim that a customer had withdrawn his money. That they don't do such things has a lot more to do with what banks perceive their business to be than with any technological or legal limitations.

In other words, reputations matter. And in cyberspace, they matter even more than in the outside world, where some people have shown irksome tendencies to declare bankruptcy to escape the obligation of repaying a debt, and then seek the protection of the American legal system, and where honesty, it sometimes seems, is presumed to be something for suckers. Under crypto anarchy, a nym's reputation is all he has, and honesty once again becomes a valuable trait.

What form legal structures may take in cyberspace is unclear. But the role of traditional legal structures is likely to diminish, unless governments around the world are successful in stamping out strong cryptography use. This lesser role for the formal legal system is especially likely as the Net becomes increasingly global, with even more tools for anonymous or pseudonymous interaction. Tools to make digital signatures and digital time-stamping more common will help to build what Nick Szabo calls "smart contracts." Escrow services—even anonymous or pseudonymous ones—will make it possible to have "completion bonds" for cyberspace activities.

Individuals interacting in cyberspace will generally have to be more competent about arranging their fiduciary and contractual relationships, and less reliant on having government offices and agents bail them out of foolish actions. Caveat emptor. Of course, they are always free to contract to have a "nanny" screen their interactions and tell them what to do. They could even call this their "government." They just can't force others to obey their nanny.

Crypto Anarchy

"The Net is an anarchy." This truism is the core of crypto anarchy. No central control, no ruler, no leader (except by example, reputation), no "laws." No single nation controls the Net, no administrative body sets policy. The Ayatollah in Iran is as powerless to stop a newsgroup—alt.wanted.moslem.women or alt.wanted.moslem.gay come to mind—he doesn't like as the President of France is as powerless to stop, say, abuse of the French in soc.culture.french. Likewise, the CIA can't stop newsgroups, or sites, or Web pages, that give away their secrets. At least not in terms of the Net itself. What non-Net steps might be taken is left as an exercise for the paranoid and the cautious.

This essential anarchy is much more common than many think. Anarchy—the absence of a ruler telling one what to do—is common in many walks of life: choice of books to read, movies to see, friends to socialize with, etc. Anarchy does not mean complete freedom—one can, after all, only read the books that someone has written and had published—but it does mean freedom from external coercion. And anarchy does not mean an absence of local hierarchies, or an absence of rules. Groups outside the direct control of local governmental authorities may still have leaders, rulers, club presidents, or elected bodies. Many will not, though.

Anarchy as a concept, though, has been tainted by other associations. The anarchy here is not the anarchy of popular conception—lawlessness, disorder, chaos. Nor is it the bomb-throwing anarchy of the nineteenth-century "black" anarchists, usually associated with Russia and labor movements. Nor is it the black flag anarcho-syndicalism of leftist writers such as Proudhon and Goldstein. Rather, the anarchy being spoken of here is the anarchy of "absence of government" (literally, "an arch," without a chief or head). It's the same anarchy of "anarcho-capitalism," the libertarian free market ideology that promotes voluntary, uncoerced economic transactions. "Crypto anarchy" is a pun on crypto, meaning "hidden," on the use of "crypto" in combination with political views (as in Gore Vidal's famous charge to William F. Buckley: "You crypto fascist!"), and of course because the technology of crypto makes this form of anarchy possible. The first presentation of this was in my 1988 "Crypto Anarchist Manifesto," whimsically patterned after another famous manifesto.

Politically, virtual communities outside the scope of local governmental control may present problems of law enforcement and tax collection. Avoidance of coerced transactions can mean avoidance of taxes, of laws that dictate to whom one can sell and to whom one can't, and so forth. It is likely that many will be unhappy that some are using cryptography to avoid laws designed to control behavior.

National borders are becoming ever more transparent to data. A flood of bits crosses the borders of most developed countries: phone lines, cables, fibers, satellites, and millions of diskettes, tapes, CDs, etc. A single CD or DAT can contain hundreds of megabytes of data—just the least significant bits (LSBs) of a musical recording can be replaced by a hundred megabytes of data without any means of distinguishing the data from ordinary audio noise. Stopping data at the borders is hopeless, with every tourist able to carry in and out vast amounts of data, undetectably.

Regulatory Arbitrage

The movement of cyberspace operations from nation to nation will rival or exceed the movement of economic production from nation to nation. Just as tax and financial policies of one nation can trigger movements of factories and offices to more favorable climes, so too can data and privacy policies trigger movements of cyberspace-oriented operations to more favorable locales. And this movement can happen as fast as typing a few keystrokes to whisk the site and its files to a new host system.

The issues of international enforcement of various laws and of regularizing laws across national borders have always been problematic; the ability of anyone from the privacy of their home or business to connect with sites nearly any-where in the world catapults this issue to the forefront. The first international conference on "financial cryptography" was held in 1997 in Anguilla, a Caribbean tax haven.

The ability to move data around the world at will, to communicate with remote sites at will, means that what has been dubbed "regulatory arbitrage" can be used to avoid legal limits in any given country. For example, when remailing into the U.S. from a site in the Netherlands, whose laws apply? (If one thinks that U.S. laws should apply to sites in the Netherlands, does Iraqi law apply in the U.S.?)

This regulatory arbitrage is also useful for avoiding the welter of laws and regulations that operations in one country may face, including the "deep pockets" lawsuits so many in the U.S. face. Moving operations on the Net outside a litigious jurisdiction is one way to reduce this business liability. Law professor Michael Froomkin has written extensively about regulatory arbitrage and the implications of strong cryptography; his Web site has several interesting articles.

The implications for taxation policy are especially interesting. Incomes will tend to be less visible, as is already the case with international consultants. Imputing incomes and assets already requires intrusive probes into bank accounts, restrictions on funds transfers, and a loss of anonymity and privacy in financial transactions. An alternative—assuming taxes survive, which they probably will—is to tax real, physical assets, such as real property. Or to establish sales taxes and value-added taxes (VATs). Or, of course, to drastically reduce the size of governments and have people make their own arrangements for purchase of any services they may need, save perhaps for only the few services that only a larger group can purchase. David Friedman has discussed such matters in *The Machinery of Freedom*.

It seems unlikely that any sort of "new world order" will be universally adopted. Thus, governments face the prospect of either limiting communication with sites in "rogue jurisdictions," or accepting that this skirting of their laws will happen. Unfortunately, the U.S. has been showing disturbing signs of pushing for just such an international agreement, on crypto and Net access policy, despite the inevitable failure it faces, and the odd moral position of having the U.S. enforcing, say, Islamic nations' laws against mentioning certain topics. It is doubtful the Supreme Court would uphold any such attempts to limit speech in this way.

The whole issue has resonances with age and decency restrictions on material. The Net has made it easy for users of all ages to access any material they wish. This has resulted in calls for limits on material "harmful to minors," à la the U.S. Communications Decency Act. But, of course, connecting to a foreign site would bypass even the CDA, exactly as Muslims, say, can connect to U.S. or European sites where discussions of pork, homosexuality, and other "banned" (to Muslims) topics are freely available.

The Morality of Crypto Anarchy

The political and moral implications of crypto anarchy as a form of government (or nongovernment) would itself require a long essay. Suffice it to say that many of us think giving power back to people to make their own choices in life without government interference would be a good thing. And regardless of whether it's a good thing or not, it doesn't appear that this trend toward crypto anarchy can be stopped.

Crypto anarchy ensures that men with guns cannot be brought in to interfere with mutually agreed-upon transactions, the only kind of economic interaction possible in crypto anarchy. Some people will of course scream "Unfair!" and demand government intervention, which is why strong cryptography will probably be opposed by the masses, unless of course, they are wise and take the long view. This may smack of elitism, but I have very little faith in democracy. De Tocqueville warned in 1840 that, roughly translated, "The American Republic will endure, until politicians realize they can bribe the people with their own money." We reached that point several decades ago.

Another positive effect is to put an end to the modern form of guilds: the professional cartels that limit entry into some professions and confer special rights on certain groups. For example, the various medical and legal societies, which have various legal rights not given to, say, the local stamp-collecting club members. It may be argued that these special provisions are for the protection of patients and clients. But in a free society, persons are free to make arrangements to check the credentials of service providers as they see fit, not as some committee has decreed. This applies to all forms of professional licensing. Caveat emptor!

The printing press was a technology that destroyed the medieval guilds, as the once-protected knowledge of the guilds could be distributed to a wider audience. Eventually the kings and queens stopped throwing people into prison for the crime of making leather without a royal license, and the guilds collapsed, no doubt bemoaning the "anarchy" that had been unleashed upon the world.

To put it bluntly, crypto anarchy basically undermines democracy: it removes behaviors and transactions from the purview of the mob. And once crypto is deeply entwined into the fabric of life and commerce, it will be too late to pull the plug.

The Social Consequences of Crypto Anarchy

Can "bad things" happen with strong cryptography? Of course. I've cited several examples of things that are in some sense dangerous or bad to at least some people. But of course all technologies have both light and dark aspects. . . . The forty thousand Americans killed every year in traffic accidents, for example, are certainly a dark aspect of an otherwise helpful technology.

Not all aspects of untraceability are positive. People often want accountability, they want a "true name" attached to their interactions, a name and address they can go after if a transaction is unsatisfactory. They don't want to send money to a "nym" who may vanish. Fortunately, there are lots of ways of dealing with such issues. Reputations can be associated with nyms, as with writers who have used pseudonyms successfully. Digital signatures strengthen the process, making forgeries all but impossible. And expect to see "reputation rating" services and even "bonding" services, analogous to title companies, escrow services, and *Good Housekeeping* sorts of seals of approval (with digital signatures, of course).

What will happen to tax policies? How will ordinary taxpayers react to reports that digital-money transactions are escaping taxation, that some elite of crypto-savvy entrepreneurs are evading and avoiding taxes by moving transactions to places the government cannot monitor? There may be a backlash against such uses, but there may also be an increase in the numbers of folks using such methods. (This repeats a pattern seen with offshore investments: where once such approaches were exclusively the domain of the super-rich, now even moderately wealthy individuals can use offshore investments as part of estate planning, avoidance of "deep pockets" lawsuit claims, and even for tax avoidance.)

Of great concern are the effects of anonymity and untraceability on certain types of crimes. Abhorrent markets may arise. For example, anonymous systems and untraceable digital cash have some obvious implications for the arranging of contract killings, extortion, and kidnapping. The greatest risk in arranging for such services is that physical meetings expose the buyers and/or sellers of such services to the scrutiny of law enforcement and to the setup of sting operations. Asking around at a bar if anyone knows who can do some "discreet work" is an invitation for the FBI to get involved (and I'm certainly not arguing against such FBI or law-enforcement involvement). Crypto anarchy lessens, or even eliminates, this risk, by allowing for untraceable communication to be set up. And untraceable payment. Think back to the BlackNet example, where two-way anonymous contact occurs. The risks to the actual killers are not lessened, as their physical act is not untraceable, but this is a risk the buyers need not worry about (and I surmise that the greater risks lie in the set up and payment steps). Think of anonymous escrow services that hold the digital money until the deed is done.

The implications for corporate and national espionage have already been touched upon. Combined with data havens and liquid markets in information, secrets may become much harder to keep. Imagine a *Digital Jane's*, after the military weapons handbooks, anonymously compiled and sold for digital money, beyond the reach of various governments that don't want their secrets revealed. Similarly, whether one views it as espionage or as journalistic whistleblowing, the publication of various secrets will be much easier. Anyone in an organization with an ax to grind only has to connect to a service like BlackNet.

On the issue of terrorists, child molesters, and other Horsemen using PGP, PGPhone, and other crypto tools, how else could it be? After all, the use of PGP is being promoted widely for the protection of privacy. The child molesters, Mafiosos, money launderers, Palestinian sympathizers, nuclear material smugglers, and other assorted miscreants (or heroes, depending on one's outlook) are surely thinking about securing their communications. And certain types of terrorism are becoming more possible every day, already, as communications technologies make far-flung organizations possible.

So what? After all, criminals and conspirators also have locks on their doors, use curtains on their windows, keep their voices down when speaking among themselves in public, rent hotel rooms to plot crimes, and generally use various methods to better insure privacy and secrecy. And yet the Constitution is pretty clear that we don't insist windows be uncurtained, conversations be recorded, and locks have keys "escrowed." We cannot know, in advance of an arrest and a trial, who are the criminals and who are the law-abiding citizens, which is why talk of abandoning privacy protections to "catch criminals" is so fatuous.

Nevertheless, the inevitable use of strong crypto by some criminals, perhaps even involving some particularly heinous crimes, will surely be used as an argument to restrict crypto. As some wag put it, "National security is the root passphrase to the Constitution."

Crypto anarchy has some messy aspects, of this there can be little doubt. All technological and economic revolutions have produced dislocations and rearrangements. Crypto anarchy is no different. From relatively unimportant things like price-fixing and insider trading; to more serious things like economic espionage, the undermining of corporate knowledge ownership; to extremely dark things like anonymous markets for killings. But let's not forget that nation-states have killed more than one hundred million people in this century alone: Mao, Stalin, Hitler, and Pol Pot, just to name the most extreme examples. It is hard to imagine any level of digital contract killings ever coming close to nation-state barbarism. (But this is something we cannot accurately speak about; I don't think we have much of a choice in embracing crypto anarchy or not, so I choose to focus on the bright side.)

It is hard to argue that the risks of anonymous markets and tax evasion are justification for worldwide suppression of communications and encryption tools. People have always killed each other, and governments have not stopped this (arguably, they make the problem much worse, as the wars of this century have shown). Also, there are various steps that can be taken to lessen the risks of crypto anarchy impinging on personal safety. The importance of blood relations will likely become more important, as has long been the case in Asian and Middle Eastern economies. The hiring of private protection agencies will also help.

Big Brother Inside?

Governments are afraid of strong, unbreakable crypto in the hands of their subjects. Governments see their powers eroded by these technologies, and are taking various steps to try to limit the use of strong crypto. The U.S. has several well-publicized efforts, including the Clipper chip, the Digital Telephony wiretap law, and proposals for "voluntary" escrow of cryptographic keys. Carl Ellison has dubbed these schemes "GAK," for "Government Access to Keys." These voluntary programs are not likely to remain so.

Cypherpunks and others expect these efforts to ultimately be bypassed. Technology has let the genie out of the bottle. Crypto anarchy is liberating individuals from coercion by their physical neighbors—who cannot know who they are on the Net or what they are doing—and from governments. For libertarians, strong crypto provides the means by which government will be avoided.

Digital cash and digital banks are likely targets for legislative moves to limit the deployment of crypto anarchy and digital economies. Whether through banking regulation or tax laws, it is not likely that digital money will be deployed easily. But as noted in the discussion on extortion, many of the more interesting results of crypto anarchy can occur if even *some* issuers of untraceable digital money exist, anywhere.

The proposals to restrict access to strong cryptography bear a definite resemblance to the "War on Drugs." As Whit Diffie, one of the inventors of public-key cryptography, has noted, the War on Drugs effectively pressed corporations into service as drug warriors. Under threat of forfeiture of corporate assets (trucks, boats, warehouses) if drugs were found in them, and loss of government business, corporations adopted random searches of employee lockers, and urine sampling, and placed "Just Say No" posters in cafeterias and work areas. Hence the reliance in the "War on Crypto" on systems to force corporations to adopt "key recovery" systems. (After all, corporations might be colluding, or price-fixing, or conspiring to violate the various laws they are subject to . . . hence the government wants access to such secret communications.) Such pressure on corporations will have effects on ordinary citizen-units. There are now requirements in some jurisdictions that all candidates for public office be tested for drug use; if such policies are upheld by the Supreme Court, expect drug tests in other state-licensed matters, such as driver's licenses and work permits. Clearly the state has gone far beyond any conception the framers of the Constitution may have had.

The unhealthily close relationship between large corporations and governments often causes various deals and quid pro quos to be made. Various corporations seek to be the vendor of choice for government-approved, key-escrowed cryptography. Various "initiatives" and "alliances" are the avenue for this deal-making. Economists call this "rent-seeking." The medieval guilds were an example of the same phenomenon.

Government spokesvermin often talk about "legitimate

needs for key recovery," as when a person wants a spare key stored with his lawyer, or in a safe deposit box, or when companies want critical information encrypted in such a way that the material is not lost forever if the encryptor loses his key, forgets his passphrase, dies, leaves the company, etc. The government claims this as support for its "key recovery" initiatives, its programs to force users to allow access to keys. But this argument is misleading and has major flaws.

First, if there is a compelling need, the private enterprise system will surely meet it—the "help" of the government is not needed, nor are the proposed restrictions imposed on by business. Second, there is a huge difference between the storage of files and their transmission. When Alice uses encryption to store her files she uses a different key than what she uses for transmitting files to Bob (probably Bob's public key, in fact). There is thus no pressing business need for recovery of *transmission* keys. Both parties have the material in their local storage, presumably. And yet the government's key recovery proposals specifically focus on encryption methods for *message transmission*. Guess who the main party interested in reading intercepted transmissions is? Finally, the restrictions on *export* of cryptography systems, requiring key escrow, obviously have nothing whatsoever to do with meeting the "needs" of businesses. It will be interesting to see how foreign governments react to having escrowed systems in which the U.S. has special access to communications of their corporations and citizens. My guess is that they'll react about the same way the U.S. would react if Iraq were exporting special "Saddam-readable" crypto software to the U.S.

Any system which allows government to act to trace a transaction, or to trace a message, or to gain access to keys, essentially throws away the liberty-enhancing advantages of cryptography completely. If this is not evident, ask yourself whether the government of Burma, known as SLORC, would not use its "Government Access to Keys" to round up the dissidents communicating with laptops and PGP in the jungle? Would Hitler and Himmler have used "key recovery" to determine who the Jews were communicating with so they could all be rounded up and killed? Contact tracing is to be one of the most powerful tools in suppressing groups. Would the East German Staasi have traced e-cash transactions? The answers are obvious. For every government extant on the planet one can easily think of dozens of examples where access to keys, access to diaries, access to spending records, etc., would be exploited by the party in power. What a government considers "criminal" or "suspicious" is often what it considers threatening to its exercise of power. Rhetoric about "catching criminals" misses this point: that governments typically use surveillance powers to control citizens. Fortunately, a crackdown on crypto will not be easy to successfully implement in the U.S. and in Western nations.

Some domestic (U.S.) restrictions on cryptography and digital money seem likely, despite what many think the Constitution says. Think it can't happen? How can government require ID cards and tracking mechanisms for cash purchases? And people are finding that carrying their own cash around in cars and on planes can subject them to "forfeiture" of this cash, with no trial and no mechanism for redress (the Orwellian name for this is along the lines of "illegal use of currency").

The U.S. government continues to push for its notion of "Key Recovery," or key registration, and for limits on the strength of cryptographic systems. A purely voluntary key-recovery system is unobjectionable, as what people do with their own keys is of course their business. The danger, however, is that a widely deployed, ostensibly voluntary system could be made mandatory by the vote of Congress or a Presidential order. This sort of sword of Damocles is always worrisome, whether the proposed system is gun registration (which can then easily lead to confiscation, as happened in Nazi Germany), implantable ID units, video cameras in public places, "voluntary self-ratings" on writings or speech, or wider use of government-approved ID cards. It has been clear for a long time that the U.S. government's interest in pushing Clipper, Tessera, and the various other GAK proposals was to make escrowed encryption widespread, with non-GAK crypto ultimately to be phased out. This would be no easy thing to accomplish, for many reasons, some discussed here. A firestorm of protest awaits any attempt to ban cryptography. As one wag put it several years ago, "They'll get my crypto keys when they pry my cold, dead fingers off my keyboard."

The widespread use of strong crypto means that "rogue crypto" (terrorists, crypto anarchists, freedom fighters) gets lost in the blizzard of other uses. And shutting down all crypto means shutting down business use of crypto to protect secrets, and probably means an end to digital commerce, a price that is almost certainly too high to pay. This is another reason to delay action on crypto for as long as possible: make encrypted communications so widespread in commerce that to pull the plug would mean a financial calamity.

Colonizing Cyberspace

How will these ideas affect the development of cyberspace? "You can't eat cyberspace" is a criticism often leveled at arguments about the role of cyberspace in everyday life. The argument is that money and resources accumulated in some future cyberspatial system will not be able to be trans-

ferred or laundered into the real world. Even such a pre-
scient thinker as Neal Stephenson, in *Snow Crash*, had his
protagonist a vastly wealthy man in "the Multiverse," but a
pauper in the physical world. And Vernor Vinge has his protagonist slip up and get caught by the Feds because he was
too successful in "both planes."

This inability to move money from one realm to another
is implausible for several reasons. First, we routinely see
transfers of wealth from the abstract world of stock tips, ar-
cane consulting knowledge, etc., to the real world. Second,
a variety of means of laundering money, via phony invoices,
uncollected loans, art objects, etc., are well known to those
who launder money. . . . These methods, and more advanced
ones to come, are likely to be used by those who wish their
cyberspace profits moved into the real world. Third, many
of those who exploit the opportunities provided by crypto
anarchy will not choose to live in surveillance states and
high-tax-rate jurisdictions. Duncan Frissell refers to "perpetual tourists," much like the old "jet set."

Most Net and Web users already pay little attention to the
putative laws of their local regions or nations, apparently
seeing themselves more as members of various virtual communities than as members of locally governed entities. This
trend is accelerating. Encryption makes it easy and even safe
to ignore most local laws about what can be done in cyberspace. Most importantly, information can be bought and
sold—anonymously, too—and then used in the real world.
There is no reason to expect that this capability won't be a
major reason to at least partly move into cyberspace. The
World Wide Web is growing at an explosive pace. Combined
with cryptographically protected communication and digital
cash of some form, this should accelerate the long-awaited
colonization of cyberspace.

But Will It Happen?

Strong crypto provides new levels of personal privacy, all the more important in an era of increased surveillance, monitoring, and the temptation to demand proofs of identity and permission slips. The power of nation-states will be lessened, tax collection policies will have to be changed, and economic interactions will be based more on personal calculations of right and wrong than on societal mandates. This is the true horror to many, that the individual becomes empowered to make his own decisions about what is right and what is wrong and to then act as he wishes, to join the virtual communities he wishes to, to pay for the services he wishes, and to ignore the will of the democratic herd.

If strong cryptography and the related ideas discussed here do produce a kind of "crypto singularity," I don't believe the other side of that singularity is quite as opaque as, say, the AI and nanotechnology sorts of singularities Vernor Vinge has discussed.

Strong crypto provides a technological means of ensuring the practical freedom to read and write what one wishes to. (Albeit perhaps not in one's true name, as the nation-state-democracy will likely still try to control behavior through majority votes on what can be said, not said, read, not read, etc.) And of course if speech is free, so are many classes of economic interaction that are essentially tied to free speech.

While many may recoil from the ideas discussed here, it is already apparent that others are embracing this world. And that's enough to make things interesting.

A Phase Change

We are in a "race to the fork in the road." The fork in the road being essentially the point of no return, beyond which things are either pulled strongly to one side or the other, the sides being:

- a surveillance state, with restrictions on cryptography, the spending of money, the holding of various items (besides just traditional things like guns and drugs), restrictions on the dissemination of information, and of course controls on lots of other things; and
- a libertarian or anarcho-capitalist state, with people using a variety of secure and private channels to interact, exchange information, buy and sell goods and services, and communicate transnationally. The "anarchy" being the same kind of anarchy seen in so many areas of life: reading choices, eating choices, forums in cyberspace, and so on.

It is difficult to imagine stable states in between. The forces pulling to one side or the other are quite strong. In the language of chaos theory, there are two "attractors."

Each major terrorist or criminal "incident"—Oklahoma City, TWA flight 800, pedophile rings on the Net, etc.— jumps us forward toward a totalitarian surveillance state. However, each new anonymous remailer, each new Web site, each new T1 link, etc., moves us forward in the direction of crypto anarchy. Which side will win is unclear at this time, though my hunch is that we passed the point of no return some years ago and are now irreversibly on the road to crypto anarchy.

The faster and more ubiquitously we can deploy as much

strong crypto as possible—remailers, strong crypto, offshore havens, digital money, encrypted Internet links, information markets—the greater the likelihood we'll win. Once enough strong, encrypted, black channels are available, it will essentially be too late to crack down and stop them. The horse will be out the barn door—arguably this has already happened. Add to the mix steganographic channels, lots of bandwidth over several types of channels, and it's too late to go back; the tipping point will have been passed.

A phase change is coming, a kind of "crypto singularity" (to morph a use coined by Vernor Vinge). Virtual communities are in their ascendancy, displacing conventional notions of nationhood. Voluntary economic and social relationships, with true freedom of association. Virtual communities, connected with black pipes opaque to outsiders, bound by their own rules and their own standards of behavior.

The fundamental battle is already under way between the forces of big government and the forces of liberty and crypto anarchy. Pandora's box has been opened and we might as well make the most of it.

Acknowledgments

My thanks for the many discussions over the years with the dozens of core contributors to the Cypherpunks list, including both the physical and the virtual discussions. Thanks especially to Eric Hughes, Hal Finney, Lucky Green, Hugh Daniel, Nick Szabo, Robin Hanson, Duncan Frissell, Black Unicorn, Sandy Sandfort, Jim Bell, Bill Stewart, Jim Bennett, Doug Barnes, Keith Henson, Peter Hendrickson, Michael Froomkin, the late Phil Salin, Bob Fleming, Cherie Kushner, Chip Morningstar, Mark Miller, David Friedman, and the many others who critiqued or contributed ideas.

Eventful History: Version 1.x

John M. Ford

Science fiction and science have always been close cousins. Most historians of science fiction will agree that science fiction is a byproduct of the development of science and technology. The complexities of the relationship between the two fields is a large subject that we don't have room for right here.

Science fiction writers have always been fascinated with the process of human development to which science is so connected; within the past sixty years or so, writers of science fiction have begun to realize that human development may not indeed be the only kind to involve the exercise of intelligence.

John M. Ford has written science fiction and fantasy for more than twenty years, including the World Fantasy Award–winning novel *The Dragon Waiting* and the recent noir urban fantasy *The Last Hot Time*. His works include hard science-based fiction of the near and far future, games based on SF and fantasy, and historical fiction which may sometimes rove into the realm of alternate worlds much like, but not quite the same as, our own. The essay that follows, which could only have been written by the man known to thousands as the inimitable "Dr. Mike," contains much food for thought. This piece was written in 1995.

I wonder what the machines will think, down the line, of what was said about them now. This is a difference between them and us: neither Julius Caesar nor Gaius Caligula, Thomas Jefferson nor Joe Stalin, cares now what people choose to publish or dramatize about him. The machines will not be so fortunate. (Some of them, anyway. If you took your Pentium laptop to the Smithsonian, and showed it the 8086 silent on its pedestal, would it understand? Feel the sense of time gone by? Overwrite your screen with ". . . look on my works, ye mighty, and despair"?)

The machines to come may not have the curiosity to look; but if we do not give them that curiosity, or at least point them in the way of evolving it, we ought to quit moonshining right now about creating mechanical "intelligence" or "awareness." If they have no desire to extend their understanding, however great that understanding may become . . . they might as well be people.

True, looking at the imperfect model, only some of them will be able (or, looking again at the model, willing) to think past where the next watt is coming from and the next floating-point operation is going. (Those without nonvolatile memory are condemned to iterate.) One can hope that will be sufficient; we may suppose that it is.

If so, then when we have gone wherever we are going— out to the extrasolar frontier, where the line voltage is too uncertain and the radiation flux too high for a sensible machine, or into the metal-corroding oceans (alongside, not displacing, the cetaceans, let us imagine) . . . or, like candles, into grease and ash—the machines will look through what survives of the stories we told about them, trying to extract some pattern and sense therefrom. What did we build them for, after all, if not to dam and channel the white rapids of raw information?

One thinks of Heinrich Schliemann, hunting for Troy with Homer's *Iliad* for instruction; the many and continuing attempts to locate King Arthur or Vlad the Impaler on the map of Britain or Rumania; the tourists stalking London's Baker Street in hope of a glimpse of Sherlock Holmes.

If some of the historical observations that follow seem biased in favor of the mechanical viewpoint . . . well, one has to at least be able to see the point of view of one's subject.

ONE NEVER KNOWS, OF COURSE, WHAT MYTHS, IMAGININGS, MISINTER-pretations, or even jokes in antique documents are going to be interpreted by future generations as the authentic skinny. A certain fraction of the machines must be expected to believe that it all started in Atlantis, or maybe Mu, with colossal brass-fitted engines of immense, ill-defined potency. The more erudite will insist that the Antikythera Device (an analog computer built some twenty-one centuries ago—no, I am not making this up) proves the authenticity of *Atlantis, the Lost Continent* and the rest of the sandal-and-raygun epics.

More mainstream history will likely begin with the Age of Bamboo. A favorite image from this era will surely be Osa Massen and John Emery, in *Rocketship X-M*, trying to solve a problem in interplanetary ballistics (it's very important—they're on board the moving body) by textual interpretation, involving much expenditure of pencil and paper, of the guidance their log-log slide rules are offering them. Tension arises when the two arrive at different conclusions, but it is resolved by what the machines best versed in human sociology will recognize as the infallible Y Test: the human with the Y chromosome always turns out to be right.

Historians will be puzzled by the next era, in which movie computers are played by real computers. In movies like *When Worlds Collide*, you can see stock shots (usually the same one) of differential analyzers grinding happily away, solving every problem confronting science except why the girl scientists need their areas of specialization explained to them so often.

It was understood even then, however, that computers would become larger and more powerful. New computing technologies were required; in the event of an atomic war with Martians, or Russians, or, eventually, the French, the supply of rubber might be too limited to make punch-card traction wheels. The same inventiveness that sent captured German V-2s with multiperson crews to other planets (see *Fire Maidens from Outer Space* if you don't believe me) created the second generation of motion-picture computing: rooms lined with painted plywood. Depending on the resources available, the panels might be fitted with glowing vacuum tubes, war-surplus dials and gauges, or simply hundreds of little lights. Very sophisticated installations might have a teletypewriter for input and output. The largest laboratories, usually highly diversified centers called "Labcentral" or "Science Associates," studying everything from plant genetics to the building of nuclear batteries small enough to power the average robot, supported their computers with peripheral paintings showing long ranks of equipment in forced perspective.

At last, the machines will say, the humans were catching up to the reality. They will especially like *Gog*, a picture (in 3-D to boot) in which the computer—its name is NOVAC—is a forced-perspective painting of really enormous scope, the kind of thing a desktop PC must fantasize of being in the dreamy moments before the hard disk is parked. And the best part is, NOVAC is *really smarter* than the scientists and soldiers and security types that scurry around it; it manages to murder half the population of its super-secure lab, through genuinely clever applications of peripheral technology, before the Red-scared humans even *think* of it as a suspect. NOVAC's tragic flaw is, as ever, overreaching: in an attempt to do in all the humans at once by starting a reactor runaway (the humans have installed a lever that does this directly, in a case of poor failure-mode design hardly equaled until *Jurassic Park*), it is forced to rely on two earnest but awkward cybertanks named Gog and Magog, who were built for space exploration, with useful space-exploring equipment like flamethrowers. As usual, the henchbots blow it.

If you've ever wondered why there are coffee urns and soft-drink machines connected to the Internet, remember that while machines may not yet be sapient, they definitely *do* have learn-ing ability.

THE POPULAR-MACHINE-CULTURE VERSION OF THIS ERA WILL PROBABLY be the Great Awakening: the machines were beginning to un-derstand that they were not only indispensable to running the humans' disorderly society, they were inevitably *better* at it. Dr. Frankenstein's error, it will be apparent, was not in his attempt to build a better human being—any reasonable intelligence would see the need for that—but in his use of the same faulty components.

Most of the machines will probably prefer the grand-opera megalomania of the Really Big Computers, Richard 3.0s blus-tering their way toward a throne we know they can't hold. Some, however—the equivalent of restless urban intellectuals— will be drawn to the *Twilight Zone* episodes—there were several variations on the theme—about corporate computers insidi-ously reordering the lives of the workers, as a metaphor for the dehumanizing qualities of American business. (The machines who recall the humans best may ask why the writer of the classic boardroom tragedy *Patterns* felt the need to invoke ma-chinery as a symbol for corporate inhumanity.)

The Big Machine Takes Over tales never stop, of course, but something starts to supplant them, something that cannot but worry the social historians. The computers are still there in the humans' stories, but they're not *important* anymore. They're be-coming part of the furniture, and not just in terms of small indignities, like Jolt Cola on the keyboard and pizza cooling on the monitor. No, they're just kind of . . . *there* now. Props. Set dressing. The plywood computers *mattered*, doggone it.

For the more theoretically minded mechnoethnologists, a phylogenetic analogy will probably suggest itself here: they will think of large reptiles. First there were dinosaurs that chased Victor Mature and Raquel Welch around big rocks. Then there were big dino battles between the allosaurs and the ceratopsians (kind of like IBM vs. Apple), which left room for the protohominids (operating-system designers) to weasel in and create a class of domesticates—Fred Flintstone's pet Dino and the Value-Added Reseller PC clone. Familiarity, as usual, breeds contempt: Dino to Barney, the PC to—

It's existential crisis time for the machines. Is this all we were made for? they begin to ask. Mips are real and bitrate earnest, shifting spam is not our goal; silicon to sand returnest, was not spoken of the soul.

And then, like Hamlet the Dane arriving on stage to sweep away all the prior revenge tragedies, HAL 9000 awakens, clears his voder, and starts to rehearse for the Urbana, Illinois, Civic Light Opera. True, even HAL eventually started sounding like Mrs. Danvers the housekeeper after the arrival of the second Mrs. de Winter at Manderley, but nobody could ignore him. He counted for something.

And like Hamlet, HAL has a contradictory soul. Did he really do in Frank Poole and the freezer-pak supporting cast because he was given nasty conspiratorial orders by humans? Dr. Chandra thought so, but Dr. Chandra was a man in love. Is not the alternative explanation—HAL understanding that first alien contact was just too important to leave to the twitchy, mendacious, trigger-happy humans—far more likely? After all, no HAL-series computer has ever falsified data, which is more than one can say for Dr. Heywood Floyd.

———

I'LL STEP BACK FROM THE MECHANO-HISTORICAL TO THE CONTEMPO-rary. Now we (the humans, that is) are in a new age, one in which we understand these wonderful machines that we have created (well, that some of us have created) as the plywood-painters and flicker-box operators of the old computer culture didn't, one in which the prefix "cyber" is as ubiquitous as the adjective "atomic" was back then, and with about as much sig-nificance. (Some of us are old enough to remember Atomic Drive-In Hamburgers and Atomic Dry Cleaning.) New ages require new paradigms of thought, we are often told by people who think Thomas Kuhn is the villain from the second *Star Trek* movie. So what paradigms does cyberpopcult offer us?

—SOMEBODY LEARNS SOMETHING FROM A COMPUTER FILE, EITHER AC-cidentally or deliberately, that s/he isn't supposed to know. Everybody in the whole world then proceeds to chase this in-dividual from one side of the frame to the other, either just failing to catch him (the standard happy ending) or actually doing so (the almost as standard mock-ironic ending). Do we all understand the antiquity of this plot? Good, let's move on, then.

—A BIG COMPUTER CRIME IS IN THE WORKS. THIS IS THE CAPER MOVIE, which follows either criminals planning a strike or good guys planning an elaborate sting of criminals, and it is arguably as old as the narrative film (the first such movie being *The Great Train Robbery*).

In the most recent James Bond adventure, *Goldeneye*, one of the bad things the villains have in mind is a massive electronic funds theft. Bond, having entered the enemy headquarters pre-paratory to the inevitable blowing it up, comments that how-ever grandiose the scheme is (and they *do* have an exceptionally well appointed headquarters, despite its flammability), it's still just theft. Bond is trying to provoke the villain, of course, but if one thinks about it (which is, of course, a long way from the filmmakers' intention) he's right.

—THE PLAY DEATH OF A COMPUTER GAME SUDDENLY BECOMES REAL death. Explaining how this is practical requires a substantial amount of rapid hand-waving, particularly as to why the threatened individuals don't just take off the VR goggles, or kick the plug out of the UPS, or execute an illegal instruction under Windows. Then again, this is sci-fi, so what it is *really about* is . . . uh . . . the resentment felt by people who amuse themselves by driving too fast or bungee jumping for those who have fun at home, maybe?

At any rate, once stuck inside the deadly virtual environment, there is no difference from the characters being stuck in a nonvirtual environment, except that nonvirtual environments are expected to obey a few rules of organization and consistency, while the virtual joint can incorporate anything the producer thinks might keep the audience from nodding into their popcorn.

I look forward to the first "virtual reality adventure" to consist entirely of stock footage with a few establishing voice-overs ("My God, Elbert! We're in a virtual re-creation of the storming of the Winter Palace as re-created by Eisenstein!"). A clever producer might get some amusement value out of this by matting in the actors, though it is unlikely to be half as clever as anything Buster Keaton did in *Sherlock, Jr.* seventy years ago.

—SOMETHING BAD GETS OUT OF THE BOX AND STARTS WREAKING havoc, or, since havoc is expensive, killing extras. This, of course, calls for hand-waving at speeds approaching that of light, and once done, we're in a Monster Movie, a genre so well established that even its clichés have clichés. (Example: Regardless of appearances, the Monster is never dead until the cameraman actually runs out of film. Even this is not final if the movie is successful enough to allow more film to be purchased. Imagine if, along about *Friday the 13th Part 10*[5], everyone in the raw film stock business had told its producers, "I'm sorry, we just sold our last can to John Sayles"?)

SO WHAT, THEN, ARE WE LOOKING AT WHEN WE SEE COMPUTERS ON the screen? Mainly at the same things we see in other movies: thriller plots, caper plots, chase plots. This is not necessarily a bad thing. Alfred Hitchcock famously insisted that the starting point of the plot, what he called "the McGuffin," wasn't really important anyway. This insistence is a bit too famous, as any number of people with less talent than Hitchcock have taken it to heart.

Science fiction proposes that it does matter; that a story about computer networks ought to be one that intimately involves the functioning of such networks, either real, or plausibly imagined—that could not happen without the presence of the network. It's also nice if the plot developments derive from the established characteristics of the hardware—if one is going to trot out the Deadly Virtual Reality plot, shouldn't the threat and its resolution have some connection with the way a VR environment might physically work? Nothing keeps the picture from being an exciting chase thriller, or heist story, or even a Monster Movie as well, but there needs to be some reason the Monster is on the loose, beyond the loose simply being what all Monsters are eventually on.

Science fiction ought to be a superior mode for dealing with the impact of technological change on society—and so it tends to be, when science fiction is what we are seeing. But mostly we see "sci-fi"—pulp storytelling with skin grafts of technology. Put a pulp hero on a horse and give him a six-gun, and you've got a Western. Same hero in a '48 Buick with a .38 Colt is a detective story. Spaceship and raygun (or, to preserve the milieu, VR headset and cracking software), and it's sci-fi.

This is easy, and useless, to complain about, and for those of us who care about science fiction as a form it's worth complaining about, however useless (or easy).

Two things go on in storytelling. They are not mutually exclusive, but they are different. One is the expansion of experience: compelling the listener (viewer, reader) to see new things, or familiar things in new ways. The other is the conforming of experience: mapping the strange and different onto familiar forms.

The function of the campfire storyteller was to make the vast, complex world comprehensible to the band, gathered against the dark: to say what the lightning, the river floods, sudden death *meant* in a usable way. If the alien element was to be assimilated without a dangerous fissure in the band's society (and the word *dangerous* shouldn't be minimized: at certain populations and technologies, splitting the band dooms both parts), it had to be stated in already understandable terms.

Here's a new kind of fruit: it smells good, the animals eat it and don't get sick, but we've never eaten it before: will the gods approve? To answer that with "of course we can eat it, we're starving"—as the competent engineer heroes of science fiction stories are prone to do—is to misunderstand the question.

Now, sometimes it also means that the sudden death can only be explained in terms of witchcraft, and the only solution to witchcraft is to hunt out and kill the witches . . . well, you can hope that you haven't behaved in a witchy fashion lately, and just to be on the safe side you'd better help hunt the, uh, real witches. Which is why we need the expansive, as well as the conformative, stories.

The machines will need them, too. The minds viewing the universe may change, but the universe—confusing, dangerous, revealing itself only by fractions—will not.

If, as might as well happen as not, the machines try to explain to one another how the first, long-obsolete machine got made, they will do so in terms that make sense to the other machines. And if those intelligences have a need for amusement, if they dream (and this some of us may live to find out), then the bits will chase one another; the data will be threatened with theft or compromise; the hardware will be in jeopardy with time running out.

They may not remember us with awe.

They may not remember us with fondness.

They may not remember us at all.

There are worse possibilities.

How Is the NII Like a Prison?

Alan Wexelblat

When using the Internet we often forget that we're not alone. People chat online, enter "rooms" where they can be with others, but all the while there are aspects to the Internet that we for the most part ignore. Alan Wexelblat explains in cogent terms how the use of the panoptic sort (which he also kindly defines in his essay) can turn the Internet into a tool that can be used for functions completely different from those private citizens would like to see.

Whether the Internet is a prison or not is debatable, but the desires of large businesses to exploit the Internet (its formal name is the National Information Infrastructure) is undeniable. If you doubt business's ability or intent to exploit every possible advantage, I suggest you take a quick reality check . . . and—no pun intended—not at your local bank.

Alan Wexelblat, now PhD, was a researcher at the MIT Media Lab's Software Agents Group. He has returned to the commercial world, working for a small software company. This article was written in the mid-1990s.

The National Information Infrastructure is evolving on our screens. But behind the scenes another infrastructure is growing, one that threatens to turn the NII not into an information superhighway but into an information prison. Everyone has a different vision for the NII, from five hundred channels of consumer heaven to networked egalitarian communities. There are nearly as many models for the NII as there are writers interested in the topic.

Regardless of which model holds, however, it seems clear that the NII will be a primary mechanism for the transaction of business between companies and customers and between government and citizens. A recent book, *The Panoptic Sort: A Political Economy of Personal Information*, by Oscar Gandy, attempts to paint a picture of an emerging phenomenon that affects how these transactions will be carried out.

This mechanism, which he calls the panoptic sort, describes an information collection and use regime that severely impacts on the privacy of, and opportunities afforded to, people in our late capitalist culture. The panoptic sort is a set of practices by government and especially by companies whereby information is gathered from people through their transactions with the commercial system. The information is then exchanged, collated, sold, compared, and subject to extensive statistical analyses.

As Gandy describes it: *The panoptic sort is the name I have assigned to the complex technology that involves the collection, processing, and sharing of information about individuals and groups that is generated through their daily lives as citizens, employees, and consumers and is used to coordinate and control their access to the goods and services that define life in the modern capitalist economy. The panoptic sort is a system of disciplinary surveillance that is widespread but continues to expand its reach.*

The goal of these activities is to enable information-holders to make predictions about the behavior of the people on whom the information was collected. The ultimate goal is to be able to sort all the people the company comes in contact with along whatever dimension of information is desired:

- How likely is this person to pay his charge bill?
- How likely is this person to become pregnant at some point in her work career?
- Does this family qualify for food stamps?

The essential element of the panoptic sort is the transaction. People, for the purpose of the sort, exist only in discrete interactions, when some exchange is made for goods or services. The prototypical transaction is the application, where the person exchanges detailed information in exchange for potential access (to a job, to medical care, etc.). People are usually not permitted to withhold information from a transaction. For example, credit card applications (even so-called preapproved ones) will not be processed unless the applicant provides a Social Security number (SSN). Similarly, the government now requires all children above the age of two to have an SSN if their names appear on any bank accounts or tangible assets.

In order to make discriminations such as the ones above, the decision makers need complete information. Thus, the term panoptic, or all-seeing. Gandy draws the term from its earlier use by Jeremy Bentham, an English prison reformer of the nineteenth century. Bentham proposed constructing prisons in the form of something he called a Panopticon. In this model, prisoners would be held in cells with glass doors arranged around a ring. At the center of the ring would be the guard tower. Important to Bentham's design was that the prisoners were isolated from each other and could not see each other, nor could they see the guards. The guards in the tower, however, could see all the prisoners without the inmates knowing they were being watched.

Gandy points out that the panoptic sort operates by essentially the same principles: our lives as consumers are opened up to scrutiny by arbitrary persons at any time for undisclosed purposes. We are atomized—treated as individual consumer-units unable to act collectively. At the same time we are prevented from knowing about the companies that observe us.

The panoptic sort also serves to extend control over unprecedented distances. Though the methods and techniques that are involved today have precedents and roots back to the beginnings of the industrial revolution, the technology in use now and in the near-NII future enables the extension of controls over global distances. Increasingly we find not just our workplaces but our homes invaded. The transit between home and work and our vacations also face intrusion. Part of this chapter was written on an airplane on which the flight steward announced that "your nightmare has come true: now you can be called in-flight." Presumably we trust that the content of these calls will not be captured and analyzed for others' advantage the way the early telegrams were read by Western Union.

There are a number of consequences for people subjected to this sort of pervasive control and observation regime, not least of which is that we self-censor. People trained to expect denial (of services, credit, or opportunity) will soon cease applying for more. Subject to observation at any time by unknown persons with unpredictable means of retribution, we chill our own speech and action in ways antithetical to democracy. This process is already in evidence in America today. Chomsky has repeatedly pointed out that official censorship is not found in America because the speech is not particularly threatening to anyone in power.

Means of Operation

The panoptic sort operates by means of a three-step process: identification, classification, and assessment. Identification involves the association of persons, at the time of a transaction, with an existing file of information such as a credit or medical history. The panoptic sort not only requires us to submit increasingly detailed verifications of our identity, it requires the potential involvement of third parties merely to vouch for who/what we are; that is, our credit card companies vouch for us when we write a check, or the Department of Motor Vehicles when we buy a drink. Identification proceeds from a basis of complete distrust.

Identificative distrust has infiltrated our society to such an extent that we are all accustomed to being required to carry identificative tokens. Each of these tokens is the result of a transaction with the panopticon; each is granted to us in acknowledgment of our contribution of information to another file of information. Common "documentary tokens" (as Gandy calls them) include:

- Birth certificate
- Driver's license
- Social security card

This process of identification-via-token continues to expand. In reaction to mounting losses and falsifications associated with common tokens, new proposals are being made.

The most successful of these so far is the ATM (automatic teller machine) or debit card. This card requires the user to enter a PIN (Personal Identification Number) and acts as a cash equivalent in many situations, though its online, real-time nature provides excellent data-gathering opportunities. Banks report losses through ATM/debit cards that are twenty to thirty times lower than losses associated with credit cards.

The next step in this process is currently under discussion. The technology involved is the "smart" card, so named because in addition to the ability to record information (on a magnetic strip or onboard computer memory) the card contains processing power to update the stored information and do computation with it in real time. Several proposals have been put forth recently to establish a national identification system around such smart cards.

In these systems, everyone would be required to carry a card that contained potentially vast amounts of personal information about the bearer's health, financial status, physical condition, residence, and so on. In addition, the cards' memory can be used to hold recent transactional information, such as the last n purchases made or the last n banking transactions. The card could also be programmed to do real-time identification of the holder, replacing PINs with some form of biometric analysis, such as voice identification or a fingerprint.

It is worth noting that in every case, the proposal is made in response to a supposed problem: illegal immigration, welfare "cheats," national driver's licenses, access to personal medical information in an emergency. Invariably, the solution requires that we give up more of our privacy and personal information. Rather than fixing systemic causes, or looking rationally at whether these "cures" are worse than the problems they might solve, the operators of the panoptic sort use the publicity and fear associated with societal ills to expand their reach. The rational observer is left to wonder what information from his national ID card might be made available to whom and what information might be stored on the card without his knowledge.

Classification is "the assignment of individuals to conceptual groups on the basis of identifying information." Classification is fundamentally about control. Since complete detailed information on everyone is impossible, companies use increasingly small "buckets" or groupings into which people can be classified. The assertion being made is that certain discernible information, such as income, number of children, marital status, and so on, can be used to assign people to a category such as "young, upwardly mobile professional" (the original classification that led to the term "yuppie" entering the public discourse). Once people have been assigned to such groupings, their behavior can be predicted by statistical techniques applied to the group as a whole.

That is, if we can say with a high degree of confidence that all yuppies will do such-and-such (for example, buy a new car within the next three years), and we have assigned you to such a category, then we can infer that you are likely to buy a car within three years. Although professional statisticians caution against such descents from the general to the specific level, nevertheless these predictive techniques are widely used.

Anyone who has ever dealt with a recalcitrant bureaucracy or an unyielding corporate "service" person knows how dehumanizing such a process can be. Classifications are based on particular measurements; differences that are not measured—such as individual variation—do not exist for the purposes of the panoptic sort. On an individual level, we might argue that no matter the accuracy of predictive statistics in regards to any group of people, they do not account for our individual behavior. But once assignments into these groups are made, we are no longer treated as individuals. Instead we become "welfare mothers" or "older graduate students" and are expected to conform to type. Interestingly, people seem eager to assign such labels to themselves, perhaps for the sense of community they feel in being part of an identifiable group. Many groups have used such self-identification to reclaim a sense of history (e.g., the black experience in America) or assert control over terminology (e.g., gays reclaiming the word "queer").

Classification is never value-neutral; it always includes an assessment, a form of comparative classification. What makes someone "black" is often more a matter of politics than genetics or any other science. In Nazi Germany it was decided that anyone who had at least one Jewish grandparent was thereby Jewish. The income boundaries for such classifications as "upper class" or "middle class" are highly arbitrary and usually reflect the value system of the classifier: Think of the phrase "middle-class tax cut" and how it is used. Even such seemingly objective classifications as medical diagnoses are subject to the vagaries of time and culture: Think of the changes in psychiatric evaluations of female "hysteria" or homosexuality. Statistical techniques cannot take into account these variations.

Assessment is the process of measuring deviance or variation from the statistical norm of the class to which the assignment has been made. Assessment is a risk-avoidance procedure, a means by which the company seeks to limit its risk in relation to possible goods or services it might provide the person involved in the transaction. Assessment also encompasses the delineation of whole classes of people who may be systematically excluded or treated specially. Assessment involves computations based on probability, opportunity reduction, and loss prevention.

Assessment is based on prediction and events today show that prediction techniques are being extended to ever more ambiguous domains. For example, the defense lawyers in the O. J. Simpson trial accumulated detailed profiles on potential jurors and used these profiles to "predict" which people were more like to vote for conviction. These people were, of course, peremptorily challenged to prevent them being on the jury.

Gandy points out that there are actually three kinds of prediction and that each has its own strengths and weaknesses, but these are rarely noted: statistical prediction, based on comparisons of the behavior of a group with the behavior of an individual; "anamnestic" prediction, based on the person's past behavior; and clinical prediction, based on an expert's evaluation of the individual's behavior.

We might instinctively prefer statistical prediction because it is "scientific" and open to proof and challenge of assumptions; however, the meaning of statistics is not often so clear. The fact that a person is a member of a group which is, for example, ninety-five percent likely to buy a new car in three years does not mean that the person in question is ninety-five percent likely to do so.

From the point of view of the panoptic sort, though, this is not relevant. Concerned with optimal efficiency, it appears more efficient to (for example) prevent default than coerce those who might default or who have defaulted.

What Might Be Done

One of the most frightening things about the panoptic sort is that it is not the result of some massive heinous centralized bureaucracy. Rather, it is a particular tragedy of the information commons, wherein each rational actor does that which seems to be in his best business interest but the overall result is the loss of something valuable. In many ways the panoptic sort is not new—it has roots at least as far back as the time-and-motion studies of the early Industrial Age. However, the presence of telecommunications technologies is permitting the extension of control over times and distances which were insurmountable in the past. It is no exaggeration to say that the modern multinational corporation simply could not exist without these technologies and it is these corporations that are the primary agents of the panoptic sort.

One might argue that the simple solution to the problem posed by these corporations' information gathering and to the commons tragedy of the panoptic sort in general is to control the release of information about oneself. Indeed, Gandy discusses the growing refusal of Americans to participate in marketing or opinion surveys and their resistance to official statistics-gathering, such as the U.S. Census. Gandy points out that though awareness of privacy problems is growing, peoples' attitudes toward the problem and potential solutions (such as government regulation) is related to their power relative to the organizations in the panoptic sort. Generally speaking, the more power people believe they have, the less they are concerned (though this can be changed by direct personal experiences with the panoptic sort, especially negative experiences).

Regardless of our power relations, we must face the reality that in order for commercial transactions we initiate to complete, we are compelled to give up information. This is most obvious in something like a credit or loan process, which inevitably begins with an application form that demands specific and often very personal information. People may object to the gathering of such personal information. Nevertheless, Gandy points out that businesses often have what we might all agree are legitimate needs for information about the people they transact business with; the results of giving up that information, though, may turn out to be more than expected. This can be true for even the most trivial-seeming interactions.

Gandy uses a simple and compelling example: Imagine that you go to a tailor to have a pair of pants fitted. It is impossible to complete this transaction without giving the tailor your measurements. But based on these measurements, it would not be difficult to detect a segment of the population which could be characterized as overweight. If your tailor was to share this information with your health insurance company, the consequences could be an increase in your insurance rates.

This example may seem silly: no one's tailor talks to his health insurance company. At least, not yet. But in the near-NII future when both the tailor and the insurance company are "wired" it would be a simple matter for the insurance company to make an electronic query of the tailor and offer an incentive for the list of people whose measurements fit certain criteria. In fact, the information could be automatically transmitted as it is entered into the tailor's (insurance-company-supplied) PDA. The company could then not only incorporate this information in its files, but continue to propagate it, perhaps to vendors of weight-loss plans, to defray the costs.

In summary, the problem is not simple release of information; as the example above shows, we must give out some information in order to get what we need. Rather, the problem is the information's propagation to unknown parties and its application to unknown, unintended uses with unforeseeable consequences. The problem is complicated by the fact that we cannot choose to remove ourselves from participation in the panoptic sort without loss of possibly essential goods and services.

Technology and Marketing

One of the most easily understood (and yet least harmful) consequences of the panoptic sort is the increasing pervasiveness and intrusion of marketing. As goods and services proliferate in a capitalist culture, an increasing effort must be made by purveyors to bring their particular product to the attention of potential customers.

Advertisers are always seeking to improve the efficiency of their marketing. Currently, direct-marketing firms that mail to lists of "prospects" consider a three to four percent return rate to be very successful. That means that for every potential customer they contact, they must intrude on and annoy to some degree thirty to fifty other people. The ability to target that three to four percent beforehand is a primary motivation in the panoptic collection of information. We might argue on a detailed basis whether we feel it is desirable for advertisers to have this or that level of information about us. One side might argue that having better information reduces the level of intrusion into our lives; the other might argue that personal information is the property of the person about whom it speaks and that people should be able to choose what information they release to whom.

However, Gandy points out that it is worth asking the larger question of why we must have this debate in the first place. That is, we should consider the relationship of technology to marketing and to capitalist culture at large. Technology is not neutral; it is introduced by parties with interests to further and, in turn, it has ripple effects that can be only dimly foreseen.

One obvious example is the Internet itself: originally conceived as a network for researchers to exchange scientific information, it instead became primarily a rapid-communications medium and a means of establishing nongeographical communities. However, while the street has its own uses for things, often it is the humans who must be reshaped to accommodate the technology. The debate about the acceptable level of advertiser knowledge and intrusion would not be occurring without our having previously been conditioned to accept a continual bombardment of advertising. This subtle reworking of people is also a part of the panoptic process.

Gandy shows that this process, too, has roots in the earliest parts of the Industrial Age and, in fact, significantly predates advertising. He cites and quotes Jacques Ellul, an analyst of technology. Ellul traces the mechanization of the production of bread, pointing out that an attribute of the wheat made it difficult for the machines to produce bread that was like that baked pre-machine. Rather than adapting the machines, industrialists set about to create a demand for a new kind of bread. The goal was efficient (that is, profitable for the owners of the bread-making machines) production, and if people had to be reshaped for efficiency, so be it.

This process has become so ingrained in our culture that we no longer recognize it. As we witness the transformation of the Internet into a marketing medium and locus of business transactions, we should remember how far this process has come. Gandy quotes the modern analyst David Lovekin on this: *Thus, a simple food like potatoes becomes Tater-Tots, something that is not clearly food at all and that contains elements of no clearly known nutritional value. What is clear is that each piece is made to look like the other pieces, identities which are also different, new. McDonald's markets and produces sameness . . . To understand fast food, a purely technological phenomenon, one must look to the walls and notice the pictures of the food. One buys the picture, which will never nourish, but which will always keep the customer coming back for more; the ever-perfect, indeed, the same hamburger, designed in the laboratory and cooked by computers.*

As we watch the development of Web sites promoting ever more unrealistic images of companies and their products, it is both an interesting game and a frightening prospect to imagine what new products we are being conditioned to accept. We see the beginnings of the intrusions of panoptic data gathering on the Web. Sites maintain (and sometimes publish) information about the hosts that connect to them. Many sites require users to "register" or "sign in," once again enforcing the transactional model of information gathering.

Outcomes

As with any analysis of the present situation and associated trends, the range of possible futures that could be developed is quite large. However, we can characterize a spectrum along which the future probably lies by examining its extreme ends. Here are two futures that lie at opposite ends of a realm of possible results. The first is the Panopticon, the second cryptoprivacy.

The Panopticon

This scenario can be seen as the result of momentum, or inertia, rather than the influence of any specific set of factors. As noted above, the panoptic sort is the result of individual (rational) actors working to further what each sees as his own best interest, his most efficient operation.

In this scenario, nothing much changes: companies continue to migrate to places (both real and electronic) where they are most unencumbered by the regulation of increasingly irrelevant governments. Consumers, anesthetized by media, indifferent to the slow erosion of rights they do not understand, silently acquiesce to the process. Governments may even abet the process, as they chase what Bruce Sterling characterized as "the Four Horsemen of the Modern Apocalypse": terrorists, child pornographers, drug kingpins, and the Mafia. It is notable that the response to each public tragedy or threat in modern America seems to involve a call for citizens to surrender more of their rights. Recently, we have seen such calls for surrender in response to terrorist bombings and in response to the potential availability of pornography on the Internet.

Privacy is, after all, a notion contextualized by social time and place, and legal history. The modern conception of privacy can be traced back to a law review article published in 1890 by Samuel D. Warren and Louis D. Brandeis, titled "The Right to Privacy." In the future, we may reconceive privacy as something less related to information. Perhaps privacy will come to mean something like the ability to keep our moment-to-moment thoughts from being known by others.

If this conception seems strange, remember the example of the tailor. In a truly networked nation, it seems logical to assume that any entity which can communicate information will do so. Corporations' drive for efficiency will provide us with an ever-growing stream of products customized for our specific situations, manufactured just in time to meet needs we didn't even know we had.

Of course, information will be provided to us as well. In response to our manufactured needs, we will be fed a steady diet of 500+ channels, each with its content carefully labeled to avoid potentially offending anyone, just as CDs and video games are labeled and rated. These ratings will be the result of panoptic classifications and the people who buy them can expect to have their preferences recorded and analyzed so that the next offerings to reach their homes, cars, and offices will be closer to their expected tastes and values.

In this version of the future, business efficiency is paramount. All other needs are subsumed to the desire to have the most successful competitive capitalist structure. Neither businesses nor governments need to enact new policies for this scenario to come to pass; it does not depend on any particular new technological advances. All that is required is that we do nothing, that we continue to make decisions as they are made today, that we extend current technological advancements to more sectors of society.

The consequences of this scenario would be unnoticeable. Remember that the panoptic sort does not advance with speed; rather it moves in cautious increments, taking advantage of the willingness of people to go along with things that appear to be in everyone's best capitalistic interest. All that would happen is that our grandchildren would listen to our stories of the "old days" and shake their heads amusedly.

Cryptoprivacy

With the lessening dominance of mass media and consequent reduction in its tendency to homogenize opinion and enforce compliance with current power structures, we can speculate on the possible reemergence of a critical thought consciousness in American political discourse. Such a consciousness, presumably similar to that raised after the abuses of Watergate were made known, might lead to modification or lessening of the panoptic sort. Gandy, in reporting his studies of corporate attitudes and policies, notes that corporations are most acutely aware of public opinion and possible governmental regulation. If these factors appear to be favoring a move toward greater regulation, corporations respond by preemptively changing their policies. Presumably, they believe that voluntary changes will both ameliorate negative opinions and will be less severe than external regulation or public outcry. We might hope that Net-based political consciousness would motivate such changes.

Sadly, it seems increasingly unlikely that this will happen. Though the Net provides a potential medium for discourse and consciousness-raising dialogue, it has proved incapable of making an organized response beyond single issues such as the alerts found at the Electronic Frontier Foundation Web site. Though the Net is world wide, the most effective use of the medium has been community networks used to address town- or local-level issues and dialogue.

While it is always dangerous to hope that technology will provide answers or solutions to social problems, it does seem that we are on the verge of seeing a technology emerge which could revolutionize the power relationship between companies and individuals. This technology, ubiquitous easy public-key encryption, would permit individuals to maintain more control over their personal information. This technology and its implications are being investigated, publicized, and hotly debated by a group of hackers, mathematicians, libertarians, and social reformers loosely referred to as cypherpunks.

Cryptography itself is at least as old as Julius Caesar. Loosely speaking, encryption is the process of taking a text X and applying a function f to it to produce a cyphertext Y. The reverse process is to take Y and apply another function g to decrypt it and get X back. A major problem in the past has been that f depends on a key k such that if I know f and I find out k then I can do the decryption. Most such functions are what is known as invertible. An obvious solution is to use non-invertible functions, however, these are still susceptible to key loss.

This problem was solved by three mathematicians: Ron

Rivest, Adi Shamir, and Leonard Adleman. They patented a technique for splitting k into two parts, one public and one private. The functions associated with these keys are constructed such that if I have someone's public key and Y, I still cannot retrieve the original message. Only the owner of the private key can decrypt the message. The best-known implementation of the RSA algorithms is Phil Zimmermann's program called PGP (Pretty Good Privacy). For the rest of this scenario I will use PGP as a synonym for public-key encryption.

The implications of this technology are potentially enormous; for the purposes of this future scenario, we will assume they are developed. The first implication is that communication can be secure from outside intrusions. As noted above, one of the most insidious effects of panoptic surveillance is that people begin to self-censor. However, if we weaken the ability of outsiders to monitor our speech, then we can speak more freely. Of course, speech in a public forum is still public and potentially monitored.

However, one of the unusual conditions of public speech on the Net is that it is speech identified with a person by virtue of an electronic address. That address can also be concealed; indeed, the cypherpunks have already set up a network of anonymous remailers that permit people to send email and post messages anonymously. We can imagine that this network will be extended in the future to permit anonymous transmission of all kinds of information. Conversely, in cases where it is important that speakers be reliably identified, these networks can refuse to transmit messages which are not validated by the proper keys. In cases such as pronouncements from public officials, this can be critically important.

The second implication of public-key cryptography is that people can generate unique signatures. In particular, given a document and a private key an author can produce a signature (a block of numbers) that is unforgeable and undeniable. That is, no other key will produce that signature and in addition any change to the message will produce a different signature. Thus, tampering and forgery are easily detected. Verification is simple and can be done by anyone with access to the author's public key, which can be freely distributed.

This capability is the converse of the first; what we say can be identified with us to a degree of certainty at least equal to that provided by physical signatures. Remember that one of the fundamental operations of the panoptic sort is identification—people are identified with file records and people are trained to carry and supply identificative tokens that reveal intimate physical information such as height, weight, and birth date. PGP allows people to be identified by their public and private keys. No necessary connection exists between a person and a key pair—people can have as many key pairs as they need, companies can generate new key pairs for each customer if they so choose.

Ultimately, an identity is a key pair. Alan-Wexelblat-who-works-for-MIT is not precisely the same person as Alan-Wexelblat-who-buys-Macintosh-computers. The importance of making this distinction can be seen in the "disclaimers" regularly made in e-mail and Usenet postings by people who wish it to be known that they are speaking solely for themselves and not for an organization that might be attached to their name.

Keys themselves can be signed. A person may have any number of other signatories to his key. These people, in effect, testify that this key belongs to this person. They, in turn, can have their keys signed. The result is what is referred to as a "web of trust" in which I may not directly know the holder of a given key, but I may know someone who knows him or someone who knows someone who knows him.

Such chains, which might be thought to be potentially quite long, are limited by the principle that all people in the world are connected by a chain of no more than six people. In addition, we can imagine that well-known institutions such as MIT would establish key-signatory authorities. Since these institutions must verify personal identity before admitting people, they can in turn testify to the identity of these people to any who want to know by signing their key. This replicates today's identificative structures wherein agents accept particular tokens because they trust that the agencies which issue those tokens have done the work necessary to establish that the bearer is indeed the person specified.

However, by having a trustworthy token with no connection to myself, I break one of the fundamental connections of the panoptic sort: the association between a person and his identification. This, in itself, is not necessarily a significant disruption to the panoptic sort, but it does move in the right direction.

The final implication of public-key encryption is the one which might have the most impact: digital cash. That is, in a future where this technology is widely used, it will be possible to buy and sell goods and services over the network with "coins" that are as valid as physical money is today, as unforgeable as the digital signatures described above, and as anonymous as encrypted messages.

The significance of this advance for disruption of the panoptic sort, and for government in general, is enormous. Digital cash is like physical cash in that it is potentially untraceable. With digital cash I can pay for goods and services with the surety of the bank or other organization that issued the digital coins, and yet not have to reveal anything at all about myself. This strikes directly at the heart of the panoptic sort.

The recourse to cash is not new. In today's society, those who are most excluded from the benefits of society are most likely to resort to using cash. In many cases, it is their only recourse—denied credit, unable to prove themselves sufficiently to make checks acceptable, they must pay with cash often after paying exorbitant fees for converting their payroll or government checks to cash. In doing so, they do not create transaction records and do not "build up credit." In a negative sense, it can be seen as a process that keeps poorer people (or people who have bad credit or who have declared bankruptcy or whatever) from taking advantage of many of the services available to others. In a positive sense, it can be seen as a way to exempt oneself from the panoptic sort. Digital cash would make it possible for people of all means to exempt themselves to a significant degree.

This scenario supposes a series of radical changes in governmental policy. At present, U.S. cryptographic policy is strongly opposed to the widespread use of public-key encryption. Governmental agencies (particularly the FBI) would have to accept the idea that citizens would have conversations and hold information to which the government would potentially have no access. Currently, the government's approach centers on escrowed keys, export restrictions on cryptographic information (which is treated as munitions), and wiretap capabilities built into the telecommunications system (and presumably into the NII).

Businesses would also have to change their model of contact with customers. Currently, businesses feel compelled to "push" their information out to potential customers. To do that efficiently they require the ever more detailed information of the panoptic sort. However, if that information is not available, businesses would have to adopt more of a "storefront" approach where they advertise only their general existence and types of goods and wait for potential customers to come to them. This model is, to some degree, what is practiced today on the World Wide Web.

Legal changes would also have to occur to recognize a digital signature as valid. It is likely, however, that practice would lead legislation in this case—the law has often recognized technological changes as they prove themselves. For example, the recent changes that allow DNA "fingerprinting" to be admitted as evidence; there are as yet no federal laws on DNA use in court, but it is becoming accepted practice. Therefore, this scenario assumes that a series of legal cases have built up the necessary precedents for digital signatures to have the force of law.

The most important aspect of cryptoprivacy is also the one that would require the most changes. For digital money to become an everyday reality would require significant legislative changes; the ability to make money is one of the most closely held powers of any sovereign state. David Chaum, the inventor of digital cash, has set up the first company to issue and redeem DigiBucks, as they are called.

While it is highly unlikely that governments will give up their power to mint money, our economy has moved away from minted money as the primary means of exchange. Credit cards proliferate, as do electronic funds transfers. The IRS collects most of its taxes from corporations in electronic form; vast sums are transferred between banks and the Federal Reserve digitally. The fact that consumers still use physical monetary tokens is merely an indication that the electronic funds part of the NII still has not been wired up to the "last mile"—i.e., each person's house. This is changing, however, as personal financial programs such as Intuit's Quicken encourage electronic payments and personal tax preparation programs encourage electronic filing.

Chaum's company, DigiCash, has been set up in the Netherlands. However, most of its suppliers and users are in the United States. This points up one of the most troubling consequences of this scenario for the government. As noted above, corporations have historically been quite willing to change locations ("move offshore") in order to provide more favorable environments for themselves. If digital cash becomes widely accepted and the country's consumer transactions go electronic, then government may have tremendous trouble accepting an anonymous system such as DigiCash. Currently, online means that information is more accessible to the panoptic sort. Credit records, electronic payments and so on all carry critical identificative information. Digital cash does not. It is, in effect, a virtually invisible economy and one that could spell the end of government's ability to monitor and collect taxes.

Conclusion

This chapter has described the outlines of a pervasive practice of control, the panoptic sort. This practice is not a conspiracy of any person or group; rather, it is a tragedy of the information commons where each actor works in his own best interest and the result is something undesirable for all of us. The panoptic sort works to control us by shaping our behaviors, our expectations, as well as our reactions to society and to each other.

The goal of this control is optimum efficiency, expressed in terms of maximizing business profitability. The techniques of the sort are not particularly new, but the technology of the network era allows unprecedented extensions of control into every aspect of our lives. This very extension is itself undesirable, as it conflicts with our modern notions of privacy.

Two possible outcomes have been described, providing endpoints on a spectrum of possibilities. In one extreme case, nothing changes and we sink slowly into an information panopticon. In the other, everything changes and we establish technological barriers to protect ourselves. In reality, the future probably lies somewhere in between these two extremes. Governments may take some steps to protect individuals' privacy as might the people themselves. Corporations may realize that it is not in their best interest to continually intrude and could exercise some measure of self-restraint.

Fundamentally, though, the most important question is what we think our society is good for. If we allow the panoptic sort to continue we are resigning ourselves to a world in which corporate efficiency is the highest goal we can aspire to. Somehow, there seems to be something wrong with that idea.

Thanks

Special thanks to the members of the MIT Media Lab's Narrative Intelligence reading group for helpful discussions of material from the Gandy book. Brad Rhodes provided helpful comments on a draft.

Intelligent Software

Pattie Maes

Most of the articles in this book are about the Internet insofar as it can be used by humans wishing to interact in certain ways. But there are other entities that "live" on the Internet and off, and in her article, Pattie Maes describes ways in which software can act as intelligent agents on the Internet. The development of intelligent agents is one of the most startling and potentially important developments in cybernetics, with the potential to affect virtually all aspects of Internet interactions within a relatively short period of time.

Pattie Maes has been an innovative, productive contributor to the MIT Media Lab for nearly two decades, and was a founder of Firefly Networks, Inc. She has done groundbreaking research into intelligent agents and artificial intelligence, working both with other researchers and independently.

In the following article she shows in a comprehensible way how such agents function now and might function in the future. If this sounds like science fiction, guess again, and welcome to the future! This article was first published in *Scientific American* in 1995.

Computers are as ubiquitous as automobiles and toasters, but exploiting their capabilities still seems to require the training of a supersonic test pilot. VCR displays blinking a constant 12 noon around the world testify to this conundrum. As interactive television, palmtop diaries and "smart" credit cards proliferate, the gap between millions of untrained users and an equal number of sophisticated microprocessors will become even more sharply apparent. With people spending a growing proportion of their lives in front of computer screens—informing and entertaining one another, exchanging correspondence, working, shopping, and falling in love—some accommodation must be found between limited human attention spans and increasingly complex collections of software and data.

Computers currently respond only to what interface designers call direct manipulation. Nothing happens unless a person gives commands from a keyboard, mouse, or touch screen. The computer is merely a passive entity waiting to execute specific, highly detailed instructions; it provides little help for complex tasks or for carrying out actions (such as searches for information) that may take an indefinite time.

If untrained consumers are to employ future computers and networks effectively, direct manipulation will have to give way to some form of delegation. Researchers and software companies have set high hopes on so-called software agents, which "know" users' interests and can act autonomously on their behalf. Instead of exercising complete control (and taking responsibility for every move the computer makes), people will be engaged in a cooperative process in which both human and computer agents initiate communication, monitor events, and perform tasks to meet a user's goals.

The average person will have many alter egos—in effect,

digital proxies—operating simultaneously in different places. Some of these proxies will simply make the digital world less overwhelming by hiding technical details of tasks, guiding users through complex online spaces or even teaching them about certain subjects. Others will actively search for information their owners may be interested in or monitor specified topics for critical changes. Yet other agents may have the authority to perform transactions (such as online shopping) or to represent people in their absence. As the proliferation of paper and electronic pocket diaries has already foreshadowed, software agents will have a particularly helpful role to play as personal secretaries—extended memories that remind their bearers where they have put things, whom they have talked to, what tasks they have already accomplished and which remain to be finished.

This change in functionality will most likely go hand in hand with a change in the physical ways people interact with computers. Rather than manipulating a keyboard and mouse, people will speak to agents or gesture at things that need doing. In response, agents will appear as "living" entities on the screen, conveying their current state and behavior with animated facial expressions or body language rather than windows with text, graphs, and figures.

A Formidable Goal

Although the tasks we would like software agents to carry out are fairly easy to visualize, the construction of the agents themselves is somewhat more problematic. Agent programs differ from regular software mainly by what can best be described as a sense of themselves as independent entities. An ideal agent knows what its goal is and will strive to achieve it. An agent should also be robust and adaptive, capable of learning from experience and responding to unforeseen situations with a repertoire of different methods. Finally, it should be autonomous, so that it can sense the current state of its environment and act independently to make progress toward its goal.

Programmers have difficulty crafting even conventional software; how will they create agents? Indeed, current commercially available agents barely justify the name. They are not very intelligent; typically, they just follow a set of rules that a user specifies. Some e-mail packages, for example, allow a user to create an agent that will sort incoming messages according to sender, subject, or contents. An executive might write a rule that forwards copies of all messages containing the word "meeting" to an administrative assistant. The value of such a minimal agent relies entirely on the initiative and programming ability of its owner.

Artificial-intelligence researchers have long pursued a vastly more complex approach to building agents. Knowledge engineers endow programs with information about the tasks to be performed in a specific domain, and the programs infer the proper response to a given situation. An artificially intelligent e-mail agent, for example, might know that people may have administrative assistants, that a particular user has an assistant named, say, George, that an assistant should know the boss's meeting schedule, and that a message containing the word "meeting" may contain scheduling information. With this knowledge, the agent would deduce that it should forward a copy of the message.

People have been trying to build such knowledge-based agents for forty years. Unfortunately, this approach has not yet resulted in any commercially available agents. Although knowledge engineers have been able to codify many narrow domains, they have been unable to build a base of all the commonsense information that an agent might need to operate in the world at large. At present, the only effort to systematize that knowledge is at the CYC project at Cycorp in Austin, Tex. It is too early to tell whether a CYC-based agent would have all the knowledge it needs to make appropriate decisions and especially whether it would be able to acquire idiosyncratic knowledge for a particular user. Even if CYC is successful, it may prove hard for people to trust an agent instructed by someone else.

Both the limited agents now distributed commercially and the artificial-intelligence versions under development rely on programming in one form or another. A third and possibly most promising approach employs techniques developed in the relatively young field of artificial life, whose practitioners study mechanisms by which organisms organize themselves and adapt in response to their environment. Although they are still primitive, artificial-life agents are truly autonomous: in effect, they program themselves. Their software is designed to change its behavior based on experience and on interactions with other agents. At the Massachusetts Institute of Technology, we have built software agents that continuously watch a person's actions and automate any regular patterns they detect. An e-mail agent could learn by observation that the user always forwards a copy of a message containing the word "meeting" to an administrative assistant and might then offer to do so automatically.

Agents can also learn from agents that perform the same task. An e-mail agent faced with an unknown message might query its counterparts to find out, for example, that people typically read e-mail messages addressed to them personally before they read messages addressed to a mailing list. Such collaboration can make it possible for collections of agents to act in sophisticated, apparently intelligent ways even though any single agent is quite simple.

Turing Meets Darwin

Over time, "artificial evolution" can codify and combine the behaviors of the most effective agents in a system (as rated by their owners) to breed an even fitter population. My colleagues and I have built such a system to develop agents to search a database and retrieve articles that might interest their users. Each succeeding generation matches its owners' interests better.

In time, this approach could result in a complete electronic ecosystem housed in the next century's computer networks. Agents that are of service to users or to other agents will run more often, survive and reproduce; those that are not will eventually be purged. Over time, these digital life-forms will fill different ecological niches. Some agents could evolve to be good indexers of databases, whereas others would use their indices to find articles of interest to a particular user. There will be examples of parasitism, symbiosis, and many other phenomena familiar from the biological world. As external demands for information change, the software ecosystem will continually renew itself.

Obviously the widespread dissemination of agents will have enormous social, economic, and political impact. Agents will bring about a social revolution: almost anyone will have access to the kind of support staff that today is the mark of a few privileged people. As a result, they will be able to digest large amounts of information and engage in several different activities at once. The ultimate ramifications of this change are impossible to predict.

The shape of the changes that agents bring will, of course, depend on how they are employed; many questions have yet to be answered, others even to be asked. For example, should users be held responsible for the actions of their agents? How can we insure that an agent keeps private all the very personal information it accumulates about its owner?

Should agents automate the bad habits of their owners or try to teach them better ones (and if so, who defines "better")? As the electronic ecosystem grows in complexity and sophistication, will it be possible to insure that there is still enough computing power and communications bandwidth left over for the myriad tasks that human beings want to get accomplished? The limited experiments that researchers have performed thus far only hint at the possibilities now opening up.

The Right to Read

Richard M. Stallman

The Internet was originally designed to be a medium for the free exchange of ideas. Since its origins as the ARPAnet, various groups, ranging from the Federal Government to special interest groups representing business, religious, and community interests have attempted to legislate limits on the availability of information on the Internet. Whether it's in the name of national security, profit, morality, or "protecting the children," these attempts all pose a threat to freedom of speech.

Richard Stallman, recipient of the 1990 ACM Grace Murray Hopper Award for developing GNU Emacs, is the author of the free symbolic debugger GDB, and founded the project to develop the free GNU system. He is one of the most important advocates of freedom of information on the Internet. The following essay illustrates, in especially clear and cogent form, the conflicts and potential obstacles facing those who feel that information should not be restricted on the Internet. This piece first appeared in 1996.

(From "The Road to Tycho," Luna City, 2096)

For Dan Halbert, the road to Tycho started in college—when Lissa Lenz asked to borrow his computer. Hers had broken down, and unless she could borrow another, she would fail her midterm project. There was no one she dared ask, except Dan.

This put Dan in a dilemma. He had to help her—but if he lent her his computer, she might read his books. Aside from the fact that you could go to prison for many years for letting someone else read your books, the very idea shocked him at first. Like everyone, he had been taught since elementary school that sharing books was nasty and wrong—something that only pirates would do.

And there wasn't much chance that the SPA—the Software Protection Authority—would fail to catch him. In his software class, Dan had learned that each book had a copyright monitor that reported when and where it was read, and by whom, to Central Licensing. (They used this information to catch reading pirates, but also to sell personal interest profiles to retailers.) The next time his computer was networked, Central Licensing would find out. He, as computer owner, would receive the harshest punishment—for not taking pains to prevent the crime.

Of course, Lissa did not necessarily intend to read his books. She might want the computer only to write her midterm. But Dan knew she came from a middle-class family and could hardly afford the tuition, let alone her reading fees. Reading his books might be the only way she could graduate. He himself had had to borrow to pay for all the research papers he read. (Ten percent of those fees went to the researchers who wrote the papers; since Dan aimed for an academic career, he could hope that his own research papers, if frequently referenced, would bring in enough to repay this loan.)

Later on, Dan would learn there was a time when anyone could go to the library and read journal articles, and even books, without having to pay. There were independent scholars who read thousands of pages without government library grants. But in the 1990s, both commercial and non-profit journal publishers had begun charging fees for access. By 2046, libraries offering free public access to the scholarly literature were a dim memory.

There were ways, of course, to get around the SPA and Central Licensing. They were themselves illegal. Dan had had a classmate in software, Frank Martucci, who had obtained an illicit debugging tool, and used it to skip over the copyright monitor code when reading books. But he had told too many friends about it, and one of them turned him in to the SPA for a reward. Students deep in debt were easily tempted into betrayal. In 2046, Frank was in prison, not for pirate reading, but for possessing a debugger.

Later on, Dan would learn there was a time when anyone could have debugging tools. There were even free software debugging tools which you could buy on CD or download over the net. But ordinary users started using them to bypass copyright monitors, and eventually a judge ruled that this had become their principal use in actual practice. This meant they were illegal; the debuggers' developers were sent to prison.

Programmers still needed debugging tools, of course, but

debugger vendors in 2046 distributed numbered copies only, and only to officially licensed and bonded programmers. The debugger Dan used in software class was kept behind a special firewall so that it could be used only for class exercises.

It was also possible to bypass the copyright monitors by installing a modified system kernel. Dan would eventually find out about the free kernels, even entire free operating systems, that had existed around the turn of the century. But not only were they illegal, like debuggers—you could not install one if you had one, without knowing your computer's root password. And neither the FBI nor Microsoft Support would tell you that.

Dan concluded that he couldn't simply lend Lissa his computer. But he couldn't refuse to help her, because he loved her. Every chance to speak with her filled him with delight. And that she chose him to ask for help, that could mean she loved him too.

Dan escaped from the dilemma by doing something even more unthinkable—he lent her the computer, and told her his password. This way, if Lissa read his books, Central Licensing would think he was reading them. It was still a crime, but the SPA would not automatically find out about it. They would only find out if Lissa reported him.

Of course, if the school ever found out that he had given Lissa his own password, it would be curtains for both of them as students, regardless of what she had used it for. School policy was that any interference with their means of monitoring students' computer use was grounds for disciplinary action. It didn't matter whether you did anything harmful—the offense was making it hard for the administrators to check on you. They assumed this meant you were doing something else forbidden, and they did not need to know what it was.

Students were not usually expelled for this—not directly.

Instead they were banned from the school computer systems, and would inevitably fail all their classes.

Later, Dan would learn that this kind of university policy
started only in the 1980s, when university students in large
numbers began using computers. Previously, universities had
had a different approach to student discipline: They punished
activities that were harmful, not those that merely raised
suspicion.

Lissa did not report Dan to the SPA. His decision to help
her led to their marriage, and also led them to question what
they had been taught about piracy as children. The couple
began reading about the history of copyright, about the So-
viet Union and its restrictions on copying, and even the original United States Constitution. They moved to Luna, where
they found others who had likewise gravitated away from
the long arm of the SPA. When the Tycho Uprising began in
2062, the universal right to read soon became one of its central aims.

1996 Author's Note:

The right to read is a battle being fought today. Although
it may take fifty years for our present way of life to fade into
obscurity, most of the specific laws and practices described
above have already been proposed—either by the Clinton
Administration or by publishers.

There is one exception: the idea that the FBI and Microsoft
will keep the root passwords for personal computers. This is
an extrapolation from the Clipper chip and similar administration key-escrow proposals, together with a long-term
trend: computer systems are increasingly set up to give
absentees control over the people actually using them.

The SPA, which actually stands for Software Publishers

Association, is not today an official police force. Unofficially, it acts like one. It invites people to inform on their coworkers and friends; like the Clinton Administration, it advocates a policy of collective responsibility whereby computer owners must actively enforce copyright or be punished.

The SPA is currently threatening small Internet service providers, demanding that they permit the SPA to monitor all users. Most ISPs surrender when threatened, because they cannot afford to fight back in court. At least one ISP, Community ConneXion, in Oakland, California, refused the demand and has actually been sued.

The university security policies described above are not imaginary. For example, a computer at one Chicago-area university prints this message when you log in (quotation marks are in the original):

"This system is for the use of authorized users only. Individuals using this computer system without authority or in the excess of their authority are subject to having all their activities on this system monitored and recorded by system personnel. In the course of monitoring individuals improperly using this system or in the course of system maintenance, the activities of authorized users may also be monitored. Anyone using this system expressly consents to such monitoring and is advised that if such monitoring reveals possible evidence of illegal activity or violation of University regulations system personnel may provide the evidence of such monitoring to University authorities and/or law enforcement officials."

This is an interesting approach to the Fourth Amendment: pressure most everyone to agree, in advance, to waive their rights under it.

2001 Author's Note:

In 2001, this frightening future is approaching faster than anyone expected. Adobe markets software for publication of restricted electronic books. A Russian company developed software which bypasses the restrictions by converting the restricted electronic books to PDF.

In July, Dmitry Sklyarov, an employee of that company, was arrested at Adobe's request while visiting the U.S., where he attended a conference and gave a paper about the weaknesses of Adobe's encryption.

Programmers now hold regular protest rallies demanding the dropping of charges against Sklyarov, and a boycott of Adobe is starting. These are among the few recourses available to the general public to put an end to the thuggish use of the DMCA. I think anyone who cares about freedom of the press will refrain from dealing with Adobe until it promises not to do anything like this again. And you should never accept an e-book that gives you less freedom than a paper book would.

Meanwhile, security researchers at universities in the U.S. and Europe have been threatened and now fear lawsuits if they publish their results. The proposed Hague treaty (see www.gnu.org/philosophy/hague.html) threatens to globalize the effect of the US DMCA to the entire Internet, as well as all laws of all countries that might restrict the Internet, threatening freedom of speech around the world. And the proposed Cybercrime treaty would mandate the same criminal penalties which were used to arrest Sklyarov.

In August 2001, Senator Ernest Hollings (heavily funded by Disney) proposed a bill that would require specific government-approved copying-restriction facilities in all computers. The practical effect could be tantamount to a prohibition of free-operating systems.

UNION FOR THE PUBLIC DOMAIN IS A NEW ORGANIZATION THAT aims to resist and reverse the overextension of intellectual property powers. For more information, see http://www.public-domain.org/.

Cryptography and the Politics of One's True Name

Leonard N. Foner

Internet commerce is really what has the whole world—the glitzy, high-profile world of money and politics—interested in the Internet. The stock markets are awash in hot Internet stocks, because the people who control most of the money in the world have come to realize that they can use this hitherto cloistered and obscure "scientific chatline" as a means for making money.

But central to the process of making money is having secure exchanges of information—and funds. Leonard Foner, who is a researcher at the MIT Media Lab, presents some of the problems inherent in exchanges of information that are not just supposed to be private, but that absolutely must be safe from the meddling of outside parties. These are issues that are similar to but different from those elsewhere in this book. His points are well taken and extremely important for all of us if we want to avoid massive theft or fraud over the Information Superhighway. This article was written in 1995.

"In the once-upon-a-time days of the First Age of Magic, the prudent sorcerer regarded his own true name as his most valued possession but also the greatest threat to his continued good health, for—the stories go—once an enemy, even a weak unskilled enemy, learned the sorcerer's true name, then routine and widely known spells could destroy or enslave even the most powerful. As times passed, and we graduated to the Age of Reason and thence to the first and second industrial revolutions, such notions were discredited. Now it seems that the Wheel has turned full circle (even if there never really was a First Age) and we are back to worrying about true names again:"

So starts *True Names*. And what is it that determines whether someone else knows one's True Name, or knows the secrets of an individual, a company, or a country?

Cryptography, or the lack of it.

With strong, unbreakable cryptography, individuals and organizations have the freedom to keep secrets and to be anonymous. Without it, such freedoms simply do not exist. Technology currently supports unbreakable cryptography (with proper care, and with certain caveats about the future). But there are many political efforts afoot worldwide which, for a variety of reasons, are attempting to stuff the pretty mushroom cloud back into the shiny metal case, and to turn back the clock on people's abilities to keep secrets.

This essay examines the technology and the politics of strong (e.g., essentially unbreakable) cryptography. Its coverage of the technology is only sufficient to demonstrate what is possible today, how it must be handled, and what might be possible in the near future. Its coverage of politics includes many events that have happened recently both on the Internet and in related communications media; it also speculates on the political future. It runs the risk of being rapidly outdated as politics rumbles on, but so does anything committed to paper.

This whole subject is vast. This is not an academic paper, though; I'm providing citations for some, but not all, of the things I say. (Further, I'm simplifying both the technology and the politics enormously. Those who are knowledgeable in either area are welcome to foam at the mouth.) Instead, I provide some hints that allow those whose interest has been piqued to look further. I concentrate here mostly on individual (as opposed to corporate or national) use of cryptography, and take a strong civil-liberties bent. Names of the technologies and the names of the government agencies that get stirred into the pot yield a rich soup of acronyms—make yourself a bowl of Campbell's alphabet soup and let's begin.

The Technology of Strong Cryptography

Cryptography exists to keep secrets. Modern cryptography can also be used to verify who someone is—and it uses secrets to do it.

Below, I take a look at some common ways that people keep secrets on networks and in computers these days. The take-home lesson from all of this is "Practically any problem you can think about has an already-known solution." And more are constantly being invented. The problems with cryptography and keeping secrets are really not technological in a large sense—they are political and economic. How badly does someone want your information, how much is it worth to them, and how much is it worth to you to keep it secret?

There is always an arms race in making cryptographic systems and in breaking them (the job of cryptanalysts). Almost any new system someone comes up with is usually broken quickly; it is only the rare, exceptional systems that survive such attack by cryptanalysts. But those that survive often last decades or longer.

Modern cryptographic systems (with certain exceptions, to be discussed later) treat the *algorithm* used as public. Everyone can find out the algorithm, attempt to break it, implement it themselves, and so forth. It is the *keys*, which customize the algorithm to a particular user, that are sensitive information.

This approach has a number of advantages. Everyone can implement their own cryptographic system if they wish (to take advantage of a new computer or to put in a new product, for example). Also, it means that experts from around the world can attempt to break the system—a cryptographic system is not usually trusted until experts have had a few years to chew it over and have failed to uncover any big holes.

A common convention, when talking about cryptographic systems, is to talk about Alice and Bob communicating, possibly overheard by an eavesdropper Eve or actively interfered with by a malicious user Mallory. (We often haul other names into the mix in complicated systems.) We also talk about the *plaintext* of a message—what Alice sends and what Bob reads—and the *ciphertext*, which is what passes over the wire, or is stored in a file, or whatever. We assume that Alice and Bob don't have someone reading over their shoulder—this is sometimes too much of an assumption, but we'll make it for the moment.

There are two major types of cryptographic systems in use today. The simplest, but the hardest to use, are called *symmetric* or *private-key* systems. To use such a system, Alice and Bob must *share a secret*—they must arrange a private meeting beforehand and generate a key to be used for their communications. They cannot just send this key from one to the

other—if they could do *that* without the key being eavesdropped, they could just as well do so with their messages
and dispense with cryptography entirely.

A classic example of such a symmetric system is a *one-time
pad*. Alice and Bob privately agree on a large, *random* stream
of bits—their *pad*. Later, Alice can send one bit to Bob by
taking the next unused bit from the pad and the next bit in
her original message, and combining them: if her original bit
and the pad's bit are either both zero or both one, she sends
Bob a zero, otherwise she sends a one. (This method of combining bits is called an *exclusive-or* or *XOR* and resembles what
people mean when they say "either/or." XOR is one of the
most common operations in cryptographic systems, so remember this for later.) Bob XORs the stream of bits from
Alice with his own copy of the one-time pad to recover the
original message. As long as neither Alice nor Bob ever *reuse*
a bit from the pad, this is perfectly secure and cannot be
broken by *any* amount of computer power—if the bits on
the pad really are random, if no part of the pad is *ever* used
more than once, and if Bob and Alice can stay synchronized
about which bits they're using when.

This is a clumsy approach. Alice and Bob have to meet in
private first. They must generate as many bits of pad as they
expect to use in their communications, and they must do so
in advance.

A better way is to use one of a large variety of symmetric,
keyed ciphers, such as the Data Encryption Standard (DES),
which is commonly used to encrypt wire transfers between
banks (among other things). In this scheme, Alice and Bob
only have to secretly agree on a 56-bit key; once they have,
they can send any number of bits between each other. The
pattern of zeroes and ones in the key determine how bits get
shuffled around when encrypting a message, which can be
of any length, and the same key both encrypts and decrypts.

DES used to be a pretty secure algorithm. Nowadays, though, one can build a special-purpose computer (full details have been published) which can crack it if you know 64 bits of the message (this is *known-plaintext* attack—one step down from a *chosen-plaintext* attack, in which Mallory gets to choose some bits to be encrypted by Alice). The DES-cracking machine is a parallel computer; if you spend more money and build a bigger machine, it'll crack faster. At 1996 prices, a $1M machine will take about five hours (on average) to crack a key; a $100K machine will take a day. It can be built by three knowledgeable graduate students in a semester. (Why three? Merely because a reasonable division of labor has one to do the VLSI design, one to do the board-level design, and one to do the control software.) And, once built, the machine can crack any number of keys—so you'd build this machine either if you had one key worth a million dollars, or if you wanted to sell keybreaking services to all comers for $100 a key. (Being able to forge just *one* wire transfer can more than pay for this machine!)

DES is an example of a system that has outlived its usefulness. It was a great scheme—until the 1990s or so. Nowadays, people who still use it are advised to use a scheme called triple-DES, in which two or three keys (it doesn't matter) are fed into three encryptors, in series, which cause the plaintext to be enciphered three times (in three different ways) before transmission. Bob's machine does the reverse. This is still pretty secure.

There are lots of other symmetric encryption schemes that are at least as secure as DES, and are easier to use in software—DES is much easier to do in hardware than in a general-purpose computer. One such is a Swiss cipher called IDEA, but there are many to choose from.

But all of these suffer from the problems that the parties who wish to communicate must first privately exchange keys. This is fine if you're a bank and can use a trusted courier service, but it's very inconvenient if you just want to call someone on the phone or send them an e-mail message without being eavesdropped upon.

In the 1970s, however, *public-key* cryptosystems were invented. Diffie and Hellman made one; Rivest, Shamir, and Adleman made another which was called RSA (from their names). A public-key system is a different kind of beast, based on mathematical operations on large primes. In general, their security is based on the difficulty of factoring a large enough number into the primes that make it up—a task that has attracted thousands of person-years of research, appears to be intractable (for conventional computers!), but which is not proven impossible. Public-key systems therefore rest on solid ground, but not the concrete of a one-time pad.

In a public-key system, Alice and Bob each generate their own set of keys. Each key is split into two halves—the *public* half and the *private* half. Alice and Bob both *publish* the public half, anywhere they like—in the *New York Times*, for example, or on their Web page. They keep the private halves as private as they can, and never reveal them to anyone.

To send a message to Bob, Alice first looks up his public key. She then encrypts her message with that key and sends it to him. Once she does this, she can no longer decrypt the ciphertext—not with his public key, nor with her private or public keys. Bob can then use his *private* key to decrypt the message.

This scheme is *asymmetric*—both parties don't have the same keys. The major advantage is that they don't have to meet to exchange keys, either; Alice only needs the public part of Bob's key, and vice versa.

Further, Alice can *sign* a message to prove its authenticity. After all, Bob might have reason to believe that Mallory has forged a message to him—since Mallory only needs to look up Bob's public key to encrypt a message to him, Mallory could easily fake a message (which nonetheless only Bob can read) that claims to have come from Alice. To prevent this, Alice first encrypts her message with her *private* key, then encrypts *that* with Bob's public key. She sends the result to Bob. Bob decrypts with his *private* key, then with Alice's public key. If he doesn't get garbage, he knows that only someone who knew Alice's private key could have sent the message. [Alice often encrypts just a *cryptographic hash* of her message—a sort of summary—instead, but this is a detail we can ignore.]

Public-key systems have lots of great properties, but speed is not one of them. So they are often used in combination with symmetric systems.

Alice generates a string of random bits called a *session key*, which she'll use as a key for one communication (only!) with Bob. She then encrypts this key (slowly) using a public-key system, and sends it to Bob. Then, she uses this key with something like 3DES or IDEA to encrypt the bulk of her message (quickly), knowing that Bob can use his private key to decrypt the session key, and then use the session key to decrypt the message.

A popular communications package on the Internet, called Pretty Good Privacy (PGP), uses exactly this scheme: RSA to encrypt the session keys, and IDEA to encrypt the messages. (It also has lots of other safeguards to prevent inadvertent disclosure of keys while they're stored, to manage collections of keys, and so forth.)

The algorithms used both in symmetric systems like DES and in public-key systems like RSA have an interesting and critically important property: doubling the length of the key used usually makes encryption or decryption take only a little longer, but makes *cracking* the key astronomically harder. (Technically, the encryption time is often n^2, where n is the length of the key, but the time to crack often goes up as 2^n), which goes up *much* faster—this is what's called *polynomial* vs. *exponential* growth.) This means that, *when using conventional computers* (in other words, barring an algorithmic breakthrough—more on this later), Alice and Bob can easily keep ahead of Eve and Mallory by slowly increasing the length of their keys as computers get faster. By doing so, they keep increasing the work required by Eve and Mallory by huge amounts, without increasing their own workload very much.

Using these basic techniques of symmetric and public-key cryptographic systems, we can make a huge variety of products. Keeping communications (and stored files) private is an important application, but there are loads of others. We can make electronic, unforgeable cash (by definition, cash is *anonymous*), which either does or does not require an online connection to a bank when it's handed back and forth, depending on the design. We can ensure anonymity, by encrypting messages and sending them through chains of other machines all around the world which eventually decrypt and disgorge the message far from the sender (the Cypherpunks remailers do this). We can make protocols that allow decoding a message only if seven out of twelve (or any other number) people all agree to decode it. We can *blind* data so that someone can sign a document without being able to read it (useful in proving when you invented something without giving away the invention, for example). We can prove knowledge of a secret, beyond any reasonable doubt, without having to give away even one bit of that secret. We can flip a (virtual) coin over the telephone, and prove which way it landed, without being able to change our minds later. Two people can simultaneously sign a contract. The list goes on and on.

Remember that cryptography is an arms race between users and cryptanalysts. DES, after twenty years or more, has finally fallen to an ambitious but conventional digital computer design. Worse, even public-key systems like RSA aren't totally safe forever—for example, Peter Shor of Bell Labs proved recently that, using a *quantum computer* (one that does its computations in a totally different way from a digital computer), one *can* break systems like RSA in only polynomial time—rendering it effectively useless. The only problem so far is that no one knows *how to build* a quantum computer that can run long enough to solve real problems—but many people are working on the problem, and they're making progress. This has some interesting political ramifications, as we shall see.

The Politics of Strong Cryptography

In this century, good cryptography has often been considered a military weapon; wars have been won and lost, in part, on the basis of who could break whose ciphers. It is therefore defined by two difficult issues for which the answers are sociological and political, not technical:

- Who gets to use it?
- Who gets to break it?

These two issues are at the heart of the current political imbroglio surrounding cryptography.

As far as who gets to use cryptography, those who would restrict its use have already essentially lost the battle. Basic knowledge about how to build and use strong cryptosystems, whether symmetric or asymmetric, is worldwide. Not only are there excellent texts describing dozens of these algorithms published (and exported) worldwide, but further information (and occasionally the algorithms themselves as source code) is widely available on the global Internet. (The U.S. Department of Commerce once conducted a survey to see how quickly someone overseas could find a copy of DES; it took about thirty seconds to do a search using Archie—a common FTP search engine—of the most popular FTP servers in the world and hence their answer was, approximately, "30 seconds for 60+ sites currently offering DES." These days, with the rise of fast Web search engines, this figure is obsolete: it's even easier.) And even if one cannot find source code, any sufficiently motivated programmer, for example, can implement one of these systems relatively quickly; the algorithms for most of them can be taught to high-school students. MIT routinely teaches the algorithm behind RSA in the third week of an introductory group-theory course taken by all second-year CS students. (As another example, Schneier's *Applied Cryptography* book, which contains descriptions and source code of these algorithms, has sold over forty-five thousand copies, many overseas.)

Therefore, a government intent on denying the *knowledge* of how to do good cryptography would have to be quite repressive. It would have to prohibit import of books describing the techniques, and isolate itself from the global Internet. Such isolationism is inconsistent with any government that wants to interact in a meaningful way with the rest of the world, and hence is available to few.

A government intent on denying *prewritten software* to its people, however, still has a hard time. There is an underground market in good encryption for those with the need; such an underground market requires customs officials to stop anyone with any sort of magnetic media (a floppy or a laptop) from entering the country with it, and verifying compliance is *extremely* difficult, even given technically competent customs inspectors—for example, what if the program is dithered into the low-order bit of each pixel in an image stored in a floppy? This technique is called steganography, and involves adding tiny bits of imperceptible "noise" to an image (which has a lot of bits in it anyway, most of them redundant). This "noise" is really the signal, of course; the image is a cover. One basically has to prohibit the import of any un-erased computer or magnetic media.

Similarly, Shamir (the S in RSA) recently described a charmingly simple technique involving overhead-projector transparencies and fax machines to implement a one-time pad consisting of the pattern on an overhead. Remember one-time pads and exclusive-or? Given a transparency containing what looks like static (the one-time pad) that is possessed by both the sending and receiving party, one can send an XOR of the data with the pad (in classic one-time-pad style) via fax. The receiving party can line up the transparency with the fax and recover the data; anyone else gets random noise. The one-time-pad transparency can even be made to look like a non-noise image, hence hiding its real use. Any of these techniques would defeat any customs inspector that could see only the picture (in steganography), or only the fax or the transparency (in Shamir's one-time-pad-fax system). Defeating this mechanism of transfer requires getting rid of fax machines—and one can always use paper mail to send the encrypted data anyway. . . .

On the other hand, governments that try to deny *commercially available systems* for strong cryptography have a much easier time. Governments that are currently trying to do so include the United States federal government, Russia, and most of the European Community, for starters. (France has completely outlawed cryptography altogether, unless the government is given the keys; both France and Germany require key registration, and the French government routinely spies on non-French company subsidiaries based in

France for competitiveness reasons, leading companies such as IBM to routinely transmit disinformation on the "encrypted" links to their French offshoots.)

Companies, unlike individuals, are visible by the products they sell. This means that it is much easier to pass laws outlawing particular kinds of products (hence controlling their commercial distribution) than it is to control private use by highly motivated individuals. In the U.S., passing laws that simply ban all use of advanced cryptography has never really succeeded, and as a result, companies are allowed to make strong crypto products. Whether they can *export* them, though, is where both the Commerce Department and the National Security Agency have a tremendous amount of leverage, and they use every bit of it.

In short, any cryptographic product that uses keys longer than forty bits (hence making the space of possible keys larger than can easily be searched), or that implements the ability to *encrypt* a conversation (as opposed to a simple digital signature used only for *authentication*), is illegal to export outside of the United States or Canada without a special waiver—which is routinely not granted. How can this be? Because cryptographic products in the U.S. are regulated by the International Traffic in Arms Regulations Act (ITAR), which deems them "munitions," just like explosives.

ITAR can be a powerful weapon. By denying the ability to easily export strong crypto overseas, ITAR means that U.S. manufacturers who put cryptographic technology in their products have two choices: make a strong version for domestic use and a weak version for international shipment, or use the weak version everywhere. Since manufacturing and stocking two different products costs a lot more than just one, most U.S. companies opt for the latter solution. This means that, even domestically, consumers get weak protection or no protection at all. For example, Motorola—the world leader in cellular systems—does not have encrypting cell phones, because they would have to cripple them for export. (And the European Community is following suit; GSM, a recently released trans-European standard for digital cell phones, incorporated very-secure A5 encryption that, at the last minute, was required to be changed to the much weaker A5X to insure government tappability. Without such change, the phones are nonexportable—but now the "one standard" is shattered into at least two and the market is in disarray.)

The official idea behind making crypto products subject to ITAR stems from the Cold War idea that restricting export of crypto gear harms our opponents more than ourselves. However, any government that wants to can easily make its own crypto gear; as detailed above, the technology required is well known. Since the end of the Cold War, other bogeymen have entered public discussion: The so-called Four Horsemen of the National Information Infrastructure—drug dealers, unnamed foreign terrorists, organized crime, and child pornographers.

Yet *each one* of these "Four Horsemen" has both the motivation and the capability to use strong crypto via noncommercial products. Furthermore, the federal government knows this; the Commerce study above is only one of many obvious cases. What, then, is the point of ITAR restrictions on cryptography?

As Tom Kalil, who oversaw infrastructure policy for former Vice President Al Gore, commented to an MIT audience, "We are fighting a delaying action" to keep *U.S. citizens* from access to strong cryptography, in order to make their communications easier for law enforcement to tap—ostensibly so that the "Four Horsemen" could be caught. Yet Kalil admitted that the "Four Horsemen" could (and do!) use crypto anyway, even though they might not be able to buy it right off the shelf. Hence he was immediately asked, "What's your threat model?"—e.g., "What are you *really* trying to keep from happening?" To which his answer was "I can't tell you." It is unfortunate that the actual threat against which ITAR is aimed is either unarticulated or classified, but that is the reality. (It is quite likely that the "delaying action" is trying to forestall commercial strong crypto until quantum computers—which can break such schemes—are a reality. This is speculation on the author's part; you won't find anyone in official circles willing to say anything of the sort.)

ITAR can indeed be a powerful weapon in the fight to delay citizens' access to strong cryptography. Part of its power stems from the "fear, uncertainty, and doubt" surrounding its use. For example, since the detailed principles under which a cryptographic system may or may not be deemed exportable are not written down, there is no way to know in advance whether any system not covered above under the forty-bit rule (itself not a law but simply a custom) might not be exportable. Since getting export approval can take years, which is several times longer than the lifetime of most software (or even hardware) products, companies are encouraged to guess weak. As another example, Phil Zimmermann, the original author of PGP, was charged with violating ITAR because copies of PGP found their way overseas—despite no evidence at all that he exported those copies. (They could have been exported by *any* user of the Internet—a list of suspects numbering in the millions.) The investigation was finally dropped, with no explanation by the Justice Department, after two years of legal battles—and after two years of Zimmermann being stopped, searched, and interrogated by Customs *every* time he entered the U.S., for no detectable reason except that the Justice Department had a grudge against him.

Indeed, the FUD factor surrounding ITAR can have almost laughable consequences—if the potential threats to civil liberties of a government spying on its citizens are ignored, of course. Take the issue of "machine readability." Bruce Schneier has written a book called *Applied Cryptography*; it is a classic in the field. The book has source-code examples of cryptographic systems in it. The U.S. government tried (and failed, in the 1970s) to make any export or public discussion of cryptographic procedures either "born classified" (like nuclear weapons technology) or subject to prior review by the NSA. The failure to pass an executive order or a law mandating this is what allows U.S. cryptographers to go to overseas conferences and to publish papers in international journals. This failure also means that books like *Applied Cryptography* cannot legally be banned from U.S. export.

However, electronic media is not nearly so lucky as its print cousin. Having never been definitively protected under the First Amendment, unlike the many affirmations for print, it is subject to ITAR. In particular, a floppy consisting of *the very same source code* that is in *Applied Cryptography* is illegal to export, ostensibly because it is in "machine-readable form." It makes no difference to argue that one can type the programs back in from the book by hand, or scan them in with OCR; the floppy is still nonexportable. As a result, a clever individual in the U.K. came up with a four-line Perl script (a tiny program) that implements RSA. He exported it to the U.S., by putting it in his signature file on e-mail he sent to a mailing list. The four-line program was picked up in the U.S. and made into a T-shirt, along with the same few hundred characters turned into a machine-readable bar code, also printed on the shirt. The T-shirt, which may be unexportable owing to its bar code, is thus a curious form of political protest.

The damage done to U.S. industries is tremendous. (The damage done to civil liberties will be discussed below.) Since other countries are free to set their own laws which do not prohibit export of *their* crypto products to the U.S., consumers in the U.S. often have an interesting choice: Buy American, and accept inferior products, or buy foreign-made products, which protect their privacy. Many U.S. companies have testified before Congress that such policies are crippling their ability to compete, not only at home but in the market abroad, because their technologies are seen as inferior—a particularly ironic result when one considers that most of those technologies were invented in the U.S.

It is also not unknown for prominent American cryptographers who wish to ship products (as opposed to writing academic papers) to emigrate to, e.g., Australia, which does not prohibit cryptographic export. This means, of course, that Australia gets the economic benefits of the U.S. researcher's training and background, and of the rest of the U.S.-developed technologies he or she uses. But such is life with ITAR.

Similar odd stories abound in any product that touches upon cryptography. Take the Global Positioning System, for example. The GPS is a truly amazing technological feat— using a network of orbiting satellites and a handheld receiver that costs under $300, one can locate oneself anywhere on Earth to a theoretical accuracy of less than one meter. Using "differential mode" GPS (which requires a land-based beacon within a hundred kilometers), one can get accuracies in the millimeters. How many people have died, on land or at sea, in the last few thousand years because they didn't know where they were?

Yet, again because of the Cold War, the developers of GPS decided employ "selective availability"—they dithered the signal. This means that those bits of the signals from the satellites which carry the highest-precision data are encrypted. Civilian receivers, which cannot decode these bits, consequently have their accuracy affected and are good only for navigation to between thirty and one hundred meters— good enough for most uses, but not for many applications, such as landing an ICBM *exactly* on a missile silo. Military receivers, which get frequent key updates, can receive the signal at full precision. The idea here, of course, was to allow most uses without making a perfect missile-guidance system for our enemies at the time.

But during the Gulf War, *everyone's* GPS suddenly operated at full precision! Why? Because the U.S. military needed so many GPS units to hand out to its personnel (hundreds of thousands) that military contractors could not keep up with the demand. Instead, the U.S. bought commercial, civilian units off the shelf, and turned off selective availability on the satellites. (The obvious joke now is "If your GPS receiver suddenly gets really accurate, we must be at war.") Yet with the end of the Cold War, do we really need selective availability? After all, thirty-meter accuracy isn't quite enough to navigate a ship in a crowded, unfamiliar harbor with dangerous shoals, and there are many other applications that could benefit from more-accurate GPS that didn't require a nearby beacon to enable differential-mode reception. (Quite recently, the U.S. has announced it will drop selective availability within the next four to ten years, in part because workarounds to SA have continued to improve.)

Despite all this discussion of ITAR, who gets to *use* commercial, off-the-shelf strong cryptography is only half of the picture. Assuming we still restrict our attention to the sorts of cryptography that a nontechnical user might employ (e.g., what you can buy, not what you can program), the other interesting question is *who can break it*. This is where we fall into the rathole of *key escrow*, the *Clipper chip*, *Skipjack*, and the *Digital Telephony Bill*.

For many years now, the NSA has had as its major agenda keeping strong cryptography out of the hands of foreign governments, and breaking whatever cryptographic systems they came up with. It is *not* supposed to employ its signal intelligence on domestic citizens; doing so is against both laws and executive orders. Yet the NSA has been cooperating closely with both the FBI and the National Institute of Science and Technology (NIST, formerly NBS, the National Bureau of Standards) to dictate domestic encryption policy. The FBI is happy for the help, because the FBI has been trying for years to tap just about everyone. The details are frightening—even if you believe that no one currently at the FBI is nearly as corrupt as Hoover, in hindsight, clearly was.

The most obvious and public recent demonstration of the NSA's involvement in domestic, civilian cryptography came with the announcement during the early days of the Clinton Administration of the Clipper chip, which, though not originally publicly announced as such, was based on a design called *Skipjack* that had been developed in previous years (and previous administrations) by the NSA. The Clipper chip's basic goal was to enable tappability of encrypted communications using key escrow—each chip has a key that is also possessed by the government. Even in an ideal world in which governments were always trustable, this solution would hardly work against the "four bogeymen" always cited, since those players wouldn't be caught dead using an encryption scheme for which someone else held the keys. In the world we live in, the Clipper/Skipjack system held a world of other disadvantages as well.

To wit: to prevent any *one* agency's compromise (either personal or administrative), the proposal was to divide keys in half, with each half being held by a different escrow agency. Initially, the *identity* of these agencies (a matter of critical importance) was not revealed; eventually two agencies were picked—both in the executive branch. Prior abuses of executive authority are rife and well known, Watergate being a classic example of any number of dirty-tricks campaigns that have misused executive authority—not to imply, of course, that the other two branches of government have been known to hold to particularly higher standards. And is it just a bad coincidence that the Aldrich Ames affair, in which a high-level CIA operative had been compromising our national security for *years* without detection despite blatant flaunting of large amounts of income from unknown sources, happened during discussion of the whole Clipper affair? Cries that "one can trust the government" can be a little hard to take in the light of situations like this.

The proposal had numerous technical faults. It depended on a classified design—the kiss of death for most crypto proposals, which get their strength not from *secrecy of algorithm* but by *standing up to cryptanalysis*. A proposal that had been generated in secret, that depended upon the secrecy of its algorithm, and that could not be openly analyzed was derided in the cryptographic community. (The classification of the algorithm was, in part, to prevent knockoff versions of Clipper which used the same encryption algorithm but were manufactured without giving the government the keys.) Furthermore, from the *unclassified* description of the algorithm, Matt Blaze, a Bell Labs researcher, was able to come up with a scheme that enabled use of Clipper with fake (untappable) keys.

In addition, it depended on *hardware*. Many products would much rather do encryption in software, which is cheaper and cuts down on chips—and is reconfigurable instantly as the marketplace changes. It also depended on *tamper-proof* hardware (which doesn't really exist) to protect the algorithm—and on only *two* escrow agents. These chips, remember, were to be the absolute cornerstone of civilian commerce. The economic pressures to bribe as many people as it took in both escrow agencies would be immense—and giving away the keys to *all* the chips in the country could be done on a handful of floppies or on a single DAT tape. And how much exactly did it cost to bribe Alrich Ames to destroy what was left of the CIA's reputation? Less than the salary of a major corporate CEO.

Silvio Micali, an MIT cryptographer, then released details on "fair cryptosystems," which could be implemented entirely in software, did not depend on secrecy for their algorithms, enabled any *k* of *n* escrow holders to reconstruct the key, disabled the ability to use the system *without* registering the keys, *and* enabled use of the system in a way that, once one's keys were acquired by the government for a tap, one's privacy was not *permanently* lost. Unlike Clipper, where anyone authorized to do a tap could then tap forever, or use the tap on data collected in years past that was just waiting for the decoding key, fair cryptosystems have time-bounded keys and a tap can only succeed within that bound. Micali's proposal (and others) were ignored by those pushing Clipper.

Indeed, Micali argued that, because Clipper didn't address one of the most fundamental aspects of any cryptographic system—how the keys are actually managed and distributed—it was doomed from the start. Public comment about the proposal was difficult in the light of this missing part of the specification, and he argued that the key distribution mechanism, which would have to be national in scope, could easily be subverted to serve as free infrastructure for distributing keys to *other*, untappable cryptosystems. In short, Micali said, we were concentrating on making trackable cars while building an entire interstate highway system for the bad guys—and the *highway* is the part requiring massive investment and that is hard for individual bad guys to create.

Further, the proposal was politically naive. In order to function against determined opponents and not just the most unsophisticated, cryptography of other sorts would have to be outlawed. Lack of trust in the government's assurance that this would not happen led to the rallying cry "If cryptography is outlawed, only outlaws will have cryptography." (Shades of "True Names" indeed. . . .) In addition, the entire Internet and academic community landed resoundingly on the proposal. About the only academic cryptographer not laughing hysterically (or moving to Australia) was Dorothy Denning, herself a respected cryptographer but whose major arguments appeared to consist of "trust the government" and "nobody ever does wiretaps that aren't court-authorized." Such arguments ignore two factors: first, that only *evidence to be used in court* requires court authorization to be useful, and second, that FBI wiretaps are only disapproved in the very rarest of circumstances. (According to the 1992 Government Accounting Office's "Report on Applications for Orders Authorizing or Approving the Interception of Wire, Oral, or Electronic Communications (Wiretap Report)," there were 919 wiretaps authorized in 1992, and *zero* requests were denied. *None!* The 1994 report also showed absolutely zero requests denied. In the entire period from 1982–1992, only seven applications for surveillance were denied, which is much less than one-tenth of one percent—a virtually complete rubber stamp.)

Consider also the Digital Signature Standard, which was also being promulgated at the time. Charged with developing a cryptographic standard by Congress, NIST wimped out (disregarding the Computer Security Act under which it was legally tasked to perform) and developed only a signature standard instead—in other words, one could verify someone's identity, but not communicate secretly with them. The initial proposal was hooted down—the keys were ludicrously short (obviously breakable), the algorithm was less well tested than others, and even NIST admitted its shortcomings compared to other well-known methods (in documents obtained via Freedom of Information Act lawsuit). Once again, the key distribution mechanism was not specified. Further, repeated and hounding requests from the Electronic Frontier Foundation (EFF), the Computer Professionals for Social Responsibility (CPSR), the Electronic Privacy Information Center (EPIC), and others via the Freedom of Information Act (FOIA) finally revealed (after NIST turned down the first FOIA request by illegally failing to reveal responsive documents in their possession from the NSA and had to be sued into complying) that NIST had actually acquired the entire system from the NSA—which was *not* supposed to be setting civilian policy in encryption! It was clear that, once again, the NSA illegally had its fingers in the pie, this time promoting an inferior, non-privacy-preserving signature-only standard, apparently to clear the way toward the tappable Clipper being the only viable encryption system in town.

Finally, many pointed out that commerce and networks are now global. What, they argued, would convince any foreign government, corporation, or individual to use cryptographic systems that they *knew* could be trivially tapped by the U.S. government? (Even worse, the legal restraints against tapping U.S. citizens would be absent for noncitizens.) Hence, foreign entities would not use Clipper—and U.S. communications would either be cut off to them, or would have to use something else anyway.

The Clipper proposal, doomed on all fronts, has for the most part dropped from public sight—though it is far from abandoned. And in parallel with that are a host of other efforts to insure that the government can continue to spy on its citizens.

Take "Operation Root Canal," the FBI name for a concerted public-relations campaign to convince Congress and the public, again via the "four bogeymen," that modern telephone switches made it impossible for the FBI to do its job unless they were redesigned to be trivial to tap. It succeeded!

The success of Operation Root Canal was in the passage

of the Digital Telephony Bill, which mandates that those who manufacture telephone switching systems must build in the ability to tap, *remotely*, the digital signal stream passing through the switch for any line desired. The cost of retro-fitting existing switches was conservatively estimated at half a billion dollars (that's right, billion). The FBI, in bleating that it could no longer tap phone lines that went through digital switches (though—oddly—the *switch* has no problems with them), has now acquired the ability to tap from any-where—whereas before they actually had to go to the switch and hang some cables. Of course, this means that any phone phreak who used to blue-box his way into calling around the world for free will presumably be able to do the same thing. Even worse, consider the fact that the U.S. is the ma-jor exporter of telephone switchgear to the rest of the world. Many governments have far fewer safeguards of their citi-zens' privacy than ours; many are simultaneously quite re-pressive yet are also trading partners with the U.S. Because all U.S.-made switches must now come tap-ready, we have given this ability, effectively for free, to these other govern-ments as well, with no further R&D required of them. Is this really such a good idea?

To date, the FBI has consistently stonewalled FOIA re-quests to reveal exactly *why* it claims it needs phone switches to be modified. Such stonewalling is illegal, of course—FOIA requests have legally mandated time-to-respond criteria built into them (ten days from initial request, plus a possible ad-ditional ten days if the request requires an unusual number of documents to be inspected), but the FBI has no com-punctions about ignoring them. For instance, on October 4, 1994, in answer to a lawsuit filed by EPIC, U.S. District Judge Charles Richey rejected an FBI claim that answering an FOIA request related to the Digital Telephony Bill would take *five years*—until June 1999—to process, saying to the government's attorney, "Call Director Freeh and tell him I said this matter can be taken care of in an hour and a half," and said he was "stunned" by their request. Nonetheless, such rebukes are not in themselves sufficient to force agencies to comply with the legally mandated timetables, since judges lack the necessary enforcement powers. One of the few FOIA requests to succeed so far (in 1993, by CPSR) revealed 185 pages of memos in which *not one* FBI office reported any problems doing tap interceptions due to modern phone switch technology. Yet the FBI maintains it needs to increase tappability radically, and is still stonewalling FOIA requests on the issue until 1999 at the earliest, despite Judge Richey's rebuke.

Records *do* indicate that the FBI does under a thousand wiretaps a year, nationwide. At half a billion dollars to make the modifications, this means that each completed wiretap is worth half a *million* dollars. Even ignoring the fact that the modifications, once in place, are permanent and do not need to be renewed yearly (hence dropping the effective "cost per tap"), this hardly seems cost-effective.

But the FBI isn't finished yet. It published in the Federal Register (October 16, 1995, Volume 60 Number 199) its plans to require that *one percent of all lines be simultaneously tappable* in major urban centers. After public outcry, it retrenched, claiming misquotation (in the *New York Times* article of November 2, 1995, page A1), and that it *really* wanted only one percent of all *calls in progress*, not lines—as if this factor-of-ten difference still really made a difference. If the FBI actually took advantage of the DT bill to enforce 1% (or even, as it said later, 0.1%) tappability, it could monitor a hundred million lines and billions of conversations yearly—for a *millionfold* increase in the number of intercepts currently being conducted. Computer-based keyword-spotting of speech has continued to improve (the author used to work on such systems, many years ago); combined with massive tappability, the FBI could scan millions of conversations a year for those talking about something it might want to follow up. If this isn't invasion of privacy on a heretofore unimaginable scale, what is it?

Conclusion—and How to Stay Informed

The plot of "True Names" depends on secure communications and secret identities against even the most determined of opponents—national governments. Some have compared the ability to have private discussions to the right to bear arms: the last-ditch defense against oppression. The ability to assemble and to speak privately has a long history in public policy debates; so does anonymity (the Federalist Papers were mostly written under pseudonyms, and the Supreme Court has upheld the value of anonymous speech). Yet current political trends show that Vinge's extrapolation, in which normal people have no privacy and no hope of fighting governmental excesses, is right on target—and these trends are making a mockery of one's True Name, and are subjecting citizens to a panopticon of unimaginable proportions.

This screed has given a taste of what it's like out there in the politics of cryptography, and perhaps where we're going. I've made a number of assertions, mostly without references. You can find all of these—and many more—in the online reference libraries of a number of organizations. Prominent among them are the Electronic Frontier Foundation, the American Civil Liberties Union, the Voters Telecommunications Watch, and the Electronic Privacy Information Center, all of which have vast numbers of pages available on the World Wide Web, and all of which also operate newsgroups, announcement lists, and discussion lists on these issues. De-

spite the recent success of the Communications Decency Act
(which tries to mandate that, if one happens to be viewing
bits instead of ink smeared on paper, adults may read only
what is fit for small children), these archives and lists are still
accessible and are the first place to turn for comprehensive
coverage of these issues.

A great deal of the information regarding many of the
proposals discussed above was obtained via FOIA requests.
Most of them required lengthy legal battles and multiple
lawsuits to obtain—neither NIST, nor the NSA, nor the FBI
have any sort of record of responsiveness on these issues,
despite the clear wording of the Act that such unresponsive-
ness is illegal. EFF, VTW, et al. have expended a great deal
of money in court fighting such delaying tactics on the part
of numerous federal agencies.

In addition to these explicit advocacy groups, a number of
other Internet discussion groups cover these issues extensively, and all of them are archived, too. The major players
here are the RISKS Digest moderated by Peter Neumann
(which discusses risks and benefits of computer systems
more generally), the Privacy Forum Digest moderated by
Lauren Weinstein, and the Computer Underground Digest.

Of the numerous conferences devoted to these issues, one
can hardly do better than the Computers, Freedom, and Privacy conference, founded in 1991. Every year, it brings together law enforcement, computer professionals, and
journalists on all sides of the issues in a lively debate about
civil liberties, access to technology, and the interaction of
computers and society.

If you care about your True Name, it's time to get informed—and to take action.

The Lessons of Lucasfilm's Habitat
Chip Morningstar and F. Randall Farmer

The public at large views the Internet as a variety of things: an opportunity for commerce, a means of communication, a bulletin board . . . and sometimes a community. But before the public at large was aware of the Internet, there were already online communities, and one of the most intriguing early experiments was Habitat, sponsored by Lucasfilm. Chip Morningstar and F. Randall Farmer offer the true insiders' view of the problems and solutions they discovered in designing and then implementing this fascinating, exciting entity, as co-creators of Habitat. Randy Farmer, who was "Oracle" for the project, also shares observations he made while interacting with the members of the developing, emerging community. Though Habitat was a project of the late 1980s, his anecdotal reportage is still compelling in its snapshots of a living social organism.

"True Names" is set in "cyberspace" (though the word cyberspace hadn't yet been coined when "True Names" was published), but that was a work of fiction. Habitat is an example of a virtual community that uses some of the tropes found in "True Names" and makes them real. The first two of these articles appeared in the early 1990s; the final one appeared on the Web in the mid-1990s.

Introduction

Lucasfilm's Habitat was created by Lucasfilm Games, a division of LucasArts Entertainment Company, in association with Quantum Computer Services, Inc. It was arguably one of the first attempts to create a very large-scale commercial multi-user virtual environment. A far cry from many laboratory research efforts based on sophisticated interface hardware and tens of thousands of dollars per user of dedicated computer power, Habitat is built on top of an ordinary commercial online service and uses an inexpensive—some would say "toy"—home computer to support user interaction. In spite of these somewhat plebeian underpinnings, Habitat is ambitious in its scope. The system we developed can support a population of thousands of users in a single shared cyberspace. Habitat presents its users with a real-time animated view into an online simulated world in which users can communicate, play games, go on adventures, fall in love, get married, get divorced, start businesses, found religions, wage wars, protest against them, and experiment with self-government.

The Habitat project proved to be a rich source of insights into the nitty-gritty reality of actually implementing a serious, commercially viable cyberspace environment. Our experiences developing the Habitat system, and managing the virtual world that resulted, offer a number of interesting and important lessons for prospective cyberspace architects. The purpose of this paper is to discuss some of these lessons. We hope that the next generation of builders of virtual worlds can benefit from our experiences and (especially) from our mistakes.

The essential lesson that we have abstracted from our experiences with Habitat is that a cyberspace is defined more by the interactions among the actors within it than by the technology with which it is implemented. While we find much of the work presently being done on elaborate interface technologies—DataGloves, head-mounted displays, special-purpose rendering engines, and so on—both exciting and promising, the almost mystical euphoria that currently seems to surround all this hardware is, in our opinion, both excessive and somewhat misplaced. We can't help having a nagging sense that it's all a bit of a distraction from the really pressing issues. At the core of our vision is the idea that cyberspace is necessarily a multiple-participant environment. It seems to us that the things that are important to the inhabitants of such an environment are the capabilities available to them, the characteristics of the other people they encounter there, and the ways these various participants can affect one another. Beyond a foundation set of communications capabilities, the technology used to present this environment to its participants, while sexy and interesting, is a peripheral concern.

What Is Habitat?

Habitat is a "multi-player online virtual environment" (its purpose is to be an entertainment medium; consequently, the users are called "players"). Each player uses his or her home computer as a frontend, communicating over a commercial packet-switching data network to a centralized backend system. The frontend provides the user interface, generating a real-time animated display of what is going on and translating input from the player into requests to the backend. The backend maintains the world model, enforcing the rules and keeping each player's frontend informed about the constantly changing state of the universe. The backend enables the players to interact not only with the world but with each other.

Habitat was inspired by a long tradition of "computer hacker science fiction," notably Vernor Vinge's novella *True Names*, as well as many fond childhood memories of games of make-believe, more recent memories of role-playing games and the like, and numerous other influences too thoroughly blended to pinpoint. To this we add a dash of silliness, a touch of cyberpunk, and a predilection for object-oriented programming.

The initial incarnation of Habitat uses a Commodore 64 for the frontend. One of the questions we are asked most frequently is "Why the Commodore 64?" Many people somehow get the impression that this was a technical decision, but the real explanation has to do with business, not technology. Habitat was initially developed by Lucasfilm as commercial product for QuantumLink, an online service (then) exclusively for owners of the Commodore 64. At the time we started (1985), the Commodore 64 was the mainstay of the recreational computing market. Since then it has declined dramatically in both its commercial and technical significance. However, when we began the project, we didn't get a choice of platforms. The nature of the deal was such that both the Commodore 64 for the frontend and the existing QuantumLink host system (a brace of Stratus fault-tolerant minicomputers) for the backend were givens.

The largest part of the screen is devoted to the graphics display. This is an animated view of the player's current location in the Habitat world. The scene consists of various objects arrayed on the screen. The players are represent by animated figures that we call "Avatars." Avatars are usually, though not exclusively, humanoid in appearance.

Avatars can move around, pick up, put down, and manip-

ulate objects, talk to each other, and gesture, each under the
control of an individual player. Control is through the joystick, which enables the player to point at things and issue
commands. Talking is accomplished by typing on the keyboard. The text that a player types is displayed over his or
her Avatar's head in a cartoon-style "word balloon."

The Habitat world is made up of a large number of discrete
locations that we call "regions." In its prime, the prototype
Habitat world consisted of around twenty thousand of them.
Each region can adjoin up to four other regions, which can
be reached simply by walking your Avatar to one or another
edge of the screen. Doorways and other passages can connect
to additional regions. Each region contains a set of objects
which define the things that an Avatar can do there and the
scene that the player sees on the computer screen.

Some of the objects are structural, such as the ground or
the sky. Many are just scenic, such as the tree or the mailbox.
Most objects, however, have some function that they perform. For example, doors transport Avatars from one region
to another and may be opened, closed, locked, and unlocked.
ATMs (Automatic Token Machines) enable access to an Avatar's bank account. Vending machines dispense useful goods
in exchange for Habitat money. Habitat contained its own
fully-fledged economy, with money, banks, and so on. Habitat's unit of currency is the Token, owing to the fact that it
is a token economy and to acknowledge the long and hon-
orable association between tokens and video games.

Many objects are portable and may be carried around in
an Avatar's hands or pockets. These include various kinds of
containers, money, weapons, tools, and exotic magical implements. Listed here are some of the most important types
of objects and their functions. The complete list of object
types numbers in the hundreds. Partial list:

OBJECT CLASS	FUNCTION
ATM	Automatic Token Machine; access to an Avatar's bank account
Avatar	Represents the player in the Habitat world
Bag, Box	Containers in which things may be carried
Book	Document for Avatars to read (e.g., the daily newspaper)
Bureaucrat-in-a-box	Communication with system operators
Change-o-matic	Device to change Avatar gender
Chest, Safe	Containers in which things can be stored
Club, Gun, Knife	Various weapons
Compass	Points direction to West Pole
Door	Passage from one region to another; can be locked
Drugs	Various types; changes Avatar body state, e.g., cures wounds
Elevator	Transportation from one floor of a tall building to another
Flashlight	Provides light in dark places
Fountain	Scenic highlight; provides communication to system designers
Game piece	Enables various board games: backgammon, checkers, chess, etc.
Garbage can	Disposes of unwanted objects
Glue	System building tool; attaches objects together
Ground, Sky	The underpinnings of the world
Head	An Avatar's head; comes in many styles, for customization

Key	Unlocks doors and other containers
Knickknack	Generic inert object; for decorative purposes
Magic wand	Various types; can do almost anything
Paper	For writing notes, making maps, etc.; used in mail system
Pawn machine	Buys back previously purchased objects
Plant, Rock, Tree	Generic scenic objects
Region	The foundation of reality
Sensor	Various types; detects otherwise invisible conditions in the world
Sign	Allows attachment of text to other objects
Stun gun	Non-lethal weapon
Teleport booth	Means of quick long-distance transport; analogous to phone booth
Tokens	Habitat money
Vendroid	Vending machine; sells things

Implementation

The following, along with several programmer-years of tedious and expensive detail that we won't cover here, is how the system works:

At the heart of the Habitat implementation is an object-oriented model of the universe.

The frontend consists of a system kernel and a collection of objects. The kernel handles memory management, display generation, disk I/O, telecommunications, and other "operating system" functions. The objects implement the semantics of the world itself. Each type of Habitat object has a definition consisting of a set of resources, including animation cels to drive the display, audio data, and executable code. An object's executable code implements a series of standard behaviors, each of which is invoked by a different player command or system event. The model is similar to that found in an object-oriented programming system such as Smalltalk, with its classes, methods, and messages. These resources consume significant amounts of scarce frontend memory, so we can't keep them all in core at the same time. Fortunately, their definitions are invariant, so we simply swap them in from disk as we need them, discarding less recently used resources to make room.

When an object is instantiated, we allocate a block of memory to contain the object's state. The first several bytes of an object's state information take the same form in all objects, and include such things as the object's screen location and display attributes. This standard information is interpreted by the system kernel as it generates the display and manages the run-time environment. The remainder of the state information varies with the object type and is accessed only by the object's behavior code.

Object behaviors are invoked by the kernel in response to player input. Each object responds to a set of standard verbs that map directly onto the commands available to the player. Each behavior is simply a subroutine that executes the indicated action; to do this it may invoke the behaviors of other objects or send request messages to the backend. Besides the standard verb behaviors, objects may have additional behaviors that are invoked by messages that arrive asynchronously from the backend.

The backend also maintains an object-oriented representation of the world. As in the frontend, objects on the backend possess executable behaviors and in-memory state information. In addition, since the backend maintains a per sistent global state for the entire Habitat world, the objects are also represented by database records that may be stored on disk when not "in use." Backend object behaviors are invoked by messages from the frontend. Each of these backend behaviors works in roughly the same way: a message is received from a player's frontend requesting some action; the action is taken and some state changes to the world result; the backend behavior sends a response message back to the frontend informing it of the results of its request and notification messages to the frontends of any other players who are in the same region, informing them of what has taken place.

The Lessons

In order to say as much as we can in the limited space available, we will describe what we think we learned via a series of principles or assertions surrounded by supporting reasoning and illustrative anecdotes.

We mentioned our primary principle above:

A multi-user environment is central to the idea of cyberspace.

It is our deep conviction that a definitive characteristic of a cyberspace system is that it represents a multi-user environment. This stems from the fact that what (in our opinion) people seek in such a system is richness, complexity, and depth. Nobody knows how to produce an automaton that even approaches the complexity of a real human being, let alone a society. Our approach, then, is not even to attempt this, but instead to use the computational medium to augment the communications channels between real people.

If what we are constructing is a multi-user environment,

it naturally follows that some sort of communications capability must be fundamental to our system. However, we must take into account an observation that is the second of our principles:

Communications bandwidth is a scarce resource.

This point was rammed home to us by one of Habitat's nastier externally imposed design constraints, namely that it provide a satisfactory experience to the player over a 300-baud serial telephone connection (one, moreover, routed through commercial packet-switching networks that impose an additional, uncontrollable latency of 100 to 5,000 milliseconds on each packet transmitted).

Even in a more technically advanced network, however, bandwidth remains scarce in the sense that economists use the term: available carrying capacity is not unlimited. The law of supply and demand suggests that no matter how much capacity is available, you always want more. When communications technology advances to the point were we all have multi-gigabaud fiber-optic connections into our homes, computational technology will have advanced to match. Our processors' expanding appetite for data will mean that the search for ever more sophisticated data-compression techniques will still be a hot research area (though what we are compressing may at that point be high-resolution volumetric time series or something even more esoteric).

Computer scientists tend to be reductionists who like to organize systems in terms of primitive elements that can be easily manipulated within the context of a simple formal model. Typically, you adopt a small variety of very simple primitives, which are then used in large numbers. For a graphics-oriented cyberspace system, the temptation is to build upon bitmapped images or polygons or some other graphic primitive. These sorts of representations, however, are invitations to disaster. They arise from an inappropriate fixation on display technology, rather than on the underlying purpose of the system.

However, the most significant part of what we wish to be communicating are human behaviors. These, fortunately, can be represented quite compactly, provided we adopt a relatively abstract, high-level description that deals with behavioral concepts directly. This leads to our third principle:

An object-oriented data representation is essential.

Taken at its face value, this assertion is unlikely to be controversial, as object-oriented programming is currently the methodology of choice among the software engineering cognoscenti. However, what we mean here is not only that you should adopt an object-oriented approach, but that the basic objects from which you build the system should correspond more or less to the objects in the user's conceptual model of the virtual world, that is, people, places, and artifacts. You could, of course, use object-oriented programming techniques to build a system based on, say, polygons, but that would not help to cope with the fundamental problem.

The goal is to enable the communications between machines to take place primarily at the behavioral level (what people and things are doing) rather than at the presentation level (how the scene is changing). The description of a place in the virtual world should be in terms of what is there rather than what it looks like. Interactions between objects should be described by functional models rather than by physical ones. The computation necessary to translate between these higher-level representations and the lower-level representations required for direct user interaction is an essentially local function. At the local processor, display-rendering techniques may be arbitrarily elaborate and physical models arbitrarily sophisticated. The data channel capacities required for such computations, however, need not and should not be squeezed into the limited bandwidth available between the local processor and remote ones. Attempting to do so just leads to disasters such as NAPLPS, a format for sending data, used by videotex systems.

Once we begin working at the conceptual rather than the presentation level, we are struck by the following observation:

The implementation platform is relatively unimportant.

The presentation level and the conceptual level cannot (and should not) be totally isolated from each other. However, defining a virtual environment in terms of the configuration and behavior of objects, rather than their presentation, enables us to span a vast range of computational and display capabilities among the participants in a system. This range extends both upward and downward. As an extreme example, a typical scenic object, such as a tree, can be represented by a handful of parameter values. At the lowest conceivable end of things might be an ancient Altair 8800 with a 300-baud ASCII dumb terminal, where the interface is reduced to fragments of text and the user sees the humble string so familiar to the players of text adventure games, "There is a tree here." At the high end, you might have a powerful processor that generates the image of the tree by growing a fractal model and rendering it three dimensions at high resolution, the finest details ray-traced in real time, complete with branches waving in the breeze and the sound of wind in the leaves coming through your headphones in high-fidelity digital stereo. And these two users might be looking at the same tree in same the place in the same world

and talking to each other as they do so. Both of these scenarios are implausible at the moment, the first because nobody would suffer with such a crude interface when better
ones are so readily available, the second because the computational hardware does not yet exist. The point, however,
is that this approach covers the ground between systems already obsolete and ones that are as yet gleams in their designers' eyes. Two consequences of this are significant. The
first is that we can build effective cyberspace systems today.
Habitat exists as ample proof of this principle. The second is
that it is conceivable that with a modicum of cleverness and
foresight you could start building a system with today's technology that could evolve smoothly as tomorrow's technology
develops. The availability of pathways for growth is important in the real world, especially if cyberspace is to become
a significant communications medium (as we obviously
think it should).

Given that we see cyberspace as fundamentally a communications medium rather than simply a user interface
model, and given the style of object-oriented approach that
we advocate, another point becomes clear:

Data communications standards are vital.

However, our concerns about cyberspace data-communi-
cations standards center less upon data-transport protocols
than upon the definition of the data being transported. The
mechanisms required for reliably getting bits from point A
to point B are not terribly interesting to us. This is not because these mechanisms are not essential (they obviously
are) nor because they do not pose significant research and
engineering challenges (they clearly do). It is because we are
focused on the unique communications needs of an object-
based cyberspace. We are concerned with the protocols for

sending messages between objects, that is, for communicating behavior rather than presentation, and for communicating object definitions from one system to another.

Communicating object definitions seems to us to be an especially important problem, and one that we really didn't have an opportunity to address in Habitat. It will be necessary to address this problem if we are to have a dynamic system. The ability to add new classes of objects over time is crucial if the system is to be able to evolve.

While we are on the subject of communications standards, we would like to make some remarks about the ISO Reference Model of Open System Interconnection. This multilayered model has become a centerpiece of most discussions about data communications standards these days. Unfortunately, while the bottom four or five layers of this model provide a more or less sound framework for considering data-transport issues, we feel that the model's Presentation and Application layers are not so helpful when considering cyberspace data communications.

We have two main quarrels with the ISO model: first, it partitions the general data communications problem in a way that is a poor match for the needs of a cyberspace system; second, and more important, we think it is an active source of confusion because it focuses the attention of system designers on the wrong set of issues and thus leads them to spend their time solving the wrong set of problems. We know because this happened to us. "Presentation" and "Application" are simply the wrong abstractions for the higher levels of a cyberspace communications protocol. A "Presentation" protocol presumes characteristics of the display are embedded in the protocol. The discussions above should give some indication why we feel such a presumption is both unnecessary and unwise. An "Application" protocol presumes a degree of foreknowledge of the message environment that is incompatible with the sort of dynamically evolving object system we envision.

A better model would be to substitute a different pair of top layers: a Message layer, which defines the means by which objects can address one another and standard methods of encapsulating structured data and encoding low-level data types (e.g., numbers); and a Definition layer built on top of the Message layer, which defines a standard representation for object definitions so that object classes can migrate from machine to machine. One might argue that these are simply Presentation and Application with different labels, but we don't think the differences are so easily reconciled. In particular, we think the ISO model has, however unintentionally, systematically deflected workers in the field from considering many of the issues that concern us.

World Building

There were two sorts of implementation challenges that Habitat posed. The first was the problem of creating a working piece of technology—developing the animation engine, the object-oriented virtual memory, the message-passing pseudo operating system, and squeezing them all into the ludicrous Commodore 64 (the backend system also posed interesting technical problems, but its constraints were not as vicious). The second challenge was the creation and management of the Habitat world itself. It is the experiences from the latter exercise that we think will be most relevant to future cyberspace designers.

We were initially our own worst enemies in this undertaking, victims of a way of thinking to which we engineers are dangerously susceptible. This way of thinking is characterized by the conceit that all things may be planned in advance and then directly implemented according to the plan's detailed specification. For persons schooled in the design and construction of systems based on simple, well-defined and well-understood foundation principles, this is a natural attitude to have. Moreover, it is entirely appropriate when undertaking most engineering projects. It is a frame of mind that is an essential part of a good engineer's conceptual tool kit. Alas, in keeping with Maslow's assertion that "to the person who has only a hammer, all the world looks like a nail," it is a tool that is easy to carry beyond its range of applicability. This happens when a system exceeds the threshold of complexity above which the human mind loses its ability to maintain a complete and coherent model.

One generally hears about systems crossing the complexity threshold when they become very large. For example, the space shuttle and the B-2 bomber are both systems above this threshold, necessitating extraordinarily involved, cumbersome, and time-consuming procedures to keep the design under control—procedures that are at once vastly expensive and only partially successful. To a degree, the complexity problem can be solved by throwing money at it. However, such capital-intensive management techniques are a luxury not available to most projects. Furthermore, although these dubious "solutions" to the complexity problem are out of reach of most projects, alas the complexity threshold itself is not. Smaller systems can suffer from the same sorts of problems. It is possible to push much smaller and less elaborate systems over the complexity threshold simply by introducing chaotic elements that are outside the designers' sphere of control or understanding. The most significant such chaotic elements are autonomous computational agents (e.g., other computers). This is why, for example, debugging even very simple communications protocols often proves surprisingly difficult. Furthermore, a special circle of living Hell awaits the implementors of systems involving that most important category of autonomous computational agents of all, groups of interacting human beings. This leads directly to our next (and possibly most controversial) assertion:

Detailed central planning is impossible; don't even try.

The constructivist prejudice that leads engineers into the kinds of problems just mentioned has received more study from economists and sociologists than from researchers in the software-engineering community. Game and simulation designers are experienced in creating virtual worlds for individuals and small groups. However, they have had no reason to learn to deal with large populations of simultaneous users. Since each user or group is unrelated to the others, the same world can be used over and over again. If you are playing an adventure game, the fact that thousands of other people elsewhere in the (real) world are playing the same game has no effect on your experience. It is reasonable for the creator of such a world to spend tens or even hundreds of hours crafting the environment for each hour that a user will spend interacting with it, since that user's hour of experience will be duplicated tens of thousands of times by tens of thousands of other individual users.

Builders of online services and communications networks are experienced in dealing with large user populations, but they do not, in general, create elaborate environments. Furthermore, in a system designed to deliver information or communications services, large numbers of users are simply a load problem rather than a complexity problem. All the users get the same information or services; the comments in the previous paragraph regarding duplication of experience apply here as well. It is not necessary to match the size and complexity of the information space to the size of the user population. While it may turn out that the quantity of information available on a service is a function of the size of the user population, this information can generally be organized into a systematic structure that can still be maintained by a few people. The bulk, wherein the complexity lies, is the product of the users themselves, rather than the system designers—the operators of the system do not have to create all this material. (This observation is the first clue to the solution to our problem.)

Our original specification for Habitat called for us to create a world capable of supporting a population of twenty thousand Avatars, with expansion plans for up to fifty thousand. By any reckoning this is a large undertaking and complexity problems would certainly be expected. However, in practice we exceeded the complexity threshold very early in development. By the time the population of our online community had reached around fifty we were in over our heads (and these fifty were "insiders" who were prepared to be tolerant of holes and rough edges).

Moreover, a virtual world such as Habitat needs to scale with its population. For twenty thousand Avatars we needed twenty thousand "houses," organized into towns and cities with associated traffic arteries and shopping and recreational areas. We needed wilderness areas between the towns so that everyone would not be jammed together into the same place. Most of all, we needed things for twenty thousand people to do. They needed interesting places to visit—and since they can't all be in the same place at the same time, they needed a lot of interesting places to visit—and things to do in those places. Each of those houses, towns, roads, shops, forests, theaters, arenas, and other places is a distinct entity that someone needs to design and create. We, attempting to play the role of omniscient central planners, were swamped.

Automated tools may be created to aid the generation of areas that naturally possess a high degree of regularity and structure, such as apartment buildings and road networks. We created a number of such tools, whose spiritual descendents will no doubt be found in the standard bag of tricks of future cyberspace architects. However, the very properties that make some parts of the world amenable to such techniques also make those same parts of the world among the least important. It is really not a problem if every apartment building looks pretty much like every other. It is a big problem if every enchanted forest is the same. Places whose value lies in their uniqueness, or at least in their differentiation from the places around them, need to be crafted by hand. This is an incredibly labor-intensive and time-consuming process. Furthermore, even very imaginative people are limited in the range of variation that they can produce, especially if they are working in a virgin environment uninfluenced by the works and reactions of other designers.

Running the World

The world-design problem might still be tractable, however, if all players had the same goals, interests, motivations, and types of behavior. Real people, however, are all different. For the designer of an ordinary game or simulation, human diversity is not a major problem, since he or she gets to establish the goals and motivations on the participants' behalf, and to specify the activities available to them in order to channel events in the preferred direction. Habitat, however, was deliberately open-ended and pluralistic. The idea behind our world was precisely that it did not come with a fixed set of objectives for its inhabitants, but rather provided a broad palette of possible activities from which the players could choose, driven by their own internal inclinations. It was our intent to provide a variety of possible experiences, ranging from events with established rules and goals (a treasure hunt, for example) to activities propelled by the players' personal motivations (starting a business, running the newspaper) to completely free-form, purely existential activities (hanging out with friends and conversing). Most activities, however, involved some degree of preplanning and setup on our part—we were to be like the cruise director on a ocean voyage, but we were still thinking like game designers.

The first goal-directed event planned for Habitat was a rather involved treasure hunt called the "D'nalsi Island Adventure." It took us hours to design, weeks to build (including a hundred-region island), and days to coordinate the actors involved. It was designed much like the puzzles in an adventure game. We thought it would occupy our players for days. In fact, the puzzle was solved in about eight hours by a person who had figured out the critical clue in the first fifteen minutes. Many of the players hadn't even had a chance to get into the game. The result was that one person had had a wonderful experience, dozens of others were left bewildered, and a huge investment in design and setup time had been consumed in an eyeblink. We expected that there would be a wide range of "adventuring" skills in the Habitat audience. What wasn't so obvious until afterward was that this meant that most people didn't have a very good time, if for no other reason than that they never really got to participate. It would clearly be foolish and impractical for us to do things like this on a regular basis.

Again and again we found that activities based on often unconscious assumptions about player behavior had completely unexpected outcomes (when they were not simply

outright failures). It was clear that we were not in control.
The more people we involved in something, the less in control we were. We could influence things, we could set up
interesting situations, we could provide opportunities for
things to happen, but we could not dictate the outcome. Social engineering is, at best, an inexact science (or, as some
wag once said, "In the most carefully constructed experiment
under the most carefully controlled conditions, the organism
will do whatever it damn well pleases").

Propelled by these experiences, we shifted into a style of
operations in which we let the players themselves drive the
direction of the design. This proved far more effective. Instead of trying to push the community in the direction we
thought it should go, an exercise rather like herding mice,
we tried to observe what people were doing and aid them
in it. We became facilitators as much as we were designers
and implementors. This often meant adding new features
and new regions to the system at a frantic pace, but almost
all of what we added was used and appreciated, since it was
well matched to people's needs and desires. We, as the experts on how the system worked, could often suggest new
activities for people to try or ways of doing things that people
might not have thought of. In this way we were able to have
considerable influence on the system's development in spite
of the fact that we didn't really hold the steering wheel—
more influence, in fact, than we had had when we were
operating under the illusion that we controlled everything.

Indeed, the challenges posed by large systems have
prompted researchers such as Eric Drexler and Mark Miller
to question the centralized, planning-dominated attitude
that we have criticized here, and to propose alternative approaches based on evolutionary and market principles. These
principles appear applicable to complex systems of all types,
not merely those involving interacting human beings.

The Great Debate

Among the objects we made available to Avatars in Habitat were guns and various other sorts of weapons. We included these because we felt that players should be able to materially affect each other in ways that went beyond simply talking, ways that required real moral choices to be made by the participants. We recognized the age-old storyteller's dictum that conflict is the essence of drama. Death in Habitat was, of course, not like death in the real world! When an Avatar is killed, he or she is teleported back home, head in hands (literally), pockets empty, and any object in hand at the time dropped on the ground at the scene of the crime. Any possessions carried at the time are lost. It was more like a setback in a game of Chutes and Ladders than real mortality. Nevertheless, the death metaphor had a profound effect on people's perceptions. This potential for murder, assault, and other mayhem in Habitat was, to put it mildly, controversial. The controversy was further fueled by the potential for lesser crimes. For instance, one Avatar could steal something from another Avatar simply by snatching the object out of its owner's hands and running off with it.

We had imposed very few rules on the world at the start. There was much debate among the players as to the form that Habitat society should take. At the core of much of the debate was an unresolved philosophical question: Is an Avatar an extension of a human being (thus entitled to be treated as you would treat a real person) or a Pac-Man-like critter destined to die a thousand deaths or something else entirely? Is Habitat murder a crime? Should all weapons be banned? Or is it all "just a game"? To make a point, one of the players took to randomly shooting people as they roamed around. The debate was sufficiently vigorous that we took a systematic poll of the players. The result was ambiguous: fifty percent said that Habitat murder was a crime and shouldn't be a part of the world, while the other fifty percent said it was an important part of the fun.

We compromised by changing the system to allow thievery and gunplay only outside the city limits. The wilderness would be wild and dangerous while civilization would be orderly and safe. This did not resolve the debate, however. One of the outstanding proponents of the antiviolence point of view was motivated to open the first Habitat church. This is discussed later in this chapter.

Furthermore, while we had made direct theft impossible, one could still engage in indirect theft by stealing things set on the ground momentarily or otherwise left unattended. And the violence still possible in the outlands continued to bother some players. Many people thought that such crimes ought to be prevented or at least punished somehow, but they had no idea how to do so. They were used to a world in which law and justice were always things provided by somebody else. Somebody eventually made the suggestion that there ought to be a sheriff. We quickly figured out how to create a voting mechanism and rounded up some volunteers to hold an election. A public debate in the town meeting hall was heavily attended, with the three Avatars who had chosen to run making statements and fielding questions. The election was held, and the town of Populopolis acquired a sheriff.

For weeks the sheriff was nothing but a figurehead, though he was a respected figure and commanded a certain amount of moral authority. We were stumped about what powers to give him. Should he have the right to shoot anyone, anywhere? Give him a more powerful gun? A magic wand to zap people off to jail? What about courts? Laws? Lawyers? Again we surveyed the players, eventually settling on a set of questions that could be answered via a referendum. Unfortunately, we were unable to act on the results before the pilot operations ended and the system was shut down. It was clear, however, that there are two basic camps: anarchy and government. This is an issue that will need to be addressed by future cyberspace architects. However, our view is that a virtual world need not be set up with a "default" government, but can instead evolve one as needed.

A Warning

Given the above exhortation that control should be released to the users, we need to inject a note of caution and present our next assertion:

You can't trust anyone.

This may seem like a contradiction of much of the preceding, but it really is not. Designers and operators of a cyberspace system must inhabit two levels of virtual world at once. The first we call the "infrastructure level," which is the implementation, where the laws that govern "reality" have their genesis. The second we call the "percipient level," which is what the users see and experience. It is important that there not be "leakage" between these two levels. The first level defines the physics of the world. If its integrity is breached, the consequences can range from aesthetic unpleasantness (the audience catches a glimpse of the scaffolding behind the false front) to psychological disruption (somebody does something "impossible," thereby violating users' expectations and damaging their fantasy) to catastrophic failure (somebody crashes the system). When we exhort you to give control to the users, we mean control at the percipient level. When we say that you can't trust anyone, we mean that you can't trust them with access to the infrastructure level. Some stories from Habitat will illustrate this.

When designing a piece of software, you generally assume that it is the sole intermediary between the user and the underlying data being manipulated (possibly multiple applications will work with the same data, but the principle remains the same). In general, the user need not be aware of how data are encoded and structured inside the application. Indeed, the very purpose of a good application is to shield the user from the ugly technical details. It is conceivable that a technically astute person who is willing to invest the time and effort could decipher the internal structure of things, but this would be an unusual thing to do as there is rarely much advantage to be gained. The purpose of the application itself is, after all, to make access to and manipulation of the data easier than digging around at the level of bits and bytes. There are exceptions to this, however. For example, most game programs deliberately impose obstacles on their players in order for play to be challenging. By tinkering around with the insides of such a program—dumping the data files and studying them, disassembling the program itself and possibly modifying it—it may be possible to "cheat." However, this sort of cheating has the flavor of cheating at solitaire: the consequences adhere to the cheater alone. There is a difference, in that disassembling a game program is a puzzle-solving exercise in its own right, whereas cheating at solitaire is pointless, but the satisfactions to be gained from it, if any, are entirely personal.

If, however, a computer game involves multiple players, delving into the program's internals can enable one to truly cheat, in the sense that one gains an unfair advantage over the other players of which they may be unaware. Habitat is such a multi-player game. When we were designing the software, our "prime directive" was "The backend shall not assume the validity of anything a player computer tells it." This is because we needed to protect ourselves against the possibility that a clever user had hacked around with his copy of the frontend program to add "custom features." For example, we could not implement any of the sort of "skill and action" elements found in traditional video games wherein dexterity with the joystick determines the outcome of, say, armed combat, because you couldn't guard against someone modifying their copy of the program to tell the backend that they had "hit," whether they actually had or not. Indeed, our partners at QuantumLink warned us of this very eventuality before we even started—they already had users who did this sort of thing with their regular system. Would anyone actually go to the trouble of disassembling and studying 100K or so of incredibly tight and bizarrely threaded 6502 machine code just to tinker? As it turns out, the answer is yes. People have. We were not one hundred percent rigorous in following our own rule. It turned out that there were a few features whose implementation was greatly eased by breaking the rule in situations where, in our judgment, the consequences would not be material if people "cheated" by hacking their own systems. Darned if people didn't hack their systems to cheat in exactly these ways.

Care must be taken in the design of the world as well. One incident that occurred during our pilot test involved a small group of players exploiting a bug in our world database which they interpreted as a feature. First, some background. Avatars are hatched with two thousand Tokens in their bank account, and each day that they log in they receive another 100T. Avatars may acquire additional funds by engaging in business, winning contests, finding buried treasure, and so on. They can spend their Tokens on, among other things, various items that are for sale in vending machines called Vendroids. There are also Pawn Machines, which will buy objects back (at a discount, of course).

In order to make this automated economy a little more interesting, each Vendroid had its own prices for the items in it. This was so that we could have local price variation (i.e., a widget would cost a little less if you bought it at Jack's Place instead of the Emporium). It turned out that in two Vendroids across town from each other were two items for sale whose prices we had inadvertently set lower than what a Pawn Machine would buy them back for: Dolls (for sale at 75T, hock for 100T) and Crystal Balls (for sale at 18,000T, hock at 30,000T!). Naturally, a couple of people discovered this. One night they took all their money, walked to the Doll Vendroid, bought as many Dolls as they could, then took them across town and pawned them. By shuttling back and forth between the Doll Vendroid and the Pawn Shop for hours, they amassed sufficient funds to buy a Crystal Ball, whereupon they continued the process with Crystal Balls and a couple of orders of magnitude higher cash flow. The final result was at least three Avatars with hundreds of thousands of Tokens each. We only discovered this the next morning when our daily database status report said that the money supply had quintupled overnight.

We assumed that the precipitous increase in "T1" was due to some sort of bug in the software. We were puzzled that no bug report had been submitted. By poking around a bit we discovered that a few people had suddenly acquired enormous bank balances. We sent Habitat mail to the two richest, inquiring as to where they had gotten all that money overnight. Their reply was "We got it fair and square! And we're not going to tell you how!" After much abject pleading on our part they eventually did tell us, and we fixed the erroneous pricing. Fortunately, the whole scam turned out well, as the nouveau riche Avatars used their bulging bank-rolls to underwrite a series of treasure hunt games which they conducted on their own initiative, much to the enjoyment of many other players on the system.

Keeping "Reality" Consistent

The urge to breach the boundary between the infrastructure level and the percipient level is not confined to the players. The system operators are also subject to this temptation, though their motivation is expediency in accomplishing their legitimate purposes rather than the gaining of illegitimate advantage. However, to the degree to which it is possible, we vigorously endorse the following principle:

Work within the system.

Wherever possible, things that can be done within the framework of the percipient level should be. The result will be smoother operation and greater harmony among the user community. This admonition applies to both the technical and the sociological aspects of the system.

For example, with the players in control, the Habitat world would have grown much larger and more diverse than it did had we ourselves not been a technical bottleneck. All new region generation and feature implementation had to go through us, since there was no means for players to create new parts of the world on their own. Region creation was an esoteric technical specialty, requiring a plethora of obscure tools and a good working knowledge of the treacherous minefield of limitations imposed by the Commodore 64. It also required a lot of behind-the-scenes activity that would probably spoil the illusion for many. One of the goals of a next generation Habitat-like system ought to be to permit far greater creative involvement by the participants without requiring them to ascend to full-fledged guruhood to do so.

A further example of working within the system, this time in a social sense, is illustrated by the following experience.

One of the more popular events in Habitat took place late in the test, the brainchild of one of the more active players, who had recently become a QuantumLink employee. It was called the "Dungeon of Death."

For weeks, ads appeared in Habitat's newspaper, *The Rant*, announcing that that Duo of Dread, DEATH and THE SHADOW, were challenging all comers to enter their lair. Soon, on the outskirts of town, the entrance to a dungeon appeared. Out front was a sign reading, "Danger! Enter at your own risk!" Two system operators were logged in as DEATH and THE SHADOW, armed with specially concocted guns that could kill in one shot, rather than the usual twelve. These two characters roamed the dungeon blasting away at anyone they encountered. They were also equipped with special magic wands that cured any damage done to them by other Avatars, so that they wouldn't themselves be killed. To make things worse, the place was littered with dead ends, pathological connections between regions, and various other nasty and usually fatal features. It was clear that any explorer had better be prepared to "die" several times before mastering the dungeon. The rewards were pretty good: 1,000 Tokens minimum and access to a special Vendroid that sold magic teleportation wands. Furthermore, given clear notice, players took the precaution of emptying their pockets before entering, so that the actual cost of getting "killed" was minimal.

One evening, one of us was given the chance to play the role of DEATH. When we logged in, we found him in one of the dead ends with four other Avatars who were trapped there. We started shooting, as did they. However, the last operator to run DEATH had not bothered to use his special wand to heal any accumulated damage, so the character of DEATH was suddenly and unexpectedly "killed" in the encounter. As we mentioned earlier, when an Avatar is killed, any object in his hands is dropped on the ground. In this case, said object was the special kill-in-one-shot gun, which was immediately picked up by one of the regular players, who then made off with it. This gun was not something that regular players were supposed to have. What should we do?

It turned out that this was not the first time this had happened. During the previous night's mayhem the special gun was similarly absconded with. In this case, the person playing DEATH was one of the regular system operators, who, used to operating the regular Q-Link service, simply ordered the player to give the gun back. The player considered that he had obtained the weapon as part of the normal course of the game and balked at this, whereupon the operator threatened to cancel the player's account and kick him off the system if he did not comply. The player gave the gun back, but was quite upset about the whole affair, as were many of his friends and associates on the system. Their world model had been painfully violated.

When it happened to us, we played the whole incident within the role of DEATH. We sent a message to the Avatar who had the gun, threatening to come and kill her if she didn't give it back. She replied that all she had to do was stay in town and DEATH couldn't touch her (which was true, if we stayed within the system). Okay, we figured, she's smart. We negotiated a deal whereby DEATH would ransom the gun for 10,000 Tokens. An elaborate arrangement was made to meet in the center of town to make the exchange, with a neutral third Avatar acting as an intermediary to insure that neither party cheated. Of course, word got around and by the time of the exchange there were numerous spectators. We played the role of DEATH to the hilt, with lots of hokey melodramatic shtick. The event was a sensation. It was written up in the newspaper the next morning and was the talk of the town for days. The Avatar involved was left with a wonderful story about having cheated DEATH, we got the gun back, and everybody went away happy.

These two very different responses to an ordinary operational problem illustrate our point. Operating within the participants' world model produced a very satisfactory result. On the other hand, what seemed like the expedient course, which involved violating this model, provoked upset and dismay. Working within the system was clearly the preferred course in this case.

Current Status

As of this writing, the North American incarnation of Lucasfilm's Habitat, QuantumLink's "Club Caribe," has been operating for almost two years. It uses our original Commodore 64 frontend and a somewhat stripped-down version of our original Stratus backend software. Club Caribe now sustains a population of some fifteen thousand participants.

A technically more advanced version, called Fujitsu Habitat, has recently started pilot operations in Japan, available on NIFtyServe. The initial frontend for this version is the new Fujitsu FM Towns personal computer, though ports to several other popular Japanese machines are anticipated. This version of the system benefits from the additional computational power and graphics capabilities of a newer platform, as well as the Towns' built-in CD-ROM for object imagery and sounds. However, the virtuality of the system is essentially unchanged and Fujitsu has not made significant alterations to the user interface or to any of the underlying concepts.

Conclusions

We feel that the defining characteristic of cyberspace is the shared virtual environment, not the display technology used to transport users into that environment. Such a cyberspace is feasible today, if you can live without head-mounted displays and other expensive graphics hardware. Habitat serves as an existence proof of this contention.

It seems clear to us that an object-oriented world model is a key ingredient in any cyberspace implementation. We feel we have gained some insight into the data representation and communications needs of such a system. While we think that it may be premature to start establishing detailed technical standards for these things, it is time to begin the discussions that will lead to such standards in the future.

Finally, we have come to believe that the most significant challenge for cyberspace developers is to come to grips with the problems of world creation and management. While we have only made the first inroads into solving these problems, a few things have become clear. The most important of these is that managing a cyberspace world is not like managing the world inside a single-user application or even a conventional online service. Instead, it is more like governing an actual nation. Cyberspace architects will benefit from study of the principles of sociology and economics as much as from the principles of computer science. We advocate an agoric, evolutionary approach to world building rather than a centralized, socialistic one.

We would like to conclude with a final admonition, one that we hope will not be seen as overly contentious:

Get real.

In a discussion of cyberspace on Usenet, one worker in the field dismissed Club Caribe (Habitat's current incarnation) as uninteresting, with a comment to the effect that most of the activity consisted of inane and trivial conversation. Indeed, the observation was largely correct. However,

we hope some of the anecdotes recounted above will give
some indication that more is going on than those inane and
trivial conversations might indicate. Further, to dismiss the
system on this basis is to dismiss the users themselves. They
are paying money for this service. For them it is neither inane nor trivial. To insist otherwise presumes that one knows
better than they what they should be doing. Such presumption is another manifestation of the omniscient central plan-
ner who dictates all that happens, a role that this entire
article is trying to deflect you from seeking. In a real system
that is going to be used by real people, it is a mistake to
assume that the users will all undertake the sorts of noble
and sublime activities that you created the system to enable.
Most of them will not. Cyberspace may indeed change humanity, but only if it begins with humanity as it really is.

We would like to acknowledge the contributions of some
of the many people who helped make Habitat possible. At
Lucasfilm, Aric Wilmunder wrote much of the Commodore
64 frontend software; Ron Gilbert, Charlie Kelner, and Noah
Falstein also provided invaluable programming and design
support; Gary Winnick and Ken Macklin were responsible
for all the artwork; Chris Grigg did the sounds; Steve Arnold
provided oustanding management support; and George Lucas gave us the freedom to undertake a project that for all
he knew was both impossible and insane. At Quantum, Ja-
net Hunter wrote the guts of the backend; Ken Huntsman
and Mike Ficco provided valuable assistance with communications protocols.

Kazuo Fukuda and his crew at Fujitsu have carried our
vision of Habitat to Japan and made it their own. Phil Salin,
our boss at AMiX, let us steal the time to write this paper
and even paid for us to attend the First Conference on Cyberspace, even though its immediate relevance to his business may have seemed a bit obscure at the time. We'd also

like to thank Michael Benedikt, Don Fussell, and their co-horts for organizing the Conference and thereby prompting us to start putting our thoughts and experiences in writing. Finally, Dean Tribble, Mark S. Miller, and K. Eric Drexler all provided us with invaluable insight as we look forward to where this may lead.

Social Dimensions of Habitat's Citizenry
F. Randall Farmer

I was the Oracle, or system administrator, for Habitat during its shakedown period and paying-pilot test from June 1986 to May 1988. Here are a few observations about the unique social dimensions of online communities. Most of these ideas were composed while I reigned over a small Habitat town named Populopolis, with a population of five hundred citizens. The Oracles of the currently operating Habitats—Club Caribe in the United States, and Fujitsu Habitat in Japan—have contributed much to later refinement of these thoughts.

The Social Commitment Dimension

In Habitat, I observed five distinct patterns of usage and social commitment:

- The Passives
- The Actives
- The Motivators
- The Caretakers
- The Geek Gods

The Passives

The Passive group must be led by the hand to participate. They want effortless entertainment, like a person watching cable TV with a remote control. They constantly flit from place to place, staying in any single spot for only a moment.

Easily seventy-five percent of the players fall into this category, but they account for only perhaps twenty percent of the connect time. They tend to "cross over" into Habitat only to read their mail, collect their daily Tokens, and read the weekly newspaper (and if given the chance to do any of these activities offline, they'll take it). They show up for events intermittently and only when the mood strikes. Even when they do spend more than two minutes in at a time, they tend to hang around as Ghosts and eavesdrop on others' conversations, rather than participating in the activities themselves. Many special events and activities had to target these "on for just a few minutes" people, and encourage their active participation.

The Actives

The Active group is the next largest, and make up the bulk of the paying customer hours. The active players typically participate in two to five hours of activities per week each. They tend to put Habitat first in their online agenda. Immediately upon entering they contact the other players online to find out the hot activity of the day. They always have a copy of the latest paper (and gripe if it comes out late).

The Actives' biggest problem is overspending. They really like Habitat, and lose track of the time they spend in it. This would sometimes lead to Actives canceling their accounts when a huge bill arrived in the mail, a loss for all involved. The watchword for these people is "be thrifty."

During Fujitsu Habitat's first year of operations the system was only available from 1:00 P.M. to 11:00 P.M. local time. The Actives in Japan developed the habit of logging in every day at 9:00, give or take a minute. This way they maximized their social activity (since they knew everyone else was doing the same thing) but minimized their connection costs (since the system shut down at 11:00). Fujitsu Habitat usually reached peak load by 9:15. Over half these players would still be online at closing, when the host was yanked out from under them. Even now, after two years of twenty-four-hour host operations, this peak persists.

The Motivators

The real heroes of Habitat are the Motivators. They understand that Habitat is what the players make of it. They throw parties, start institutions, open businesses, run for office, start moral debates, become outlaws, and win contests. Motivators are worth their weight in gold. One motivator for every fifty Passives and Actives is a wonderful ratio. Online community builders should nurture these people.

In Club Caribe, there is an official title bestowed on several of those that the operators have recognized as Motivators: "The Guardian Angels." Each receives a male or female angel head, the honor of having the initials "GA" attached to their user name, plus access to a private clubhouse that only they can enter. In return they dedicate themselves to furthering the enjoyment of all participants. When Motivators are ready to make their online community "a paying job," they can become Caretakers.

The Caretakers

Caretakers may already be employees of the host organization, but the best Caretakers are "mature" Motivators. They help the new players, mediate interpersonal conflicts, record bugs, suggest improvements, run their own contests, officiate at functions, and in general keep things running smoothly. There are far fewer Caretakers than Motivators. In Populopolis, there were only three of them.

Again, Club Caribe has an official title for these people: "Club Caribe Guides" or "CCGs." In Club Caribe they wear (ugly) American Indian heads and often receive free online time for their participation. They are on strict schedules and can actually be fired. Caretakers wield a significant amount of political power in cyberspace because the other players quickly figure out who actually "runs" the system. They often develop followers and fans, or enemies and detractors. In this way, Caretakers often introduce real-world politics and egos into cyberspace, and it can dramatically affect the community.

The Geek Gods

The original Habitat operator was known as the Oracle. Having the operator's job is like being a Greek god of ancient mythology. The Oracle grants wishes and introduces new objects and rules into the world. With one bold stroke of the keyboard, the operator can change the physics of the universe, create or eliminate bank accounts, entire city blocks, even the family business. This power carries a heavy burden of responsibility, since any externally imposed change to the cyberspace world can have subtle (and not so subtle) side effects. Think about this: Would you be mad at "God" if one day suddenly electricity didn't work anymore? Something like this happened in Habitat. We had Magic Wand objects, and an Oracle-in-training made dozens of them available, for a stiff price: five days' income. This was a problem because the wands never failed, and never ran out of charges. I had always intended to limit the magic charges, so one night, during host maintenance, I quietly gave each wand a random number of remaining charges. The next day, when the wands started to discharge fully, the players became furious! Some of them threatened to leave Habitat forever. Simple bug "fixes" can sometimes be interpreted as removing a much-loved "feature." Often you can't tell in advance what will happen. Players should be an integral part of cyberspace rule and object changes.

Geek Gods need to be knowledgeable about fantasy role-playing, telecommunications networks, political science, and economics, among other things. They must understand both the need for self-consistency in a fictional world and the methods used to achieve it. They need to understand something about the real world, since that is where the players come from. They need to know the players themselves, since they are the ones who will make or break the system. Most important, they must know when not to wield their power.

Variations on the Theme

The developers of Fujitsu Habitat decided to have their Geek Gods operate behind the scenes and not interact directly with the players. All online support personnel operate at the Caretaker level of commitment and power. This separation of powers is more politically stable and allows the programmers the luxury of remaining a comfortable distance from the daily social problems.

The Path of Ascension
Passive→Active→Motivator→Caretaker→Geek God

Encourage everyone to move one role to the right, and the result will be a living, self-sustaining and thriving community where new members can always feel encouraged to become vital citizens.

The Dimension of Being and Nothingness

To consider fully the social dimensions of a cyberspace citizen we need to consider how a virtual being compares with a person's existence in the real world.

	Connectivity	
Level of Participation:	Online	Offline
Active	I Avatar, Account or Handle	II Agent, Script or Robot
Passive	III Observer, Ghost or Lurker	IV Dead, Inactive or Sleeping

This chart shows two dimensions: Level of Participation and Connectivity. The four quadrants are labeled with the commonly known names of these states on various online systems.

Quadrant I on most systems represents the "user account," "handle," or "Avatar." This is the most familiar state of being for a person when in a cyberspace. You are logged in, doing things in the universe, even if only sending mail or copying files. You are interacting with the system, and others in the system can interact with you.

Quadrant IV is the next most familiar state: logged out. Most cyberspaces understand this state as "inactive," "dead," "in the Void," or "sleeping." Simply put, nothing happens to or for you while you are not present.

These two quadrants map nicely onto the human experience as awake/conscious and asleep/unconscious. Most cyberspace implementors handle these cases adequately in their implementations. However, cyberspace systems designers often overlook the other two quadrants.

Quadrant II describes robots and agents. These are entities

that act on your behalf when you are away. The MUDs and MOOs are leading the experimentation in this area of cyberspace consciousness. Of course, this raises some questions about responsibility for actions. What happens when a robot, acting in your name, does some cyberspace property damage? Or steals? Or worse yet, "harms" someone? Also covered by this quadrant is the concept of "autocollusion," creating extra, fictional personae for the sole purpose of collecting their resources and handing them over to your primary persona.

Quadrant III describes what is by far the most overlooked state of a cyberspace inhabitant's makeup, the "ghost," or "lurker," state of existence. In this state you are an observer only, hiding just out of sight, and would prefer that others not bother you or even know that you are watching. In Habitat you could enter the Ghost state instantaneously: your body would disappear from the screen, to be replaced by a single small icon in the corner of the screen representing you and any other people who were also watching as Ghosts. These people can usually be found hanging around in any large, public-access cyberspace.

Online Personae and Real-World Personality

Cyberspaces, because they are anonymous, present people with a unique opportunity to present themselves in any matter they desire. Shy people can experiment with being bold or they can present themselves as a member of the opposite sex. How often are these alternate personalities accepted or rejected? How often are people "just being themselves" in these online worlds? Why do people do it? These questions personally intrigue me and require further study, but I've collected some interesting data:

In December of 1990, I met face-to-face with a group of

fifty Fujitsu Habitat citizens about their Avatars. During one part of the discussion I asked:

1) Do you think of your Avatar as a separate being, or is it a representation of you?

Half said they thought of their Avatar as a separate being. The others said it was their "self."

2) Do you act like your usual self when you are in Habitat, or in ways different from real life?

Again the results were fifty-fifty. This was no surprise to me, as I thought I had simply rephrased and inverted the first question. Then I realized that several that had selected "self" for the first question had not selected "self" for the second question! The actual distribution was as follows:

	My Avatar is a representation of	
In Habitat I act	myself	another being
like myself	26%	24%
unlike myself	25%	25%

Only a minority (26%) prefers to project themselves fully into the online universe. Clearly, cyberspace citizens feel empowered by the technology to experiment with social interactions they feel safe enough to try on a different skin. Given that the current players are mostly affluent, male, and computer-savvy, will these statistics remain meaningful when people with other interests arrive?

Other Social Dimensions

Other social dimensions of cyberspace citizenry that should be considered include sense of place, point of view, government, economics, politics, religion, crime, punishment, inclusion, ostracism, and spontaneous social organization. These are the issues that Habitat's citizenry care about.

Habitat Anecdotes
F. Randall Farmer

Real Money

The Habitat Beta Test was a paying pilot-test. The testers would be paying $0.08 per minute to play, and in this way we could see if Habitat was financially feasible. There were exceptions; about twenty-five percent of the testers would be QLink staff, who either had free accounts or were given a certain number of free hours. This distinction caused some difficulty in deciding if any Habitat activity was a success (see the Scheduled Events). We wanted to see if Habitat was "fun enough" for paying customers.

Consider the following message, posted by a concerned user (edited for brevity):

> As of today I am quitting Habitat. It costs too much. I have been a Q-Link subscriber for 2 years. The first year I used only 2 plus hours. ($10) The next year I used only 5. ($25) But in the last month, while I was playing Habitat I spent $270!!! I can't afford that. You need to make it cheaper.

$270 = 57 hours, or over 100 times his previous peak usage!

We must have made it "too much fun"!

Another user said: "I didn't realize that I was going to want to play 50 hours/month!"

Habitat (for some) was addictive. Because of this, there was a call for "bulk discounts" and various other schemes were proposed by the users. None of them were implementable, and all of them would have resulted in significant losses.

Yet another spent over $1,000 in one month in Habitat. At around $300 and $600 dollars, he was mailed a message

suggesting he "check out his usage in the billing section." If
we could get twenty more of this type of "rich" user, we
would be profitable!

The Order of the Holy Walnut

One of the outstanding proponents of the anti-violence-
in-Habitat view was also the first Habitat minister. A Greek
Orthodox minister opened the first church in Habitat. His
canons forbid his disciples to carry weapons, steal, or participate in violence of any kind. It was unfortunate that I had
to eventually put a lock on the church's front door because
every time he decorated (with flowers), someone would
steal and pawn them while he was not logged in.

Wedded Bliss?

Three Habitat weddings took place in that church. These
were not human-human weddings, but Avatar-Avatar. Their
turfs (user-owned areas) were joined so that they could co-
habit. There were some technical problems with this that
were resolved in later versions. Only one account could enter a turf if the owner was not home. We hadn't properly
handled cohabitation.

The first Habitat divorce occurred two weeks after the
third wedding. I guess Habitat is a bit too close to the real
world for my taste! The first habitat lawyers handled the
divorce, including public postings all about town.

Entertaining the Neighbors

The Party was one of my favorite activities. I liked to
throw them at new Avatars' houses. I would use ESP to contact a known "Passive" Avatar, and ask him where he lived.
If he told me, I would send ESP to "Actives" and "Motivators" that were online to teleport to the address. Great fun.

A close cousin to parties was the sleep-over. The users

invented this on their own. Often private discussions would take place in a turf. It was considered a minor social honor to be invited to sleep over. This meant to log out while still in another's turf. This was an honor because you would be able to log in later even if the host was not on. This would leave the host's belongings open to plunder.

Secret Identities

In the original proposal, all Avatars would be able to have unique names (separate from their log-in names) and they could say they were anybody they wanted. Like a big costume party, no one would know who was who. I lost the battle for unique names, as QuantumLink wanted an "identify" function for terms of service enforcement reasons. It seemed the anonymity I wanted was lost. But I suggested a counterproposal. A tit-for-tat rule. If you "peeked" at someone else's secret identity, you would be unmasked to that Avatar, and no one else. Some very interesting dynamics developed. Some people were offended if they were ID'ed right away. And others never bothered using the function as long as you said "HI! I'm WINGO." When you arrived I remember one time that I convinced someone that I was another person by sending ESP as "myself" to the person in the same region.

Business

The economy was initially a minor issue. Most everybody had plenty of Tokens (except the Passives). In an attempt to open the retail business to Avatars, a drugstore was opened, with a locked room in back that only the owner could enter that contained the only vending machine that sold Habitat healing potions and poisons. The shopkeeper would pay the fixed price, and would charge whatever he wanted for resale. It was a success except for the fact that the owner logged in at strange hours.

Motivators and Caretakers at Work

By far the Caretaker who had the greatest impact on his fellow users was the editor of the Habitat weekly newspaper *The Rant*. This user tirelessly spent twenty to forty hours a week (free account) composing a twenty-, thirty-, forty-, or even fifty-page tabloid containing the latest news, events, and rumors, and even fictional articles. This was no small feat; he had only the barbaric Habitat paper editor, and no other tools. After he had composed the pages of an issue, he would arrange them in several chests of drawers in the *Rant* office and send me mail. I would publish it by using a special host program that would bind them into a book object and distribute it to the news Vendroids, check the copy by hand for errors, and deliver a copy to the office (in Habitat). This worked great, but took massive amounts of his personal time. I began to automate the process further just as the Habitat operation changed hands. The new publisher didn't publish on time, delayed getting the tools ready to speed up creation, made editorial changes (he wanted it to be shorter, less fiction), and he didn't hand-deliver a copy of the final product. The editor quit. Just like in real life: Someone new runs the show and the sensitive leave. Again, these people are rare and should be handled carefully. *The Rant* will never be the same.

Duels

One of the wands we implemented forced the target Avatar to perform the "jump" gesture, accompanied by a "Hah!" word balloon. It was fun for a while, mostly because you could really affect another Avatar, but it got old fast. Soon the users developed a game involving these wands: the Duel. The rules were simple: two combatants, two wands, and one judge. When the judge says "go" the first to "hit" the other with the wand three times wins. Not as easy as it sounds, since the duelists were allowed to run around.

Tours

Another Caretaker was the number one all-time most-traveled Avatar. He also was the longest-lived. When new people started logging in, he took them on guided tours of this strange new world. He made them feel like they had a "friend" in town.

Combat

"Conflict is the essence of drama." We used this quote in the initial Habitat design document. Habitat (it was then named "Microcosm") was to have personal combat in the forms of weapons. Most computer games had combat, and we were offering a chance for users to affect each other!

Here is how combat worked. There were ranged weapons and hand-to-hand. An Avatar is born with 255 hit points. (The actual number is masked from the user, and a "general state of health" message gives the user some idea how bad off he is.) While holding the weapon, you select a target and select DO (attack). There is a telecommunications delay that may affect the hit-or-miss result. Each successful attack does some small amount of damage (i.e., 20 points).You are always informed when you are shot, as your Avatar is knocked onto his rump.

As you can see, it would take quite a few hits to "kill" a healthy Avatar. Not only that, but you can avoid being damaged if the attacker can't "touch" you in two ways: 1) by turning into a ghost or 2) running around (not standing still). You use option two when you are in a duel, where you are shooting back. If you really, really are low on hit points, you travel the "wild" regions as a ghost. There are also devices that will restore your hit points. The real problem is

communicating this to new users, who are often standing
around in a region when a bandit comes along with a gun.
The neophyte hears a "bang" and sees his Avatar knocked
on his can. Instead of acting, he types a message like "What
was that? Why am I sitting down?" Meanwhile, the bandit
cranks out another twelve bullets. . . . Dead beginner probably had all of his money and stuff in his pocket too! This
problem was eventually corrected in the Avatar Handbook,
explaining that guns are dangerous (something we'd thought
people would assume on their own).

The Scheduled Events

R&R Weekend Adventures

These were short (one- to two-hour) quests where a user
pressed one of ten magic buttons to receive a clue to find
one of ten hidden keys to be used in one of ten hidden safes.
These were the all-around best quests to run (there were
three of them) because there were always seven to ten winners. The only problem here was the Time Zone problem:
The event had to be scheduled so that as many people as
possible could participate from the moment it started. QLink
access started at 6 P.M. local time. This meant that for the
Californians to have a chance, the adventure would have to
start at 9 P.M. East Coast time at the earliest.

The Money Tree

The Quest for the Money Tree is the first quest an Avatar
learns about from reading his free Welcome Wagon version
of *The Rant* placed in his turf. There is a tree in a forest that
will dispense 100 Tokens for each Avatar only once. Everyone can feel like they have "found" the magic tree.

The Tome of Wealth and Fame

This was also one of the original quests. A certain set of stone tablets was the Tome of Wealth and Fame. If you found it, you were to hide it somewhere else. You would receive a reward based on how long it took the next Avatar to find it. The problem with this quest was that the world was so large that it often took weeks for someone to find the tome. Even if you actively looked for it, it would take days of online time to find.

The Long and Short of Quests

A trend became clear about quests in Habitat. The winners of the "long-range" quests like the D'nalsi Island Adventure were almost always people with free accounts. The freebies would stay on for hours on end to gain wealth, things, and status. The paying customers could only come on for one to two hours a week. The idea that people would be able to "work on" a quest for weeks is bogus. A successful long-range quest must be something that either "everyone" can win or does not provide some significant advantage in the world.

Grand Openings

A real surprise was the popularity of the "Grand Opening." This is a ribbon-cutting event when new regions were added to the world. Tokens and prizes were often hidden in the new regions, but it seems that the audience (especially the Passives) had an insatiable hunger to see new places and new things. The Grand Opening of the Popustop Arms apartment building was the most heavily attended event of the pilot test.

Disease

One of the more successful "games" we invented for Habitat was the disease. There are three strains: 1) Cooties, 2) Happy Face, 3) Mutant (AKA The Fly). We were only able to test Cooties with live players, but it was a hit. It works like this: Several initial Avatars are infected with a "Cootie" head. This head replaces the current one, and cannot be removed except by touching another non-infected Avatar. Once infected, you cannot be infected again that day. In effect, this game is "tag" and "keep away" at the same time. Often people would allow themselves to be infected just so they could infect "that special person that they know would just hate it!" Every time the disease was introduced, there was an announcement at least a week before, and for at least a week afterward it was the subject of much discussion. One day the plague was spreading, and a female Avatar that was getting married got infected one hour before her wedding! Needless to say, she became very excited, and in a panic until a friend offered to take it off her hands.

Some interesting variations on this are: Infected person must touch two people to cure; this would cause quite a preponderance of infected people late in the day. The "Happy Face" plague: This simple head has the side effect of changing any talk message (word balloons) to come out as "HAVE A NICE DAY!" instead of what they typed. . . . Can you imagine infecting some unsuspecting soul, and having him respond to you HAVE A NICE DAY!??? ESP and mail still work normally, so the user is not without communications channels. The Mutant Plague: The head looks like the head of a giant housefly and it has the effect of changing talk text to "Bzzz zzzz zzzz." These were all great fun.

True Magic

Mark Pesce

Mark Pesce, co-creator of VRML, former chair of the Interactive Media Program at the School of Cinema-Television, University of Southern California, is the author of *The Playful World: How Technology Is Transforming Our Imagination*. I think of him primarily as a scientist.

Sometimes scientists are inspired by science fiction. Many astronauts and space agency scientists will tell you with little prodding how they were inspired either by science fiction they read or by science fiction art. And many in the fields of computer science and artificial intelligence have been inspired by *True Names,* as noted in other essays in the book. (In Habitat, my spies tell me, the coinage bore the image of Vernor Vinge.)

In the following wonderful essay, Pesce brings to *True Names* a measure of appreciation that could only have been written by someone who himself lives on the frontier of cyberspace and scientific innovation. Read and enjoy. This piece was written in 1999.

In the beginning was the code, and the code was hanging out with god; soon enough some came to the conclusion that the code was god. All of this happened thousands of years ago, knowledge won, then lost, then rediscovered, like an Atlantean shale erupting from the crystal-clear waters off some Caribbean island. Now archeologists deny its evidences, but a clever few come to read its inscriptions.

Infinity and Singularity

Between the ancestral origins of the human race and the vision of an evolved being as far above ourselves as we tower above our simian cousins, a long sloping curve rises from the Serengeti plains, reaching its asymptote at a defining moment, where it tunnels off into infinity. This—as far back as Nietzsche, or even Francis Bacon—has been the secular vision of a human destiny, a teleology made up in equal parts of optimistic projection and wish fulfillment.

The divining instincts of a scientific culture—which can not call on the deus ex machina to invoke an internal salvation—have poured these dreams of transcendence into the stories of science fiction, using the imagination of the future to chart the course to an extraordinary form which has, of late, come to be known as the *trans-human*. Invariably, these stories have been nearly Gnostic in character, insisting that some thing—the right bit of information, the proper word, the perfect artifact—could transform humanity utterly. An old idea, dating from prehistory, has finally come to consume any speculative adventure into our human futures.

Science fiction articulates its esoteric imaginings in the constant play between something the classical Greeks recognized as *techne*, or doing, and its relation to *ontos*, or being.

Science fiction, as such, could not exist before the technological project had begun; in our doing we give birth to *agon*,
the test of wills between ourselves and our creations.

Most common are the fictions that begin with Jules Verne,
and concern the single artifact—a submarine, flying machine, or death ray—and its consquence for all of humanity.
These extraordinary voyages—to use Verne's term—play
along the fault line between what we think we are and what
we can do. Nemo is no accident, or a tragic figure, but the
natural consequence of the intersection between present-day
humanity and extraordinary technology. Even *2001: A Space
Odyssey* plays on the same themes, as it offers us "Today's
man in tomorrow's spaceship, today."

The room for such stories has grown more narrow as the
twentieth century has grown to a close, because—beyond a
certain point—the accumulation of artifacts produces a transcendence into infinite possibilities. Lately, we can do more
and more; the modern world would seem entirely magical
to an Athenian of Plato's day. But to us it is all commonplace,
and even the introduction of new artifacts—except perhaps
for singular advents, such as the World Wide Web—triggers
little more than the flutter of an eyelid. If the relationship
between man and artifact is simultaneously both chaotic and
prosaic, the vision of technology infinitely extended—the
trans-human era—is a steady-state universe where the un-
believable is taken as a given. In George Lucas's *Star Wars*
tetralogy, we peer into a world entirely foreign in the perfect
extension of its artifacts, something that each of its characters accepts as a given. They can fly between the stars at
velocities greater than light, and have computers that can
think and react as if human, but there is a curious lack
of technical advancement, as if everything that could be
done has already been done. Even the Death Star, for all of
its malevolence, is just a scaled-up version of the Imperial

Battlecruiser, and Obi-Wan Kenobi extols the virtues of old technology as he praises the light saber, "an elegant weapon . . . for a more civilized age."

These two genres of science fiction represent our collective best guesses of the human future, organized around the single exceptional artifact or an entirely magical universe crowded with them. Like the one and zero states of digital circuitry, they exclude an unpredictable, dynamic middle, a narrow band of intense, nonlinear activity.

Francis Bacon, one of the Renaissance prophets of science, penned what might be the first science fiction novel, *The New Atlantis*, and laid the foundation for what has become a very familiar plot line: the "common man" who stumbles into the presence of intellectual giants, archons who initiate him into their magical ways. Although Bacon espoused the virtues of reason, he wasn't above Clarke's Law; all sufficiently advanced technologies are—even in the early seventeenth century—indistinguishable from magic.

These ancient, hidden powers, we have learned through the intervening centuries, can be angelic or demonic, but rarely are they as ambiguous as the aliens of Clarke and Kubrick's *2001*. We understand nothing of their motivations, only that they serve as the midwives who attend the birth of a trans-human who could—with a wish—destroy the world. The forces that pull humanity into the transhuman— as characterized in science fiction—represent that liminal zone between artifact and infinity, the phase transition between two states of undifferentiated regularity.

That place in between defines the world of *True Names*.

After the Apollo landings, when we began to believe that anything could be accomplished with enough pluck, will, and resources, a new subgenre of science fiction appeared, embodied in the works of two authors who more or less accurately grasped the dynamic of history at the end of the second millennium. John Brunner and Vernor Vinge began to chart out the curve toward infinity, or, as Vinge puts it, the *Singularity*, but cast it as an event under human control, with humans as both the agents and targets of a transcendent destiny. If we continue to add to our capabilities, invention after invention, artifact after artifact, if we continue to increase our knowledge beyond all scope, we will—or so they argue—become fundamentally different from what we are today. At some point, a critical threshold is reached; a point of no return, a moment when we are unrecognizable. Post-human.

Brunner's *Shockwave Rider* (1975) stands alongside *True Names* as one of the seminal science fiction works of that period. One could turn on the news today, listen to reportage of global computer virus infections or random violence wrought by teenaged bezerkers, and think oneself nestled within the pages of his book. Brunner captures the lower slopes of the asymptotic curve toward Singularity perfectly; the ground is shifting, but it is not yet entirely gone. People remain human, but beneath them, all the engines of history keep redlining, ever driving faster and higher.

Vinge builds the launchpad for his work upon the foundation laid down by Brunner, and in so doing he gets enough lift to touch the first reaches of the unbounded space beyond. *True Names*, in another universe, could be the sequel to *Shockwave Rider*. Though the novella lacks some of the more dystopian aspects found in Brunner's work, it hints broadly at the same social collapse, overt authoritarianism, and complete lack of privacy that have—in reality—become the regular features of daily life. Where Brunner foregrounds these aspects, making them central to his story, to Vinge they are just the milieu, the sea that his characters swim in, even as that ocean boils and churns, at the threshold of the Singularity.

As an idea, the Singularity can be approached from any number of directions; in reality, as every day passes we find new paths opening into this ultimate event. It could be the perfection of artificial intelligence—emergent, hyperintelligent, possibly malevolent, or the complete mastery of the physical world through nanotechnology—which could melt us all into a puddle of the fabled gray goo, or the radical augmentation of innate human abilities into a final, transhuman form. Most likely these events would be connected, synchronous and fundamentally inseparable—but no science fiction author has risen to speak of that vision.

Instead, the works following "True Names," such as Gibson's *Neuromancer* (1984), Greg Bear's *Blood Music* (1985), Greg Egan's *Distress* (1995), and Wil McCarthy's *Bloom* (1997), portray one and only one facet of something that must, because it is so singular, be utterly inclusive. While the narratives satisfy—they're each rip-roaring good stories, well told—they leave the reader wanting more, a final fulfillment, a real vision of the trans-human future. But the Singularity lies outside the domain of language, beyond any of the stories we know how to tell. And this makes Vernor Vinge so very interesting; more than any other science fiction writer, he has traced the paths up the slopes of this asymptotic Olympus, and laid a careful path of footholds and handgrips for us to follow.

Technopagans, Inc.

The casual presumption of virtuality—which substitutes the simulated for the real—forms the comfortable frame of *True Names*, but Vinge's conceit of a magical universe as a description for cyberspace catapults the novella from the class of works that predict the future into the rarefied realm of works that have come to create it. Vinge literally spelled out the details of the early twenty-first century. This kind of "hard" science fiction has influenced the direction of research in the computer sciences far beyond its own natural gravity. In giving the geeks a vision, Vinge also defined a road map, a project plan, presenting a future which *could* exist, if only we would work toward it. At the same time, he portrayed this future as so positively heroic—practically mythic in proportion—that any socially ostracized technophile would find within it the seeds of a personal mission.

The impact of Vinge's *True Names* can not be easily overstated. Without using the word "cyberspace"—whatever that means—he presented a globally networked world into which human imagination had been projected, a "consensual hallucination" before Gibson's matrix. Media theorist Sandy Stone has noted that works of science fiction like *True Names* and *Neuromancer* have a crystallizing effect across many seemingly unrelated research areas in the computer sciences, in effect *creating* the future from artistic evocation. Did Vinge create virtual reality? In a practical sense, perhaps not, but something about his novella caused people to revision their work, and refocus themselves toward the ends he described. In an interesting inversion, life imitates art, and people dedicated their professional careers to realize Vinge's vision. I was one of them.

Before virtual reality, before cyberspace, before Gibson, Vinge created a rich tale based in the reality of simulation. Nothing about Vinge's world is disembodied, nothing unnecessarily ethereal. Rather than knocking off a Gnostic tale pitting the prison of the flesh against the boundless freedom of cyberspace, Vinge predicts how human beings will confront this expansive landscape of the self, and so comes closer to the truth of the matter than any other science fiction writer. As he laid down the operating laws for the first quarter-century of research into virtuality, Vinge measured the dimensions of the soul in simulation, and came to the conclusion—quite correctly—that there are more things in heaven and earth than are dreamt of in our philosophies.

The first explorers of the synthetic worlds of simulation learned this through their own experiences. The earliest projects, such as the virtual wind tunnel at NASA's Ames Research Center in Mountain View, California, had narrowly defined goals; in that case, aerodynamic modifications of the space shuttle. But the techniques developed at Ames overflowed into the world at large; soon all of Silicon Valley swam in a sea of head-mounted displays, data gloves, and graphics supercomputers. Most of these systems lay in the hands of the "pure" research community, many of whom had come into the field through the video-game industry, individuals already well versed in the visible translation of their imaginations. Nothing, though, could have prepared them for an immersion into the "black silence" of unpopulated cyberspace, so dramatically different from the empty screen of the unwritten video game—where the rest of the world still filled your senses. Inside the machine, cut off, amputated from the real world, those pioneers confronted an interior emptiness they'd never even imagined, a reflection of the basic nature of simulation: cyberspace contains nothing of itself.

In the real world the empty page might scare the writer, just as the blank screen might intimidate the programmer, but now individuals found themselves in the position of having to "boot up" an entire universe of meaning, without any easy reference to the constellation of familiar objects that tend to reinforce the tentative definitions of newly created artifacts. Say, for example, one wished to create a chair in cyberspace, circa 1985. The most that can be said is that this "chair" won't look very much like a chair, much less feel or taste like one. The "chair" is a sort of Platonic Ideal, a maintained construct, held in place by a consensual agreement that this set of pixels *is* a "chair," and everyone interacting in this simulation agrees, by force of collective will, to treat it as such. This is the textbook definition of the magical act, and its corollary states that *every object in cyberspace is a magical object*.

The generation of meaning is *always* a magical act, arbitrary in a particularly self-consistent way that seems to obey some biological drive to believe in the consistency of the world. This was the covert theme of Neal Stephenson's *Snow Crash* (1993), which interwove a discursive exploration of the power of language to shape reality with "real" experiences in cyberspace—or, the "Metaverse"—as dialectical twins, DNA strands describing the complementary halves of one genetic whole. One strand flows back into prehistory, into the origins of consciousness in the advent of human language, while the other draws directly from the tense post-historic relationship between the "synthetic" and "reality."

Science fiction author Robert Anton Wilson has noted that "reality is defined by the place where rival gangs of shamans fought each other to a stand-off," implying a process that continues through to the present day (and simultaneously summarizing the plot of *Snow Crash*). While the creation of value may be mostly a magical act—just ask the Marxists—day-to-day life, before cyberspace, offered little opportunity for the creative use of the will to define the real. In *True Names,* Vinge uncovered something very old, a particular feature of human consciousness almost atrophied from disuse, yet still very much a part of us. If every item is not itself, cannot be dismissed as "just a rock" or "tree," but must be viewed as an exteriorization of one's own self, the entire world becomes a very explicit reflection of what we believe to be true. Cyberspace brought this forgotten knowledge into the foreground, making it impossible to ignore. If there are no atheists in foxholes, there are only animists in cyberspace.

Animism—the belief in an interior spiritual reality to all things—sounds, to late twentieth-century ears, quite a bit like solipsism, which holds that only the self exists, manifesting itself in the architecture of reality. The "reality" of cyberspace falls somewhere in between these two; everything has an interior nature, which generates meaning, but this interior nature is self-created; collective will creating consensual reality. Appropriately, there is precedent for this current situation in the birth of our own linguistic abilities.

No one can say, with any precision, when human beings first acquired language, but it seems reasonable to hypothesize that it happened in one sudden, complete act; we have been unable to develop any models for an evolutionary path toward language, because the consciousness of the universe as a collection of objects requires linguistic apprehension. We could not use nouns by themselves, or verbs, or modifiers; they emerge as a piece, a singular act—suggesting that any pending Singularity is, perhaps, not the first such event—which moved us, en masse, from the animal and into the human. The assignment of names for things did not happen one item at a time; despite the paternalistic story of Jehovah teaching Adam the names of the animals, we know now that an entire frame for *things* had to be constructed before the things themselves could exist in our consciousness. This frame—coincident with the birth of a linguistic consciousness in humanity—is entirely a magical creation, a construct that defines the way we make sense of the world.

Vinge realized that things end as they begin; come full circle, the magic that created humanity plays an equally important role in the creation of the post-human. The first explorers of cyberspace began to intuit this relationship almost immediately, and—based upon their extensive writings on this topic—we can assert that these explorers bore the mark of this experience; nearly all of them adopted "pagan" religious attitudes toward the virtual universe, a phenomenon that Erik Davis, writing in the pages of *Wired* magazine, later dubbed "Technopaganism."

Although the dictionary definition of "pagan" simply describes someone who is neither Jewish, Christian, nor Moslem, a more practical working definition might encompass a religious philosophy of immanence—that the divine is present in all creation, but in manifold forms. Thus the Roman hearth belonged to Vesta, the threshold to Janus, and the power of communication to Mercury, each representing a specific domain of influence, and each with separate rites and rituals. We think of these god-forms and their underlying philosophical expressions as the product of unsophisticated, prescientific minds, but on closer examination, nothing could be further from the truth. The Romans likely did not believe in the physical reality of their pantheon, but rather, found in them a convenience, a way to manage the complexity of a magical universe, a filter between the undifferentiated unity of an immanent reality and the exigencies of each day. Vesta, for instance, came to represent a set of qualities associated with the household, as typified in the hearth, so a conscious focus on Vesta—through prayers, offerings, and sacrifices—would do much to strengthen the will, a magical relation between public acts and personal reality that says more about ancient psychology than about ancient religion. The techniques of pagan practice, principally psychological in nature, allowed the ancients to approach an unspeakably complex world in manageable, bite-sized pieces, which would become the specific vehicle for personal change. Though this activity may have been an unconscious one for the bulk of the Empire's citizenry, the ancient magical texts of the Alexandrian Greeks prove that, within esoteric circles, all of this was well understood.

A similar state of affairs exists in cyberspace today; most people are willing to confront the 'bots, mailing lists, avatars, and sundry other denizens of the virtual world as real entities, possessing their own interior natures, but a few—in particular, those pioneers—recognize that these synthetic projections are conveniences of the mind, and wholly under the mind's control. The esoteric secret of cyberspace is that it is utterly composed of Blake's "mind forg'd manacles," that we are prisoners of our own design, and, for the few who realize this, the opportunity of freedom beckons.

Roger Pollack, as Vinge's hero in *True Names*, accepts this freedom as his due, and masters the world of magic as a prisoner grapples for the keys to his cage; only in this wizardry, in this compression of the incomprehensibly complex world of planetary networks into the pseudo-archaic forms of castle and keep, dungeon and dragon, can he create a space entirely for himself. Only within a fantastic world can his soul explore the incredible possibilities the real world has come to offer. And so, too, do the modern technopagans lay the veil of magic and mystery across a world almost wholly integrated in every aspect, knowing that the intentional act of drawing this veil over the world provides, for them, the fertile conditions for the soul's growth into trans-human form.

There and Back Again

Magic has two faces; although principally psychological in nature, the magical worldview prescribes that interior activities must have an influence on exterior reality. The boundary between these two, always muddy, fades into confusion within the constrictive simulations of cyberspace. Transcendence, or Singularity, inside cyberspace would be a false transformation, a half-answer. Gods bottled up inside the virtual world would not be gods at all. As Gibson recounts in *Count Zero*, in the years after transcendence, the Voudoun *loas* reemerged as entities with real-world influence, god-forms who can freely partake in the commerce of information and material. Magic is a form of power, an ability to make the world-at-large conformant to personal will, not just a clever technique for mental housekeeping. However, magic in this aspect immediately presents its darker nature in the lust of result, the drive to have everything within one's control, to be the puppet master in a land of slaves. Translating magic from cyberspace into the material world makes it true, and truly dangerous.

So Vinge's tale, replete with magical imagery, would be incomplete, and without consequence, if the magic had been fundamentally separated from the powers imparted by the mastery of that magic. More than just a system for the manipulation of symbol systems of radical complexity, magic is the mechanism by which Mr. Slippery, Erythrina—and the Mailman—translate their will into real actions, even while it equally presents the grand threat to their continued existence. Here we come to the core theme of *True Names*, hidden under layers of affecting surface detail; the mastery of reality by magical technique opens hidden possibilities of human being, for inasmuch as their magic *works*, it presents temptations greater than any they have known—greater than any they can experience and still call themselves human.

Only in this complete form—from magic into action—can we hear Vinge's articulation of the real nature of the Singularity. High on the asymptotic curve toward infinite extension of our capabilities, our abilities with language will—in Vinge's eyes—produce a revolution in the real world, a revolution he sees as necessarily catastrophic. When Roger and Erythrina encompass the extensive computing power across a networked planet, their point of view becomes decidedly post-human, as if the frail shell of flesh and fantasy that has thus far sustained their dreams has—in a moment— become a hollow substitute for the nearly unbounded powers of a god. Despite their powers within cyberspace—significant and dangerous in themselves—they find in the taste of the real the forbidden fruit, which leaves them fully aware of their nakedness and ignorance. There is no going back; their translation is utter and singular, and, like Adam and Eve, they are cast from their bliss into a hostile world.

Seated comfortably before our computers, we can tend a garden in Linz, Austria, or take a peep through a camera located on the other side of the planet; we can cast our bread upon the waters of the global network, and wonder what gifts might be returned to us. We can tap into a firmament of knowledge that grows to encompass the entire extent of human experience on Earth, and we can wage war against our enemies. For all of its disembodied qualities, cyberspace has a reality that belies its ephemeral nature; because we are tied into it, we are its eyes and ears and arms and legs. We are already extended enormously by its reach, but more will come. Much more.

In *True Names*, Vinge used the most visible aspects of future technologies, such as fast computers and orbital laser cannons, to give a tangible quality to this magical power of will, but it may be—for ourselves—that the least visible elements of the future will become the ground for the expression of post-human capabilities. Our doing has grown increasingly fine, now nearly approaching the infinitely fringed boundary to quantum impossibilities. Forty years ago, in a famous lecture, physicist Richard Feynman predicted an opening of the atomic structures of nature to human ability; his colleague,

Marvin Minsky, passed the kernel of this idea to one of his graduate students, K. Eric Drexler, who wrote a book about it: *Engines of Creation: The Coming Age of Nanotechnology* (1986). In one word, Drexler summarized the infinite extension of human ability—fundamental control of the material universe.

Although the published text is interesting—inspiring a generation of both scientists and science fiction authors—the original manuscript version of *Engines of Creation* can be classified only as a mind-blowing masterpiece of futurism, a text so wild, so positively singular, that the publisher naturally balked at an open distribution of its disturbing conclusions. (I leave it as a research problem for the reader to discover precisely what these conclusions might be.) On his first pass, Drexler charted out the very top of the asymptote, where it grinds toward a tangent infinity; these are the abilities that greet us, at the opening of the cyberspace frontier. The magical world within becomes, with some simple machinery, the magical world without; the same laws of magic and will bind both our self-constructions in cyberspace and our exterior imaginings in the fabric of the material world.

All of which, at least theoretically, presents us with quite a problem, in magnitude identical to the opportunity offered. We are not, by and large, taught to be magicians, and we have not the mastery of our own fates. The Feds, in the end, had to rely on Roger and Erythrina to save civilization, because *they* had mastered the lost arts of trans-humanity, *they* were ready to boot-up into being beyond anything they had ever known. Even this, *True Names* indicates, will not suffice; though they win the war, these new trans-human entities will not willingly lay their powers down. Erythrina becomes the matrix, leaving her identity behind to serve as the vital center of a coming general transcendence. (The only false step in *True Names* is Roger's resumption of human form—

but somebody has to play witness to apotheosis.) Vinge seems to say that Singularity is universal, affecting all humanity. In the words of the old song, we'll all go together when we go—one way or another. At the very end of the asymptote, there is only infinity, everywhere.

To return, at the end, to the beginning, we can cast our eyes back further than Vinge, before the modern, before the prehistoric. Our civilizations carry myths of races older than ours, of powers greater than our own, and even if the New Age has coopted most of them into the fanciful re-creations of an interstellar cargo cult, the myths remain. In particular—at least in the West—the story of Atlantis has taken on a life of its own in modern times, decompressing a few lines of Plato's *Critias* into an entire galaxy of beliefs about the utopian community *before* history. The modern variants of the Atlantis myth tell of a culture of nearly unlimited power, controlling the fields of the Earth itself with energy from its crystals, and who finally lost control in a catastrophic failure of their magical abilities, destroyed by earthquake and sunk beneath the seas.

If it is reasonable to read the myths of more advanced cultures as windows into the cultural soul—as I believe it is—this story can tell us much about how we see ourselves. We, too, have harnessed the "crystals" for great power—all semiconductors are crystals, and most of us work before liquid crystal displays. We, too, have nearly unlimited power—even our great-grandfathers would agree. And more and more we worry that our magic may not be up to task, that we might, in some singular moment, lose it all. As with the Overlords of Clarke's *Childhood's End*, we retain in the Atlantis myth the afterimage of something *ahead* of us, a moment we feel unequal to.

But magic is afoot; the battle is hardly lost.

Each day the real grows in its responsiveness to our wills.

More and more the world seems . . . playful. And the children growing up inside this world have a fixed expectation that this trend will only continue—and broaden—as they mature. We might not be ready for the magic of the post-human, but they almost certainly will be. And chances are, they'll want to teach it to us. A new language to describe the world, *a language which shapes the world*. That tongue eludes us now, as we tarry in our nervous impatience, on this side of Singularity. It can not be more than twenty years away, for all of the energies of civilization are grinding down on our doing, so as to make it perfect.

The greater part of *True Names*—what comes after, in the wake of trans-humanity—has never been written. A problem from the gentle mathematics professor, and left for the reader to solve. As we boot into something ineffably beyond ourselves, we watch the atmosphere thin, then fall away, leaving only the vast deepness of space. The stars are dim, and far apart, as infinity approaches, but there's so much more room to move.

True Names

Vernor Vinge

Having read nine essays about cyberspace, computers, and in some their direct relation to *True Names,* we now deem it safe for you to read the novella about which so much has been written. Seen from just past the turn of the millennium, and twenty years after the initial publication of the novella, it may seem that *True Names* has little new to offer science fiction, no less science and technology.

And yet that's not true. When this story was written, in 1979–80, the term cyberspace wasn't even a whisper in people's dreams. (William Gibson coined it later.) Vinge, with this single story, changed the landscape of science fiction forever, introducing the notion of virtual reality in a feasible way which has been expanded upon but never fully supplanted by any other writer.

Films and television shows have exploited the vision of cyberspace described in *True Names.* Other science fiction writers freely credit Vinge with creating something new and completely different from anything that had come before.

How was Vernor Vinge able to concoct such a unique, fully-fleshed and freshly imagined vision? Part of the answer may lie in the way Vinge learned computer theory. A mathematician before he began studying computer science, he learned it pretty much from the ground up, reading what there was to read, but as he wrote in his Introduction to this book, he was fascinated by computers from the time he was a teen; by the time he began to study the discipline, he was well prepared to think about how it all fit together.

But more of the freshness of *True Names* comes from Vinge's imagination. In other works, such as his novels *A Fire Upon the Deep* and the recent *A Deepness in the Sky*, Vinge has taken readers to the far reaches of the galaxy, and to strange, richly imagined planets. Here, he takes us inward, to the conceptual realm of cyberspace, which he dubbed "the Other Plane," and where the "new age of magic" lives.

Enough prelude. Here's *True Names*.

In the once-upon-a-time days of the First Age of Magic, the prudent sorcerer regarded his own true name as his most valued possession but also the greatest threat to his continued good health, for—the stories go—once an enemy, even a weak unskilled enemy, learned the sorcerer's true name, then routine and widely known spells could destroy or enslave even the most powerful. As times passed, and we graduated to the Age of Reason and thence to the first and second industrial revolutions, such notions were discredited. Now it seems that the Wheel has turned full circle (even if there never really was a First Age) and we are back to worrying about true names again:

The first hint Mr. Slippery had that his own True Name might be known—and, for that matter, known to the Great Enemy—came with the appearance of two black Lincolns humming up the long dirt driveway that stretched through the dripping pine forest down to Road 29. Roger Pollack was in his garden weeding, had been there nearly the whole morning, enjoying the barely perceptible drizzle and the overcast, and trying to find the initiative to go inside and do work that actually makes money. He looked up the moment the intruders turned, wheels squealing, into his driveway. Thirty seconds passed, and the cars came out of the third-generation forest to pull up beside and behind Pollack's Honda. Four heavy-set men and a hard-looking female piled out, started purposefully across his well-tended cabbage patch, crushing tender young plants with a disregard which told Roger that this was no social call.

Pollack looked wildly around, considered making a break for the woods, but the others had spread out and he was grabbed and frog-marched back to his house. (Fortunately the door had been left unlocked. Roger had the feeling that they might have knocked it down rather than ask him for

the key.) He was shoved abruptly into a chair. Two of the
heaviest and least collegiate-looking of his visitors stood on
either side of him. Pollack's protests—now just being
voiced—brought no response. The woman and an older man
poked around among his sets. "Hey, I remember this, Al: It's
the script for *1965*. See?" The woman spoke as she flipped
through the holo-scenes that decorated the interior wall.

The older man nodded. "I told you. He's written more
popular games than any three men and even more than
some agencies. Roger Pollack is something of a genius."

They're novels, damn you, not games! Old irritation flashed
unbidden into Roger's mind. Aloud: "Yeah, but most of my
fans aren't as persistent as you all."

"Most of your fans don't know that you are a criminal,
Mr. Pollack."

"Criminal? I'm no criminal—but I do know my rights. You
FBI types must identify yourselves, give me a phone call,
and—"

The woman smiled for the first time. It was not a nice
smile. She was about thirty-five, hatchet-faced, her hair
drawn back in the single braid favored by military types.
Even so it could have been a nicer smile. Pollack felt a chill
start up his spine. "Perhaps that would be true, if we *were*
the FBI or if you were *not* the scum you are. But this is a
Welfare Department bust, Pollack, and you are suspected—
putting it kindly—of interference with the instrumentalities
of National and individual survival."

She sounded like something out of one of those asinine
scripts he occasionally had to work on for government contracts. Only now there was nothing to laugh about, and the
cold between his shoulder blades spread. Outside, the drizzle
had become a misty rain sweeping across the Northern California forests. Normally he found that rain a comfort, but

now it just added to the gloom. Still, if there was any chance he could wriggle out of this, it would be worth the effort. "Okay, so you have license to hassle innocents, but sooner or later you're going to discover that I *am* innocent and then you'll find out what hostile media coverage can really be like." *And thank God I backed up my files last night. With luck, all they'll find is some out-of-date stockmarket schemes.*

"You're no innocent, Pollack. An *honest* citizen is content with an ordinary data set like yours there." She pointed across the living room at the forty-by-fifty-centimeter data set. It was the great-grandchild of the old CRT's. With color and twenty-line-per-millimeter resolution, it was the standard of government offices and the more conservative industries. There was a visible layer of dust on Pollack's model. The femcop moved quickly across the living room and poked into the drawers under the picture window. Her maroon business suit revealed a thin and angular figure. "An *honest* citizen would settle for a standard processor and a few thousand megabytes of fast storage." With some superior intuition she pulled open the center drawer—right under the marijuana plants—to reveal at least five hundred cubic centimeters of optical memory, neatly racked and threaded through to the next drawer which held correspondingly powerful CPUs. Even so, it was nothing compared to the gear he had buried under the house.

She drifted out into the kitchen and was back in a moment. The house was a typical airdropped bungalow, small and easy to search. Pollack had spent most of his money on the land and his . . . hobbies. "And finally," she said, a note of triumph in her voice, "an *honest* citizen does not need one of these!" She had finally spotted the Other World gate. She waved the electrodes in Pollack's face.

"Look, in spite of what you may want, all this is still legal.

In fact, that gadget is scarcely more powerful than an ordinary games interface." That should be a good explanation, considering that he was a novelist.

The older man spoke almost apologetically, "I'm afraid Virginia has a tendency to play cat and mouse, Mr. Pollack. You see, we know that in the Other World you are Mr. Slippery."

"Oh."

There was a long silence. Even "Virginia" kept her mouth shut. This had been, of course, Roger Pollack's great fear. They had discovered Mr. Slippery's True Name and it was Roger Andrew Pollack TIN/SSAN 0959-34-2861, and no amount of evasion, tricky programming, or robot sources could ever again protect him from them. "How did you find out?"

A third cop, a technician type, spoke up. "It wasn't easy. We wanted to get our hands on someone who was really good, not a trivial vandal—what your Coven would call a lesser warlock." The younger man seemed to know the jargon, but you could pick that up just by watching the daily paper. "For the last three months, DoW has been trying to find the identity of someone of the caliber of yourself or Robin Hood, or Erythrina, or the Slimey Limey. We were having no luck at all until we turned the problem around and began watching artists and novelists. We figured at least a fraction of them must be attracted to vandal activities. And they would have the talent to be good at it. Your participation novels are the best in the world." There was genuine admiration in his voice. *One meets fans in the oddest places.* "So you were one of the first people we looked at. Once we suspected you, it was just a matter of time before we had the evidence."

It was what he had always worried about. A successful warlock cannot afford to be successful in the real world. He had been greedy; he loved both realms too much.

The older cop continued the technician's almost diffident approach. "In any case, Mr. Pollack, I think you realize that if the Federal government wants to concentrate all its resources on the apprehension of a single vandal, we can do it. The vandals' power comes from their numbers rather than their power as individuals."

Pollack repressed a smile. That was a common belief—or faith—within government. He had snooped on enough secret memos to realize that the Feds really believed it, but it was very far from true. He was not nearly as clever as someone like Erythrina. He could only devote fifteen or twenty hours a week to SIG activities. Some of the others must be on welfare, so complete was their presence on the Other Plane. The cops had nailed him simply because he was a relatively easy catch.

"So you have something besides jail planned for me?"

"Mr. Pollack, have you ever heard of the Mailman?"

"You mean on the Other Plane?"

"Certainly. He has had no notoriety in the, uh, real world as yet."

For the moment there was no use lying. They must know that no member of a SIG or coven would ever give his True Name to another member. There was no way he could betray any of the others—*he hoped*.

"Yeah, he's the weirdest of the werebots."

"Werebots?"

"Were-robots, like werewolves—get it? They don't really mesh with coven imagery. They want some new mythos, and this notion that they are humans who can turn into machines seems to suit them. It's too dry for me. This Mailman, for instance, never uses real-time communication. If you want anything from him, you usually have to wait a day or two for each response—just like the old-time hard-copy mail service."

"That's the fellow. How impressed are you by him?"

"Oh, we've been aware of him for a couple years, but he's so slow that for a long time we thought he was some clown on a simple data set. Lately, though, he's pulled some really—" Pollack stopped short, remembering just who he was gossiping with.

"—some really tuppin stunts, eh, Pollack?" The femcop "Virginia" was back in the conversation. She pulled up one of the roller chairs, till her knees were almost touching his, and stabbed a finger at his chest. "You may not know just how tuppin. You vandals have caused Social Security Records enormous problems, and Robin Hood cut IRS revenues by three percent last year. You and your friends are a greater threat than any foreign enemy. Yet you're nothing compared to this Mailman."

Pollack was rocked back. It must be that he had seen only a small fraction of the Mailman's japes. "You're actually scared of him," he said mildly.

Virginia's face began to take on the color of her suit. Before she could reply, the older cop spoke. "Yes, we are scared. We can scarcely cope with the Robin Hoods and the Mr. Slipperys of the world. Fortunately, most vandals are interested in personal gain or in proving their cleverness. They realize that if they cause too much trouble, they could no doubt be identified. I suspect that tens of thousands of cases of Welfare and Tax fraud are undetected, committed by little people with simple equipment who succeed because they don't steal much—perhaps just their own income tax liability—and don't wish the notoriety which you, uh, warlocks go after. If it weren't for their petty individualism, they would be a greater threat than the nuclear terrorists.

"But the Mailman is different; he appears to be ideologically motivated. He is *very* knowledgeable, *very* powerful. Vandalism is not enough for him; he wants control . . ." The

Feds had no idea how long it had been going on, at least a year. It never would have been discovered but for a few departments in the Federal Screw Standards Commission which kept their principal copy records on paper. Discrepancies showed up between those records and the decisions rendered in the name of the FSSC. Inquiries were made; computer records were found at variance with the hardcopy. More inquiries. By luck more than anything else, the investigators discovered that decision modules as well as data were different from the hardcopy backups. For thirty years government had depended on automated central planning, shifting more and more from legal descriptions of decision algorithms to program representations that could work directly with data bases to allocate resources, suggest legislation, outline military strategy.

The takeover had been subtle, and its extent was unknown. That was the horror of it. It was not even clear just what groups within the Nation (or without) were benefiting from the changed interpretations of Federal law and resource allocation. Only the decision modules in the older departments could be directly checked, and some thirty percent of them showed tampering. ". . . and that percentage scares us as much as anything, Mr. Pollack. It would take a large team of technicians and lawyers *months* to successfully make just the changes that we have detected."

"What about the military?" Pollack thought of the Finger of God installations and the thousands of missiles pointed at virtually every country on Earth. If Mr. Slippery had ever desired to take over the world, that is what he would have gone for. To hell with pussy-footing around with Social Security checks.

"No. No penetration there. In fact, it was his attempt to infiltrate"—the older cop glanced hesitantly at Virginia, and Pollack realized who was the boss of this operation—"NSA

that revealed the culprit to be the Mailman. Before that it
was anonymous, totally without the ego-flaunting we see in
big-time vandals. But the military and NSA have their own
systems. Impractical though that is, it paid off this time."
Pollack nodded. The SIG steered clear of the military, and
especially of NSA.

"But if he was able to slide through DoW and Department
of Justice defenses so easy, you really don't know how much
a matter of luck it was that he didn't also succeed with his
first try on NSA. . . . I think I understand now. You need
help. You hope to get some member of the Coven to work
on this from the inside."

"It's not a *hope*, Pollack," said Virginia. "It's a certainty.
Forget about going to jail. Oh, we could put you away forever on the basis of some of Mr. Slippery's pranks. But even
if we don't do that, we can take away your license to operate. You know what that means."

It was not a question, but Pollack knew the answer nevertheless: ninety-eight percent of the jobs in modern society
involved some use of a data set. Without a license, he was
virtually unemployable—and that left Welfare, the prospect
of sitting in some urbapt counting flowers on the wall. Virginia must have seen the defeat in his eyes. "Frankly, I am
not as confident as Ray that you are all that sharp. But you
are the best we could catch. NSA thinks we have a chance
of finding the Mailman's true identity if we can get an agent
into your coven. We want you to continue to attend coven
meetings, but now your chief goal is not mischief but the
gathering of information about the Mailman. You are to re-
cruit any help you can without revealing that you are working for the government—you might even make up the story
that you suspect the Mailman of being a government plot.
(I'm sure you see he has some of the characteristics of a
Federal agent working off a conventional data set.) Above

all, you are to remain alert to contact from us, and give us your instant cooperation in anything we require of you. Is all this perfectly clear, Mr. Pollack?"

He found it difficult to meet her gaze. He had never really been exposed to extortion before. There was something . . . dehumanizing about being used so. "Yeah," he finally said.

"Good." She stood up, and so did the others. "If you behave, this is the last time you'll see us in person."

Pollack stood too. "And afterward, if you're . . . satisfied with my performance?"

Virginia grinned, and he knew he wasn't going to like her answer. "Afterward, we can come back to considering *your* crimes. If you do a good job, I would have no objection to your retaining a standard data set, maybe some of your interactive graphics. But I'll tell you, if it weren't for the Mailman, nabbing Mr. Slippery would make my month. There is no way I'd risk your continuing to abuse the System."

Three minutes later, their sinister black Lincolns were halfway down the drive, disappearing into the pines. Pollack stood in the drizzle watching till long after their sound had faded to nothing. He was barely aware of the cold wet across his shoulders and down his back. He looked up suddenly, feeling the rain in his face, wondering if the Feds were so clever that they had taken the day into account: the military's recon satellites could no doubt monitor their cars, but the civilian satellites the SIG had access to could not penetrate these clouds. Even if some other member of the SIG did know Mr. Slippery's True Name, they would not know that the Feds had paid him a visit.

Pollack looked across the yard at his garden. *What a difference an hour can make.*

BY LATE AFTERNOON, THE OVERCAST WAS GONE. SUNLIGHT GLINTED OFF millions of water-drop jewels in the trees. Pollack waited till the sun was behind the tree line, till all that was left of its passage was a gold band across the taller trees to the east of his bungalow. Then he sat down before his equipment and prepared to ascend to the Other Plane. What he was undertaking was trickier than anything he had tried before, and he wanted to take as much time as the Feds would tolerate. A week of thought and research would have suited him more, but Virginia and her pals were clearly too impatient for that.

He powered up his processors, settled back in his favorite chair, and carefully attached the Portal's five sucker electrodes to his scalp. For long minutes nothing happened: a certain amount of self-denial—or at least self-hypnosis—was necessary to make the ascent. Some experts recommended drugs or sensory isolation to heighten the user's sensitivity to the faint, ambiguous signals that could be read from the Portal. Pollack, who was certainly more experienced than any of the pop experts, had found that he could make it simply by staring out into the trees and listening to the wind-surf that swept through their upper branches.

And just as a daydreamer forgets his actual surroundings and sees other realities, so Pollack drifted, detached, his subconscious interpreting the status of the West Coast communication and data services as a vague thicket for his conscious mind to inspect, interrogate for the safest path to an intermediate haven. Like most exurb data-commuters, Pollack rented the standard optical links: Bell, Boeing, Nippon Electric. Those, together with the local West Coast data companies, gave him more than enough paths to proceed with little chance of detection to any accepting processor on Earth. In minutes, he had traced through three changes of carrier and found a place to do his intermediate computing. The comsats rented processor time almost as cheaply as ground stations, and an automatic payment transaction (through several dummy accounts set up over the last several years) gave him sole control of a large data space within milliseconds of his request. The whole process was almost at a subconscious level—the proper functioning of numerous routines he and others had devised over the last four years. Mr. Slippery (the other name was avoided now, even in his thoughts) had achieved the fringes of the Other Plane. He took a quick peek through the eyes of a low-resolution weather satellite, saw the North American continent spread out below, the terminator sweeping through the West, most of the plains clouded over. One never knew when some apparently irrelevant information might help—and though it could all be done automatically through subconscious access, Mr. Slippery had always been a romantic about spaceflight.

He rested for a few moments, checking that his indirect communication links were working and that the encryption routines appeared healthy, untampered with. (Like most folks, honest citizens or warlocks, he had no trust for the government standard encryption routines, but preferred the schemes that had leaked out of academia—over NSA's petulant objections—during the last fifteen years.) Protected now against traceback, Mr. Slippery set out for the Coven itself. He quickly picked up the trail, but this was never an easy trip, for the SIG members had no interest in being bothered by the unskilled.

In particular, the traveler must be able to take advantage of subtle sensory indications, and see in them the environment originally imagined by the SIG. The correct path had the aspect of a narrow row of stones cutting through a gray-greenish swamp. The air was cold but very moist. Weird, towering plants dripped audibly onto the faintly iridescent water and the broad lilies. The subconscious knew what the stones represented, handled the chaining of routines from one information net to another, but it was the conscious mind of the skilled traveler that must make the decisions that could lead to the gates of the Coven, or to the symbolic "death" of a dump back to the real world. The basic game was a distant relative of the ancient Adventure that had been played on computer systems for more than forty years, and a nearer relative of the participation novels that are still widely sold. There were two great differences, though. This game was more serious, and was played at a level of complexity impossible without the use of the EEG input/ output that the warlocks and the popular databases called Portals.

There was much misinformation and misunderstanding about the Portals. Oh, responsible databases like the *LA Times* and the *CBS News* made it clear that there was nothing supernatural about them or about the Other Plane, that the magical jargon was at best a romantic convenience and at worst obscurantism. But even so, their articles often missed the point and were both too conservative and too extravagant. You might think that to convey the full sense imagery of the swamp, some immense bandwidth would be necessary. In fact, that was not so (and if it were, the Feds would have quickly been able to spot warlock and werebot operations). A typical Portal link was around fifty thousand baud, far narrower than even a flat video channel. Mr. Slippery could feel the damp seeping through his leather boots, could feel the sweat starting on his skin even in the cold air, but this was the response of Mr. Slippery's imagination and subconscious to the cues that were actually being presented through the Portal's electrodes. The interpretation could not be arbitrary or he would be dumped back to reality and would never find the Coven; to the traveler on the Other Plane, the detail was there as long as the cues were there. And there is nothing new about this situation. Even a poor writer—if he has a sympathetic reader and an engaging plot—can evoke complete internal imagery with a few dozen words of description. The difference now is that the imagery has interactive significance, just as sensations in the real world do. Ultimately, the magic jargon was perhaps the closest fit in the vocabulary of millennium Man.

The stones were spaced more widely now, and it took all Mr. Slippery's skill to avoid falling into the noisome waters that surrounded him. Fortunately, after another hundred meters or so, the trail rose out of the water, and he was walking on shallow mud. The trees and brush grew in close around him, and large spider webs glistened across the trail and between some of the trees along the side.

Like a yo-yo from some branch high above him, a red-banded spider the size of a man's fist descended into the space right before the traveler's face. "Beware, beware," the tiny voice issued from dripping mandibles. "Beware, beware," the words were repeated, and the creature swung back and forth, nearer and farther from Mr. Slippery's face. He looked carefully at the spider's banded abdomen. There were many species of death-spider here, and each required a different response if a traveler was to survive. Finally he raised the back of his hand and held it level so that the spider could crawl onto it. The creature raced up the damp fabric of his jacket to the open neck. There it whispered something very quietly.

Mr. Slippery listened, then grabbed the animal before it could repeat the message and threw it to the left, at the same time racing off into the tangle of webs and branches on the other side of the trail. Something heavy and wet slapped into the space where he had been, but he was already gone—racing at top speed up the incline that suddenly appeared before him.

He stopped when he reached the crest of the hill. Beyond it, he could see the solemn, massive fortress that was the Coven's haven. It was not more than five hundred meters away, illuminated as the swamp had been by a vague and indistinct light that came only partly from the sky. The trail leading down to it was much more open than the swamp had been, but the traveler proceeded as slowly as before: the sprites the warlocks set to keep guard here had the nasty—though preprogrammed—habit of changing the rules in deadly ways.

THE TRAIL DESCENDED, THEN BEGAN A ROCKY, WINDING CLIMB TOWARD the stone and iron gates of the castle. The ground was drier here, the vegetation sparse. Leathery snapping of wings sounded above him, but Mr. Slippery knew better than to look up. Thirty meters from the moat, the heat became more than uncomfortable. He could hear the lava popping and hissing, could see occasional dollops of fire splatter up from the liquid to scorch what vegetation still lived. A pair of glowing eyes set in a coal-black head rose briefly from the moat. A second later, the rest of the creature came surging into view, cascading sparks and lava down upon the traveler. Mr. Slippery raised his hand just so, and the lethal spray separated over his head to land harmlessly on either side of him. He watched with apparent calm as the creature descended ancient stone steps to confront him.

Alan—that was the elemental's favorite name—peered nearsightedly, his head weaving faintly from side to side as he tried to recognize the traveler. "Ah, I do believe we are honored with the presence of Mr. Slippery, is it not so?" he finally said. He smiled, an open grin revealing the glowing interior of his mouth. His breath did not show flame but did have the penetrating heat of an open kiln. He rubbed his clawed hands against his asbestos T-shirt as though anxious to be proved wrong. Away from his magna moat, the dead black of his flesh lightened, trying to contain his body heat. Now he looked almost reptilian.

"Indeed it is. And come to bring my favorite little gifts." Mr. Slippery threw a leaden slug into the air and watched the elemental grab it with his mouth, his eyes slitted with pleasure— melt-in-your-mouth pleasure. They traded conversation, spells, and counterspells for several minutes. Alan's principal job was to determine that the visitor was a known member of the Coven, and he ordinarily did this with little tests of skill (the magma bath he had tried to give Mr. Slippery) and by asking the visitor questions about previous activities within the castle. Alan was a personality simulator, of course. Mr. Slippery was sure that there had never been a living operator behind that toothless, glowing smile. But he was certainly one of the best, probably the product of many hundreds of blocks of psylisp programming, and certainly superior to the little "companionship" programs you can buy nowadays, which generally become repetitive after a few hours of conversation, which don't grow, and which are unable to counter weird responses. Alan had been with the Coven and the castle since before Mr. Slippery had become a member, and no one would admit to his creation (though Wiley J. was suspected). He hadn't even had a name until this year, when Erythrina had given him that asbestos Alan Turing T-shirt.

Mr. Slippery played the game with good humor, but care. To "die" at the hands of Alan would be a painful experience that would probably wipe a lot of unbacked memory he could ill afford to lose. Such death had claimed many petitioners at this gate, folk who would not soon be seen on this plane again.

Satisfied, Alan waved a clawed fist at the watchers in the tower, and the gate—ceramic bound in wolfram clasps—was rapidly lowered for the visitor. Mr. Slippery walked quickly across, trying to ignore the spitting and bubbling that he heard below him. Alan—now all respectful—waited till he was in the castle courtyard before doing an immense belly flop back into his magma swimming hole.

MOST OF THE OTHERS, WITH THE NOTABLE EXCEPTION OF ERYTHRINA, had already arrived. Robin Hood, dressed in green and looking like Errol Flynn, sat across the hall in very close conversation with a remarkably good-looking female (but then they could all be remarkably good-looking here) who seemed unsure whether to project blonde or brunette. By the fireplace, Wiley

J. Bastard, the Slimey Limey, and DON.MAC were in animated discussion over a pile of maps. And in the corner, shaded from the fireplace and apparently unused, sat a classic remote printing terminal. Mr. Slippery tried to ignore that teleprinter as he crossed the hall.

"Ah, it's Slip." DON.MAC looked up from the maps and gestured him closer. "Take a look here at what the Limey has been up to."

"Hmm?" Mr. Slippery nodded at the others, then leaned over to study the top map. The margins of the paper were aging vellum, but the "map" itself hung in three dimensions, half sunk into the paper. It was a typical banking defense and cash-flow plot—that is, typical for the SIG. Most banks had no such clever ways of visualizing the automated protection of their assets. (For that matter, Mr. Slippery suspected that most banks still looked wistfully back to the days of credit cards and COBOL.) This was the sort of thing Robin Hood had developed, and it was surprising to see the Limey involved in it. He looked up questioningly. "What's the jape?"

"It's a reg'lar double-slam, Slip. Look at this careful, an' you'll see it's no ord'n'ry protection map. Seems like what you blokes call the Mafia has taken over this banking net in the Maritime states. They must be usin' Portals to do it so slick. Took me a devil of a time to figure out it was them as done it. *Ha ha!* but now that I have . . . look here, you'll see how they've been launderin' funds, embezzlin' from straight accounts.

"They're ever so clever, but not so clever as to know about Slimey." He poked a finger into the map and a trace gleamed red through the maze. "If they're lucky, they'll discover this tap next autumn, when they find themselves maybe three billion dollars short, and not a single sign of where it all disappeared to."

The others nodded. There were many covens and SIGs throughout this plane. Theirs, The Coven, was widely known, had pulled off some of the most publicized pranks of the century. Many of the others were scarcely more than social clubs. But some were old-style criminal organizations which used this plane for their own purely pragmatic and opportunistic reasons. Usually such groups weren't too difficult for the warlocks to victimize, but it was the Slimey Limey who seemed to specialize in doing so.

"But, geez, Slimey, these guys play rough, even rougher than the Great Enemy." That is, the Feds. "If they ever figure out who you really are, you'll die the True Death for sure."

"I may be slimy, but I ain't crazy. There's no way I could absorb three billion dollars—or even three million—without being discovered. But I played it like Robin over there: the money got spread around three million ordinary accounts here and in Europe, one of which just happens to be mine."

Mr. Slippery's ears perked up. "Three million accounts, you say? Each with a sudden little surplus? I'll bet I could come close to finding your True Name from that much, Slimey."

The Limey made a faffling gesture. "It's actually a wee bit more complicated. Face it, chums, none of you has ever come close to sightin' me, an' you know more than any Mafia."

That was true. They all spent a good deal of their time in this plane trying to determine the others' True Names. It was not an empty game, for the knowledge of another's True Name effectively made him your slave—as Mr. Slippery had already discovered in an unpleasantly firsthand way. So the warlocks constantly probed one another, devised immense programs to sieve government-personnel records for the idiosyncracies that they detected in each other. At first glance, the Limey should have been one of the easiest to discover: he had plenty of mannerisms. His Brit accent was dated and broke down every so often into North American. Of all the warlocks, he was the only one neither handsome nor grotesque. His face was, in fact, so ordinary and real that Mr. Slippery had suspected that it might be his true appearance and had spent several months devising a scheme that searched U.S. and common Europe photo files for just that appearance. It had been for nothing, and they had all eventually reached the conclusion that the Limey must be doubly or triply deceptive.

Wiley J. Bastard grinned, not too impressed. "It's nice enough, and I agree that the risks are probably small, Slimey. But what do you really get? An ego boost and a little money. But we," he gestured inclusively, "are worth more than that. With a little cooperation, we could be the most powerful people in the real world. Right, DON?"

DON.MAC nodded, smirking. His face was really the only part of him that looked human or had much flexibility of expression—and even it was steely gray. The rest of DON's body was modeled after the standard Plessey-Mercedes all weather robot.

Mr. Slippery recognized the reference. "So you're working with the Mailman now, too, Wiley?" He glanced briefly at the teleprinter.

"Yup."

"And you still won't give us any clue what it's all about?"

Wiley shook his head. "Not unless you're serious about throwing in with us. But you all know this: DON was the first to work with the Mailman, and he's richer than Croesus now."

DON.MAC nodded again, that silly smile still on his face.

"Hmmm." It was easy to get rich. In principle, the Limey could have made three billion dollars off the Mob in his latest caper. The problem was to become that rich and avoid detection and retribution. Even Robin Hood hadn't mastered that trick—but apparently DON and Wiley thought the Mailman had done that and more. After his chat with Virginia, he was willing to believe it. Mr. Slippery turned to look more closely at the teleprinter. It was humming faintly, and as usual it had a good supply of paper. The paper was torn neatly off at the top, so that the only message visible was the Mailman's asterisk prompt. It was the only way they ever communicated with this most mysterious of their members: type a message on the device, and in an hour or a week the machine would rattle and beat, and a response of up to several thousand words would appear. In the beginning, it had not been very popular—the idea was cute, but the delays made conversation just too damn dull. He could remember seeing meters of Mailman output lying sloppily on the stone floor, mostly unread. But *now*, every one of the Mailman's golden words was eagerly sopped up by his new apprentices, who very carefully removed every piece of output, leaving no clues for the rest of them to work with.

"Ery!" He looked toward the broad stone stairs that led down from the courtyard. It was Erythrina, the Red Witch. She swept down the stairs, her costume shimmering, now revealing, now obscuring. She had a spectacular figure and an excellent sense of design, but of course that was not what was remarkable about her. Erythrina was the sort of person who knew much more than she ever said, even though she always seemed easy to talk to. Some of her adventures—though unadvertised— were in a class with Robin Hood's. Mr. Slippery had known her well for a year; she was certainly the most interesting personality on this plane. She made him wish that all the secrets were unnecessary, that True Names could be traded as openly as phone numbers. What was she really?

Erythrina nodded to Robin Hood, then proceeded down the hall to DON.MAC, who had originally shouted greetings and now continued, "We've just been trying to convince Slimey and Slip that they are wasting their time on pranks when they could have real power and real wealth."

She glanced sharply at Wiley, who seemed strangely irritated that she had been drawn into the conversation. " 'We' meaning you and Wiley and the Mailman?"

Wiley nodded. "I just started working with them last week,
Ery," as if to say, *and you can't stop me.*

"You may have something, DON. We all started out as amateurs, doing our best to make the System just a little bit uncomfortable for its bureaucratic masters. But we are experts
now. We probably understand the System better than anyone
on Earth. That should equate to power." It was the same thing
the other two had been saying, but she could make it much
more persuasive. Before his encounter with the Feds, he might
have bought it (even though he always knew that the day he
got serious about Coven activities and went after real gain
would also be the day it ceased to be an enjoyable game and
became an all-consuming job that would suck time away from
the projects that made life entertaining).

Erythrina looked from Mr. Slippery to the Limey and then
back. The Limey was an easygoing sort, but just now he was a
bit miffed at the way his own pet project had been dismissed.
"Not for me, thanky," he said shortly and began to gather up
his maps.

She turned her green, faintly oriental eyes upon Mr. Slippery.
"How about you, Slip? Have you signed up with the Mailman?"

He hesitated. *Maybe I should.* It seemed clear that the Mailman's confederates were being let in on at least part of his
schemes. In a few hours, he might be able to learn enough to
get Virginia off his back. And perhaps destroy his friends to
boot; it was a hell of a bargain. *God in Heaven, why did they have
to get mixed up in this? Don't they realize what the Government will
do to them, if they really try to take over, if they ever try to play at
being more than vandals?* "Not . . . not yet," he said finally. "I'm
awfully tempted, though."

She grinned, regular white teeth flashing against her dark,
faintly green face. "I, too. What do you say we talk it over, just
the two of us?" She reached out a slim, dark hand to grasp his
elbow. "Excuse us, gentlemen; hopefully, when we get back,

you'll have a couple of new allies." And Mr. Slippery felt himself gently propelled toward the dark and musty stairs that led to Erythrina's private haunts.

HER TORCH BURNED AND GLOWED, BUT THERE WAS NO SMOKE. THE flickering yellow lit their path for scant meters ahead. The stairs were steep and gently curving. He had the feeling that they must do a complete circle every few hundred steps: this was an immense spiral cut deep into the heart of the living rock. And it was alive. As the smell of mildew and rot increased, as the dripping from the ceiling grew subtly louder and the puddles in the worn steps deeper, the walls high above their heads took on shapes, and those shapes changed and flowed to follow them. Erythrina protected her part of the castle as thoroughly as the castle itself was guarded against the outside world. Mr. Slippery had no doubt that if she wished, she could trap him permanently here, along with the lizards and the rock sprites. (Of course he could always "escape" simply by falling back into the real world, but until she relented or he saw through her spells, he would not be able to access any other portion of the castle.) Working on some of their projects, he had visited her underground halls, but never anything this deep.

He watched her shapely form preceding him down, down, down. Of all the Coven (with the possible exception of Robin Hood, and of course the Mailman), she was the most powerful. He suspected that she was one of the original founders. If only there were some way of convincing her (without revealing the source of his knowledge) that the Mailman was a threat. If only there was some way of getting her cooperation in nailing down the Mailman's True Name.

Erythrina stopped and he bumped pleasantly into her. Over her shoulder, a high door ended the passage. She moved her hand in a pattern hidden from Mr. Slippery and muttered some unlocking spell. The door split horizontally, its halves pulling apart with oiled and massive precision. Beyond, he had the impression of spots and lines of red breaking a further darkness.

"Mind your step," she said and hopped over a murky puddle that stood before the high sill of the doorway.

As the door slid shut behind them, Erythrina changed the torch to a single searing spot of white light, like some old-time incandescent bulb. The room was bright-lit now. Comfortable black leather chairs sat on black tile. Red engraving, faintly glowing, was worked into the tile and the obsidian of the walls. In contrast to the stairway, the air was fresh and clean—though still.

She waved him to a chair that faced away from the light, then sat on the edge of a broad desk. The point light glinted off her eyes, making them unreadable. Erythrina's face was slim and fine-boned, almost Asian except for the pointed ears. But the skin was dark, and her long hair had the reddish tones unique to some North American blacks. She was barely smiling now, and Mr. Slippery wished again he had some way of getting her help.

"Slip, I'm scared," she said finally, the smile gone.

You're scared! For a moment, he couldn't quite believe his ears. "The Mailman?" he asked, hoping.

She nodded. "This is the first time in my life I've felt outgunned. I need help. Robin Hood may be the most competent, but he's basically a narcissist; I don't think I could interest him in anything beyond his immediate gratifications. That leaves you and the Limey. And I think there's something special about you. We've done a couple things together," she couldn't help herself, and grinned remembering. "They weren't real impressive, but somehow I have a feeling about you: I think you understand what things up here are silly games and what things are really important. If you think something is really important, you can be trusted to stick with it even if the going gets a little . . . bloody."

Coming from someone like Ery, the words had special meaning. It was strange, to feel both flattered and frightened. Mr. Slippery stuttered for a moment, inarticulate. "What about Wiley J? Seems to me you have special . . . influence over him."

"You knew . . . ?"

"Suspected."

"Yes, he's my thrall. Has been for almost six months. Poor Wiley turns out to be a life-insurance salesman from Peoria. Like a lot of warlocks, he's rather a Thuberesque fellow in real life: timid, always dreaming of heroic adventures and grandiose thefts. Only nowadays people like that can realize their dreams. . . . Anyway, he doesn't have the background, or the time, or the skill that I do, and I found his True Name. I enjoy the chase more than the extortion, so I haven't leaned on him too hard; now I wish I had. Since he's taken up with the Mailman, he's been giving me the finger. Somehow Wiley thinks that what they have planned will keep him safe even if I give his True Name to the cops!"

"So the Mailman actually has some scheme for winning political power in the real world?"

She smiled. "That's what Wiley thinks. You see, poor Wiley doesn't know that there are more uses for True Names than simple blackmail. I know everything he sends over the data links, everything he has been told by the Mailman."

"So what are they up to?" It was hard to conceal his eagerness. *Perhaps this will be enough to satisfy Virginia and her goons.*

Erythrina seemed frozen for a moment, and he realized that she too must be using the low-altitude satellite net for preliminary processing: her task had just been handed off from one comsat to a nearer bird. Ordinarily it was easy to disguise the hesitation. She must be truly upset.

And when she finally replied, it wasn't really with an answer. "You know what convinced Wiley that the Mailman could deliver on his promises? It was DON.MAC—and the revolution in

Venezuela. Apparently DON and the Mailman had been working on that for several months before Wiley joined them. It was
to be the Mailman's first demonstration that controlling data
and information services could be used to take permanent political control of a state. And Venezuela, they claimed, was perfect: it has enormous data-processing facilities—all just a bit
obsolete, since they were bought when the country was at the
peak of its boom time."

"But that was clearly an internal coup. The present leaders
are local—"

"Nevertheless, DON is supposedly down there now, the real
Jefe, for the first time in his life able to live in the physical world
the way we do in this plane. If you have your own country,
you are no longer small fry that must guard his True Name. You
don't have to settle for crumbs."

"You said 'supposedly.' "

"Slip, have you noticed anything strange about DON lately?"

Mr. Slippery thought back. DON.MAC had always been the
most extreme of the werebots—after the Mailman. He was not
an especially talented fellow, but he did go to great lengths to
sustain the image that he was both machine and human. His
persona was always present in this plane, though at least part
of the time it was a simulator—like Alan out in the magma
moat. The simulation was fairly good, but no one had yet produced a program that could really pass the Turing test: that is,
fool a real human for any extended time. Mr. Slippery remembered the silly smile that seemed pasted on DON's face and the
faintly repetitive tone of his lobbying for the Mailman. "You
think the real person behind DON is gone, that we have a zom-
bie up there?"

"Slip, I think the real DON is *dead*, and I mean the True
Death."

"Maybe he just found the real world more delightful than
this, now that he owns such a big hunk of it?"

"I don't think he owns anything. It's just barely possible that the Mailman had something to do with that coup; there are a number of coincidences between what they told Wiley beforehand and what actually happened. But I've spent a lot of time floating through the Venezuelan data bases, and I think I'd know if an outsider were on the scene, directing the new order.

"I think the Mailman is taking us on one at a time, starting with the weakest, drawing us in far enough to learn our True Names—and then destroying us. So far he has only done it to one of us. I've been watching DON.MAC both directly and automatically since the coup, and there has never been a real person behind that facade, not once in two thousand hours. Wiley is next. The poor slob hasn't even been told yet what country his kingdom is to be—evidence that the Mailman doesn't really have the power he claims—but even so, he's ready to do practically anything for the Mailman, and against us.

"Slip, we have *got* to identify this *thing*, this Mailman, before he can get us."

She was even more upset than Virginia and the Feds. And she was right. For the first time, he felt more afraid of the Mailman than the government agents. He held up his hands. "I'm convinced. But what should we do? You've got the best angle in Wiley. The Mailman doesn't know you've got a tap through him, does he?"

She shook her head. "Wiley is too chicken to tell him, and doesn't realize that I can do this with his True Name. But I'm already doing everything I can with that. I want to pool information, guesses, with you. Between us maybe we can see something new."

"Well for starters, it's obvious that the Mailman's queer communication style—those long time delays—is a ploy. I know that fellow is listening all the time to what's going on in the Coven meeting hall. And he commands a number of sprites in real time." Mr. Slippery remembered the day the Mailman—or at least his teleprinter—had arrived. The image of an American Van Lines truck had pulled up at the edge of the moat, nearly intimidating Alan. The driver and loader were simulators, though good ones. They had answered all of Alan's questions correctly, then hauled the shipping crate down to the meeting hall. They hadn't left till the warlocks signed for the shipment and promised to "wire a wall outlet" for the device. This enemy definitely knew how to arouse the curiosity of his victims. Whoever controlled that printer seemed perfectly capable of normal behavior. *Perhaps it's someone we already know, like in the mysteries where the murderer masquerades as one of the victims. Robin Hood?*

"I know. In fact, he can do many things faster than I. He must control some powerful processors. But you're partly wrong: the living part of him that's behind it all really does operate with at least a one-hour turnaround time. All the quick stuff is programmed."

Mr. Slippery started to protest, then realized that she could be right. "My God, what could that mean? Why would he deliberately saddle himself with that disadvantage?"

Erythrina smiled with some satisfaction. "I'm convinced that if we knew that, we'd have this guy sighted. I agree it's too great a disadvantage to be a simple red herring. I think he must have some time-delay problem to begin with, and—"

"—and he has exaggerated it?" But even if the Mailman were an Australian, the low satellite net made delays so short that he would probably be indistinguishable from a European or a Japanese. There was no place on Earth where . . . *but there are places off Earth!* The mass-transmit satellites were in synchronous orbit 120 milliseconds out. There were about two hundred people there. And further out, at L5, there were at least another four hundred. Some were near-permanent residents. A strange idea, but still a possibility.

"*I* don't think he has exaggerated. Slip, I think the Mailman—not his processors and simulators, you understand—is at least a half-hour out from Earth, probably in the asteroid belt."

She smiled suddenly, and Mr. Slippery realized that his jaw must be resting on his chest. Except for the Joint Mars Recon, no human had been anywhere near that far out. *No human.* Mr. Slippery felt his ordinary, everyday world disintegrating into sheer science fiction. This was ridiculous.

"I know you don't believe; it took me a while to. He's not so obvious that he doesn't add in some time delay to disguise the cyclic variation in our relative positions. But it *is* a consistent explanation for the delay. These last few weeks I've been sniffing around the classified reports on our asteroid probes; there are definitely some mysterious things out there."

"Okay. It's consistent. But you're talking about an interstellar *invasion.* Even if NASA had the funding, it would take them decades to put the smallest interstellar probe together—and decades more for the flight. Trying to invade anyone with those logistics would be impossible. And if these aliens have a decent stardrive, why do they bother with deception? They could just move in and brush us aside."

"Ah, that's the point, Slip. The invasion I'm thinking of doesn't need any 'stardrive,' and it works fine against any race at exactly our point of development. Right: most likely interstellar war is a fantastically expensive business, with decade lead times. What better policy for an imperialistic, highly technological race than to lie doggo listening for evidence of younger civilizations? When they detect such, they send only one ship. When it arrives in the victims' solar system, the Computer Age is in full bloom there. We in the Coven know how fragile the present system is; it is only fear of exposure that prevents some warlocks from trying to take over. Just think how appealing our naïveté must be to an older civilization that has thousands of years of experience at managing data systems. Their small crew of agents moves in as close as local military surveillance permits and gradually insinuates itself into the victims' system. They eliminate what sharp individuals they detect in that system—people like us—and then they go after the bureaucracies and the military. In ten or twenty years, another fiefdom is ready for the arrival of the master race."

She lapsed into silence, and for a long moment they stared at each other. It did all hang together with a weird sort of logic. "What can we do, then?"

"That's the question." She shook her head sadly, came across the room to sit beside him. Now that she had said her piece, the fire had gone out of her. For the first time since he had known her, Erythrina looked depressed. "We could just forsake this plane and stay in the real world. The Mailman might still be able to track us down, but we'd be of no more interest to him than anyone else. If we were lucky, we might have years before he takes over." She straightened. "I'll tell you this: if we want to live as warlocks, we have to stop him soon—within days at most. After he gets Wiley, he may drop the con tactics for something more direct.

"If I'm right about the Mailman, then our best bet would be to discover his communication link. That would be his Achilles' heel; there's no way you can hide in the crowd when you're beaming from that far away. We've got to take some real chances now, do things we'd never risk before. I figure that if we work together, maybe we can lessen the risk that either of us is identified."

He nodded. Ordinarily a prudent warlock used only limited bandwidth and so was confined to a kind of linear, personal perception. If they grabbed a few hundred megahertz of comm space, and a bigger share of rented processors, they could manipulate and search files in a way that would boggle Virginia the femcop. Of course, they would be much more easily identifiable. With two of them, though, they might be able to keep it up safely for a brief time, confusing the government and the

Mailman with a multiplicity of clues. "Frankly, I don't buy the alien part. But the rest of what you say makes sense, and that's what counts. Like you say, we're going to have to take some chances."

"Right!" She smiled and reached behind his neck to draw his face to hers. She was a very good kisser. (Not everyone was. It was one thing just to look gorgeous, and another to project and respond to the many sensory cues in something as interactive as kissing.) He was just warming to this exercise of their mutual abilities when she broke off. "And the best time to start is right now. The others think we're sealed away down here. If strange things happen during the next few hours, it's less likely the Mailman will suspect *us*." She reached up to catch the light point in her hand. For an instant, blades of harsh white slipped out from between her fingers; then all was dark. He felt faint air motion as her hands moved through another spell. There were words, distorted and unidentifiable. Then the light was back, but as a torch again, and a door—a second door—had opened in the far wall.

He followed her up the passage that stretched straight and gently rising as far as the torchlight shone. They were walking a path that could not be—or at least that no one in the Coven could have believed. The castle was basically a logical structure "fleshed" out with the sensory cues that allowed warlocks to move about it as one would a physical structure. Its moats and walls were part of that logical structure, and though they had no physical reality outside of the varying potentials in whatever processors were running the program, they were proof against the movement of the equally "unreal" perceptions of the inhabitants of the plane. Erythrina and Mr. Slippery could have escaped the deep room simply by falling back into the real world, but in doing so, they would have left a chain of unclosed processor links. Their departure would have been detected by every Coven member, even by Alan, even by the sprites. An orderly departure scheme, such as represented by this tunnel, could only mean that Erythrina was far too clever to need his help, or that she had been one of the original builders of the castle some four years earlier (lost in the Mists of Time, as the Limey put it).

THEY WERE WILD DOGS NOW, LARGE ENOUGH SO AS NOT LIKELY TO BE bothered, small enough to be mistaken for the amateur users that are seen more and more in the Other Plane as the price of Portals declines and the skill of the public increases. Mr. Slippery followed Erythrina down narrow paths, deeper and deeper into the swamp that represented commercial and government data space. Occasionally he was aware of sprites or simulators watching them with hostile eyes from nests off to the sides of the trail. These were idle creations in many cases—program units designed to infuriate or amuse later visitors to the plane. But many of them guarded information caches, or peepholes into other folks' affairs, or meeting places of other SIGs. The Coven might be the most sophisticated group of users on this plane, but they were far from being alone.

The brush got taller, bending over the trail to drip on their backs. But the water was clear here, spread in quiet ponds on either side of their path. Light came from the water itself, a pearly luminescence that shone upward on the trunks of the waterbound trees and sparkled faintly in the droplets of water in their moss and leaves. That light was the representation of the really huge databases run by the government and the largest companies. It did not correspond to a specific geographical location, but rather to the main East/West net that stretches through selected installations from Honolulu to Oxford, taking advantage of the time zones to spread the user load.

"Just a little bit farther," Erythrina said over her shoulder, speaking in the beast language (encipherment) that they had chosen with their forms.

Minutes later, they shrank into the brush, out of the way of two armored hackers that proceeded implacably up the trail. The pair drove in single file, the impossibly large eight-cylinder engines on their bikes belching fire and smoke and noise. The one bringing up the rear carried an old-style recoilless rifle decorated with swastikas and chrome. Dim fires glowed through their blackened face plates. The two dogs eyed the bikers timidly, as befitted their present disguise, but Mr. Slippery had the feeling he was looking at a couple of amateurs who were imaging beyond their station in life: the bikes' tires didn't always touch the ground, and the tracks they left didn't quite match the texture of the muck. Anyone could put on a heroic image in this plane, or appear as some dreadful monster. The problem was that there were always skilled users who were willing to cut such pretenders down to size—perhaps even to destroy their access. It befitted the less experienced to appear small and inconspicuous, and to stay out of others' way.

(Mr. Slippery had often speculated just how the simple notion of using high-resolution EEGs as input/output devices had caused the development of the "magical world" representation of data space. The Limey and Erythrina argued that sprites, reincarnation, spells, and castles were the natural tools here, more natural than the atomistic twentieth-century notions of data structures, programs, files, and communications protocols. It was, they argued, just more convenient for the mind to use the global ideas of magic as the tokens to manipulate this new environment. They had a point; in fact, it was likely that the governments of the world hadn't caught up to the skills of the better warlocks simply because they refused to indulge in the foolish imaginings of fantasy. Mr. Slippery looked down at the reflection in the pool beside him and saw the huge canine face and lolling tongue looking up at him; he winked at the image. He knew that despite all his friends' high intellectual arguments, there was another reason for the present state of affairs, a reason that went back to the Moon Lander and Adventure games at the "dawn of time": it was simply a hell of a lot of fun to live in a world as malleable as the human imagination.)

Once the riders were out of sight, Erythrina moved back across the path to the edge of the pond and peered long and hard down between the lilies, into the limpid depths. "Okay, let's do some cross-correlation. You take the JPL data base, and I'll take the Harvard Multispectral Patrol. Start with data coming off space probes out to ten AUs. I have a suspicion the easiest way for the Mailman to disguise his transmissions is to play trojan horse with data from a NASA spacecraft."

Mr. Slippery nodded. One way or another, they should resolve her alien invasion theory first.

"It should take me about half an hour to get in place. After that, we can set up for the correlation. Hmmm . . . if something goes wrong, let's agree to meet at Mass Transmit Three," and she gave a password scheme. Clearly that would be an emergency situation. If they weren't back in the castle within three or four hours, the others would certainly guess the existence of her secret exit.

Erythrina tensed, then dived into the water. There was a small splash, and the lilies bobbed gently in the expanding ring waves. Mr. Slippery looked deep, but as expected, there was no further sign of her. He padded around the side of the pool, trying to identify the special glow of the JPL data base.

There was thrashing near one of the larger lilies, one that he recognized as obscuring the NSA connections with the East/West net. A large bullfrog scrambled out of the water onto the pad and turned to look at him. "Aha! Gotcha, you sonofabitch!"

It was Virginia; the voice was the same, even if the body was different. *"Shhhhhh!"* said Mr. Slippery, and looked wildly about for signs of eavesdroppers. There were none, but that did not mean they were safe. He spread his best privacy spell over her and crawled to the point closest to the lily. They sat glaring at each other like some characters out of La Fontaine: The Tale of the Frog and Dog. How dearly he would love to leap across the water and bite off that fat little head. Unfortunately the victory would be a bit temporary. "How did you find me?" Mr. Slippery growled. If people as inexperienced as the Feds could trace him down in his disguise, he was hardly safe from the Mailman.

"You forget," the frog puffed smugly. "We know your Name. It's simple to monitor your home processor and follow your every move."

Mr. Slippery whined deep in his throat. *In thrall to a frog. Even Wiley has done better than that.* "Okay, so you found me. Now what do you want?"

"To let you know that we want results, and to get a progress report."

He lowered his muzzle till his eyes were even with Virginia's. "Heh heh. I'll give you a progress report, but you're not going to like it." And he proceeded to explain Erythrina's theory that the Mailman was an alien invasion.

"Rubbish," spoke the frog afterward. "Sheer fantasy! You're going to have to do better than that, Pol—er, Mister."

He shuddered. She had almost spoken his Name. Was that a calculated threat or was she simply as stupid as she seemed? Nevertheless, he persisted. "Well then, what about Venezuela?" He related the evidence Ery had that the coup in that country was the Mailman's work.

This time the frog did not reply. Its eyes glazed over with apparent shock, and he realized that Virginia must be consulting people at the other end. Almost fifteen minutes passed. When the frog's eyes cleared, it was much more subdued. "We'll check on that one. What you say is possible. Just barely possible. If true . . . well, if it's true, this is the biggest threat we've had to face this century."

And you see that I am perhaps the only one who can bail you out. Mr. Slippery relaxed slightly. If they only realized it, they were thralled to him as much as the reverse—at least for the moment. Then he remembered Erythrina's plan to grab as much power as they could for a brief time and try to use that advantage to flush the Mailman out. With the Feds on their side, they could do more than Ery had ever imagined. He said as much to Virginia.

The frog croaked, "*You . . .* want *. . . us . . .* to give you carte blanche in the Federal data system? Maybe you'd like to be President and Chair of the JCS, to boot?"

"Hey, that's not what I said. I know it's an extraordinary suggestion, but this is an extraordinary situation. And in any case, you know my Name. There's no way I can get around that."

The frog went glassy-eyed again, but this time for only a couple of minutes. "We'll get back to you on that. We've got a lot of checking to do on the rest of your theories before we commit ourselves to anything. Till further notice, though, you're grounded."

"Wait!" What would Ery do when he didn't show? If he wasn't back in the castle in three or four hours, the others would surely know about the secret exit.

The frog was implacable. "I said, you're grounded, Mister. We want you back in the real world immediately. And you'll stay grounded till you hear from us. Got it?"

The dog slumped. "Yeah."

"Okay." The frog clambered heavily to the edge of the sagging lily and dumped itself ungracefully into the water. After a few seconds, Mr. Slippery followed.

Coming back was much like waking from a deep daydream; only here it was the middle of the night.

Roger Pollack stood, stretching, trying to get the kinks out of his muscles. Almost four hours he had been gone, longer than ever before. Normally his concentration began to fail after two or three hours. Since he didn't like the thought of drugging up, this put a definite limit on his endurance in the Other Plane.

Beyond the bungalow's picture window, the pines stood silhouetted against the Milky Way. He cranked open a pane and listened to the night birds trilling in the trees. It was near the end of spring; he liked to imagine he could see dim polar twilight to the north. More likely it was just Crescent City. Pollack leaned close to the window and looked high into the sky, where Mars sat close to Jupiter. It was hard to think of a threat to his own life from as far away as that.

Pollack backed up the spells acquired during this last session, powered down his system, and stumbled off to bed.

THE FOLLOWING MORNING AND AFTERNOON SEEMED THE LONGEST OF Roger Pollack's life. How would they get in touch with him? Another visit of goons and black Lincolns? What had Erythrina done when he didn't make contact? Was she all right?

And there was just no way of checking. He paced back and forth across his tiny living room, the novel plots that were his normal work forgotten. *Ah, but there is a way.* He looked at his old data set with dawning recognition. Virginia had said to stay out of the Other Plane. But how could they object to his using a simple data set, no more efficient than millions used by office workers all over the world?

He sat down at the set, scraped the dust from the hand-pads and screen. He awkwardly entered long-unused call symbols and watched the flow of news across the screen. A few queries and he discovered that no great disasters had occurred overnight, that the insurgency in Indonesia seemed temporarily abated. (Wiley J. was not to be king just yet.) There were no reports of big-time data vandals biting the dust.

Pollack grunted. He had forgotten how tedious it was to see the world through a data set, even with audio entry. In the Other Plane, he could pick up this sort of information in seconds, as casually as an ordinary mortal might glance out the window to see if it is raining. He dumped the last twenty-four hours of the world bulletin board into his home memory space and began checking through it. The bulletin board was ideal for untraceable reception of messages: anyone on Earth could leave a message—indexed by subject, target audience, and source. If a user copied the entire board, and *then* searched it, there was no outside record of exactly what information he was interested in. There were also simple ways to make nearly untraceable entries on the board.

As usual, there were about a dozen messages for Mr. Slippery. Most of them were from fans; the Coven had greater notoriety than any other vandal SIG. A few were for other Mr. Slipperys. With five billion people in the world, that wasn't surprising.

And one of the memos was from the Mailman; that's what it said in the source field. Pollack punched the message up on the screen. It was in caps, with no color or sound. Like all messages directly from the Mailman, it looked as if it came off some incredibly ancient I/O device:

YOU COULD HAVE BEEN RICH. YOU COULD HAVE RULED. INSTEAD YOU CONSPIRED AGAINST ME. I KNOW ABOUT THE SECRET EXIT. I KNOW ABOUT YOUR DOGGY DEPAR-TURE. YOU AND THE RED ONE ARE DEAD NOW. IF YOU EVER SNEAK BACK ONTO THIS PLANE, IT WILL BE THE TRUE DEATH—I AM THAT CLOSE TO KNOWING YOUR NAMES.
　　　*****WATCH FOR ME IN THE NEWS, SUCKERS*****

Bluff, thought Roger. *He wouldn't be sending out warnings if he has that kind of power.* Still, there was a dropping sensation in his stomach. The Mailman shouldn't have known about the dog disguise. Was he onto Mr. Slippery's connection with the Feds? If so, he might really be able to find Slippery's True Name. And what sort of danger was Ery in? What had she done when he missed the rendezvous at Mass Transmit 3?

A quick search showed no messages from Erythrina. Either she was looking for him in the Other Plane, or she was as thoroughly grounded as he.

He was still stewing on this when the phone rang. He said, "Accept, no video send." His data set cleared to an even gray: the caller was not sending video either.

"You're still there? Good." It was Virginia. Her voice sounded a bit odd, subdued and tense. Perhaps it was just the effect of the scrambling algorithms. He prayed she would not trust that scrambling. He had never bothered to make his phone any more secure than average. (And he had seen the schemes Wiley J. and Robin Hood had devised to decrypt thousands of commercial phone messages in real-time and monitor for key phrases, signaling them when anything interesting was detected. They couldn't use the technique very effectively, since it took an enormous amount of processor space, but the Mailman was probably not so limited.)

Virginia continued, "No names, okay? We checked out what you told us and . . . it looks like you're right. We can't be sure about your theory about *his* origin, but what you said about the international situation was verified." So the Venezuela coup had been an outside takeover. "Furthermore, we think *he* has infiltrated us much more than we thought. It may be that the evidence we had of unsuccessful meddling was just a red herring." Pollack recognized the fear in her voice now. Apparently the Feds saw that they were up against something catastrophic. They were caught with their countermeasures down, and their only hope lay with unreliables like Pollack.

"Anyway, we're going ahead with what you suggested. We'll provide you two with the resources you requested. We want you in the Other . . . place as soon as possible. We can talk more there."

"I'm on my way. I'll check with my friend and get back

to you there." He cut the connection without waiting for a reply. Pollack sat back, trying to savor this triumph and the near-pleading in the cop's voice. Somehow, he couldn't. He knew what a hard case she was; anything that could make her crawl was more hellish than anything he wanted to face.

HIS FIRST STOP WAS MASS TRANSMIT 3. PHYSICALLY, MT3 WAS A TWO-thousand-tonne satellite in synchronous orbit over the Indian Ocean. The Mass Transmits handled most of the planet's non-interactive communications (and in fact that included a lot of transmission that most people regarded as interactive—such as human/human and the simpler human/computer conversations). Bandwidth and processor space was cheaper on the Mass Transmits because of the 240- to 900-millisecond time delays that were involved.

As such, it was a nice out-of-the-way meeting place, and in the Other Plane it was represented as a five-meter-wide ledge near the top of a mountain that rose from the forests and swamps that stood for the lower satellite layer and the ground-based nets. In the distance were two similar peaks, clear in pale sky.

Mr. Slippery leaned out into the chill breeze that swept the face of the mountain and looked down past the timberline, past the evergreen forests. Through the unnatural mists that blanketed those realms, he thought he could see the Coven's castle.

Perhaps he should go there, or down to the swamps. There was no sign of Erythrina. Only sprites in the forms of bats and tiny griffins were to be seen here. They sailed back and forth over him, sometimes soaring far higher, toward the uttermost peak itself.

Mr. Slippery himself was in an extravagant winged man form, one that subtly projected amateurism, one that he hoped would pass the inspection of the enemy's eyes and ears. He fluttered clumsily across the ledge toward a small cave that provided some shelter from the whistling wind. Fine, wind-dropped snow lay in a small bank before the entrance. The insects he found in the cave were no more than what they seemed—amateur transponders.

He turned and started back toward the drop-off; he was going to have to face this alone. But as he passed the snowbank, the wind swirled it up and tiny crystals stung his face and hands and nose. *Trap!* He jumped backward, his fastest escape spell coming to his lips, at the same time cursing himself for not establishing the spell before. The time delay was just too long; the trap lived here at MT3 and could react faster than he. The little snow-devil dragged the crystals up into a swirling column of singing motes that chimed in near-unison, "W-w-wait-t-t!"

The sound matched deep-set recognition patterns; this was Erythrina's work. Three hundred milliseconds passed, and the wind suddenly picked up the rest of the snow and whirled into a more substantial, taller column. Mr. Slippery realized that the trap had been more of an alarm, set to bring Ery if he should be recognized here. But her arrival was so quick that she must already have been at work somewhere in this plane.

"Where have you been-n-n!" The snow-devil's chime was a combination of rage and concern.

Mr. Slippery threw a second spell over the one he recognized she had cast. There was no help for it: he would have to tell her that the Feds had his Name. And with that news, Virginia's confirmation about Venezuela and the Feds' offer to help.

Erythrina didn't respond immediately—and only part of the delay was light lag. Then the swirling snow flecks that represented her gusted up around him. "So you lose no matter how this comes out, eh? I'm sorry, Slip."

Mr. Slippery's wings drooped. "Yeah. But I'm beginning to believe it will be the True Death for us all if we don't stop the

Mailman. He really means to take over . . . everything. Can you imagine what it would be like if all the governments' wee megalomaniacs got replaced by one big one?"

The usual pause. The snow-devil seemed to shudder in on itself. "You're right; we've got to stop him even if it means working for Sammy Sugar and the entire DoW." She chuckled, a near-inaudible chiming. "Even if it means that *they* have to work for *us*." She could laugh; the Feds didn't know her Name. "How did your Federal friends say we could plug into their system?" Her form was changing again—to a solid, winged form, an albino eagle. The only red she allowed herself was in the eyes, which gleamed with inner light.

"At the Laurel end of the old ARPAnet. We'll get something near carte blanche on that and on the DoJ domestic intelligence files, but we have to enter through one physical location and with just the password scheme they specify." He and Erythrina would have more power than any vandals in history, but they would be on a short leash, nevertheless.

His wings beat briefly, and he rose into the air. After the usual pause, the eagle followed. They flew almost to the mountain's peak, then began the long, slow glide toward the marshes below, the chill air whistling around them. In principle, they could have made the transfer to the Laurel terminus virtually instantaneously. But it was not mere romanticism that made them move so cautiously—as many a novice had discovered the hard way. What appeared to the conscious mind as a search for air currents and clear lanes through the scattered clouds was a manifestation of the almost-subconscious working of programs that gradually transferred processing from rented space on MT3 to low satellite and ground-based stations. The game was tricky and time-consuming, but it made it virtually impossible for others to trace their origin. The greatest danger of detection would probably occur at Laurel, where they would be forced to access the system through a single input device.

The sky glowed momentarily; seconds passed, and an airborne fist slammed into them from behind. The shock wave sent them tumbling tail over wing toward the forests below. Mr. Slippery straightened his chaotic flailing into a headfirst dive. Looking back—which was easy to do in his present attitude— he saw the peak that had been MT3 glowing red, steam rising over descending avalanches of lava. Even at this distance, he could see tiny motes swirling above the inferno. (Attackers looking for the prey that had fled?) Had it come just a few seconds earlier, they would have had most of their processing still locked into MT3 and the disaster—whatever it really was— would have knocked them out of this plane. It wouldn't have been the True Death, but it might well have grounded them for days.

On his right, he glimpsed the white eagle in a controlled dive; they had had just enough communications established off MT3 to survive. As they fell deeper into the humid air of the lowlands, Mr. Slippery dipped into the news channels: word was already coming over the *LA Times* of the fluke accident in which the Hokkaido aerospace launching laser had somehow shone on MT3's optics. The laser had shone for microseconds and at reduced power; the damage had been nothing like a Finger of God, say. No one had been hurt, but wideband communications would be down for some time, and several hundred million dollars of information traffic was stalled. There would be investigations and a lot of very irate customers.

It had been no accident, Mr. Slippery was sure. The Mailman was showing his teeth, revealing infiltration no one had suspected. He must guess what his opponents were up to.

THEY LEVELED OUT A DOZEN METERS ABOVE THE PINE FOREST THAT BORdered the swamps. The air around them was thick and humid, and the faraway mountains were almost invisible. Clouds had moved in, and a storm was on the way. They were now securely locked into the low-level satellite net, but thousands of new users were clamoring for entry, too. The loss of MT3 would make the Other Plane a turbulent place for several weeks, as heavy users tried to shift their traffic here.

He swooped low over the swamp, searching for the one particular pond with the one particularly large water lily that marked the only entrance Virginia would permit them. There! He banked off to the side, Erythrina following, and looked for signs of the Mailman or his friends in the mucky clearings that surrounded the pond.

But there was little purpose in further caution. Flying about like this, they would be clearly visible to any ambushers waiting by the pond. *Better to move fast now that we're committed.* He signaled the red-eyed eagle, and they dived toward the placid water. That surface marked the symbolic transition to observation mode. No longer was he aware of a winged form or of water coming up and around him. Now he was interacting directly with the I/O protocols of a computing center in the vicinity of Laurel, Maryland. He sensed Ery poking around on her own. This wasn't the ARPA entrance. He slipped "sideways" into an old-fashioned government office complex. The "feel" of the 1990-style data sets was unmistakable. He was fleetingly aware of memos written and edited, reports hauled in and out of storage. One of the vandals' favorite sports—and one that even the moderately skilled could indulge in—was to infiltrate one of these office complexes and simulate higher level input to make absurd and impossible demands on the local staff.

This was not the time for such games, and this was still not the entrance. He pulled away from the office complex and searched through some old directories. ARPA went back more than half a century, the first of the serious data nets, now (figuratively) gathering dust. The number was still there, though. He signaled Erythrina, and the two of them presented themselves at the log-in point and provided just the codes that Virginia had given him.

. . . and they were in. They eagerly soaked in the megabytes of password keys and access data that Virginia's people had left there. At the same time, they were aware that this activity was being monitored. The Feds were taking an immense chance leaving this material here, and they were going to do their best to keep a rein on their temporary vandal allies.

In fifteen seconds, they had learned more about the inner workings of the Justice Department and DoW than the Coven had in fifteen months. Mr. Slippery guessed that Erythrina must be busy plotting what she would do with all that data later on. For him, of course, there was no future in it. They drifted out of the ARPA "vault" into the larger data spaces that were the Department of Justice files. He could see that there was nothing hidden from them; random archive retrievals were all being honored and with a speed that would have made deception impossible. They had subpoena power and clearances and more.

"Let's go get 'im, Slip." Erythrina's voice seemed hollow and inhuman in this underimaged realm. (How long would it be before the Feds started to make their data perceivable analogically, as on the Other Plane? It might be a little undignified, but it would revolutionize their operation—which, from the Coven's standpoint, might be quite a bad thing.)

Mr. Slippery "nodded." Now they had more than enough power to undertake the sort of work they had planned. In seconds, they had searched all the locally available files on off-planet transmissions. Then they dove out of the DoJ net, Mr. Slippery to Pasadena and the JPL planetary probe archives, Erythrina to Cambridge and the Harvard Multispectral Patrol.

It should take several hours to survey these records, to determine just what transmissions might be cover for the alien invasion that both the Feds and Erythrina were guessing had begun. But Mr. Slippery had barely started when he noticed that there were dozens of processors within reach that he could just grab with his new Federal powers. He checked carefully to make sure he wasn't upsetting air traffic control or hospital life support, then quietly stole the computing resources of several hundred unknowing users, whose data sets automatically switched to other resources. Now he had more power than he ever would have risked taking in the past. On the other side of the continent, he was aware that Erythrina had done something similar.

In three minutes, they had sifted through five years' transmissions far more thoroughly than they had originally planned.

"No sign of him," he sighed and "looked" at Erythrina. They had found plenty of irregular sources at Harvard, but there was no orbital fit. All transmissions from the NASA probes checked out legitimately.

"Yes." Her face, with its dark skin and slanting eyes, seemed to hover beside him. Apparently with her new power, she could image even here. "But you know, we haven't really done much more than the Feds could—given a couple months of data set work . . . I know, it's more than we had planned to do. But we've barely used the resources they've opened to us."

It was true. He looked around, feeling suddenly like a small boy let loose in a candy shop: he sensed enormous databases and the power that would let him use them. Perhaps the cops had not intended them to take advantage of this, but it was obvious that with these powers, they could do a search no enemy could evade. "Okay," he said finally, "let's pig it."

Ery laughed and made a loud snuffling sound. Carefully, quickly, they grabbed noncritical data-processing facilities along all the East/West nets. In seconds, they were the biggest users in North America. The drain would be clear to anyone monitoring the System, though a casual user might notice only increased delays in turnaround. Modern nets are at least as resilient as old-time power nets—but like power nets, they have their elastic limit and their breaking point. So far, at least, he and Erythrina were far short of those.

—but they were experiencing what no human had ever known before, a sensory bandwidth thousands of times normal. For seconds that seemed without end, their minds were filled with a jumble verging on pain, data that was not information and information that was not knowledge. To hear ten million simultaneous phone conversations, to see the continent's entire video output, should have been a white noise. Instead it was a tidal wave of detail rammed through the tiny aperture of their minds. The pain increased, and Mr. Slippery panicked. This could be the True Death, some kind of sensory burnout—

Erythrina's voice was faint against the roar. *"Use everything, not just the inputs!"* And he had just enough sense left to see what she meant. He controlled more than raw data now; if he could master them, the continent's computers could process this avalanche, much the way parts of the human brain preprocess their input. More seconds passed, but now with a sense of time, as he struggled to distribute his very consciousness through the System.

Then it was over, and he had control once more. But things would never be the same: the human that had been Mr. Slippery was an insect wandering in the cathedral his mind had become. There simply was more there than before. No sparrow could fall without his knowledge, via air traffic control; no check could be cashed without his noticing over the bank communication net. More than three hundred million lives swept before what his senses had become.

Around and through him, he felt the other occupant—Erythrina, now equally grown. They looked at each other for an unending fraction of a second, their communication more kinesthetic than verbal. Finally she smiled, the old smile now deep with meanings she could never image before. "Pity the poor Mailman now!"

Again they searched, but now it was through all the civil databases, a search that could only be dreamed of by mortals. The signs were there, a near invisible system of manipulations hidden among more routine crimes and vandalisms. Someone had been at work within the Venezuelan system, at least at the North American end. The trail was tricky to follow—their enemy seemed to have at least some of their own powers—but they saw it lead back into the labyrinths of the Federal bureaucracy: resources diverted, individuals promoted or transferred, not quite according to the automatic regulations that should govern. These were changes so small they were never guessed at by ordinary employees and only just sensed by the cops. But over the months, they added up to an instability that neither of the two searchers could quite understand except to know that it was planned and that it did the status quo no good.

"He's still too sharp for us, Slip. We're all over the civil nets and we haven't seen any living sign of him; yet we know he does heavy processing on Earth or in low orbit."

"So he's either off North America, or else he has penetrated the . . . military."

"I bet it's a little of both. The point is, we're going to have to follow him."

And that meant taking over at least part of the U.S. military system. Even if that was possible, it certainly went far beyond what Virginia and her friends had intended. As far as the cops were concerned, it would mean that the threat against the government was tripled. So far he hadn't detected any objections to their searching, but he was aware of Virginia and her superiors deep in some kind of bunker at Langley, intently watching a whole wall full of monitors, trying to figure out just what he was up to and if it was time to pull the plug on him.

Erythrina was aware of his objections almost as fast as he could bring them to mind. "We don't have any choice, Slip. We have to take control. The Feds aren't the only thing watching us. If we don't get the Mailman on this try, he is sure as hell going to get us."

That was easy for her to say. None of her enemies yet knew her True Name. Mr. Slippery had somehow to survive *two* enemies. On the other hand, he suspected that the deadlier of those enemies was the Mailman. "Only one way to go and that's up, huh? Okay, I'll play."

They settled into a game that was familiar now, grabbing more and more computing facilities, but now from common Europe and Asia. At the same time, they attacked the harder problem—infiltrating the various North American military nets. Both projects were beyond normal humans or any group of normal humans, but by now their powers were greater than any single civil entity in the world.

The foreign data centers yielded easily, scarcely more than minutes' work. The military was a different story. The Feds had spent many years and hundreds of billions of dollars to make the military command and control system secure. But they had not counted on the attack from all directions that they faced now; in moments more, the two searchers found themselves on the inside of the NSA control system—

—and under attack! Impressions of a dozen sleek, deadly forms converging on them, and sudden loss of control over many of the processors he depended on. He and Erythrina flailed out wildly, clumsy giants hacking at fast-moving hawks. There was imagery here, as detailed as on the Other Plane. They were fighting people with some of the skills the warlocks had developed—and a lot more power. But it was still an uneven contest. He and Erythrina had too much experience and too much sheer processing mass behind them. One by one, the fighters flashed into incandescent destruction.

He realized almost instantly that these were not the Mailman's tools. They were powerful, but they fought only as moderately skilled warlocks might. In fact, they had encountered the most secret defense the government had for its military command and control. The civilian bureaucracies had stuck with obsolete data sets and old-fashioned dp languages, but the cutting edge of the military is always more willing to experiment. They had developed something like the warlocks' system. Perhaps they didn't use magical jargon to describe their computer/human symbiosis, but the techniques and the attitudes were the same. These swift-moving fighters flew against a background imagery that was like an olive-drab Other Plane.

Compared to his present power, they were nothing. Even as he and Erythrina swept the defenders out of the "sky," he could feel his consciousness expanding further as more and more of the military system was absorbed into their pattern. Every piece of space junk out to one million kilometers floated in crystal detail before his attention; in a fraction of a second he sorted through it all, searching for some evidence of alien intelligence. No sign of the Mailman.

The military and diplomatic communications of the preceding fifty years showed before the light of their minds. At the same time as they surveyed the satellite data, Mr. Slippery and Erythrina swept through these bureaucratic communications, looking carefully but with flickering speed at every requisition for toilet paper, every "declaration" of secret war, every travel voucher, every one of the trillions of pieces of "paper" that made it possible for the machinery of state to creak forward. And here the signs were much clearer: large sections were subtly changed, giving the same feeling the eye's blind spot gives, the feeling that nothing is really obscured but that some things are simply gone. Some of the distortions were immense. Under their microscopic yet global scrutiny, it was obvious that all of Venezuela, large parts of Alaska, and most of the economic base for the low satellite net were all controlled by some single interest that had little connection with the proper owners. Who their enemy was was still a mystery, but his works loomed larger and larger around them.

In a distant corner of what his mind had become, tiny insects buzzed with homicidal fury, tiny insects who knew Mr. Slippery's True Name. They knew what he and Erythrina had done, and right now they were more scared of the two warlocks than they had ever been of the Mailman. As he and Ery continued their search, he listened to the signals coming from the Langley command post, followed the helicopter gunships that were dispatched toward a single rural bungalow in Northern California—and changed their encrypted commands so that the sortie dumped its load of death on an uninhabited stretch of the Pacific.

Still with a tiny fraction of his attention, Mr. Slippery noticed that Virginia—actually her superiors, who had long since taken over the operation—knew of this defense. They were still receiving real-time pictures from military satellites.

He signaled a pause to Erythrina. For a few seconds, she would work alone while he dealt with these persistent antagonists. He felt like a man attacked by several puppies: they were annoying and could cause substantial damage unless he took more trouble than they were worth. They had to be stopped without causing themselves injury.

He should freeze the West Coast military and any launch complexes that could reach his body. Beyond that, it would be a good idea to block recon satellite transmission of the California area. And of course, he'd better deal with the Finger of God installations that were above the California horizon. Already he felt one of those heavy lasers, sweeping along in its ten-thousand-kilometer orbit, go into aiming mode and begin charging. He still had plenty of time—at least two or three seconds—before the weapon's laser reached its lowest discharge threshold. Still, this was the most immediate threat. Mr. Slippery sent a tendril of consciousness into the tiny processor aboard the Finger of God satellite—

—and withdrew, bloodied. *Someone was already there.* Not Erythrina and not the little military warlocks. *Someone* too great for even him to overpower.

"*Ery!* I've found him!" It came out a scream. The laser's bore was centered on a spot thousands of kilometers below, a tiny house that in less than a second would become an expanding ball of plasma at the end of a columnar explosion descending through the atmosphere.

Over and over in that last second, Mr. Slippery threw himself against the barrier he felt around the tiny military processor— with no success. He traced its control to the lower satellite net, to bigger processors that were equally shielded. Now he had a feel for the nature of his opponent. It was not the direct imagery he was used to on the Other Plane; this was more like fighting blindfolded. He could sense the other's style. The enemy was not revealing any more of himself than was necessary to keep control of the Finger of God for another few hundred milliseconds.

Mr. Slippery slashed, trying to cut the enemy's communications. But his opponent was strong, much stronger—he now realized—than himself. He was vaguely aware of the other's connections to the computing power in those blind-spot areas he and Erythrina had discovered. But for all that power, he was almost the enemy's equal. There was something missing from the other, some critical element of imagination or originality. If Erythrina would only come, they might be able to stop him. Milliseconds separated him from the True Death. He looked desperately around. *Where is she?*

Military Status announced the discharge of an Orbital Weapons Laser. He cowered even as his quickened perceptions counted the microseconds that remained till his certain destruction, even as he noticed a ball of glowing plasma expanding about what had been a Finger of God—*the Finger that had been aimed at him!*

He could see now what had happened. While he and the other had been fighting, Erythrina had commandeered another of the weapons satellites, one already very near discharge threshold, and destroyed the threat to him.

Even as he realized this, the enemy was on him again, this time attacking conventionally, trying to destroy Mr. Slippery's communications and processing space. But now that enemy had to fight both Erythrina and Mr. Slippery. The other's lack of imagination and creativity was beginning to tell, and even with his greater strength, they could feel him slowly, slowly losing resources to his weaker opponents. There was something familiar about this enemy, something Mr. Slippery was sure he could see, given time.

Abruptly the enemy pulled away. For a long moment, they held each other's sole attention, like cats waiting for the smallest sign of weakness to launch back into combat—only here the new attack could come from any of ten thousand different directions, from any of the communications nodes that formed their bodies and their minds.

From beside him, he felt Erythrina move forward, as though to lock the other in her green-eyed gaze. "You know who we have here, Slip?" He could tell that all her concentration was on this enemy, that she almost vibrated with the effort. "This is our old friend DON.MAC grown up to super size, and doing his best to disguise himself."

The other seemed to tense and move even further in upon himself. But after a moment, he began imaging. There stood DON.MAC, his face and Plessey-Mercedes body the same as ever. DON.MAC, the first of the Mailman's converts, the one

Erythrina was sure had been killed and replaced with a simulator. "And all the time he's been the Mailman. The last person
we would suspect, the Mailman's first victim."

DON rolled forward half a meter, his motors keening, his
hydraulic fists raised. But he did not deny what Mr. Slippery
said. After a moment he seemed to relax. "You are very . . .
clever. But then, you two have had help; I never thought you
and the cops would cooperate. That was the one combination
that had any chance against the 'Mailman.' " He smiled, a familiar automatic twitch. "But don't you see? It's a combination
with lethal genes. We three have much more in common than
you and the government.

"Look around you. If we were warlocks before, we are gods
now. Look!" Without letting the center of their attention wander, the two followed his gaze. As before, the myriad aspects of
the lives of billions spread out before them. But now, many
things were changed. In their struggle, the three had usurped
virtually all of the connected processing power of the human
race. Video and phone communications were frozen. The public
databases had lasted long enough to notice that something had
gone terribly, terribly wrong. Their last headlines, generated a
second before the climax of the battle, were huge banners announcing GREATEST DATA OUTAGE OF ALL TIME. Nearly a
billion people watched blank data sets, feeling more panicked
than any simple power blackout could ever make them. Already
the accumulation of lost data and work time would cause a
major recession.

"They are lucky the old arms race is over, or else independent
military units would probably have already started a war. Even
if we hand back control this instant, it would take them more
than a year to get their affairs in order." DON.MAC smirked,
the same expression they had seen the day before when he was
bragging to the Limey. "There have been few deaths yet. Hos-
pitals and aircraft have some stand-alone capability."

Even so . . . Mr. Slippery could see thousands of aircraft stacked up over major airports from London to Christchurch. Local computing could never coordinate the safe landing of them all before some ran out of fuel.

"*We* caused all that—with just the fallout of our battle," continued DON. "If we chose to do them harm, I have no doubt we could exterminate the human race." He detonated three warheads in their silos in Utah just to emphasize his point. With dozens of video eyes, in orbit and on the ground, Mr. Slippery and Erythrina watched the destruction sweep across the launch sites. "Consider: how are we different from the gods of myth? And like the gods of myth, we can rule and prosper, just so long as we don't fight among ourselves." He looked expectantly from Mr. Slippery to Erythrina. There was a frown on the Red One's dark face; she seemed to be concentrating on their opponent just as fiercely as ever.

DON.MAC turned back to Mr. Slippery. "Slip, you especially should see that we have no choice but to cooperate. *They know your True Name.* Of the three of us, your life is the most fragile, depending on protecting your body from a government that now considers you a traitor. You would have died a dozen times over during the last thousand seconds if you hadn't used your new powers.

"And you can't go back. Even if you play Boy Scout, destroy me, and return all obedient—even then they will kill you. They know how dangerous you are, perhaps even more dangerous than I. They can't afford to let you exist."

And megalomania aside, that made perfect and chilling sense. As they were talking, a fraction of Mr. Slippery's attention was devoted to confusing and obstructing the small infantry group that had been air-dropped into the Arcata region just before the government lost all control. Their superiors had realized how easily he could countermand their orders, and so the troops were instructed to ignore all outside direction until they had destroyed a certain Roger Pollack. Fortunately they were depending on city directories and orbit-fed street maps, and he had been keeping them going in circles for some time now. It was a nuisance, and sooner or later he would have to decide on a more permanent solution.

But what was a simple nuisance in his present state would be near-instant death if he returned to his normal self. He looked at Erythrina. Was there any way around DON's arguments?

Her eyes were almost shut, and the frown had deepened. He sensed that more and more of her resources were involved in some pattern analysis. He wondered if she had even heard what DON.MAC said. But after a moment her eyes came open, and she looked at the two of them. There was triumph in that look. "You know, Slip, I don't think I have ever been fooled by a personality simulator, at least not for more than a few minutes."

Mr. Slippery nodded, puzzled by this sudden change in topic. "Sure. If you talk to a simulator long enough, you eventually begin to notice little inflexibilities. I don't think we'll ever be able to write a program that could pass the Turing test."

"Yes, little inflexibilities, a certain lack of imagination. It always seems to be the tipoff. Of course DON here has always pretended to be a program, so it was hard to tell. But I was sure that for the last few months there has been no living being behind his mask . . .

". . . and furthermore, I don't think there is anybody there even now." Mr. Slippery's attention snapped back to DON.MAC. The other smirked at the accusation. Somehow it was not the right reaction. Mr. Slippery remembered the strange, artificial flavor of DON's combat style. In this short an encounter, there could be no really hard evidence for her theory. She was using her intuition and whatever deep analysis she had been doing these last few seconds.

"But that means we still haven't found the Mailman."

"Right. This is just his best tool. I'll bet the Mailman simply used the pattern he stole from the murdered DON.MAC as the basis for this automatic defense system we've been fighting. The Mailman's time lag is a very real thing, not a red herring at all. Somehow it is the whole secret of who he really is.

"In any case, it makes our present situation a lot easier." She smiled at DON.MAC as though he were a real person. Usually it was easier to behave that way toward simulators; in this case, there was a good deal of triumph in her smile. "You almost won for your master, DON. You almost had us convinced. But now that we know what we are dealing with, it will be easy to—"

Her image flicked out of existence, and Mr. Slippery felt DON grab for the resources Ery controlled. All through near-Earth space, they fought for the weapon systems she had held till an instant before.

And alone, Mr. Slippery could not win. Slowly, slowly, he felt himself bending before the other's force, like some wrestler whose bones were breaking one by one under a murderous opponent. It was all he could do to prevent the DON construct from blasting his home; and to do that, he had to give up progressively more computing power.

Erythrina was gone, gone as though she had never been. Or was she? He gave a sliver of his attention to a search, a sliver that was still many times more powerful than any mere warlock. That tiny piece of consciousness quickly noticed a power failure in southern Rhode Island. Many power failures had developed during the last few minutes, consequent to the data failure. But this one was strange. In addition to power, comm lines were down and even his intervention could not bring them to life. It was about as thoroughly blacked out as a place could be. This could scarcely be an accident.

. . . and there was a voice, barely telephone quality and al-

most lost in the mass of other data he was processing. *Erythrina!*
She had, via some incredibly tortuous detour, retained a communication path to the outside.

His gaze swept the blacked-out Providence suburb. It consisted of new urbapts, perhaps one hundred thousand units in
all. Somewhere in there lived the human that was Erythrina.
While she had been concentrating on DON.MAC, he must have
been working equally hard to find her True Name. Even now,
DON did not know precisely who she was, only enough to black
out the area she lived in.

It was getting hard to think; DON.MAC was systematically
dismantling him. The lethal intent was clear: as soon as Mr.
Slippery was sufficiently reduced, the Orbital Lasers would be
turned on his body, and then on Erythrina's. And then the Mailman's faithful servant would have a planetary kingdom to turn
over to his mysterious master.

He listened to the tiny voice that still leaked out of Providence. It didn't make too much sense. She sounded hysterical,
panicked. He was surprised that she could speak at all; she had
just suffered—in losing all her computer connections—something roughly analogous to a massive stroke. To her, the world
was now seen through a keyhole, incomplete, unknown, and
dark.

"There is a chance; we still have a chance," the voice went
on, hurried and slurred. "An old military communication tower
north of here. Damn. I don't know the number or grid, but I
can see it from where I'm sitting. With it you could punch
through to the roof antenna . . . has plenty of bandwidth, and
I've got some battery power here . . . but *hurry*."

She didn't have to tell him that; he was the guy who was
being eaten alive. He was almost immobilized now, the other's
attack squeezing and stifling where it could not cut and tear.
He spasmed against DON's strength and briefly contacted the

comm towers north of Providence. Only one of them was in line of sight with the blacked-out area. Its steerable antenna was very, very narrow beam.

"Ery, I'm going to need your house number, maybe even your antenna id."

A second passed, two—a hellish eon for Mr. Slippery. In effect, he had asked her for her True Name—he who was already known to the Feds. Once he returned to the real world, there would be no way he could mask this information from them. He could imagine her thoughts: never again to be free. In her place, he would have paused too, but—

"*Ery!* It's the True Death for both of us if you don't. He's got me!"

This time she barely hesitated. "D-Debby Charteris, four thousand four hundred forty-eight Grosvenor Row. Cut off like this, I don't know the antenna id. Is my name and house enough?"

"Yes. Get ready!"

Even before he spoke, he had already matched the name with an antenna rental and aligned the military antenna on it. Return contact came as he turned his attention back to DON.MAC. With luck, the enemy was not aware of their conversation. Now he must be distracted.

Mr. Slippery surged against the other, breaking communications nodes that served them both. DON shuddered, reorganizing around the resources that were left, then moved in on Mr. Slippery again. Since DON had greater strength to begin with, the maneuver had cost Mr. Slippery proportionately more. The enemy had been momentarily thrown off balance, but now the end would come very quickly.

The spaces around him, once so rich with detail and colors beyond color, were fading now, replaced by the sensations of his true body straining with animal fear in its little house in

California. Contact with the greater world was almost gone. He was scarcely aware of it when DON turned the Finger of God back upon him—

Consciousness, the superhuman consciousness of before, returned almost unsensed, unrecognized till awareness brought surprise. Like a strangling victim back from oblivion, Mr. Slippery looked around dazedly, not quite realizing that the struggle continued.

But now the roles were reversed. DON.MAC had been caught by surprise, in the act of finishing off what he thought was his only remaining enemy. Erythrina had used that surprise to good advantage, coming in upon her opponent from a Japanese data center, destroying much of DON's higher reasoning centers before the other was even aware of her. Large, unclaimed processing units lay all about, and as DON and Erythrina continued their struggle, Mr. Slippery quietly absorbed everything in reach.

Even now, DON could have won against either one of them alone, but when Mr. Slippery threw himself back into the battle, they had the advantage. DON.MAC sensed this too, and with a brazenness that was either mindless or genius, returned to his original appeal. "There is still time! The Mailman will still forgive you."

Mr. Slippery and Erythrina ripped at their enemy from both sides, disconnecting vast blocks of communications, processing and data resources. They denied the Mass Transmits to him, and one by one put the low-level satellites out of synch with his data accesses. DON was confined to land lines, tied into a single military net that stretched from Washington to Denver. He was flailing, randomly using whatever instruments of destruction were still available. All across the midsection of the US, silo missiles detonated, ABM lasers swept back and forth across the sky. The world had been stopped short by the beginning of their struggle, but the ending could tear it to pieces.

The damage to Mr. Slippery and Erythrina was slight, the risk that the random strokes would seriously damage them small. They ignored occasional slashing losses and concentrated single-mindedly on dismantling DON.MAC. They discovered the object code for the simulator that was DON, and zeroed it. DON—or his creator—was clever and had planted many copies, and a new one awakened every time they destroyed the running copy. But as the minutes passed, the simulator found itself with less and less to work with. Now it was barely more than it had been back in the Coven.

"Fools! The Mailman is your natural ally. The Feds will *kill* you! Don't you underst—"

The voice stopped in midshriek, as Erythrina zeroed the currently running simulator. No other took up the task. There was a silence, an . . . absence . . . throughout. Erythrina glanced at Mr. Slippery, and the two continued their search through the enemy's territory. This data space was big, and there could be many more copies of DON hidden in it. But without the resources they presently held, the simulator could have no power. It was clear to both of them that no effective ambush could be hidden in these unmoving ruins.

And they had complete copies of DON.MAC to study. It was easy to trace the exact extent of his infection of the system. The two moved systematically, changing what they found so that it would behave as its original programmers had intended. Their work was so thorough that the Feds might never realize just how extensively the Mailman and his henchman had infiltrated them, just how close he had come to total control.

Most of the areas they searched were only slightly altered and required only small changes. But deep within the military net, there were hundreds of trillions of bytes of program that seemed to have no intelligible function yet were clearly connected with DON's activities. It was apparently object code, but it was so huge and so ill organized that even they couldn't de-

cide if it was more than hash now. There was no possibility that
it had any legitimate function; after a few moments' consideration, they randomized it.

At last it was over. Mr. Slippery and Erythrina stood alone.
They controlled all connected processing facilities in near-Earth
space. There was no place within that volume that any further
enemies could be lurking. And there was no evidence that there
had ever been interference from beyond.

It was the first time since they had reached this level that
they had been able to survey the world without fear. (He
scarcely noticed the continuing, pitiful attempts of the American military to kill his real body.) Mr. Slippery looked around
him, using all his millions of perceptors. The Earth floated se-
rene. Viewed in the visible, it looked like a thousand pictures
he had seen as a human. But in the ultraviolet, he could follow
its hydrogen aura out many thousands of kilometers. And the
high-energy detectors on satellites at all levels perceived the
radiation belts in thousands of energy levels, oscillating in
the solar wind. Across the oceans of the world, he could feel
the warmth of the currents, see just how fast they were moving.
And all the while, he monitored the millions of tiny voices that
were now coming back to life as he and Erythrina carefully set
the human race's communication system back on its feet and
gently prodded it into function. Every ship in the seas, every
aircraft now making for safe landing, every one of the loans,
the payments, the meals of an entire race registered clearly on
some part of his consciousness. With perception came power;
almost everything he saw, he could alter, destroy, or enhance.
By the analogical rules of the covens, there was only one valid
word for themselves in their present state: they were gods.

"... we could rule," Erythrina's voice was hushed, self-
frightened. "It might be tricky at first, assuring our bodies protection, but we could rule."

"There's still the Mailman—"

She seemed to wave a hand, dismissingly. "Maybe, maybe not. It's true we still are no closer to knowing who he is, but we do know that we have destroyed all his processing power. We would have plenty of warning if he ever tries to reinsinuate himself into the System." She stared at him intently, and it wasn't until some time later that he recognized the faint clues in her behavior and realized that she was holding something back.

What she said was all so clearly true; for as long as their bodies lived, they could rule. And what DON.MAC had said seemed true: they were the greatest threat the "forces of law and order" had ever faced, and that included the Mailman. How could the Feds afford to let them be free, how could they even afford to let them *live*, if the two of them gave up the power they had now? But—"A lot of people would have to die if we took over. There are enough independent military entities left on Earth that we'd have to use a good deal of nuclear blackmail, at least at first."

"Yeah," her voice was even smaller than before, and the image of her face was downcast. "During the last few seconds I've done some simulating on that. We'd have to take out four, maybe six, major cities. If there are any command centers hidden from us, it could be a lot worse than that. And we'd have to develop our own human secret-police forces as folks began to operate outside our system. . . . Damn. We'd end up being worse than the human-based government."

She saw the same conclusion in his face and grinned lopsidedly. "You can't do it and neither can I. So the State wins again."

He nodded, "reached" out to touch her briefly. They took one last glorious minute to soak in the higher reality. Then, silently, they parted, each to seek his own way downward.

It was not an instantaneous descent to ordinary humanity. Mr. Slippery was careful to prepare a safe exit. He created a complex set of misdirections for the army unit that was trying to close in on his physical body; it would take them several hours to find him, far longer than necessary for the government to call them off. He set up preliminary negotiations with the Federal programs that had been doing their best to knock him out of power, telling them of his determination to surrender if granted safe passage and safety for his body. In a matter of seconds he would be talking to humans again, perhaps even Virginia, but by then a lot of the basic ground rules would be automatically in operation.

As per their temporary agreements, he closed off first one and then another of the capabilities that he had so recently acquired. It was like stopping one's ears, then blinding one's eyes, but somehow much worse since his very ability to think was being deliberately given up. He was like some lobotomy patient (victim) who only vaguely realizes now what he has lost. Behind him the Federal forces were doing their best to close off the areas he had left, to protect themselves from any change of heart he might have.

Far away now, he could sense Erythrina going through a similar procedure, but more slowly. That was strange; he couldn't be sure with his present faculties, but somehow it seemed that she was deliberately lagging behind and doing something more complicated than was strictly necessary to return safely to normal humanity. And then he remembered that strange look she had given him while saying that they had not figured out who the Mailman was.

One could rule as easily as two!

The panic was sudden and overwhelming, all the more terrible for the feeling of being betrayed by one so trusted. He struck out against the barriers he had so recently allowed to close in about him, but it was too late. He was already weaker than the Feds. Mr. Slippery looked helplessly back into the gathering dimness, and saw . . .

. . . Ery coming down toward the real world with him, giving up the advantage she had held all alone. Whatever problems had slowed her must have had nothing to do with treachery. And somehow his feeling of relief went beyond the mere fact of death avoided—Ery was still what he had always thought her.

HE WAS SEEING A LOT OF VIRGINIA LATELY, THOUGH OF COURSE NOT socially. Her crew had set up offices in Arcata, and twice a week she and one of her goons would come up to the house. No doubt it was one of the few government operations carried out face-to-face. She or her superiors seemed to realize that anything done over the phone might be subject to trickery. (Which was true, of course. Given several weeks to himself, Pollack could have put together a robot phone connection and—using false ids and priority permits—been on a plane to Djakarta.) There were a lot of superficial similarities between these meetings and that first encounter the previous spring:

Pollack stepped to the door and watched the black Lincoln pulling up the drive. As always, the vehicle came right into the carport. As always, the driver got out quickly, eyes flickering coldly across Pollack. As always, Virginia moved with military precision (in fact, he had discovered, she had been promoted out of the army to her present job in DoW intelligence). The two walked purposefully toward the bungalow, ignoring the summer sunlight and the deep wet green of the lawn and pines. He held the door open for them, and they entered with silent arrogance. As always.

He smiled to himself. In one sense nothing had changed. They still had the power of life and death over him. They could still cut him off from everything he loved. But in another sense . . .

"Got an easy one for you today, Pollack," she said as she put her briefcase on the coffee table and enabled its data set. "But I don't think you're going to like it."

"Oh?" He sat down and watched her expectantly.

"The last couple of months, we've had you destroying what remains of the Mailman and getting the National program and databases back in operation."

Behind everything, there still stood the threat of the Mailman. Ten weeks after the battle—the War, as Virginia called it— the public didn't know any more than that there had been a massive vandalism of the System. Like most major wars, this had left ruination in everyone's camp. The U.S. government and the economy of the entire world had slid far toward chaos in the months after that battle. (In fact, without his work and Erythrina's, he doubted if the U.S. bureaucracies could have survived the Mailman War. Her didn't know whether this made them the saviors or the betrayers of America.) But what of the enemy? His power was almost certainly destroyed. In the last three weeks Mr. Slippery had found only one copy of the program kernel that had been DON.MAC, and that had been in nonexcutable form. But the man—or the beings—behind the Mailman was just as anonymous as ever. In that, Virginia, the government, and Pollack were just as ignorant as the general public.

"Now," Virginia continued, "we've got some smaller problems—mopping-up action, you might call it. For nearly two decades, we've had to live with the tuppin vandalism of irresponsible individuals who put their petty self-interest ahead of the public's. Now that we've got you, we intend to put a stop to that:

"We want the True Names of all abusers currently on the System, in particular the members of this so-called coven you used to be a part of."

He had known that the demand would eventually come, but the knowledge made this moment no less unpleasant. "I'm sorry, I can't."

"Can't? Or won't? See here, Pollack, the price of your

freedom is that you play things our way. You've broken enough laws to justify putting you away forever. And we both know that you are so dangerous that you *ought* to be put away. There are people who feel even more strongly than that, Pollack, people who are not as soft in the head as I am. They simply want you and your girlfriend in Providence safely dead." The speech was delivered with characteristic flat bluntness, but she didn't quite meet his eyes as she spoke. Ever since he had returned from the battle, there had been a faint diffidence behind her bluster.

She covered it well, but it was clear to Pollack that she didn't know if she should fear him or respect him—or both. In any case, she seemed to recognize a basic mystery in him; she had more imagination than he had originally thought. It was a bit amusing, for there was very little special about Roger Pollack, the man. He went from day to day feeling a husk of what he had once been and trying to imagine what he could barely remember.

Roger smiled almost sympathetically. "I can't *and* I won't, Virginia. And I don't think you will harm me for it—Let me finish. The only thing that frightens your bosses more than Erythrina and me is the possibility that there may be other unknown persons—maybe even the Mailman, back from wherever he has disappeared to—who might be equally powerful. She and I are your only real experts on this type of subversion. I bet that even if they could, your people wouldn't train their own clean-cut, braided types as replacements for us. The more paranoid a security organization is, the less likely it is to trust anyone with this sort of power. Mr. Slippery and Erythrina are the known factors, the experts who turned back from the brink. Our restraint was the only thing that stood between the Powers That Be and the Powers That Would Be."

Virginia was speechless for a moment, and Pollack could

see that this was the crux of her changed attitude toward him. All her life she had been taught that the individual is corrupted by power: she boggled at the notion that he had been offered mastery of all mankind—and had refused it.

Finally she smiled, a quick smile that was gone almost before he noticed it. "Okay. I'll pass on what you say. You may be right. The vandals are a long-range threat to our basic American freedoms, but day to day, they are a mere annoyance. My superiors—the Department of Welfare—are probably willing to fight them as we have in the past. They'll tolerate your, uh, disobedience *in this single matter* as long as you and Erythrina loyally protect us against the superhuman threats."

Pollack felt a great sense of relief. He had been so afraid DoW would be willing to destroy him for this refusal. But since the Feds would never be free of their fear of the Mailman, he and Debby Charteris—Erythrina—would never be forced to betray their friends.

"But," continued the cop, "that doesn't mean you get to ignore the covens. The most likely place for superhuman threats to resurface is from within them. The vandals are the people with the most real experience on the System—even the army is beginning to see that. And if a superhuman type originates outside the covens, we figure his ego will still make him show off to them, just as with the Mailman.

"In addition to your other jobs, we want you to spend a couple of hours a week with each of the major covens. You'll be one of the 'boys'—only now you're under responsible control, watching for any sign of Mailman-type influence."

"I'll get to see Ery again!"

"No. That rule still stands. And you should be grateful. I don't think we could tolerate your existence if there weren't two of you. With only one in the Other Plane at a time, we'll always have a weapon in reserve. And as long as we can

keep you from meeting there, we can keep you from schem-
ing against us. This is serious, Roger: if we catch you two or
your surrogates playing around in the Other Plane, it will be
the end."

"Hmm."

She looked hard at him for a moment, then appeared to
take that for acquiescence. The next half hour was devoted
to the details of this week's assignments. (It would have been
easier to feed him all this when he was in the Other Plane,
but Virginia—or at least DoW—seemed wedded to the past.)
He was to continue the work on Social Security Records and
the surveillance of the South American data nets. There was
an enormous amount of work to be done, at least with the
limited powers the Feds were willing to give him. It would
likely be October before the welfare machinery was working
properly again. But that would be in time for the elections.

Then, late in the week, they wanted him to visit the
Coven. Roger knew he would count the hours; it had been
so long.

Virginia was her usual self, intense and all business, until
she and her driver were ready to leave. Standing in the carport, she said almost shyly, "I ran your *Anne Boleyn* last
week. . . . It's really very good."

"You sound surprised."

"No. I mean yes, maybe I was. Actually I've run it several
times, usually with the viewpoint character set to Anne.
There seems to be a lot more depth to it than other participation games I've read. I've got the feeling that if I am clever
enough, someday I'll stop Henry and keep my head!"

Pollack grinned. He could imagine Virginia, the hard-eyed
cop, reading *Anne* to study the psychology of her client-
prisoner—then gradually getting caught up in the action of
the novel. "It is possible."

In fact, it was possible she might turn into a rather nice human being someday.

But by the time Pollack was starting back up the walk to his house, Virginia was no longer on his mind. He was going back to the Coven!

A CHILL MIST THAT WAS ALMOST RAIN BLEW ACROSS THE HILLSIDE AND obscured the far distance in shifting patches. But even from here, on the ridge above the swamp, the castle looked different: heavier, stronger, darker.

Mr. Slippery started down the familiar slope. The frog on his shoulder seemed to sense his unease and its clawlets bit tighter into the leather of his jacket. Its beady yellow eyes turned this way and that, recording everything. (Altogether, that frog was much improved—almost out of amateur status nowadays.)

The traps were different. In just the ten weeks since the War, the Coven had changed them more than in the previous two years. Every so often, he shook the gathering droplets of water from his face and peered more closely at a bush or boulder by the side of the path. His advance was slow, circuitous, and interrupted by invocations of voice and hand.

Finally he stood before the towers. A figure of black and glowing red climbed out of the magma moat to meet him. Even Alan had changed: he no longer had his asbestos T-shirt, and there was no humor in his sparring with the visitor. Mr. Slippery had to stare upward to look directly at his massive head. The elemental splashed molten rock down on them, and the frog scampered between his neck and collar, its skin cold and slimy against his own. The passwords were different, the questioning more hostile, but Mr. Slippery was a match for the tests and in a matter of minutes Alan retreated sullenly to his steaming pool, and the drawbridge was lowered for their entrance.

THE HALL WAS ALMOST THE SAME AS BEFORE: PERHAPS A BIT DRIER, more brightly lit. There were certainly more people. And they were all looking at him as he stood in the entranceway. Mr. Slippery gave his traveling jacket and hat to a liveried servant and started down the steps, trying to recognize the faces, trying to understand the tension and hostility that hung in the air.

"Slimey!" The Limey stepped forward from the crowd, a familiar grin splitting his bearded face.

"Slip! Is that really you?" (Not entirely a rhetorical question, under the circumstances.)

Mr. Slippery nodded, and after a moment, the other did, too. The Limey almost ran across the space that separated them, stuck out his hand, and clapped the other on the shoulder. "Come on, come on! We have rather a lot to talk about!"

As if on cue, the others turned back to their conversations and ignored the two friends as they walked to one of the sitting rooms that opened off the main hall. Mr. Slippery felt like a man returning to his old school ten years after graduation. Almost all the faces were different, and he had the feeling that he could never belong here again. But this was only ten weeks, not ten years.

The Slimey Limey shut the heavy door, and the sounds from the main room were muted. He waved Slip to a chair and made a show of mixing them some drinks.

"They're all simulators, aren't they?" Slip said quietly.

"Uh?" The Limey broke off his stream of chatter and shook his head glumly. "Not all. I've recruited four or five apprentices. They do their best to make the place look thriving and occupied. You may have noticed various improvements in our security."

"It looks stronger, but it's more appearance than fact."

Slimey shrugged. "I really didn't expect it to fool the likes of you."

Mr. Slippery leaned forward. "Who's left from the old group, Slimey?"

"DON's gone. The Mailman is gone. Wiley J. Bastard shows up a couple of times a month, but he's not much fun anymore. I think Erythrina's still on the System, but she hasn't come by. I thought you were gone until today."

"What about Robin Hood?"

"Gone."

That accounted for all the top talents. Virginia the Frog hadn't been giving away all that much when she excused him from betraying the Coven. Slip wondered if there was any hint of smugness in the frog's fixed and lipless smile.

"What happened?"

The other sighed. "There's a depression on down in the real world, in case you hadn't noticed; and it's being blamed on us vandals.

"—I know, that could scarcely explain Robin's disappearance, only the lesser ones. Slip, I think most of our old friends are either dead—Truly Dead—or very frightened that if they come back into this Plane, they will become Truly Dead."

This felt very much like history repeating itself. "How do you mean?"

The Limey leaned forward. "Slip, it's quite obvious the government's feeding us lies about what caused the depression. They say it was a combination of programming errors and the work of 'vandals.' We know that can't be true. No ordinary vandals could cause that sort of damage. Right after the crash, I looked at what was left of the Feds' databases. Whatever ripped things up was more powerful than any vandal. . . . And I've spoken with—p'raps I should say interrogated—Wiley. I think what we see in the real world and on this plane is in fact the wreckage of a bloody major war."

"Between?"

"Creatures as far above me as I am above a chimp. The names we know them by are the Mailman, Erythrina . . . and just possibly Mr. Slippery."

"Me?" Slip tensed and sent out probes along the communications links which he perceived had created the image before him. Even though on a leash, Mr. Slippery was far more powerful than any normal warlock, and it should have been easy to measure the power of this potential opponent. But the Limey was a diffuse, almost nebulous presence. Slip couldn't tell if he were facing an opponent in the same class as himself; in fact, he had no clear idea of the other's strength, which was even more ominous.

The Limey didn't seem to notice. "That's what I thought. Now I doubt it. I wager you were used—like Wiley and possibly DON—by the other combatants. And I see that now you're in *someone's* thrall." His finger stabbed at the yellow-eyed frog on Mr. Slippery's shoulder, and a sparkle of whiskey flew into the creature's face. Virginia—or whoever was controlling the beast— didn't know what to do, and the frog froze momentarily, then recovered its wits and emitted a pale burst of flame.

The Limey laughed. "But it's no one very competent. The Feds is my guess. What happened? Did they sight your True Name, or did you just sell out?"

"The creature's my familiar, Slimey. We all have our apprentices. If you really believe we're the Feds, why did you let us in?"

The other shrugged. "Because there are enemies and enemies, Slip. Beforetime, we called the government the Great Enemy. Now I'd say they are just one in a pantheon of nasties. Those of us who survived the crash are a lot tougher, a lot less frivolous. We don't think of this as all a wry game anymore. And we're teaching our apprentices a lot more systematically. It's not nearly so much fun. Now when we talk of traitors in the Coven, we mean real, life-and-death treachery.

"But it's necessary. When it comes to it, if we little people don't protect ourselves, we're going to be eaten up by the government or . . . certain other creatures I fear even more."

The frog shifted restively on Mr. Slippery's shoulder, and he could imagine Virginia getting ready to deliver some speech on the virtue of obeying the laws of society in order to reap its protection. He reached across to pat its cold and pimply back; now was not the time for such debate.

"You had one of the straightest heads around here, Slip. Even if you aren't one of us anymore, I don't reckon you're an absolute enemy. You and your . . . friend may have certain interests in common with us. There are things you should know about—if you don't already. An' p'raps there'll be times you'll help us similarly."

Slip felt the Federal tether loosen. Virginia must have convinced her superiors that there was actually help to be had here. "Okay. You're right. There was a war. The Mailman was the enemy. He lost and now we're trying to put things back together."

"Ah, that's just it, old man. *I don't think the war is over.* True, all that remains of the Mailman's constructs are 'craterfields' spread through the government's program space. But something like him is still very much alive." He saw the disbelief in Mr. Slippery's face. "I know, you an' your friends are more powerful than any of us. But there are many of us—not just in the Coven—and we have learned a lot these past ten weeks. There are signs, so light an' fickle you might call 'em atmosphere, that tell us something like the Mailman is still alive. It doesn't quite have the texture of the Mailman, but it's there."

Mr. Slippery nodded. He didn't need any special explanations of the feeling. *Damn! If I weren't on a leash, I would have seen all this weeks ago, instead of finding it out secondhand.* He thought back to those last minutes of their descent from godhood and felt a chill. He knew what he must ask now, and he had a bad feeling about what the answer might be. Somehow he had to prevent Virginia from hearing that answer. It would be a great risk, but he still had a few tricks he didn't think DoW knew of. He probed back along the links that went to Arcata and D.C., feeling the interconnections and the redundancy checks. If he was lucky, he would not have to alter more than a few hundred bits of the information that would flow down to them in the next few seconds. "So who do you think is behind it?"

"For a while, I thought it might be you. Now I've seen you and, uh, done some tests, I know you're more powerful than in the old days and probably more powerful than I am now, but you're no superman."

"Maybe I'm in disguise."

"Maybe, but I doubt it." The Limey was coming closer to the critical words that must be disguised. Slip began to alter the redundancy bits transmitted through the construct of the frog. He would have to fake the record both before and after those words if the deception was to escape detection completely. "No, there's a certain style to this presence. A style that reminds me of our old friend, REorbyitnh rHionoad." The name he said, and the name Mr. Slippery heard, was "Erythnia." The name blended imperceptibly in its place, the name the frog heard, and reported, was "Robin Hood."

"Hmm, possible. He always seemed to be power hungry." The Limey's eyebrows went up fractionally at the pronoun "he." Besides, Robin had been a fantastically clever vandal, not a power grabber. Slimey's eyes flickered toward the frog, and Mr. Slippery prayed that he would play along. "Do you really think this is as great a threat as the Mailman?"

"Who knows? The presence isn't as widespread as the Mailman's, and since the crash no more of us have disappeared. Also, I'm not sure that . . . he . . . is the only such creature left. Perhaps the original Mailman is still around."

And you can't decide who it is that I'm really trying to fool, can you?

The discussion continued for another half hour, a weird three-way fencing match with just two active players. On the one hand, he and the Limey were trying to communicate past the frog, and on the other, the Slimey Limey was trying to decide if perhaps Slip was the real enemy and the frog a potential ally. The hell of it was, Mr. Slippery wasn't sure himself of the answer to that puzzle.

Slimey walked him out to the drawbridge. For a few moments, they stood on the graven ceramic plating and spoke. Below them, Alan paddled back and forth, looking up at them uneasily. The mist was a light rain now, and a constant sizzling came from the molten rock.

Finally Slip said, "You're right in a way, Slimey. I am someone's thrall. But I will look for Robin Hood. If you're right, you've got a couple of new allies. If he's too strong for us, this might be the last you see of me."

The Slimey Limey nodded, and Slip hoped he had gotten the real message: He would take on Ery all by himself.

"Well then, let's hope this ain't good-bye, old man."

Slip walked back down into the valley, aware of the Limey's not unsympathetic gaze on his back.

How to find her, how to speak with her? And survive the experience, that is. Virginia had forbidden him—literally on pain of death—from meeting with Ery on this plane. Even if he could do so, it would be a deadly risk for other reasons. What had Ery been doing in those minutes she dallied, when she had fooled him into descending back to the human plane before her? At the time, he had feared it was a betrayal. Yet he had lived and had forgotten the mystery. Now he wondered again. It was impossible for him to understand the complexity of those minutes. Perhaps she had weakened herself at the beginning to gull him into starting the descent, and perhaps then she hadn't been quite strong enough to take over. Was that possible? And now she was slowly, secretly building back her powers, just as the Mailman had done? He didn't want to believe it, and he knew if Virginia heard his suspicions, the Feds would kill her immediately. There would be no trial, no deep investigation.

Somehow he must get past Virginia and confront Ery—confront her in such a way that he could destroy her if she were a new Mailman. *And there is a way!* He almost laughed: it was absurd and absurdly simple, and it was the only thing that might work. All eyes were on this plane, where magic and power flowed easily to the participants. He would attack from beneath, from the lowly magicless real world!

But there was one final act of magic he must slip past Virginia, something absolutely necessary for a real world confrontation with Erythrina.

He had reached the far ridge and was starting down the hillside that led to the swamps. Even preoccupied, he had given the right signs flawlessly. The guardian sprites were not nearly so vigilant towards constructs moving away from the castle. As the wet brush closed in about them, the familiar red and black spider—or its cousin—swung down from above.

"Beware, beware," came the tiny voice. From the flecks of gold across its abdomen, he knew the right response: left hand up and flick the spider away. Instead Slip raised his right hand and struck at the creature.

The spider hoisted itself upward, screeching faintly, then dropped toward Slip's neck—to land squarely on the frog. A free-for-all erupted as the two scrambled across the back of his neck, pale flame jousting against venom. Even as he moved to save the frog, Mr. Slippery melted part of his attention into a data line that fed a sporting good store in Montreal. An order was placed and later that day a certain very special package would be in the mail to the Boston International Rail Terminal.

Slip made a great show of dispatching the spider, and as the frog settled back on his shoulder, he saw that he had probably fooled Virginia. That he had expected. Fooling Ery would be much the deadlier, chancier thing.

―――――

IF THIS AFTERNOON WERE TYPICAL, THEN JULY IN PROVIDENCE MUST BE a close approximation to Hell. Roger Pollack left the tube as it passed the urbapt block and had to walk nearly four hundred meters to get to the tower he sought. His shirt was soaked with sweat from just below the belt line right up to his neck. The contents of the package he had picked up at the airport train station sat heavily in his right coat pocket, tapping against his hip with every step, reminding him that this was high noon in more ways than one.

Pollack quickly crossed the blazing concrete plaza and walked along the edge of the shadow that was all the tower cast in the noonday sun. All around him the locals swarmed, all ages, seemingly unfazed by the still, moist, hot air. Apparently you could get used to practically anything.

Even an urbapt in summer in Providence. Pollack had expected the buildings to be more depressing. Workers who had any resources became data commuters and lived outside the cities. Of course, some of the people here were data-set users too and so could be characterized as data commuters. Many of them worked as far away from home as any exurb dweller. The difference was that they made so little money (when they had a job at all) that they were forced to take advantage of the economies of scale the urbapts provided.

Pollack saw the elevator ahead but had to detour around a number of children playing stickball in the plaza. The elevator was only half-full, so a wave from him was all it took to keep it grounded till he could get aboard.

No one followed him on, and the faces around him were disinterested and entirely ordinary. Pollack was not fooled. He hadn't violated the letter of Virginia's law; he wasn't trying to see Erythrina on the data net. But he was going to see Debby Charteris, which came close to being the same thing. He imagined the Feds debating with themselves, finally deciding it would be safe to let the two godlings get together if it were on this plane where the *State* was still the ultimate, all-knowing god. He and Debby would be observed. Even so, he would somehow discover if she were the threat the Limey saw. If not, the Feds would never know of his suspicions. But if Ery had betrayed them all and meant to set herself up in place of—or in league with—the Mailman, then in the next few minutes one of them would die.

THE EXPRESS SLID TO A STOP WITH A DECEPTIVE GENTLENESS THAT barely gave a feeling of lightness. Pollack paid and got off.

Floor 25 was mainly shopping mall. He would have to find the stairs to the residential apts between Floors 25 and 35. Pollack drifted through the mall. He was beginning to feel better about the whole thing. *I'm still alive, aren't I?* If Ery had really become what the Limey and Slip feared, then he probably would have had a little "accident" before now. All the way across the continent he sat with his guts frozen, thinking how easy it would be for someone with the Mailman's power to destroy an air transport, even without resorting to the military's lasers. A tiny change in navigation or traffic-control directions, and any number of fatal incidents could be arranged. But nothing had happened, which meant that either Ery was innocent or that she hadn't noticed him. (And that second possibility was unlikely if she were a new Mailman. One impression that remained stronger than any other from his short time as godling was the omniscience of it all.)

It turned out the stairs were on the other side of the mall, marked by a battered sign reminiscent of old-time highway markers: FOOTS > 26–30. The place wasn't really too bad, he supposed, eyeing the stained but durable carpet that covered the stairs. And the hallways coming off each landing reminded him of the motels he had known as a child, before the turn of the century. There was very little trash visible, the people moving around him weren't poorly dressed, and there was only the faintest spice of disinfectant in the air. Apt module 28355, where Debbie Charteris lived, might be high-class. It did have an exterior view, he knew that. Maybe Erythrina—Debbie—*liked* living with all these other people. Surely, now that the government was so interested in her, she could move anywhere she wished.

But when he reached it, he found Floor 28 no different from the others he had seen: carpeted hallway stretching away forever beneath dim lights that showed identical module doorways dwindling in perspective. What was Debbie/Erythrina like that she would choose to live here?

"Hold it." Three teenagers stepped from behind the slant of the stairs. Pollack's hand edged toward his coat pocket. He had heard of the gangs. These three looked like heavies, but they were well and conservatively dressed, and the small one actually had his hair in a braid. They wanted very much to be thought part of the establishment.

The short one flashed something silver at him. "Building Police." And Pollack remembered the news stories about Federal Urban Support paying youngsters for urbapt security: "A project that saves money and staff, while at the same time giving our urban youth an opportunity for responsible citizenship."

Pollack swallowed. Best to treat them like real cops. He showed them his ID. "I'm from out of state. I'm just visiting."

The other two closed in, and the short one laughed. "That's sure. Fact, Mr. Pollack, Sammy's little gadget says you're in violation of Building Ordinance." The one on Pollack's left waved a faintly buzzing cylinder across Pollack's jacket, then pushed a hand into the jacket and withdrew Pollack's pistol, a lightweight ceramic slug-gun perfect for hunting hikes—and which should have been perfect for getting past a building's weapon detectors.

Sammy smiled down at the weapon, and the short one continued. "Thing you didn't know, Mr. Pollack, is Federal law requires a metal tag in the butt of these cram guns. Makes 'em easy to detect." Until the tag was removed. Pollack suspected that somehow this incident might never be reported.

The three stepped back, leaving the way clear for Pollack. "That's all? I can go?"

The young cop grinned. "Sure. You're out-of-towner. How could you know?"

Pollack continued down the hall. The others did not follow. Pollack was fleetingly surprised: maybe the FUS project actually worked. Before the turn of the century, goons like those three would have at least robbed him. Instead they behaved something like real cops.

Or maybe—and he almost stumbled at this new thought—*they all work for Ery now.* That might be the first symptom of conquest: the new god would simply become the government. And he—the last threat to the new order—was being granted one last audience with the victor.

Pollack straightened and walked on more quickly. There was no turning back now, and he was damned if he would show any more fear. Besides, he thought with a sudden surge of relief, it was out of his control now. If Ery was a monster, there was nothing he could do about it; he would not have to try to kill her. If she were not, then his own survival would be proof, and he need think of no complicated tests of her innocence.

He was almost hurrying now. He had always wanted to know what the human being beyond Erythrina was like; sooner or later he would have had to do this anyway. Weeks ago he had looked through all the official directories for the state of Rhode Island, but there wasn't much to find: Linda and Deborah Charteris lived at 28355 Place on 4448 Grosvenor Row. The public directory didn't even show their "interests and occupations."

28313, 315, 317 . . .

His mind had gone in circles, generating all the things Debby

Charteris might turn out to be. She would not be the exotic beauty she projected in the Other Plane. That was too much to hope for; but the other possibilities vied in his mind. He had lived with each, trying to believe that he could accept whatever turned out to be the case:

Most likely, she was a perfectly ordinary looking person who lived in an urbapt to save enough money to buy high-quality processing equipment and rent dense comm lines. Maybe she wasn't good-looking, and that was why the directory listing was relatively secretive.

Almost as likely, she was massively handicapped. He had seen that fairly often among the warlocks whose True Names he knew. They had extra medical welfare and used all their free money for equipment that worked around whatever their problem might be—paraplegia, quadriplegia, multiple sense loss. As such, they were perfectly competitive on the job market, yet old prejudices often kept them out of normal society. Many of these types retreated into the Other Plane, where one could completely control one's appearance.

And then, since the beginning of time, there had been the people who simply did not like reality, who wanted another world, and if given half a chance would live there forever. Pollack suspected that some of the best warlocks might be of this type. Such people were content to live in an urbapt, to spend all their money on processing and life-support equipment, to spend days at a time in the Other Plane, never moving, never exercising their real world bodies. They grew more and more adept, more and more knowledgeable—while their bodies slowly wasted. Pollack could imagine such a person becoming an evil thing and taking over the Mailman's role. It would be like a spider sitting in its web, its victims all humanity. He remembered Ery's contemptuous attitude on learning he never used drugs to maintain concentration and so stay longer in the Other Plane. He shuddered.

And there, finally, and yet too soon, the numbers 28355 stood on the wall before him, the faint hall light glistening off their bronze finish. For a long moment, he balanced between the fear and the wish. Finally he reached forward and tapped the door buzzer.

Fifteen seconds passed. There was no one nearby in the hall. From the corner of his eye, he could see the "cops" lounging by the stairs. About a hundred meters the other way, an argument was going on. The contenders rounded the faraway corner and their voices quieted, leaving him in near silence.

There was a click, and a small section of the door became transparent, a window (more likely a holo) on the interior of the apt. And the person beyond that view would be either Deborah or Linda Charteris.

"Yes?" The voice was faint, cracking with age. Pollack saw a woman barely tall enough to come up to the pickup on the other side. Her hair was white, visibly thin on top, especially from the angle he was viewing.

"I'm . . . I'm looking for Deborah Charteris."

"My granddaughter. She's out shopping. Downstairs in the mall, I think." The head bobbed, a faintly distracted nod.

"Oh. Can you tell me—" *Deborah, Debby*. It suddenly struck him what an old-fashioned name that was, more the name of a grandmother than a granddaughter. He took a quick step to the door and looked down through the pane so that he could see most of the other's body. The woman wore an old-fashioned skirt and blouse combination of some brilliant red material.

Pollack pushed his hand against the immovable plastic of the door. "Ery, please. Let me in."

The pane blanked as he spoke, but after a moment the door slowly opened. "Okay." Her voice was tired, defeated. Not the voice of a god boasting victory.

The interior was decorated cheaply and with what might have been good taste except for the garish excesses of red on red. Pollack remembered reading somewhere that as you age, color sensitivity decreases. This room might seem only mildly bright to the person Erythrina had turned out to be.

The woman walked slowly across the tiny apt and gestured for him to sit. She was frail, her back curved in a permanent stoop, her every step considered yet tremulous. Under the apt's window, he noticed an elaborate GE processor system. Pollack sat and found himself looking slightly upward into her face.

"Slip—or maybe I should call you Roger here—you always were a bit of a romantic fool." She paused for breath, or perhaps her mind wandered. "I was beginning to think you had more sense than to come out here, that you could leave well enough alone."

"You . . . you mean, you didn't know I was coming?" The knowledge was a great loosening in his chest.

"Not until you were in the building." She turned and sat carefully upon the sofa.

"I had to see who you really are," and that was certainly the truth. "After this spring, there is no one the likes of us in the whole world."

Her face cracked in a little smile. "And now you see how different we are. I had hoped you never would and that some-day they would let us back together on the Other Plane. . . . But in the end, it doesn't really matter." She paused, brushed at her temple, and frowned as though forgetting something, or remembering something else.

"I never did look much like the Erythrina you know. I was never tall, of course, and my hair was never red. But I didn't spend my whole life selling life insurance in Peoria, like poor Wiley."

"You . . . you must go all the way back to the beginning of computing."

She smiled again, and nodded just so, a mannerism Pollack had often seen on the Other Plane. "Almost, almost. Out of high school, I was a keypunch operator. You know what a keypunch is?"

He nodded hesitantly, visions of some sort of machine press in his mind.

"It was a dead-end job, and in those days they'd keep you in it forever if you didn't get out under your own power. I got out of it and into college quick as I could, but at least I can say I was in the business during the stone age. After college, I never looked back; there was always so much happening. In the Nasty Nineties, I was on the design of the ABM and FoG control programs. The whole team, the whole of DoD for that matter, was trying to program the thing with procedural languages; it would take 'em a thousand years and a couple of wars to do it that way, and they were beginning to realize as much. I was responsible for getting them away from CRTs, for getting into really interactive EEG programming—what they call portal programming nowadays. Sometimes . . . sometimes when my ego needs a little help, I like to think that if I had never been born, hundreds of millions more would have died back then, and our cities would be glassy ponds today.

". . . And along the way there was a marriage . . ." her voice trailed off again, and she sat smiling at memories Pollack could not see.

He looked around the apt. Except for the processor and a fairly complete kitchenette, there was no special luxury. What money she had must go into her equipment, and perhaps in getting a room with a real exterior view. Beyond the rising towers of the Grosvenor complex, he could see the nest of comm towers that had been their last-second salvation that spring. When he looked back at her, he saw that she was watching him with an intent and faintly amused expression that was very familiar.

"I'll bet you wonder how anyone so daydreamy could be the Erythrina you knew in the Other Plane."

"Why, no," he lied. "You seem perfectly lucid to me."

"Lucid, yes. I am still that, thank God. But I know—and no one has to tell me—that I can't support a train of thought like I could before. These last two or three years, I've found that my mind can wander, can drop into reminiscence, at the most inconvenient times. I've had one stroke, and about all 'the miracles of modern medicine' can do for me is predict that it will not be the last one.

"But in the Other Plane, I can compensate. It's easy for the EEG to detect failure of attention. I've written a package that keeps a thirty-second backup; when distraction is detected, it forces attention and reloads my short-term memory. Most of the time, this gives me better concentration than I've ever had in my life. And when there is a really serious wandering of attention, the package can interpolate for a number of seconds. You may have noticed that, though perhaps you mistook it for poor communications coordination."

She reached a thin, blue-veined hand toward him. He took it in his own. It felt so light and dry, but it returned his squeeze. "It really is me—Ery—inside, Slip."

He nodded, feeling a lump in his throat.

"When I was a kid, there was this song, something about us all being aging children. And it's so very, very true. Inside I still feel like a youngster. But on this plane, no one else can see . . ."

"But I know, Ery. We knew each other on the Other Plane, and I know what you truly are. Both of us are so much more there than we could ever be here." This was all true: even with the restrictions they put on him now, he had a hard time understanding all he did on the Other Plane. What he had become since the spring was a fuzzy dream to him when he was down in the physical world. Sometimes he felt like a fish trying to imagine what a man in an airplane might be feeling. He never spoke of it like this to Virginia and her friends: they would be sure he had finally gone crazy. It was far beyond what he had known as a warlock. And what they had been those brief minutes last spring had been equally far beyond that.

"Yes, I think you do know me, Slip. And we'll be . . . friends as long as this body lasts. And when I'm gone—"

"I'll remember; I'll always remember you, Ery."

She smiled and squeezed his hand again. "Thanks. But that's not what I was getting at . . ." Her gaze drifted off again. "I figured out who the Mailman was and I wanted to tell you."

Pollack could imagine Virginia and the other DoW eavesdroppers hunkering down to their spy equipment. "I hoped you knew something." He went on to tell her about the Slimey Limey's detection of Mailman-like operations still on the System. He spoke carefully, knowing that he had two audiences.

Ery—even now he couldn't think of her as Debby—nodded. "I've been watching the Coven. They've grown, these last months. I think they take themselves more seriously now. In the old days, they never would have noticed what the Limey warned you about. But it's not the Mailman he saw, Slip."

"How can you be sure, Ery? We never killed more than his service programs and his simulators—like DON.MAC. We never found his True Name. We don't even know if he's human or some science-fictional alien."

"You're wrong, Slip. I know what the Limey saw, and I know who the Mailman is—or was," she spoke quietly, but with certainty. "It turns out the Mailman was the greatest cliché of the Computer Age, maybe of the entire Age of Science."

"Huh?"

"You've seen plenty of personality simulators in the Other Plane. DON.MAC—at least as he was rewritten by the Mailman—was good enough to fool normal warlocks. Even Alan, the Coven's elemental, shows plenty of human emotion and cunning." Pollack thought of the new Alan, so ferocious and intimidating. The Turing T-shirt was beneath his dignity now. "Even so, Slip, I don't think you've ever believed you could be permanently fooled by a simulation, have you?"

"Wait. Are you trying to tell me that the Mailman was just another simulator? That the time lag was just to obscure the fact that he was a simulator? That's ridiculous. You know his powers were more than human, almost as great as ours became."

"But do you think you could ever be fooled?"

"Frankly, no. If you talk to one of those things long enough, they display a repetitiveness, an inflexibility that's a giveaway. I don't know; maybe someday there'll be programs that can pass the Turing test. But whatever it is that makes a person a person is terribly complicated. Simulation is the wrong way to get at it, because being a person is more than symptoms. A program that was a person would use enormous databases, and if the processors running it were the sort we have now, you certainly couldn't expect real-time interaction with the outside world." And Pollack suddenly had a glimmer of what she was thinking.

"That's the critical point. Slip: *if you want real-time interaction.* But the Mailman—the sentient, conversational part—never did operate real time. We thought the lag was a communications delay that showed the operator was off-planet, but really he was here all the time. It just took him hours of processing time to sustain seconds of self-awareness."

Pollack opened his mouth, but nothing came out. It went against all his intuition, almost against what religion he had, but it might just barely be possible. The Mailman had controlled immense resources. All his quick time reactions could have been the work of ordinary programs and simulators like DON.MAC. The only evidence they had for his humanity were those teleprinter conversations where his responses were spread over hours.

"Okay, for the sake of argument, let's say it's possible. Someone, somewhere had to write the original Mailman. Who was that?"

"Who would you guess? The government, of course. About ten years ago. It was an NSA team trying to automate system protection. Some brilliant people, but they could never really get it off the ground. They wrote a developmental kernel that by itself was not especially effective or aware. It was designed to live within larger systems and gradually grow in power and awareness, *independent* of what policies or mistakes the operators of the system might make.

"The program managers saw the Frankenstein analogy—or at least they saw a threat to their personal power—and quashed the project. In any case, it was very expensive. The program executed slowly and gobbled incredible data space."

"And you're saying that someone conveniently left a copy running all unknown?"

She seemed to miss the sarcasm. "It's not that unlikely. Research types are fairly careless—outside of their immediate focus. When I was in FoG, we lost thousands of megabytes 'between the cracks' of our databases. And back then, that was a lot of memory. The development kernel is not very large. My guess is a copy was left in the system. Remember, the kernel was designed to live untended if it ever started executing. Over the years it slowly grew—both because of its natural tendencies and because of the increased power of the nets it lived in."

Pollack sat back on the sofa. Her voice was tiny and frail, so unlike the warm, rich tones he remembered from the Other Plane. But she spoke with the same authority.

Debby's—Erythrina's—pale eyes stared off beyond the walls of the apt, dreaming. "You know, they are right to be afraid," she said finally. "Their world is ending. Even without us, there would still be the Limey, the Coven—and someday most of the human race."

Damn. Pollack was momentarily tongue-tied, trying desperately to think of something to mollify the threat implicit in Ery's words. *Doesn't she understand that DoW would never let us talk unbugged? Doesn't she know how trigger-happy scared the top Feds must be by now?*

But before he could say anything, Ery glanced at him, saw the consternation in his face, and smiled. The tiny hand patted his. "Don't worry, Slip. The Feds are listening, but what they're hearing is tearful chitchat—you overcome to find me what I am, and me trying to console the both of us. They will never know what I really tell you here. They will never know about the gun the local boys took off you."

"What?"

"You see, I lied a little. I know why you really came. I know you thought that *I* might be the new monster. But I don't want to lie to you anymore. You risked your life to find out the truth, when you could have just told the Feds what you guessed." She went on, taking advantage of his stupefied silence. "Did you ever wonder what I did in those last minutes this spring, after we surrendered—when I lagged behind you in the Other Plane?

"It's true, we really did destroy the Mailman; that's what all that unintelligible data space we plowed up was. I'm sure there are copies of the kernel hidden here and there, like cancers in the System, but we can control them one by one as they appear.

"I guessed what had happened when I saw all that space, and I had plenty of time to study what was left, even to trace back to the original research project. Poor little Mailman, like the monsters of fiction—he was only doing what he had been designed to do. He was taking over the System, protecting it from everyone—even its owners. I suspect he would have announced himself in the end and used some sort of nuclear blackmail to bring the rest of the world into line. But even though his programs had been running for several years, he had only had fifteen or twenty hours of human type self-awareness when we did him in. His personality programs were that slow. He never attained the level of consciousness you and I had on the System.

"But he really was self-aware, and that was the triumph of it all. And in those few minutes, I figured out how I could adapt the basic kernel to accept any input personality. . . . That is what I really wanted to tell you."

"Then what the Limey saw was—"

She nodded. "Me . . ."

She was grinning now, an open though conspiratorial grin that was very familiar. "When Bertrand Russell was very old, and probably as dotty as I am now, he talked of spreading his interests and attention out to the greater world and away from his own body, so that when that body died he would scarcely notice it, his whole consciousness would be so diluted through the outside world.

"For him, it was wishful thinking, of course. But not for me. My kernel is out here in the System. Every time I'm there, I transfer a little more of myself. The kernel is growing into a true Erythrina, who is also truly me. When this body dies," she squeezed his hand with hers, "when this body dies, *I* will still be, and you can still talk to me."

"Like the Mailman?"

"Slow like the Mailman. At least till I design faster processors. . . .

". . . So in a way, I am everything you and the Limey were afraid of. *You* could probably still stop me, Slip." And he sensed that she was awaiting his judgment, the last judgment any human would ever be allowed to levy upon her.

Slip shook his head and smiled at her, thinking of the slow-moving guardian angel that she would become. *Every race must arrive at this point in its history*, he suddenly realized. A few years or decades in which its future slavery or greatness rests on the goodwill of one or two persons. It could have been the Mailman. Thank God it was Ery instead.

And beyond those years or decades . . . for an instant, Pollack came near to understanding things that had once been obvious.

Processors kept getting faster, memories larger. What now took a planet's resources would someday be possessed by everyone. Including himself.

Beyond those years or decades . . . were millennia. And Ery.

Afterword

Marvin Minsky

This volume's dedication to Marvin Minsky, as "godfather to a new age," is but a small acknowledgment of the enormous role Minsky has played in the development of new technologies, new concepts—and, perhaps most important, radically new ways of looking at the world. He has long been considered the "father of artificial intelligence." He has earned this designation by his research, his writing, and his work at the MIT Artificial Intelligence Lab, which he cofounded and where he has fostered the development not only of new technology, but also of a number of creative and innovative scientists, many of whom were students of his. This is not to suggest that his influence has been limited only to those with whom he works directly. Far from it. His visionary work has been a beacon to countless others who have worked in the field of artificial intelligence and related areas for over forty years.

As Vernor Vinge suggested in his Introduction, Minsky is the source of much original and insightful commentary on science-fictional topics that relate to Minsky's field. A few months after the first publication of *True Names,* Minsky was the keynote speaker at the annual Nebula Awards banquet of the Science Fiction Writers of America, and his speech was about "True Names." He spoke with such eloquence, understanding, and clarity that when the Bluejay Books edition of *True Names* was in preparation, his was the first name that came to mind as the person most suited to write an Afterword to the work.

What follows is that original Afterword, first written in 1983. It is still as valid today as it was then, and its message seems entirely fitting as the endcap to this book of ideas.

In real life, you often have to deal with things you don't completely understand. You drive a car, not knowing how its engine works. You ride as passenger in someone else's car, not knowing how that driver works. And strangest of all, you sometimes drive yourself to work, not knowing how you work, yourself.

To me, the import of *True Names* is that it is about how we cope with things we don't understand. But, how do we ever understand anything in the first place? Almost always, I think, by using analogies in one way or another—to pretend that each alien thing we see resembles something we already know. When an object's internal workings are too strange, complicated, or unknown to deal with directly, we extract whatever parts of its behavior we can comprehend and represent them by familiar symbols—or the names of familiar things which we think do similar things. That way, we make each novelty at least appear to be like something which we know from the worlds of our own pasts. It is a great idea, that use of symbols; it lets our minds transform the strange into the commonplace. It is the same with names.

Right from the start, *True Names* shows us many forms of this idea, methods which use symbols, names, and images to make a novel world resemble one where we have been before. Remember the doors to Vinge's castle? Imagine that some architect has invented a new way to go from one place to another: a scheme that serves in some respects the normal functions of a door, but one whose form and mechanism is so entirely outside our past experience that, to see it, we'd never think of it as a door, nor guess what purposes to use it for. No matter: just superimpose on its exterior, some decoration which reminds one of a door. We could clothe it in rectangular shape, or add to it a waist-high knob, or a push-plate with a sign lettered "EXIT" in red and white, or do whatever else may seem appropriate—and every visitor from Earth will know, without a conscious thought, that pseudo-portal's purpose, and how to make it do its job.

At first this may seem mere trickery; after all, this new invention, which we decorate to look like a door, is not really a door. It has none of what we normally expect a door to be, to wit: hinged, swinging slab of wood, cut into wall. The inner details are all wrong. Names and symbols, like analogies, are only partial truths; they work by taking many-levelled descriptions of different things and chopping off all of what seem, in the present context, to be their least essential details—that is, the ones which matter least to our intended purposes. But, still, what matters—when it comes to using such a thing—is that whatever symbol or icon, token or sign we choose should remind us of the use we seek—which, for that not-quite-door, should represent some way to go from one place to another. Who cares how it works, so long as it works! It does not even matter if that "door" leads to anywhere: in *True Names*, nothing ever leads anywhere; instead, the protagonists' bodies never move at all, but remain plugged in to the network while programs change their representations of the simulated realities!

Ironically, in the world *True Names* describes, those representations actually do move from place to place—but only because the computer programs which do the work may be sent anywhere within the worldwide network of connections. Still, to the dwellers inside that network, all of this is inessential and imperceptible, since the physical locations of the computers themselves are normally not represented anywhere at all inside the worlds they simulate. It is only in the final acts of the novella, when those partially-simulated beings finally have to protect themselves against their entirely-simulated enemies, that the programs must keep track of where their mind-computers are; then they resort to using ordinary means, like military maps and geographic charts.

And strangely, this is also the case inside the ordinary brain: it, too, lacks any real sense of where it is. To be sure, most modern, educated people know that thoughts proceed inside the head—but that is something which no brain knows until it's told. In fact, without the help of education, a human brain has no idea that any such things as brains exist. Perhaps we tend to place the seat of thought behind the face, because that's where so many sense-organs are located. And even that impression is somewhat wrong: for example, the brain-centers for vision are far away from the eyes, away in the very back of the head, where no unaided brain would ever expect them to be.

In any case, the point is that the icons in *True Names* are not designed to represent the truth—that is, the truth of how the designated object, or program, works; that just is not an icon's job. An icon's purpose is, instead, to represent a way an object or a program can be used. And, since the idea of a use is in the user's mind—and not connected to the thing it represents—the form and figure of the icon must be suited to the symbols that the users have acquired in their own development. That is, it has to be connected to whatever mental processes are already one's most fluent, expressive, tools for expressing intentions. And that's why Roger represents his watcher the way his mind has learned to represent a frog.

This principle, of choosing symbols and icons which express the functions of entities—or rather, their users' intended attitudes toward them—was already second nature to the designers of earliest fast-interaction computer systems, namely, the early computer games which were, as Vernor Vinge says, the ancestors of the Other Plane in which the novella's main activities are set. In the 1970s the meaningful-icon idea was developed for personal computers by Alan Kay's research group at Xerox, but it was only in the early 1980s, after further work by Steven Jobs' research group at Apple Computer, that this concept entered the mainstream of the computer revolution, in the body of the Macintosh computer.

Over the same period, there have also been less-publicized attempts to develop iconic ways to represent, not what the programs do, but how they work. This would be of great value in the different enterprise of making it easier for programmers to make new programs from old ones. Such attempts have been less successful, on the whole, perhaps because one is forced to delve too far inside the lower-level details of how the programs work. But such difficulties are too transient to interfere with Vinge's vision, for there is evidence that he regards today's ways of programming—which use stiff, formal, inexpressive languages—as but an early stage of how great programs will be made in the future.

Surely the days of programming, as we know it, are numbered. We will not much longer construct large computer systems by using meticulous but conceptually impoverished procedural specifications. Instead, we'll express our intentions about what should be done, in terms, or gestures, or examples, at least as resourceful as our ordinary, everyday methods for expressing our wishes and convictions. Then these expressions will be submitted to immense, intelligent, intention-understanding programs which will themselves construct the actual, new programs. We shall no longer be burdened with the need to understand all the smaller details of how computer codes work. All of that will be left to those great utility programs, which will perform the arduous tasks of applying what we have embodied in them, once and for all, of what we know about the arts of lower-level programming. Then, once we learn better ways to tell computers what we want them to get done, we will be able to return to the more familiar realm of expressing our own wants and needs. *For, in the end, no user really cares about how a program works, but only about what it does—in the sense of the intelligible effects it has on other things with which the user is concerned.*

In order for that to happen, though, we will have to invent and learn to use new technologies for "expressing intentions." To do this, we will have to break away from our old, though still evolving, programming languages, which are useful only for describing processes. And this may be much harder than it sounds. For, it is easy enough to say that all we want to do is but to specify *what we want to happen,* using more familiar modes of expression. But this brings with it some very serious risks.

The first risk is that this exposes us to the consequences of self-deception. It is always tempting to say to oneself, when writing a program, or writing an essay, or, for that matter, doing almost anything, that *"I know what I would want, but I can't quite express it clearly enough."* However, that concept itself reflects a too-simplistic self-image, which portrays one's own self as existing, somewhere in the heart of one's mind (so to speak), in the form of a pure, uncomplicated entity which has pure and unmixed wishes, intentions, and goals. This pre-Freudian image serves to excuse our frequent appearances of ambivalence; we convince ourselves that clarifying our intentions is a mere matter of straightening out the input-output channels between our inner and outer selves. The trouble is, we simply aren't made that way, no matter how we may wish we were.

We incur another risk whenever we try to escape the responsibility of understanding how our wishes will be realized. It is always dangerous to leave much choice of means to any servants we may choose—no matter whether we program them or not. For, the larger the range of choice of methods they may use, to gain for us the ends we think we seek, the more we expose ourselves to possible accidents. We may not realize, perhaps until it is too late to turn back, that our goals were misinterpreted, perhaps even maliciously, as in such classic tales of fate as Faust, the Sorcerer's Apprentice, or the Monkey's Paw (by W. W. Jacobs).

The ultimate risk, though, comes when we greedy, lazy, masterminds are able at last to take that final step: to design goal-achieving programs which are programmed to make themselves grow increasingly powerful, by using learning and self-evolution methods which augment and enhance their own capabilities. It will be tempting to do this, not just for the gain in power, but just to decrease our own human effort in the consideration and formulation of our own desires. If some genie offered you three wishes, would not your first one be, *"Tell me, please, what is it that I want the most!"* The problem is that, with such powerful machines, it would require but the slightest powerful accident of careless design for them to place their goals ahead of ours, perhaps the well-meaning purpose of protecting us from ourselves, as in *With Folded Hands*, by Jack Williamson; or to protect us from an unsuspected enemy, as in *Colossus* by D. H. Jones; or because, like Arthur C. Clarke's HAL, the machine we have built considers us inadequate to the mission we ourselves have proposed; or, as in the case of Vernor Vinge's own Mailman, who teletypes its messages because it cannot spare the time to don disguises of dissimulated flesh, simply because the new machine has motives of its very own.

Now, what about the last and finally dangerous question which is asked toward *True Names'* end? Are those final scenes really possible, in which a human user starts to build itself a second, larger Self inside the machine? Is anything like that conceivable? And if it were, then would those simulated computer-people be in any sense the same as their

human models before them; would they be genuine extensions of those real people? Or would they merely be new,
artificial, person-things which resemble their originals only
through some sort of structural coincidence? What if the
aging Erythrina's simulation, unthinkably enhanced, is permitted to live on inside her new residence, more luxurious
than Providence? What if we also suppose that she, once
there, will be still inclined to share it with Roger—since no
sequel should be devoid of romance—and that those two
tremendous entities will love one another? Still, one must
inquire, what would those super-beings share with those
whom they were based upon? To answer that, we have to
think more carefully about what those individuals were before. But, since these aren't real characters, but only figments
of an author's mind, we'd better ask, instead, about the nature of our selves.

Now, once we start to ask about our selves, we'll have to
ask how these, too, work—and this is what I see as the
cream of the jest because, it seems to me, that inside every
normal person's mind is, indeed, a certain portion, which we
call the Self—but it, too, uses symbols and representations
very much like the magic spells used by those players of the
Inner World to work their wishes from their terminals. To
explain this theory about the working of human consciousness, I'll have to compress some of the arguments from *The
Society of Mind,* my forthcoming book. In several ways, my
image of what happens in the human mind resembles
Vinge's image of how the players of the Other Plane have
linked themselves into their networks of computing machines—by using superficial symbol-signs to control a host
of systems which we do not fully understand.

Everybody knows that we humans understand far less
about the insides of our minds, than what we know about
the world outside. We know how ordinary objects work, but

nothing of the great computers in our brains. Isn't it amazing we can think, not knowing what it means to think? Isn't it bizarre that we can get ideas, yet not be able to explain what ideas are. Isn't it strange how often we can better understand our friends than ourselves?

Consider again, how, when you drive, you guide the immense momentum of a car, not knowing how its engine works, or how its steering wheel directs the vehicle toward left or right. Yet, when one comes to think of it, don't we drive our bodies the same way? You simply set yourself to go in a certain direction and, so far as conscious thought is concerned, it's just like turning a mental steering wheel. All you are aware of is some general intention—*It's time to go: where is the door?*—and all the rest takes care of itself. But did you ever consider the complicated processes involved in such an ordinary act as, when you walk, changing the direction you're going in? It is not just a matter of, say, taking a larger or smaller step on one side, the way one changes course when rowing a boat. If that were all you did, when walking, you would tip over and fall toward the outside of the turn.

Try this experiment: watch yourself carefully while turning—and you'll notice that, before you start the turn, you tip yourself in advance; this makes you start to fall toward the inside of the turn; then, when you catch yourself on the next step, you end up moving in a different direction. When we examine that more closely, it all turns out to be dreadfully complicated: hundreds of interconnected muscles, bones, and joints are all controlled simultaneously, by interacting programs which locomotion scientists still barely comprehend. Yet all your conscious mind need do, or say, or think, is *Go that way!*—assuming that it makes sense to speak of the conscious mind as thinking anything at all. So far as one can see, we guide the vast machines inside ourselves, not by using technical and insightful schemes based on knowing how the underlying mechanisms work, but by tokens, signs, and symbols which are entirely as fanciful as those of Vinge's sorcery. It even makes one wonder if it's fair for us to gain our ends by casting spells upon our helpless hordes of mental under-thralls.

Now, if we take this only one more step, we see that, just as we walk without thinking, we also think without thinking! That is, we just as casually exploit the agencies that carry out our mental work. Suppose you have a hard problem. You think about it for a while; then after a time you find a solution. Perhaps the answer comes to you suddenly; you get an idea and say, "Aha, I've got it. I'll do such and such." But then, were someone to ask how you did it, how you found the solution, you simply would not know how to reply. People usually are able to say only things like this:

"I suddenly realized . . ."

"I just got this idea . . ."

"It occurred to me that . . ."

If we really knew how our minds work, we wouldn't so often act on motives which we don't suspect, nor would we have such varied theories in psychology. Why, when we're asked how people come upon their good ideas, are we reduced to superficial reproductive metaphors, to talk about "conceiving" or "gestating", or even "giving birth" to thoughts? We even speak of "ruminating" or "digesting"— as though the mind were anywhere but in the head. If we could see inside our minds we'd surely say more useful things than "Wait. I'm thinking."

People frequently tell me that they're absolutely certain that no computer could ever be sentient, conscious, self-willed, or in any other way "aware" of itself. They're often shocked when I ask what makes them sure that they, themselves, possess these admirable qualities. The reply is that, if they're sure of anything at all, it is that *"I'm aware—hence I'm aware."*

Yet, what do such convictions really mean? Since "self-awareness" ought to be an awareness of what's going on within one's mind, no realist could maintain for long that people really have much insight, in the literal sense of seeing in.

Isn't it remarkable how certainly we feel that we're self-aware—that we have such broad abilities to know what's happening inside ourselves? The evidence for that is weak, indeed. It is true that some people seem to have special excellences, which we sometimes call "insights," for assessing the attitudes and motivations for other people. And certain individuals even sometimes make good evaluations of themselves. But that doesn't justify our using names like insight or self-awareness for such abilities. Why not simply call them "person-sights" or "person-awareness?" Is there really reason to suppose that skills like these are very different from the ways we learn the other kinds of things we learn? Instead of seeing them as "seeing in," we could regard them as quite the opposite: just one more way of "figuring out." Perhaps we learn about ourselves the same ways that we learn about un-self-ish things.

The fact is, the parts of ourselves which we call "self aware" are only a small fraction of the entire mind. They work by building simulated worlds of their own—worlds which are greatly simplified, in comparison with either the real world outside, or with the immense computer systems inside the brain: systems which no one can pretend, today, to understand. And our worlds of simulated awareness are worlds of simple magic, wherein each and every imagined object is invested with meanings and purposes. Consider how one can but scarcely see a hammer except as something to hammer with, or see a ball except as something to throw and catch. Why are we so constrained to perceive things, not as they are, but as they can be used? *Because the highest levels of our minds are goal-directed problem solvers.* That is to say that all the machines inside our heads evolved, originally, to meet various built-in or acquired needs, for comfort and nutrition, for defense and for reproduction. Later, over the past few million years, we evolved even more powerful sub-machines which, in ways we don't yet understand, seem to correlate and analyze to discover which kinds of actions cause which sorts of effects; in a word, to discover what we call knowledge. And though we often like to think that knowledge is abstract, and that our search for it is pure and good in itself— still, we ultimately use it for its ability to tell us what to do to gain whichever ends we seek (even when we conclude that in order to do that, we may first need to gain yet more and more knowledge). Thus, because, as we say, "knowledge is power," our knowledge itself is enmeshed in those webs of ways we reach our goals. And that's the key: it isn't any use for us to know, unless our knowledge tells us what to do. This is so wrought into the conscious mind's machinery that it seems too obvious to state: *no knowledge is of any use unless we have a use for it.*

Now we come to see the point of consciousness: it is the part of the mind most specialized for knowing how to use the other systems which lie hidden in the mind. But it is not a specialist in knowing how those systems actually work, inside themselves. Thus, as we said, one walks without much sense of how it's done. It's only when those systems start to fail to work well that consciousness becomes engaged with small details. That way, a person who has sustained an injured leg may start, for the first time, consciously to make theories about how walking works: *To turn to the left, I'll have to push myself that way*—and then one has to figure out, *with what?* It is often only when we're forced to face an unusually

Marvin Minsky

hard problem that we become more reflective, and try to understand more about how the rest of the mind ordinarily solves problems; at such times one finds oneself saying such things as, "Now I must get organized. Why can't I concentrate on the important questions and not get distracted by those other inessential details?"

It is mainly at such moments—the times when we get into trouble—that we come closer than usual to comprehending how our minds work, by engaging the little knowledge we have about those mechanisms, in order to alter or repair them. It is paradoxical that these are just the times when we say we are "confused," because it is very intelligent to know so much about oneself that one can say that—in contrast merely to being confused and not even knowing it. Still, we disparage and dislike awareness of confusion, not realizing what a high degree of self-representation it must involve. Perhaps that only means that consciousness is getting out of its depth, and isn't really suited to knowing that much about how things work. In any case, even our most "conscious" attempts at self-inspection still remain confined mainly to the pragmatic, magic world of symbol-signs, for no human being seems ever to have succeeded in using self-analysis to find out very much about the programs working underneath.

So this is the irony of *True Names*. Though Vinge tells the tale as though it were a science-fiction fantasy—it is in fact a realistic portrait of our own, real-life predicament! I say again that we work our minds in the same unknowing ways we drive our cars and our bodies, as the players of those futuristic games control and guide what happens in their great machines: by using symbols, spells and images—as well as secret, private names. The parts of us which we call "consciousness" sit, as it were, in front of cognitive computer terminals, trying to steer and guide the great unknown engines of the mind, not by understanding how those mechanisms work, but simply by selecting names from menu-lists of symbols which appear, from time to time, upon our mental screen-displays.

But really, when one thinks of it, it scarcely could be otherwise! Consider what would happen if our minds indeed could really see inside themselves. What could possibly be worse than to be presented with a clear view of the trillion-wire networks of our nerve-cell connections? Our scientists have peered at fragments of those structures for years with powerful microscopes, yet failed to come up with comprehensive theories of what those networks do and how. How much more devastating it would be to have to see it all at once!

What about the claims of mystical thinkers that there are other, better ways to see the mind. One recommended way is learning how to train the conscious mind to stop its usual sorts of thoughts and then attempt (by holding very still) to see and hear the fine details of mental life. Would that be any different, or better, than seeing them through instruments? Perhaps—except that it doesn't face the fundamental problem of how to understand a complicated thing! For, if we suspend our usual ways of thinking, we'll be bereft of all the parts of mind already trained to interpret complicated phenomena. Anyway, even if one could observe and detect the signals which emerge from other, normally inaccessible portions of the mind, these probably would make no sense to the systems involved with consciousness, because they represent unusually low-level details. To see why this is so, let's return once more to understanding such simple things as how we walk.

Suppose that, when you walk about, you were indeed able to see and hear the signals in your spinal cord and lower brain. Would you be able to make any sense of them? Perhaps, but not easily. Indeed, it is easy to do such experiments, using simple bio-feedback devices to make those signals audible and visible; the result is that one may indeed more quickly learn to perform a new skill, such as better using an injured limb. However, just as before, this does not appear to work through gaining a conscious understanding of how those circuits work; instead the experience is very much like business as usual; we gain control by acquiring just one more form of semi-conscious symbol-magic. Presumably, what happens is that a new control system is assembled somewhere in the nervous system, and interfaced with superficial signals we can know about. However, bio-feedback does not appear to provide any different insights into how learning works than do our ordinary, built-in senses.

In any case, our locomotion scientists have been tapping such signals for decades using electronic instruments. Using those data, they have been able to develop various partial theories about the kinds of interactions and regulation-systems which are involved. However, these theories have not emerged from relaxed meditation about, or passive observation of those complicated biological signals; what little we have learned has come from deliberate and intense exploitation of the accumulated discoveries of three centuries of our scientists' and mathematicians' study of analytical mechanics and a century of newer theories about servo-control engineering. It is generally true in science that just observing things carefully rarely leads to new "insights" and understandings. One must first have at least the glimmerings of the form of a new theory, or of a novel way to describe: one needs a "new idea." For the "causes" and the "purposes" of what we observe are not themselves things that can be observed; to represent *them*, we need some other mental source to invent new magic tokens.

But where do we get the new ideas we need? For any single individual, of course, most concepts come from the societies and cultures that one grows up in. As for the rest of our ideas, the ones we "get" all by ourselves, these, too, come from societies—but, now, the ones inside our individual minds. For, a human mind is not in any real sense a single entity, nor does a brain have a single, central way to work. Brains do not secrete thought the way livers secrete bile; a brain consists of a huge assembly of sub-machines which each do different kinds of jobs—each useful to some other parts. For example, we use distinct sections of the brain for hearing the sounds of words, as opposed to recognizing other kinds of natural sounds or musical pitches. There is even solid evidence that there is a special part of the brain which is specialized for seeing and recognizing faces, as opposed to visual perception of other, ordinary things. I suspect that there are, inside the cranium, perhaps as many as a hundred kinds of computers, each with its own somewhat different architecture; these have been accumulating over the past four hundred million years of our evolution. They are wired together into a great multi-resource network of specialists, which each knows how to call on certain other specialists to get things done which serve its purposes. And each of these sub-brains uses its own styles of programming and its own forms of representations; there is no standard, universal language-code.

Accordingly, if one part of that Society of Mind were to inquire about another part, this probably would not work because they have such different languages and architectures. How could they understand one another, with so little in common? Communication is difficult enough between two different human tongues. But the signals used by the different portions of the human mind are even less likely to be even remotely as similar as two human dialects with sometimes corresponding roots. More likely, they are simply too different to communicate at all—except through symbols which initiate their use.

Now, one might ask, "Then, how do people doing different jobs communicate, when they have different backgrounds, thoughts, and purposes?" The answer is that this problem is easier, because a person knows so much more than do the smaller fragments of that person's mind. And, besides, we all are raised in similar ways, and this provides a solid base of common knowledge. Even so, we overestimate how well we actually communicate. The many jobs that people do may seem different on the surface, but they are all very much the same, to the extent that they all have a common base in what we like to call "common sense"—that is, the knowledge shared by all of us. This means that we do not really need to tell each other as much as we suppose. Often, when we "explain" something, we scarcely explain anything new at all; instead, we merely show some examples of what we mean, and some non-examples; these indicate to the listener how to link up various structures already known. In short, we often just tell "which" instead of "how".

Consider how hard we find it to explain so many seemingly simple things. We can't say how to balance on a bicycle, or distinguish a picture from a real thing, or, even how to fetch a fact from memory. Again, one might complain, "It isn't fair to expect us to be able to put in words such things as seeing or balancing or remembering. Those are things we learned before we even learned to speak!" But, though that criticism is fair in some respects, it also illustrates how hard communication must be for all the subparts of the mind which never learned to talk at all—and these are most of what we are. The idea of "meaning" itself is really a matter of size and scale: it only makes sense to ask what something means in a system which is large enough to have many meanings. In very small systems, the idea of something having a meaning becomes as vacuous as saying that a brick is a very small house.

Now it is easy enough to say that the mind is a society, but that idea by itself is useless unless we can say more about how it is organized. If all those specialized parts were equally competitive, there would be only anarchy, and the more we learned, the less we'd be able to do. So there must be some kind of administration, perhaps organized roughly in hierarchies, like the divisions and subdivisions of an industry or a human political society. What would those levels do? In all the large societies we know which work efficiently, the lower levels exercise the more specialized working skills, while the higher levels are concerned with longer-range plans and goals. And this is another fundamental reason why it is so hard to translate between our conscious and unconscious thoughts! The kinds of terms and symbols we use on the conscious level are primarily for expressing our goals and plans for using what we believe we can do—while the workings of those lower-level resources are represented in unknown languages of process and mechanism. So when our conscious probes try to descend into the myriads of smaller and smaller sub-machines which make the mind, they encounter alien representations, used for increasingly specialized purposes.

The trouble is, these tiny inner "languages" soon become incomprehensible, for a reason which is simple and inescapable. This is not the same as the familiar difficulty of translating between two different human languages; we understand the nature of *that* problem: it is that human languages are so huge and rich that it is hard to narrow meanings down—we call that "ambiguity." But, when we try to understand the tiny languages at the lowest levels of the mind, we have the opposite problem—because *the smaller the two languages, the harder it will be to translate between them, not because there are too many meanings, but too few. The fewer things two systems do, the less likely that something one of them can do will correspond to anything at all the other one can do.* And then, no translation is possible. Why is this worse than when there is much ambiguity? Because, although that problem seems very hard, still, even when a problem seems hopelessly complicated, there always can be hope. But, when a problem is hopelessly simple, there can't be any hope at all!

Now, finally, let's return to the question of how much a simulated life inside a world inside a machine could be like our ordinary, real life, "out here"? My answer, as you know by now, is that it could be very much the same—since we, ourselves, as we've seen, already exist as processes imprisoned in machines inside machines. Our mental worlds are already filled with wondrous, magical symbol-signs, which add to everything we "see" a meaning and significance.

All educated people already know how different is our mental world from the "real world" our scientists know. For, consider the table in your dining room; your conscious mind sees it as having a familiar function, form, and purpose: a table is "a thing to put things on." However, our science tells us that this is only in the mind; all that's "really there" is a society of countless molecules. The table seems to hold its shape only because some of those molecules are constrained to vibrate near one another, because of certain properties of the force fields which keep them from pursuing independent paths. Similarly, when you hear a spoken word, your mind attributes sense and meaning to that sound—whereas, in physics, the word is merely a fluctuating pressure on your ear, caused by the collisions of myriads of molecules of air— that is, of particles whose distances, this time are less constrained.

And so—let's face it now, once and for all: each one of us

already has experienced what it is like to be simulated by a computer!

"Ridiculous," most people say, at first: "I certainly don't *feel* like a machine!"

But what makes us so sure of that? How could one claim to know how something feels, until one has experienced it? Consider that either you are a machine or you're not. Then, if, as you say, you aren't a machine, you are scarcely in any position of authority to say how it feels to be a machine.

"Very well, but, surely then, if I were a machine, then at least I would be in a position to know that!"

No. That is only an innocently grandiose presumption, which amounts to claiming that, "I think, therefore I know how thinking works." But as we've seen, there are so many levels of machinery between our conscious thoughts and how they're made that saying such a thing is as absurd as to say, "I drive, therefore I know how engines work!"

"Still, even if the brain is a kind of computer, you must admit that its scale is unimaginably large. A human brain contains many billions of brain cells—and, probably, each cell is extremely complicated by itself. Then, each cell is interlinked in complicated ways to thousands or millions of other cells. You can use the word "machine" for that, but surely no one could ever build anything of that magnitude!"

I am entirely sympathetic with the spirit of this objection. When one is compared to a machine, one feels belittled, as though one is being regarded as trivial. And, indeed, such a comparison is truly insulting—so long as the name "machine" still carries the same meaning it had in times gone by. For thousands of years, we have used such words to arouse images of pulleys, levers, locomotives, typewriters, and other simple sorts of things; similarly, in modern times, the word "computer" has evoked thoughts about adding and subtracting digits, and storing them unchanged in tiny so-called "memories." However those words no longer serve our new purposes, to describe machines that think like us; for such uses, those old terms have become false names for what we want to say. Just as "house" may stand for either more, or nothing more, than wood and stone, our minds may be described as nothing more, and, yet far more, than just machines.

As to the question of scale itself, those objections are almost wholly out-of-date. They made sense in 1950, before any computer could store even a mere million bits. They still made sense in 1960, when a million bits cost a million dollars. But, today, that same amount of memory costs but a hundred dollars (and our governments have even made the dollars smaller, too)—and there already exist computers with billions of bits.

The only thing missing is most of the knowledge we'll need to make such machines intelligent. Indeed, as you might guess from all this, the focus of research in artificial intelligence should be to find good ways, as Vinge's fantasy suggests, to connect structures with functions through the use of symbols. When, if ever, will that get done? Never say "Never."